Novels by Gerald Brandt
available from DAW Books:

The San Angeles Novels:
THE COURIER
THE OPERATIVE

THE OPERATIVE

A SAN ANGELES NOVEL

GERALD BRANDT

DAW BOOKS, INC.

DONALD A. WOLLHEIM, FOUNDER

375 Hudson Street, New York, NY 10014

ELIZABETH R. WOLLHEIM
SHEILA E. GILBERT
PUBLISHERS

www.dawbooks.com

First Printing, November 2016
1 2 3 4 5 6 7 8 9

DAW TRADEMARK REGISTERED
U.S. PAT. AND TM. OFF. AND FOREIGN COUNTRIES
—MARCA REGISTRADA
HECHO EN U.S.A.

PRINTED IN THE U.S.A.

For George Robert Wood
Father, Grandfather, and friend

ACKNOWLEDGMENTS

A big thanks to my beta readers this time around: Rob Riddell, Tim Rohr, Virginia O'Dine, and Troy Bucher. You all read this with an eye to detail and story that made everything better. Also, a thank-you and a heartfelt apology to Adria Laycraft whose input was much appreciated—sometimes my brain doesn't work. My writers group, Poverty of Writers: Evan Braun, Sherry Peters, and Bev Geddes worked under some strict time lines, and delivered superbly. Without your input, this would have been a different book. Cliff Nielsen has, once again, given me a cover that exceeded my expectations. His attention to detail brought the imagery in my head to life.

A huge thank-you to Reg Kovac, who finished building my shed in some sweltering heat, while I sat in my office and got this book finished. Also a thanks to his wife (my awesome sister), Gesine, who let him do it.

A special thanks to Sheila Gilbert for giving me the opportunity to continue telling Kris' story, and for having such incredible insight into what the story was about. Sheila and the rest of the team at DAW have excelled at every turn. They all work so hard to make each and every book the best it can be.

My agents Sara Megibow at kt literary and Jerry Kalajian at IPG work so hard on my behalf. You guys are great.

To Jared and Ryan, who have listened to me mutter to myself while driving, watched me pace around the house anxiously, and who have, on occasion, let me bounce ideas off of them. All this work would be pointless without you guys.

And finally, my Marnie, without whom this book would never have been completed. Your patience, your questions, your willingness to do more than your share, have enabled me to reach for the stars and chase after my dreams. None of this would have been possible without your support and indulgence.

CHAPTER 1

ACE BOOT CAMP, KANANASKIS—SUNDAY, JUNE 11, 2141
5:20 A.M.

THE NIGHTMARES ARE THE WORST.

They are always the same: I wake up in total darkness, crammed into a wooden box too small to hold me. Every nook and cranny is filled with shards of glass and metal. My skin weeps blood from a million tiny cuts. When I lift my head, my forehead scrapes against the rough-hewn wood of the lid.

Outside the box I can sense someone moving. I try to shout, to let them know I'm trapped in here. To let me out. But I can't. My breath freezes in my lungs, solidifying into a mass of fear so intense it threatens to explode from my body.

That's when the first shaft of light pierces the box. I feel the bullet enter my chest, splitting my skin, pushing through my ribs, before coming to rest against my spine.

Another shaft of light. Another bullet. More drill through the box's wooden top, until the fear melts into warm blood filling my lungs, drowning me in my dark coffin. I am dying. Can you die in a dream?

The lid opens slowly on well-oiled hinges, and all I can do is blink in the sudden brightness. My mouth opens and closes like a fish pulled from water. I can feel the hot blood running past my lips and down my cheeks, filling my ears. I gag, spitting more of the coppery, viscous fluid onto my face. Above me is a mirror, placed so I can see what's left of my body as my life seeps away.

But the reflection I see isn't mine. Instead it's Quincy. The man I killed.

I told myself—keep telling myself—that it was in self-defense. That I'd had no other choice. It doesn't make any difference.

Quincy lies in the small box, his skin sliced in a thousand places. His chest is a morass of blood and bone and flesh where the bullets—bullets that only moments ago I had felt—plowed into him.

And then the nightmare gets worse.

Quincy stares back at me, stares into my soul, and he begins to change. His black, beady eyes soften into hazel. His narrow face widens. His thin lips fill, curving into a persistent smile. It's not Quincy in the box anymore. It's Ian Miller, the man I love. The fine lace pattern of old scars on the left side of his face make him more beautiful rather than less. His hazel eyes—eyes I'd lost myself in so many times—slowly lose their light, until they are as dull as the Level 1 ceiling.

I used to wake up screaming. Thrashing in sheets wrapped so tight around me that it took two people to unwind them. My heart pounding so hard I thought it would burst through my chest. They moved me out of the bunkhouse until I learned to control myself better.

It took almost six months, half the time I'd been at the ACE training compound.

While the other ACE trainees bonded over bunkhouse chats and shared spaces, I learned how to squeeze more into the dark corner of my mind where I kept the other memories. Memories of being told I'd never see my parents again, of my uncle and aunt. Of Quincy's handiwork.

I was moved to a small room off the cookhouse. I'd lock myself in early at the end of the day, avoiding the others, avoiding everyone. Sometimes I'd hear the other students come in for a late night snack, chatting and happy; smell the fresh coffee and biscuits the cook, Pat, made for them. All I had to look forward to was another agonizing night. After they left, I'd hear a soft knock on my door and footsteps walking away. Pat would always leave a little snack for me.

We'd all been here almost a year, and I was bunking with the others now. The beds, hard, lumpy, and smelly, reminded me of the halfway house I was placed in after my parents were killed, adding more fuel to the nightmares that still came almost every night.

Only the screaming had stopped.

At the compound, I learned it helped to be outside, to feel the sun beating on my skin, the sky open above me. In winter, I walked from the bunkhouse to the cookhouse in just a t-shirt and shorts, wanting . . . *needing* to feel the wind and sun on my bare skin, no matter what the temperature.

There were no ceilings here, no putrid water dripping from the Ambients and girders, no recycled air. I'd grown to love the huge open expanse, no longer scared by a sky that stretched on forever. There was nothing to break the silent splendor of the mountains. Even transports were forbidden from flying overhead by the Canadian government, to keep the wilderness as pristine as possible.

ACE BOOT CAMP, KANANASKIS—SUNDAY, JUNE 11, 2141 5:35 A.M.

I woke up early again this morning, the nightmare's sweat still cling-ing to my skin, making the sheets cold and clammy. Turning over onto my side, I stared at the bunk beside me as the tendrils of fear slipped back into hiding. In the dim morning light, filtered through frayed red and white checked curtains, I could see the blanket rise and fall as the bunk's occupant slept. I knew her name. I knew she did well in physical challenges and poorly in others. But I didn't know *her*. I had missed that chance. I'm not sure I would have taken it even if it was offered.

It wasn't.

From what I'd been able to pick up, we'd all come from below Level 3. None of us had family or real friends that would miss us. Emma seemed to be the only exception; she'd been recruited from a small group of insurgents creating havoc on Level 2 near San Francisco.

The room stank of old shoes and sweaty clothes. Yesterday after-noon we'd done endurance training, tasked with running the moun-tain's trails while carrying our own food and water. We'd gotten back well after the sun had gone down, using small headlamps to light the way, and fallen into our bunks, exhausted. It was a relief not to hear the other girls talk. Not to be ignored, excluded yet again.

Janice, one of the other students, walked in from outside and silently crept back to her bed. I lay still, not wanting her to know I was awake, until her breathing evened out. I cautiously raised my head off the pillow. For the last three days, I'd felt nauseous in the mornings, barely making it to the latrines before throwing up. Things seemed to be better this morning. Hopefully, whatever had made me sick was gone. At least I didn't have to hide it from anyone today. I didn't want to be sick this close to graduation.

Even completely wiped out, I'd remembered to take Oscar out of my pocket and slip him under my pillow last night. Oscar was my small golden figurine, a vague image of a man with his arms crossed holding what I always thought was a sword. It was passed down from mother to daughter for generations. No one remembered why they called him that, but the name stuck. I'd been using him as a key chain when I was a courier. Now the chain and ring attached to Oscar's back were empty, my bike safely stored at Kai's restaurant.

Mom didn't give him to me. I'd snatched anything I could when the police dragged me from our small apartment—when the corporations killed Mom and Dad. It was all I had of them now.

Knowing I wasn't going to sleep anymore, I crept out of bed with Oscar in my hand, the cold floor raising goose bumps on my skin. Pulling on a pair of sweatpants, I grabbed my climbing gear off the hook by the door and slipped out of the bunkhouse into the chill morning air. I pulled on my sneakers, stiff and cold with yesterday's sweat. The sun had risen over the low hills at end of the valley. By the time I reached the western cliffs, it would have warmed up the rock well enough to get some climbing in.

One of the first things we were told when we got here was that we were never allowed to leave the compound without authorization. I hadn't let anyone control my life that way since I ran away from my aunt's house at fourteen, and I wasn't going to start. I'd been heading out since the first week, and kept on doing it. Either the instructors had gotten used to me, or they had finally given up. I walked across the yard, but barely got halfway across when I heard the cookhouse door slam shut.

Over time, Pat's late night offerings of food had turned into talks—and tears. After we shared our names, we shared our opinions on the camp students and staff. Eventually we became close enough to share our nightmares.

Hers were worse than mine.

I angled over to the cookhouse entrance. On the bench outside the door, Pat had left a muffin and a bottle of water. She didn't come out to see me. She knew I needed my time alone in the mornings. Time to get over the nightmares. Good friends did that. If I had a chance to head back to the cliffs after dinner, she'd probably join me.

Pat had been Black Ops before she became a cook. Before her breakdown. ACE had kept her on, and she was happy. For the most part. Sometimes her stories made me second-guess being here, but I really had nowhere else to go. She made me wonder if my nightmares would turn me into a cook instead of an operative.

I left the compound, pulling the crisp mountain air deep into my lungs until they hurt, trying to get rid of the smell of the bunkhouse, and took the path heading to the cliffs. The muffin, still warm from the oven, was gone before I hit the band of trees surrounding the valley. Some of the nausea I'd felt for the last few days came back, and I hoped the food would help quell it. It didn't, but at least I didn't feel like I was going to throw up. The sun had risen enough for me to feel its heat through the leaves. By the time I finished the steep half-hour hike, I was sweating and breathing hard. I stopped at the bottom of the cliff and took a swig of water.

Sitting on a rock, the morning sun warming my face, I stared at the valley below. The compound hid behind the trees I'd just hiked through. Low hills in the east turned rocky as they moved up the valley toward me, eventually becoming small peaks before growing into the cliff face and mountains behind me. I knew if I sat long enough, letting the silence permeate my skin, I would almost believe I was alone in the world. Six weeks ago I'd wanted to believe anything but. Ian had joined me; one of his rare visits to the compound. We had sat up here, the sun warming our naked skin. We didn't climb that day.

Pulling myself from the memory with difficulty, I took off my runners and socks, squeezed my bare feet into climbing shoes, and laced them up.

I stood and faced the cliff. It rose almost thirty meters here, slowly gaining height until it was more than double that at the far end. I'd been up and down the cliff face so many times the rock was like an old friend. The mornings I came here alone, I never climbed higher than three meters off the ground, my route traversing the rock face from right to left. When you put a new climb on a cliff, you got to name it. I called this one *Eyes of Hazel*.

I moved to the route's start, stretching my back. The large scar between my shoulder blades felt tight, as it always did first thing in the morning. I got it last year when the black box that blocked my tracker had melted into my skin. The trackers were active devices, injected into us at birth. They sent out a low power signal with every heartbeat. The good thing was we had to go near a sensor for them to be read. The bad was San Angeles was littered with sensors. I had control of mine; we all did if we worked for ACE. I was injected with a modified transmitter that I could control with my comm unit, letting me be anyone I wanted. Or no one at all, invisible to the sensors.

ACE still made the occasional offer to remove the scar. I always refused. I might try to shovel all my memories into a box where they couldn't hurt me anymore, but the burn was part of me. Part of who I was. Like Ian's scarred face. But on days like today, when it really bothered me, I wondered what it would be like without it. It was something I thought of more and more often.

I climbed up a meter before starting the traverse. My fingers slid over the rough limestone, finding the tiny fingerholds. I'd done this route so many times, they knew where to go by themselves. My feet moved from positive edges to gentle slopers, and I lost myself in the workout, the only sound my breathing. As I traversed, the sun casting my shadow on the rock in front of me, the tension slipped from my shoulders, the nightmare's memories slowly fading into the background.

Climbing wasn't part of the training process, but when an instructor had found me on one of my early forays from the compound, I'd been right here, touching the rock, feeling the captured heat of the sun seeping into my hand. It almost felt like the rock was alive, with a beating heart of its own. I wanted to know if there was a way to get to the top. Over time, the instructor brought Pat out to meet me. She showed me holds and routes. We progressed to real climbing, using ropes and cams and nuts and other types of protection against falling I'd never heard of. I'd learned to lead, to boulder, how to protect my second on a traverse. And through it all, I got stronger.

More recently, Pat had preferred running the mountain's trails, trying to best her time of slightly less than twenty-five minutes for the five-kilometer loop, and I climbed alone.

Looking back at the girl I was, the one who had walked into the compound almost a year ago, I saw someone weaker, mentally and physically. Her skin had been so pale it was almost translucent—the result of living under a roof and Ambients her entire life. Today, I could feel my muscles tense as I moved across the rock face. I knew when I pulled sideways on a hold that my lats would kick in to take the load. My skin had tanned under the not-so-gentle sun. The only thing that hadn't changed was my height. Being just over a meter and a half tall made me try even harder at climbing. At everything.

My ambition, my dedication, didn't help me win over the other students. They all tried hard, all wanted to be here, but while they were outside around a campfire, I was in my bunk studying. All of that disappeared when I was on the rock. The cool breeze coming up from the valley floor blew through my short hair, the sun warming me, and the silence becoming part of me. This was why I left the compound as often as I could. I wasn't here to make friends. According to the instructors, we were here for Agent training. Like Ian, I called it boot camp. Black Ops boot camp.

Across the valley, the unexpected *thrum* of a transport shuttle interrupted the quiet.

―――――

ACE BOOT CAMP, KANANASKIS—SUNDAY, JUNE 11, 2141
6:15 A.M.

Miller tossed and turned in the small bed. The mattress was horrible, and no matter which way he moved, something jabbed into his back or his side or his chest. He sighed. The crap he would put up with just to surprise his girl.

The surprise was supposed to have been yesterday, but when he'd gotten here, the recruits had all been out on training. When they weren't back by sundown, he'd waited another hour before it had become clear they'd still be a couple more. Miller had crawled into bed at 11:00 P.M. He'd see Kris tomorrow, his last chance before she graduated.

Next week, the recruits would start survival training. A week of hell in the mountains followed by another week in a fake city built into nearby caves. Simulated Level 1 and Level 2 environs, complete with gangs, food and water shortages, and filth. A lot of the recruits had come from Levels 1 and 2 and knew what it was like, but this was worse, intentionally worse, and made more so by almost a full year outdoors in the mountains. Some of them came out quivering heaps of flesh, others pure psychopaths.

When Miller had gone through it, it had changed him. He had come out stronger, quieter. Willing to do whatever it took to help the people who were forced to live on those Levels. In the intervening years, his resolve had been tested over and over. He did whatever it took to win.

Meeting Kris, falling in love with her, had changed him again. His resolve had deepened and shifted more toward fighting the corporations that made the world the way it was, instead of the individuals he had dealt with before. The change had moved him up the ranks, letting him see how corrupt the corporations truly were. ACE was the only sane thing in the world, working toward diminishing the corporations' power and reversing the damage they'd done to the world's ecosystem.

The recruits didn't know how lucky they were that ACE had chosen them. Sure, they'd all been alone, eking out what life they could on the lower levels, but they hadn't had to face the corporations. Didn't see the damage the corporations were causing. Kris had, though. She'd been through it, seen what the corporations did, and had come out the other side stronger. Like him.

His plan was to get Kris away for the weekend, just the two of them. They would be alone together for the first time in over a month. He missed holding her in his arms. Missed how she tasted.

He had booked a cabin at Baker Creek Resort down near Lake Louise. Tourism was still a big thing up here, and there were plenty of places to go. He'd almost picked the Lake Louise Chateau itself, an old, majestic place that wrapped around half the lake, overlooking the cool milky water with its faint hints of green from the winter runoff. The lake used to be a vibrant blue, back when it was glacier fed. That had been a long time ago. Miller wanted time alone with

Kris, and the hundred or so cabins at Baker Creek offered that more than the Chateau. It had cost him almost a month's salary to book one night. Clean outdoor space was something only the rich could afford on a regular basis.

Miller flipped onto his back and sighed. Fuck it. He didn't remember the beds being so bad. But then, after a tough day of training, sleeping on hard-packed dirt would have felt good. He was pretty sure they hadn't changed the mattresses since he'd been through. Sleep was moving further and further away. He might as well get up and see what the kitchen was offering for breakfast. When you had hungry recruits, the food had to be hearty and good, and it always was, at least as far as he remembered. It would make up for the crappy bed. He got dressed, keeping quiet so he wouldn't wake the instructors, and moved the backup gun he always carried from under his pillow to its ankle holster.

Leaving the bunkhouse, Miller walked across the grounds, heading for the kitchen directly opposite. He paused by the flagpole in the center of the quadrangle outside the cookhouse. Its base was surrounded by stunted lilacs, their scented flowers long since gone. The Canadian maple leaf, red against a white background, moved gently at the top. He looked left to the men's bunkhouse. The women stayed in a separate building behind it, and he waited a minute, hoping Kris would walk around the corner. The wind shifted, and the smell of bacon and fresh baked bread wafted through the compound.

Miller sighed and took a step away from the pole before coming to an abrupt stop. Something wasn't right . . . didn't feel right. He'd been Black Ops long enough to trust his instincts. He stepped back to the shrubs and scanned the compound's perimeter, not seeing anything out of the ordinary.

That's when he heard it. The sound of a transport coming from the east.

Transports didn't fly here. The Canadian government had declared all of their wilderness areas national historic sites. That meant no-fly zones. No exceptions. Miller dropped to a knee, minimizing his profile, and continued to scan the eastern horizon.

Suddenly, another sound punched through the air. Miller threw himself to the ground and rolled under the bushes, burying his head in his arms.

A single rocket cut over his head, screaming in the thin mountain air. The bunkhouse he'd just left disintegrated in slow motion. The rocket pierced the wall. The walls sucked inward before the explosion threw them back out. The sound of the detonation numbed his senses. Wind from the blast hit him, driving him deeper into the lilacs. Seconds later, his hiding place was pummeled by falling debris, shredding the leaves above him.

Miller lay still, his ears ringing in the silence that settled throughout the valley. His breath came in short, sharp bursts and he forced himself to slow it down, to breathe deeply. As he got his breathing under control, his pounding heart followed suit.

No one should have known this was an ACE training facility. But there was no reason to destroy it unless they did. What the fuck was going on?

A second scream pierced the air, the sound distant, cutting through the ringing in his ears. The cookhouse disappeared into shards of plastiwood that pelted the compound's central square. This shot had been lower. The transport was coming in for a landing. Miller thought their intent wasn't complete destruction. They'd destroyed the cookhouse, almost guaranteed to be empty this early in the morning, and the instructors. That left the rookies to protect what remained. It was either a fluke or they had more information than they should have.

They wanted something else.

The now almost leafless lilacs above Miller shook as the transport looped around the flagpole. The intense heat from its thrusters barely missed his back. For an instant, a shadow blotted out the sun. More grit was thrown into the air. The transport came in fast, blowing everything in its path out of the way. Miller shuffled backward, putting more of the bushes between him and the machine. He groped for the gun in its ankle holster, using the flying dust as cover, before peering through the bare branches, protecting his eyes against the grit with his hand. A third explosion shook the ground—the fuel tank used by the cookhouse stoves spewed black acrid smoke into the air.

The transport was fairly small, the type used for quick raids and extractions. Four rotatable thrusters pointed toward the ground. Two stubby wings holding more air-to-ground missiles sat above the open doors. At most, Miller figured it could carry ten people, including the pilot. Since they didn't destroy everything from the air, they must have come for an extraction, which meant only a handful of personnel at the most. Miller's first thought was of Kris.

Pieces of the cookhouse flew through the air, forced aside by the power of the engines. The branches still offered at least some protection from the onslaught. Miller squinted, trying to keep an eye on the transport. Dark figures jumped to the ground from the open door barely four meters from where he lay. He didn't move, hoping they wouldn't see him through the confusion they'd created.

The transport hadn't landed. It hovered above the ground, ready for a quick exit. Whoever these guys were, they knew their shit. Miller closed his eyes and forced himself to relax. A sense of calm washed through him, as it always did when he was working. This was what he knew.

He opened his eyes and moved slowly, using the cover provided by the hovering transport, and crouched beside the destroyed lilac.

His first objective would be the pilot. Get the transport out of the picture, and the men on the ground would have no place to run.

The shadowy figures split into two teams of four and jogged away, keeping low to the ground. As he watched them, Miller realized where they were going. There was only one thing in that direction: the recruits' bunks. As the men disappeared into the blowing dust, he heard two gunshots, crisp and clean even over the sound of the thrusters.

He threw his plan away and followed the men.

———

ACE BOOT CAMP, KANANASKIS—SUNDAY, JUNE 11, 2141 6:17 A.M.

I checked the ground below me. It was clear except for a small tree stump nestled against the rock face. I let go of my handholds, pushing gently away from the limestone, and landed in a crouch. Staying close to the ground, I spun to face the compound. I could barely see it from where I was, just a speck of red from the top of the flagpole and a corner of the cookhouse between a gap in the trees. I stood slowly, and more of the compound came into view.

Without warning one of the buildings, the one the instructors lived in, disintegrated in complete silence before the sound of the explosion ricocheted off the crag behind me. I flinched and scrambled behind an old lodgepole pine. Its rough bark pressed into my cheek. For a second I was back on Level 3, standing outside Internuncio as it disappeared into flames and rubble.

I remembered Howie's blue hand-painted motorcycle sitting outside the doors.

I remembered Quincy's grin.

I couldn't breathe. My arms wrapped around the pine, its rough, sticky bark anchoring me in the real world. Everything lost its color, changing to dull shades of gray. I had to get away. Run from the flames that licked through my memories. I stumbled, and everything went from gray to black.

The sound of a second explosion rolled up the valley like thunder, pulling me back from the edge of the abyss. I had fallen backward. The tree stump pressed into the small of my back. My head pushed against the limestone. I lurched to my feet and starting running, following the trail back to the compound. I didn't give myself the chance to fucking think.

If I did, I wasn't sure I'd be racing toward the destruction.

I knew I would never make it back in time to help. By the time I got there, the damn thing would be over. They'd taught us that the first week we were here. A successful attack, whether on friendly or enemy ground, should be over almost before it began. Get in and get out. The longer you hung around, the more chance for something to go wrong.

The best I would be able to do was look for survivors. I never thought I'd need my first aid training before I'd even graduated.

If there was anyone left.

I was halfway down before my brain registered the pain. The rocks and tree roots sticking up from the trail stabbed into the bottom of my feet with every step. In my rush to leave, I'd left my sneakers at the cliff. The tight climbing shoes were great on vertical rock, but sucked for anything else. The thin soles were designed to let you feel the nuances. They weren't meant for the trail. Each step slammed my toes into the pointy tips, sending harsh pangs into my feet. I pushed on, trying to ignore it.

Gunfire echoed through the valley. It sounded as though a full battle was taking place. The transports I knew were usually designed to carry about twenty people, but it sounded like there were a hundred or more down there. Was the transport the only source of intruders? What if they'd brought in ground troops during the night? For all I knew, there could be guns trained on me right now, waiting for a clean shot. My step faltered and I almost froze.

What the hell was I doing? I didn't have a gun, or a knife. Or anything else for that matter.

A third explosion hammered through the air, and a ball of flame roiled into the sky. Black smoke billowed up, filling the horizon and spreading across the valley. The compound disappeared behind the black smudge, briefly obscuring my view. The smoke cleared in a sudden *whump*, and the transport lifted away, turning back in the direction it had come from. With its departure, the thick cloud rose back into the sky.

Silence filled the air.

The ground leveled out and I pushed harder, picking up my pace before reaching the compound gate. My heart beat to the rhythm of my feet, my lungs pulling in as much of the thin mountain air as they could.

Except for Pat, I wasn't friends with anyone in the compound. But they were still my *people*.

I'd do whatever I could to help them.

ACE BOOT CAMP, KANANASKIS—SUNDAY, JUNE 11, 2141
6:22 A.M.

There were two bunkhouses and two teams. Each team was dressed in mottled gray, their forms vague, blending with the dirt thrown up by the transport. Ski goggles covered their eyes. They'd be able to see a lot better in this mess than Miller would. Each person carried an assault rifle and had what looked like a handgun strapped to their waist. They were definitely here for business.

Miller didn't know which group he should follow. Which team was heading for the women's bunkhouse? He picked the one curving to the left. By the track they were following, it seemed they would go around the first building. The transport still hovered behind him, its side door facing the bunkhouses. At that angle, the pilot shouldn't be able to see him. Miller could barely make out the people he was following. It would be worse near the thrusters.

He tripped over something and staggered forward. A pistol skittered across the ground in front of him. He scooped it up and looked back. He'd kicked the weapon out of one of the instructors' hands. Dirt blown up by the transport had started to mound against her body. Miller went back to the prone form, checking for a pulse. There wasn't one. Two holes punctured the instructor's shirt, dead center of the body mass. The blood had a layer of grit sticking to it.

Miller checked the gun. Its magazine had been ejected and the mechanism was filled with sand and grit, making it useless to anyone that tried to use it. Even if he could find the magazine, he doubted it would work. He dropped the weapon beside the body and pivoted back toward the bunkhouses, sprinting after the gray uniforms. The farther he got from the transport, the better the visibility. Which wasn't a good thing. With no cover, he was vulnerable. He pressed on anyway.

The team in front of him split again, two of them running around the back of the men's bunkhouse. He had followed the wrong group. The other two moved to either side of the front door. Miller dropped to the ground and watched, not sure if he should stay to see what they did, or loop around to the women's bunkhouse.

If he engaged them now, chances were he would be dead in

seconds. The fact that they split up helped a lot. Two against one was always better than four.

Suddenly, the door to the bunkhouse burst open, taking the men standing beside it by surprise. The door slammed into one of the intruders, banging his head against the outside wall. Two students stumbled out still dressed in running shorts and t-shirts from last night's exercise. They blindly ran past the attackers, not stopping to check if anyone was waiting for them. They only made it a few steps before one of the front door team put bullets into their backs.

How could these guys be only two weeks away from graduating? Miller thought. He mentally shrugged. They'd never make it now.

More shots came from the back of the bunkhouse, and the two attackers regrouped, preparing to storm through the open door.

Miller barely hesitated before making up his mind. There wasn't much he could do for Kris now, and he couldn't leave a bunch of trainees to fend for themselves. That's not who he was.

Miller stood and fired three quick shots, two to the body and one to the head—the training taking over without him thinking about it.

One of the attackers at the front door pitched forward, falling onto his partner. The back of his uniform darkened with blood. The second attacker ducked and spun, bringing his rifle to bear on Miller. The split second it took him to maneuver around his partner's body gave Miller all the time he needed. He took another three shots and the second attacker fell, joining his partner in death.

The gunfire from the back entrance had stopped, and Miller waited, out of bullets. The silence meant that either all the trainees inside were dead and he was in big trouble, or the students had everything under control. Either way, he'd done all he could, and was only wasting his time hanging around.

Miller rushed to the attackers' bodies and grabbed the handgun and a comm unit from the closest one. Close-quarter fighting was no place for a rifle. For a moment, he thought he recognized the man he was stealing the equipment from. Miller pushed the thought away—now was not the time. As he raced toward the second bunkhouse, he jammed the comm unit's earbud into his ear.

The women's dorm was farther out. He hadn't heard any gunfire, so maybe they hadn't been hit yet. If he was in charge, he would have synchronized both teams. It was possible the two dead recruits had stopped that. Miller hadn't even made it halfway to the dorm when he heard the bullets start to fly again.

The comm unit in Miller's ear came to life.

"Over their heads, just get them under control."

"Roger that."

Under control? That was a different ploy than he had seen in the men's quarters, unless they hadn't had time to implement it. What the hell was going on?

"We're in. Looking now."

Miller changed his tactics yet again. His plan had been to get in and start shooting. Take them by surprise and take them out. Now it sounded more like a hostage situation.

He slowed down as he approached the bunkhouse. The front door was open, swinging slightly in the wind. He'd lost any advantage the swirling dust had given him—the second bunkhouse was blocked from the transport by the first building. Putting his back to the faded exterior wall, Miller peeked between the gap created by the door's hinges.

He saw four women on their knees with their hands clasped behind their heads. They were in the aisle between the beds that lined the walls. Miller changed his angle and saw the four attackers leaning over them, their guns trained on the women. Their gray fatigues seemed out of place against the red checked curtains of the dorm.

One attacker stepped forward, toward the first trainee in line, roughly grabbing her blonde hair that was still tousled by sleep. He jerked her head back and pointed her face to the ceiling. She cried out in pain. Miller watched as he did the same to the other three. From his angle, he couldn't see the faces of the women, but he knew who was missing. Kris's height would have given her away. These women were too tall.

"She's not here."

"Then find out where she is."

The attacker yanked at the first woman's hair again, forcing her to look at him.

"Where is she?"

Miller didn't hear the answer.

"You know exactly who I'm talking about." The man raised his gun, pointing it at her head. *"Last chance."*

He waited for maybe half a second before pulling the trigger, reaching for the next person in line before the body had hit the ground.

Fuck! He hadn't even given her time to answer. This was getting out of control fast.

Miller moved, crouching behind the door, and fired two shots through the wood. He rolled back out of the way before the return shots riddled the door from top to bottom.

Miller risked a quick glance through the hinge gap again. One of the men was down. The distraction he'd provided was all two of the recruits needed. They launched themselves toward the attackers, aiming low for the knees, and brought them down. Miller stood and kicked the door out of his way, firing more shots over the women's heads. The interrogator fell onto one of the beds and lay still. Miller put another bullet into the body, just to be sure.

One of the men struggled back to his feet, pushing away the

writhing figure on top of him. He kicked her in the gut and ran, making it to the back door before Miller had a chance to take a shot.

"We're down. I don't think we got all the instructors with the missile hits. I'm coming in."

Both women were now on the last guy, their fists swinging as fast as they could. Half the time they got in each other's way.

Miller ran toward them. "Keep him alive. We need him."

They ignored him, pummeling the still form of the attacker. Miller grabbed one of them by her arm, hauling her off the man. Her fists were covered in blood.

"I said we need him."

The third student finally moved from her kneeling position, taking the woman from his arms and dragging her to an empty bed. Miller pulled at the second trainee, knowing it was already too late. There had been enough power in the punches to make the face barely recognizable as human.

A shadow flickered in the corner of Miller's eye. He ducked and twisted, aiming his gun at the front door. His finger twitched on the trigger before he recognized the compound's cook. She stood in the open doorway, a gun in her shaking hand.

"I . . . I just stepped out to pee . . ." Her face was pale, her eyes unfocused, staring at nothing.

Miller strode toward her. He'd heard stories of the cook. How she'd had to be pulled from the field. He didn't know much about post-traumatic stress, but he knew he didn't want her to have a gun.

The sound of the transport taking off pulsed through the open door, followed by a wave of dark, acrid smoke. Miller relaxed a little. They were leaving.

He gently removed the gun from the cook's hand and pulled her out of the doorway. She backed against the wall and slid down, sitting hunched over, not moving.

Walking back to the bodies, Miller collected their weapons and laid them on a bed far from the trainees. He had three handguns now, and there was no one in the room he wanted to give one to. It was a personal thing; he didn't trust recruits until they'd seen some field time. One of the trainees pulled blankets off the bed and covered the bodies.

Miller sat, running his fingers through his hair. Dirt and small pieces of plastiwood fell into his lap.

Where the hell was Kris?

CHAPTER 2

ACE BOOT CAMP, KANANASKIS—SUNDAY, JUNE 11, 2141
6:27 A.M.

THE SOUND OF ANOTHER TRANSPORT echoed across the valley. I kept running until I reached the boulder that marked the compound's entrance. I huddled in its shadow, struggling to catch my breath, wishing for some time to think.

I cringed as the transport flew overhead, washing me in the heat of its thrusters. I wanted to run back to the protection of the forest. If these were more fucking attackers, I'd never make it. My training didn't allow it. I knew I had to go in, find a weapon, and do what I could to help. I squeezed my eyes shut against the flying grit and waited.

The pitch of the engines changed. I forced my eyes open and peered around the boulder. The transport, a large one that could seat twenty or more, settled lightly to the ground beside the flagpole. The thrusters cycled down to an idle. A hush fell over the valley. If I closed my eyes again—and I desperately wanted to—I could almost believe the morning had been a dream.

But I wasn't about to do that.

Someone ran out of the billowing smoke, holding a cloth to their face. I didn't recognize them, but they wore shorts and a t-shirt. A trainee from yesterday's run. I waited for the sound of gunfire. When none came, I guessed the unmarked transport was from ACE.

I left the rock and ran through the gate, back to what was left of my home. Inside the entrance on my left was nothing but rubble. The instructor's bunkhouse, the one Miller always used when he came for a visit, was gone. A pit opened in the bottom of my stomach, threatening to swallow me whole. I lost control of my legs and almost fell. I slowed to a walk.

What if he had been here when this had happened?

Forcing myself to regain control, I turned and stared past the transport at the cookhouse. The pit in my gut deepened. Pat!

I followed the fence, staying as far from the transport as possible. I didn't want to have to see or talk to anyone. Not yet.

Black smoke poured from a hole in the ground. The fuel tanks for the cookhouse stoves had blown, leaving a burning pit. The air was thick with the smell of chemicals and smoke, making my eyes water. I took a step closer to what was left of the structure. Through the smoke, I thought I saw people moving. I didn't know if they were survivors or rescuers from the transport.

Maybe one of them was Pat. Maybe she'd gotten out. I took another few steps, and the smoke thinned. My hope disappeared. No one could have made it out of there.

The loss of Pat felt like someone had reached through my skin and grabbed my heart, twisting it into a hard knot. Tears threatened to stream down my face. I turned my back on the rubble, no longer able to look at it, and kneaded my eyes.

I'd come too far to be this weak.

There would be time to mourn later, when this was over. A single thought rose through the chaos and emotion; at least Pat wasn't my fault. I wasn't sure I could handle another burden like that. The thought immediately made me feel guilty.

By the flagpole, people jumped out of the transport carrying medi-kits. They ran away from me, toward the still-standing buildings. Some of them came back with people, helping them walk and talking to them. Others came back in teams, awkwardly carrying long black bags between them that slumped in the middle. The bodies of the dead.

I didn't want to know why the recruit bunkhouses were left standing. I could already feel the paranoia setting in.

The sound of gunfire made me turn away from the cookhouse, and I tripped over a shattered window frame. I dropped to my hands and knees and struggled to get back up, ending up kneeling on the ground, my mind empty but traveling a million kilometers an hour.

Heavy black boots came into view, and I glanced up. Three men pointed their weapons at my head, their faces smeared with green and black paint. Through the haze I noticed they all wore camouflage, and though it seemed like they were uniforms, I couldn't see any markings or insignia.

Two of them stepped forward and hoisted me to my feet. No one spoke. They led me toward the transport while the third one fell in behind us. I felt the cold metal of his gun pointing between my shoulder blades. My melted skin twitched.

They ended up almost dragging me. My body was shutting down. I couldn't feel their grip. I forced myself to concentrate to keep my feet moving. It wasn't quite working. My mind kept slipping back to last year when Internuncio had blown up. The sounds and smells that filled the air were the same.

I tried to pull myself from the stupor that threatened to take me over. The compound was a mess. Gray smoke from the buildings mingled with the dark cloud billowing from the hole. I had moved from the clean mountains into hell in only a few steps.

I knew I should have been here to help. But I had to be selfish. Had to have things my own way. Maybe if I had been here, I could have done something and things wouldn't have ended so badly. I shook my head again. This wasn't my fault. Not this time. I couldn't let myself think that way.

We stopped in front of a medic and another woman. I stared, barely recognizing her. It was Janice, one of the other recruits. She seemed to have aged ten years. Her face was smeared with blood, her eyes sunken and flat.

Until she looked at me.

Suddenly I saw fire and hate with such intensity that I stumbled back. The men gripping my arms pulled me back in line.

"You know her?" His voice was gruff, like he wasn't used to talking.

Janice nodded and walked past us, leaving the medic behind. He rushed to follow her. As she entered the shadow of the transport's stunted wing, I could swear I saw her hand move to a bulge at the back of her shirt. She turned back to face me, staring into my eyes with the same hatred I'd seen moments earlier, before letting her empty hand drop. Janice turned her back on me and entered the transport, as if I didn't exist anymore. As if I didn't matter.

A single thought forced itself through the fog in my head. Pat had liked her. It didn't make me feel better.

The men let go of me and shoved me toward the transport. "Get on board, we're evacuating everyone." They didn't stick around long enough to know if I was able to stay standing or not.

I shambled closer to the open door, unsure of what else to do.

When I got close, a medic pulled me aboard and shoved a bottle of water into my hands. He pointed to the hard plastic seats behind him.

I picked one as far away from Janice as I could.

ACE BOOT CAMP, KANANASKIS—SUNDAY, JUNE 11, 2141
6:25 A.M.

Miller knew the bunkhouse wasn't the best place to stay. Visibility was limited, and it was too easy to block any of the exits. He had heard a second, bigger transport fly overhead a short time ago. His best guess was that it was an ACE evac unit or the Canadian military. It didn't make much sense for it to be anything else. If the smaller ship had been expecting reinforcements, it wouldn't have left.

Still, it was in their best interest to move someplace more defensible. The only problem was that this was a training facility. Even worse, it was disguised as guest camp for people who wanted to enjoy the Canadian wilderness. There wasn't any place that was defensible, except maybe the underground weapons bunker. And they didn't have access to that.

Time to make do with what he had.

Miller sat on one of the beds, his gun reloaded and back in its ankle holster, the others sitting on the bed beside him. He'd checked the rifles. They were loaded and ready as well. Miller was familiar with how they worked; ACE used the same kind for assaults where body count was a high priority. It really wasn't the best weapon for what he'd seen today.

The rifles, K-3700s, were designed to be simple and dependable. Accuracy wasn't one of their strong points. Capable of over seven hundred 9mm rounds a minute, devastation was their main goal. There were more modern weapons out there, but nothing seemed to stop another human being better than a bullet.

His hands started shaking; they always did at the end of a mission. Miller did his best to hide them from the others in the bunkhouse. It wasn't fear or hate that made him shake. It was the adrenaline still coursing through his veins, searching for release.

The student he'd pulled off the body was sitting on a bed across the center aisle. She rubbed her hands, desperately trying to get rid of the dried blood that covered them. The other two women were rifling through the dead man's clothes, hoping for something that indicated who or what he was.

Miller knew they wouldn't find anything; these guys were professionals.

The cook still sat on the floor by the front door, her legs curled under her dirty apron, staring at nothing. Her face exposed a world of pain and memories. He couldn't bear to watch.

That made three out of five who could help if the attack wasn't over yet. Maybe the one on the bed would snap out of it. That would make four. One more look at the cook convinced Miller she wouldn't be any help at all.

The women searching the body came up empty. Miller scooped two of the handguns and two rifles off the bed and walked over to them. They stood as he got closer.

"Here, you may need these," he said, handing them a handgun and a rifle each.

The women took the weapons. One of them immediately checked the handgun's clip and verified there was one in the chamber. When she was done, she reached out a hand.

"Janice."

"Miller." Her handshake was firm and steady.

Janice pointed her thumb over her shoulder. "She's Emma."

Emma glanced up from making sure the safety was on and smiled.

"I'm pretty sure the second transport is friendly," Miller said. "But if it isn't, can you two handle those?" He nodded toward the rifles. Weapons training was part of the course, but he wanted them to actually think about it and answer.

Janice nodded. "Emma's best in class on the range. She'll trim your nose hairs from three hundred meters. You might lose some skin at four hundred, though."

"Not with this piece of shit," Emma said, holding the K-3700 at arm's length as though it was the most disgusting thing she'd ever seen. The blood on her hands didn't seem to bother her.

Miller ignored her. "Good. We need to get out of here. We'll head out the back door and follow the fence to the gate. Once we're in the woods, we'll have a better chance."

"What if the transport is ours?" Janice asked.

"Then we're better off than we started."

"We'll have cover once we get behind the instructor bunkhouse," Emma said. "But when we get outside the fence, we won't have anything until we reach the trees."

"It's worse than that. The bunkhouse is gone. And we've got these two to take care of."

Janice glanced over to the cook with a look hovering between pity and disgust. "I say leave 'em. They'll slow us down if we really need to move."

Miller felt like decking her. "Then it's a good thing you're not in charge, recruit. Now sling your rifles and grab them. We're moving out."

Janice blanched at the tone in Miller's voice, but she didn't hesitate to follow his orders. She double-checked the safety on the handgun and shoved it down the back of her pants before slinging the rifle. She strode to the cook while Emma grabbed their bunkmate. Miller peeked out the front window, watching the corners of the men's bunkhouse for any movement.

"Okay, let's go. Stay low and move as fast as you can. It may be friendlies out there, so don't shoot until we're sure who they are."

"You mean until one of us is dead," said Janice.

"If it takes you that long to figure it out, we've wasted a year on you. Now move!" Miller was pretty sure Janice would have made it out of the simulated city as a pure killer. There was a time and a place for people like that, but he hated working with them.

He was the last to leave, closing the door quietly behind him.

Where the fuck was Kris?

Even though the compound was disguised as a resort, there were protocols to follow. The fence was chain-link, interwoven with plastiwood to make it seem more natural. You could still see through it in spots. There were no bushes or long grasses to hide in, either inside or outside the fence. Miller hoped the transport was friendly.

They managed to keep the men's bunkhouse between them and the transport for half the trip. That left them about eighteen meters of exposure before they had a chance to hide behind what was left of Miller's bunkhouse. After that was the gate.

Miller hunkered down, keeping his rifle aimed at the portion of the transport he could see. He sent Emma first. She ran, half dragging, half carrying the other recruit. Once she got behind the diminishing smoke from the explosion, she dropped her load and duplicated Miller's stance.

Janice made it most of the way before someone climbed out of the rubble.

She dropped the cook and unslung her rifle.

Miller saw the white medic armband, covered in soot from the bunkhouse. Janice lifted the rifle and clicked off the safety.

Miller stood and yelled, "Hold your fire."

Janice pulled the trigger. The ground between her and the medic ruptured, spraying dirt into the air.

Miller ran toward Janice. He was too far away. "Hold your fire!"

The path of the bullets moved closer to the medic.

Janice fell, her bullets spraying harmlessly into the wreckage of the bunkhouse. The cook grappled her legs with one arm and reached for the rifle with the other. Janice fought back, trying to break free.

Three men in full camouflage ran from the corner of the men's bunkhouse.

"Hold your fire." Miller tackled Janice, helping the cook pin her to the ground. "They're fucking ours!"

As fast as it had begun, it was over.

Emma was herded back to Miller by the men. Janice lay stunned on the ground, her finger still twitching over an imaginary trigger. The cook had let go and scurried to the fence, sitting with her back against it. Miller could hear her gasping for air.

One of the men in camouflage looked down at Miller and grinned. "What the hell got you into this mess, Miller?"

Miller stood, letting go of Janice. "Wrong place, wrong time, Liam." He'd worked with Liam and his team multiple times over the last few years. "How the hell did you guys get here so fast?"

"We monitor the airspace, same as the Canadian government. As soon as we figured out the path of the transport, we launched."

Another medic came, helping Janice to her feet, and started a slow walk to the transport.

"You under control here?" Liam asked. "We need to finish securing the compound before the Canadians get here from Cold Lake or

Comox to find out who broke the no fly zone. We scrambled out of Calgary, so they can't be more than a few minutes behind us."

Miller surveyed the area, stopping briefly at Emma and the cook. "Yeah, we're good. I'll get this group to the transport."

Without another word, the three men left, heading back to the bunkhouses.

Miller watched them leave. Kris wasn't here. If she was hiding anywhere in the compound, the rescue crew would find her. If she wasn't, then either she was safe outside the compound or they'd gotten her. But why her? Why here? Why now? In another few weeks, she would have been back in San Angeles or on a mission. A one-on-one encounter on the street would have been easier and safer. This attack was almost personal, but who would have the resources to do it?

Only the corporations.

Emma approached him. "They were looking for Kris," she said.

He nodded. "Where is she?"

Emma shrugged. "Sometimes she gets up early and heads for the cliffs. Sometimes she heads for an early breakfast."

Miller's empty stomach knotted. He forced himself to walk to the cook. "Was Kris in the cookhouse?"

She didn't respond.

Miller nudged her with his foot and she stared up at him, struggling to get the words out.

"I saw her heading out and gave her some food. Sometimes she changes her mind and comes in for breakfast, though." She sucked in a deep breath and looked back at the ground. "I heard the door slam when I left to pee. I don't know who it was."

The cook's words cut through Miller. His hands started shaking again. This time, it wasn't the adrenaline. He stumbled away, sucking in deep breaths to stop the nausea that threatened to take over.

Kris had to have gone climbing this morning. It was the only solution he was willing to accept. Despite trying to convince himself, Miller ended up standing beside what was left of the cookhouse. A couple of medics sifted through the rubble, pulling a body from the wreckage. The face was blackened beyond recognition. They rolled the body into a bag and lifted it. Miller's insides churned as they carried the body out. It was too big to be Kris. He stumbled backward. She *had* to have gone climbing.

Another medic touched Miller on the shoulder. "We need to be gone in ninety seconds. Canadian military aircraft have been spotted on radar. They're moving fast."

Miller nodded. He had a decision to make, and not much time to make it. Stay and look for Kris, or leave and never know. It wasn't much of a decision. One look in the transport, and then he'd head into the woods. The cliff band was west of here.

If Kris was out there, he'd find her.

⟫⟩

ACE BOOT CAMP, KANANASKIS—SUNDAY, JUNE 11, 2141
6:28 A.M.

The transport filled up quickly. Three more students got in: Emma from my bunkhouse and two of the male students, Isaac and Andrew. They all shuffled past me, choosing to sit farther toward the back. Emma gave me a weak smile, almost stopping as if to talk to me before Janice grabbed her arm, pulling her past my seat.

Medics tossed their bags through the open door and climbed in after them. They all moved to the front, leaving room for the soldiers to follow. I didn't know if ACE actually had any true soldiers, but it's how I thought of them.

I stared at each face as it came in the door, still hoping that Pat would walk in. After most of the soldiers' seats were filled, I sunk deeper into misery. At one point, I looked behind me, believing I heard Pat's calming voice. All I saw were the other trainees. Janice caught me searching and I quickly swept past her.

At the very back, wedged between the seats, were the body bags. Once I realized they were back there, I faced forward again.

I didn't see Pat.

Pain from my feet drove through my dejection. I reached down to take off my climbing shoes. Pulling my feet from the tight confines of the shoes was almost more painful than the run down from the cliffs. Blood rushed back to my toes, flushing them with heat. Pat sometimes said that taking off your climbing shoes was better than sex. I'd always laughed, thinking she couldn't have been doing it right, then.

My hand slid into my pocket on reflex, digging for Oscar. I gripped him in my fingers and rubbed his inscrutable face with my thumb. Sometimes I wondered what secrets his gaze held. What had he seen in the generations he'd been in my family? Today, I envied his ability to not feel. To stand apart from what went on around him.

Shadows blocked the light coming from the door and I glanced up, my eyes taking a second to adjust to the change. The first thing that came into focus was a white apron. Pat climbed on board and dropped into a seat across the aisle from me. I couldn't stop the smile that stretched across my face before I saw the pain etched on hers.

I reached out and grabbed her hand, squeezing. She jerked away, going almost fetal in her chair. My elation at seeing her evaporated instantly, turning to concern. If what had happened had given me flashbacks to last year, I couldn't imagine what they had done to her. I knew enough to leave her alone for a while, whispering that I was here when she needed me. Some demons had to be fought solo. A medic gently placed a blanket over her.

The pitch of the thrusters changed and I felt a slight lurch. We were out of here. One of the soldiers reached a hand down through the still open door. Instead of pulling someone in, a head appeared, scanning the people in the transport. My heart jumped into my throat and I stood in my seat.

"Ian!"

His eyes found mine, and he grabbed the soldier's hand. The door shut behind him and the transport lifted into the air. I fell back into my seat as the transport sped forward, the hard plastic pressing against my spine. Ian grabbed onto the seatbacks, using them for support, and made his way down the aisle.

He climbed over me, collapsing next to the window before grabbing me in a hug so tight I almost couldn't breathe. For the first time since this whole thing had started, I felt safe. A sense of disappointment swept through me when he let go. He held my face in his hands, examining me as if I was somehow damaged.

"I thought I'd lost you," he said.

I raised my hand, running my fingers down the scars on his face. A tear fell from his eye, and I wiped it gently away with my thumb. "Yeah, not gonna happen anytime soon," I said with fake bravado. We sat like that a while longer as the transport raced through the valley, bobbing and weaving as it followed the contours of the land. The sound of someone behind us throwing up pulled us apart. I kind of hoped it was Janice that was sick.

I glanced at Pat. She was sleeping across the hard seats, the blanket pulled over her head. I turned back to Ian.

"What are you doing here?" I asked.

He leaned back. "Long story."

I listened as he explained what he had planned for the coming weekend, my head resting on his shoulder. When he reached the part about the women's bunkhouse, I pulled away, suddenly cold and tense. I sat up straight.

"They were looking for me? Why? Who?"

"I don't know. None of their team made it long enough for me to question them. Have you contacted anyone outside of the compound?"

"No, of course not. Who would I talk to?"

"Did anyone come through the compound on another course? Maybe just for a week or so?"

"No one I talked to."

Miller nodded his head. "Okay." He took my hand in his. "We'll figure it out."

I buried my face into his shirt, and I knew. This *was* all my fault. How many people had died today?

All because of me.

LOS ANGELES, LEVEL 4—SUNDAY, JUNE 11, 2141 7:00 A.M.

Jeremy Adams sat behind the small, battered desk, a far cry from what he was used to when he was in charge of Meridian defenses. He ran his fingers over the rough surface, tracing the outlines of names of people long since forgotten, forcing himself to stay calm. It never used to be this hard.

"What do you mean, you didn't get her?" His voice came out as a soft purr, and he smiled inwardly, quite proud of himself. His pleasure increased when the man in front of him cringed. This was the way it should be.

"The pilot and one guy managed to get out. The pilot has no clue what happened but the guy does."

"And does this . . . *guy* have a name?" Jeremy heard his voice rising and he struggled to maintain control. Anger was a constant force that lived under his skin, and he'd lost control of it too many times recently.

"Yes, of course. Sorry." Another cringe. "Corporal Marl. He came from Meridian when we made the call."

"Get his complete story. Corroborate what you can. Then kill him. We don't need people who run at the first sign of trouble."

"The others were killed. He barely escaped."

"Did he come back with the girl?" Jeremy asked.

"N—no."

"Then he is a failure on more than one front." Jeremy jerked to his feet, scraping the old desk across the floor, and his voice rose into a scream. "And failure will not . . ." Realizing he'd lost control yet again, he forced himself to sit back down and reached for the water bottle in front of him. His face felt flushed, hot. He took a slow sip before he risked talking again. In a much softer voice, he continued. "And failure will not be tolerated. Neither will argument."

Everything about the man in front of him reeked of fear. Normally it would have made Jeremy feel good, but nothing had been the same since the courier had destroyed everything he'd worked so hard to achieve. Instinctively, he reached for his shoulder, stopping himself before he began to massage it. He'd started the habit after they'd shot him with the dart last year. Back when he was torturing Miller as retribution for killing his best sniper, Abby. Habits made for a weak man, and he was not weak.

The man in front of him let out a hasty "Yes, sir," and backed toward the door. Jeremy froze him in his tracks by simply looking at him. Jeremy let the smile show this time.

"I want the girl. Don't fail me again."

The man continued backing out of the small room, closing the door as he crossed the threshold.

Jeremy's fingers returned to tracing the names etched into the desk. The girl had done this to him. It was her fault he was down here, stuck between Levels 3 and 4 in a room with no windows. Not controlling Meridian. Her and her asshole boyfriend. He was next on the list.

A war was beginning to build above Earth—war that he had planned, had prepared for—and that . . . that *fucking bitch* had taken it away from him.

Jeremy pulled the small desk closer to him and took another sip of water.

Careful, old man. You can't afford to lose it now. You'll get back everything she took from you. It will all get better when she's gone.

He wanted Kris. She had been a throwaway. Someone with no family and no friends, someone that wouldn't be missed, the perfect sacrificial pawn. Instead, she'd destroyed everything he'd worked for. Taken it away from him the moment it had come into his grasp.

He'd planned this attack so well, even placing Janice in the camp to give him the lay of the land. It was supposed to be a quick in and out. Get the girl and chalk up the attack to one of the corporations. Janice had given the signal this morning, an early attack would surprise everyone. Nothing had worked out right.

Killing Kris was his first step to redemption. And if not redemption, then at least satisfaction. Nothing was going to get in his way.

KADOKAWA SAT CITY 2 (FORMERLY MERIDIAN SAT CITY)— SUNDAY, JUNE 11, 2141 7:20 A.M.

Bryson Searls stood in the airlock of his lab, waiting for the air to cycle through the systems. He'd spent the better part of the last ten years ensconced between the lab's brilliant white walls and stainless steel work surfaces. This morning was the last time he would walk through the pressurized doors and take off his white face mask, booties, and matching full-body suit with its damn integrated hoodie.

At least he hoped it was.

He remembered the day he had come to the lab for the first time. A young kid fresh out of university, riding the wave of a fantastical thesis on quantum teleportation and uncertainty. The first time he'd stepped across the eight-centimeter gap that segregated the lab from the rest of the Sat City, allowing the room to float free of the constant vibrations the satellite generated. That's when he'd made his choice. Back then, it had seemed like a miracle. He'd been courted by all the corporations, offered more money than he would be able to spend in a single lifetime. Hell, ten lifetimes. In the end, he'd decided to go with Meridian, a small corporation that made most of its money maintaining the Sat Cities for the big three: SoCal, IBC, and Kadokawa.

But none of them had *this* lab. His lab. Meridian had given it to him, and anything he thought it needed to get the job done. He'd been their wunderkind, and he could do no wrong. He'd performed miracles for them, going from instantaneously moving photons across a room to moving ships across the vastness of space in the short time he'd been here.

Only a year ago, Jeremy had insisted on performing a quantum jump drive test with humans, over Bryson's strenuous objections. Rats were no longer good enough for Jeremy. The test had succeeded, but only long enough for the wrong decisions to be made.

A month after the pilot and the two crew had returned, they started showing signs of mental degradation. A couple of weeks later, they couldn't even remember their own names. A week after that, they were dead.

An autopsy, which Bryson insisted on attending despite his

aversion to blood, showed an almost Alzheimer's-like degradation of the hippocampus and posterior cerebral cortex. A dangerous combination that had led to the speedy deaths of the crew. He'd researched medical terminology and case studies, hoping they would lead him to an answer. Once, he'd even called his dad to get more information, closing the link before the connection could be made. That was a bridge he'd burned long ago.

It was only recently he'd come to realize his old man, the great Doc Searls, had been right about a lot of things.

Jeremy had kept the deaths of the crew quiet for as long as he could, but after the hostile takeover by Kadokawa, it bubbled to the surface like leprosy. Kadokawa had used a lot of resources to take over Meridian, and they weren't happy that the drive turned out to be a failure. Jeremy had disappeared, a ghost into the night, leaving Bryson to fend for himself. That was when he had found out Jeremy's true plans.

He felt foolish now. He had believed, truly believed, that Meridian wanted the quantum drive to help the people of Earth. When huge quantities of water were found in Andromeda, he'd thrown a party for everyone who worked in the lab. His inventions, his discoveries, were going to make the world a better place.

With ample access to water, no one would die of thirst or hunger just because they couldn't afford to pay for it. Farms that were closed because they could no longer irrigate their fields could reopen. The world could become green again. He hadn't thought about it then, but maybe there was more of his dad in him than he'd believed.

Jeremy's plans had been different. He had wanted war. The ability to move troops almost instantaneously with no chance for the enemy to predict when or where they would arrive was a powerful tool. Now the war was on its way, and Jeremy's plans were coming to fruition without him or the drive.

Kadokawa had continued where Jeremy left off, funding Bryson and his lab to find out what had gone wrong and how to fix it. Knowing why they wanted the quantum drive left Bryson feeling hollow and empty. At first, he had refused to work, believing the choice was still his to make. When Kadokawa had started threatening his staff, he still balked. After they had seriously hurt the first one—an intern with no real responsibilities named Melanie—he'd begun his work again.

He'd begun planning to get out of the prison his lab had become at the same time.

Early on, he had made it a habit to go to the executive-class ship they had outfitted for the failed test, its engines removed and disassembled in the lab. He would sit in the hollow metal shell thinking of what had gone wrong. What had they missed? The first time he went, he'd created a panic until they found him. For the next few months, guards would accompany him, standing outside the hulk as he thought about the dead crew—whether they had families or not, if they were forced to take the flight or they had volunteered. More recently, he was just left alone, free to wander around the Sat City. Kadokawa had apparently decided he had no place to go.

Through it all, Bryson had continued to do his job, keeping his staff safe and working toward a solution. He had found the answer only last week.

Everyone had gone home for the night, exhausted from the endless weeks and months of overtime. Exhausted by the repeated failures. Bryson had stayed, poring over the latest test results. The quiet of the empty lab always helped him focus, and his mind settled into the data, visualizing the ebb and flow of formulas and results. As often happened, the solution popped into his head as he lay half-asleep, the cold of the stainless steel desk pressing into his cheek.

He ran the test again that night, finishing before morning. All the data pointed to not only a successful jump over any distance, but complete safety for anything on board as well. In the end, it wasn't the drive that was the problem, but the shielding. The solution was the radical realignment of the nanofilaments in a heavy water suspension. They could respond fast enough to the quantum fluctuations to be almost one hundred percent effective.

By the time everyone else came in, he'd deleted the results and altered the data from the previous day, hiding his trail as he went. It would be difficult, if not impossible, for anyone to come to the same conclusions he had—not from the changed data.

Bryson knew that what he'd discovered would come out eventually. Rumors said that SoCal, at least, had the data Jeremy had leaked last year. But without Bryson and his years of experience, it would be a long time before they reached the same conclusions.

He shook his head, forcing himself back to the present. He'd been standing in the airlock far too long. People might start to notice. With luck, they'd chalk it up to the long nights and early mornings.

He buried the memory chip deeper into his pocket, into the folds created by the seams. The chip contained everything: every schematic, every piece of data he'd worked on in his time in this lab. It contained the working jump drive and shielding. He waited for the door to open before stepping across the gap to the station itself. He'd never gotten used to the transition. The lab was his home, insulated and protected. The rest of the Sat City was noisy and smelly in comparison. The stench of humanity living out its last days in a tin can.

Bryson had stayed a full week after he'd solved the problem, making sure his results couldn't—weren't—being duplicated. Now it was time for him to get out of here. He'd laid the groundwork by visiting the test ship on a regular basis, which got him close to the transport bay where the shuttles from Earth and the other Sat Cities came in. All it would take was luck and timing.

He felt the familiar rush of guilt slice through his body, taking care not to let it show on his face. The lives of the people in his lab would be hell when he was gone. He hoped there wouldn't be any retribution, but knowing Kadokawa, somebody would end up paying the price. But after a year of planning, of memorizing transport schedules and ground crew routes, he'd come to realize that there was no way to get everyone off. His was a solo plan, and the information he had was too important.

Walking the hallways of the city as though deep in thought, Bryson slowly made his way to the transport bays. His breathing was rough as he tried to control the fear building inside him. If he was caught . . . He buried the thought and forced himself to act natural. Today was just like every other time he had done this.

Taking the long way, Bryson meandered down a section filled with stores and offices, all closed this early in the morning, the flashing advertising that always fought for attention still turned off for the night. It was a route he'd taken many times before. As he got closer to the transports, two security guards converged on him.

He'd never seen security walking this route so early in the morning, and the first thought that raced through his already panicked brain was *They knew!*

He fought the urge to run that threatened to consume him, keeping his gaze down, watching the tips of his shoes slide across the worn gray composite that made up the floor. The guards stopped in front of him and his step faltered. Bryson looked up, expecting them to be staring back.

Instead, they were examining a window display, joking with each other as if he didn't even exist. Bryson felt the tension flow out him. He stole a glance between the women as he walked past. Behind the glass storefront was a display of mid-grade wedding rings. The stones in the gold bands showing the telltale orange tinge of the Le Verrier mines, the same type he used in his quantum experiments. How much would their value rise if the drive became reality?

Bryson continued past and started breathing again. His heart pounded in his ears, and he was sure that under his jacket, dark circles of sweat betrayed the fear he felt.

Once in the transport bay, Bryson moved closer to the executive-class ship they had used for the first test. It was nothing but an empty hulk now, a shell ready for the new engines and a new crew. For a test that, with luck, would never take place. He resisted the urge to put his hand into his pocket to feel for the chip.

When he was near the ship, it was only a short run to the shuttle scheduled to leave for Earth this morning. He had no idea where it went—looking at departure schedules might have alerted Kadokawa security to his plans—all he knew was when it would leave. Bryson waited for the crew to board the craft before he sprinted across the open space and leaped into its hold. He scampered over the baggage to the far corner and waited, his body trembling, lungs hurting from holding his breath. No one yelled. No alarms went off. No security came to drag him away.

The doors to the hold closed, and he felt the space begin to pressurize. Not to the same degree as the crew and passenger areas, but enough to keep him alive. He'd made sure of that, at least.

It wasn't until he felt the engine thrust accelerate them away from the satellite that he let himself believe he actually had a chance to escape. He'd be able to relax for a while, until they landed, about an hour from now.

If Kadokawa found out he'd left before then, his escape was already over.

CHAPTER 3

WEST COAST—SUNDAY, JUNE 11, 2141 10:15 A.M.

I **WATCHED AS IAN FELL ASLEEP,** his features softening as the tension fell away. He'd always been able to fall asleep quickly. It was a skill I'd never had. I sat in my seat, listening to the general chatter from the people behind me riding just under the buzz of the thrusters. The medics and soldiers in front of me sat silent. Occasionally one of them would shift in their seat or mumble a soft word to the people they were sitting next to, but for the most part they stayed alert and quiet.

Pat sat curled in her seat, a thin blanket pulled over her head. Every time the blanket twitched I stole a quick glance, hoping she was coming out of it.

After a while, I ended up staring out the window on the other side of Ian, not truly relaxed, but not as tense as I had been. The transport stayed low, following the contours of the land, out of sight from the Canadians. We flew over tiny lakes of the purest blue and between mountain peaks that reached above the view of my window. Eventually the mountains gave way to foothills and the wilderness to farms. At one time, every square centimeter of fertile soil had been covered with cultivated land. Now, barren patches infiltrated around the edges. Of those left, the ones closest to the rivers and lakes were greener, more lush. The farther from the water, the more the land was wrapped in irrigation pipes. Some of the pipes terminated at the closest water source. Others, larger ones, ran to the Pacific Ocean's desalinization plants.

There were places like this all over the world. Greedy corporations had stripped the planet of most of its trees and natural coverings, and water had become scarce. Once-fertile land became arid and dry. Places that used to generate more food than we knew what to do with now struggled to keep up with demand, sometimes trying to get three crops a year where there used to be only one.

By the time we reached the ocean, the view had given way to high-rise towers and fibercrete. Then it all fell away, and water sparkled below us as far as I could see.

I turned to look out Pat's window. The coastline we passed alternated between massive desalinization plants and shantytowns that pushed themselves farther and farther into the water. We were racing too fast for me to make out any details, but from what I could see, it was as though someone had ripped the roof off of Level 1 and exposed all the filth and grime and poverty to the open sky.

A flat gray wall sprang up from the ground, and my view disappeared.

We were flying lower now, almost skimming the surface of the water. The grungy gray wall of the city reached into the sky, out of my line of sight. It passed by the window in a blur. That meant we'd reached San Francisco at least, where the city started. I knew from my classes that the wall wasn't as smooth as it looked. The years had taken their toll. The wall was laced with cracks and missing pieces chipped away by weather, age, and the earthquakes that occasionally shook everything. There were special teams of repair crews that went out and worked on the wall almost daily. SoCal couldn't—wouldn't—let the average citizen see the outside world. If the low-level workers knew the outside was attainable, they wouldn't do the menial work required to keep San Angeles running. It was how things had worked for generations.

When I was young, I think I was seven or eight, Mom and Dad took me to see the wall. Back then I didn't even think of it as the inside; it was just the wall. The fact that there was an outside was something I never really thought about until I'd stood on Level 7.

My parents and I had gone to watch them replace a section damaged by an earthquake. Repair crews had built a temporary structure to support the levels above and knocked out a piece of the wall. Dad had talked about the new materials, the flexibility of the wall so it could stand up to some shaking. Mom talked about the sun, the water, how everything we knew needed both to survive. Including us. I was too young to understand.

The memory had stuck in my head. I don't know if it was because of the huge expanse of water I saw through the man-made hole, or the number of corporate soldiers standing there, each one with their back to the hole, their weapon ready, keeping the tourists—us—away.

It was one of the few outings we'd gone on as a family. Maybe I remembered it because of that, because I had felt wondrously safe and happy. It bothered me that that thought had come second, after the soldiers with their guns.

The sound of the thrusters changed, pulling me back. The transport rose and more of the wall came into view, reaching almost two hundred meters high. Seven levels of city. Faded white letters flashed by, painted six meters high on the wall. *Los Padres.*

Part of ACE training was remembering the world the way it used to be . . . before the corporations took over. Los Padres used to be what they called a national forest. Families camped and hiked under the canopy of trees, the green-speckled light warm on their skin, or amongst the scrub that used to cover most of the southern areas. All that was left of it now were faded white letters painted on an immense wall of fibercrete. Fibercrete. Another word I'm sure I learned at school, and relearned at ACE. It's what had started the cities moving up and out, until the multi-leveled structure almost covered the entire west coast of the continental United States and the individual cities became wards instead of separate entities. Even the forests disappeared, replaced by cheap housing, city-supporting infrastructure, and corporate-run factories.

They had built the first three levels quickly, starting in the city cores of San Francisco, San Jose, and Los Angeles. Building until nothing was left. Level 2 was made flat, going around the hills and mountains, cutting off access to them and taking away anything that made a place unique. In downtown Los Angeles, they chopped off anything over five stories tall to create Level 2. In San Francisco, the buildings were taller but had received the same humiliation.

Everyone who could afford it moved up, following the sun, until even that was denied them. Now only the elite could live on Level 7, the ceiling of the entire structure. Up there, the grass still grew, manmade lakes held water. And the shit settled on the lower levels. Over four generations had lived since the walls went up, never knowing how the sun felt on their skin.

Eventually Level 1 became a "hive of scum and villainy," as one of the old vids we watched described a fictional city on a fictional world. Only here it wasn't fiction. It was true. Most of Level 1 became a refuge for those who didn't fit, or want to fit, with society. Drug dealers, murderers. Rapists.

Those who lived there still needed money, and strangely enough still wanted a roof over their heads. More than what the Level's ceiling provided. So the corporations had built sewage and water treatment plants, taking up a lot of Level 1 real estate to keep those on the higher Levels happy.

That had been my world from when I was thirteen, when my parents were killed, until I was sixteen, when I managed to scramble my way out of the dirt. I became a courier, riding my motorcycle between Level 2 and Level 5, delivering whatever was given to me.

Ian had a small place on Level 5, right at the cutoff of the third build. When they'd built the last two Levels, they'd segregated the population. No one was allowed into Level 6 without permission. It took a lot to get that.

I'd been up there on Level 7, watching a real sunset for the first time, the open air making me feel exposed and small. Back then, the black box taped to my back had given me access, blocking my ID tag from transmitting its location. The box had also given me my scar.

Now I was part of ACE, and I had access without the box, thanks to my modifiable ID. I'd never tested it in the real world. The tracker IDs were a SoCal invention. A way for the corporations to track the population without their knowledge. A way to keep us in our place.

That first sunset felt like a lifetime ago, but it had been less than a year. A year spent under the open sky in the Canadian mountains, but that first sunset over the ocean outside Los Angeles still sent a thrill through me when I thought about it.

More faded letters flashed past the window. All I caught was *Barbara*. We were really moving.

The transport suddenly wallowed, nosing closer to the water

before righting itself again. The pitch of the thrusters changed. The soldiers, most of whom had been sleeping, jumped to their feet and started gathering their gear. Beside me, Ian had woken up. He reached across my body, grabbed the seatbelt, and buckled me in, cinching the belt snug. I turned to face him, my stomach tightening into a knot.

Ian's head blocked the window as he stared out across the Pacific Ocean. I looked out the wedge of window behind the seats in front of us. All I could make out was the gray water and the waves, closer now, rolling over each other in a rush to make it to shore. Ian jerked his head back, and I caught a quick glimpse of a smoke trail. I couldn't tell which way it was heading, but I was smart enough to hazard a guess.

The smoke trail got closer, disappearing under the window and out of my view. The transport shook like a dog getting out of water. There were no explosions or smoke or fire. The knot in my gut loosened. A dud. Someone was firing at us, and it seemed like they couldn't afford real equipment. I noticed that Ian hadn't relaxed yet. Instead he was reaching for his own seatbelt and muttering under his breath.

The lights went out and the world went quiet.

I lost all feeling of forward motion. My stomach reached up, nestling at the bottom of my throat. We were plummeting. People started screaming. Over the noise I heard orders being barked to the soldiers. The transport twisted, leaning to the left. Ian fell against me, still struggling to get his seatbelt on. I stared out the windows behind him. The ocean tilted at a dangerous angle.

The transport wasn't even close to being a glider. I figured the only thing keeping us in the air was our forward momentum, and without thrusters we were losing that. The sliver of window I had looked out before darkened, turning a dull matte gray. The wall. And we were heading straight for it.

The gray was replaced with white, and the transport pulled nose up. We hit the top of a sandy cliff, bouncing back into the sky. I felt my stomach dig its claws into my throat before everything went really wrong. The seats in front of us tore from their moorings, launching upward. I grabbed onto Ian's arm, but it wasn't there anymore. He floated above his seat, his head near the ceiling.

He was smiling at me.

The side of the transport disappeared in a rush of screaming air and fibercrete, leaving sharp chunks of composite pointing into the cabin. A hungry mouth with jagged teeth. I screamed and grabbed for Ian again, hoping to pull him back down. His seat was gone. So was he.

I didn't have time to think, to scream, to cry. The transport slammed to a stop and my head cracked against the seat in front of me.

WEST COAST—SUNDAY, JUNE 11, 2141 10:16 A.M.

Things are bad. Really bad. Miller knew they were in trouble the moment he saw the second aircraft. Nobody flew this close to the wall or another transport unless they wanted to. The longer he stared at it, the more he became sure it was a gunship. It couldn't be ACE protection . . . there was no reason for them to send one. Not now. No one would dare attack this close to the city. Not even SoCal, and they pretty much owned the damn place. The chance of destroying the wall and killing thousands of people was too great.

The second he saw the flash and the smoke trail snaking toward them, he knew he was wrong. Someone *would* dare. At the first sign of the approaching missile he'd reached for Kris's seatbelt, buckling her in nice and tight.

When the missile hit the transport and didn't explode, Miller breathed a small sigh of relief, then the thrusters shut down and the lights went out. Loss of power was never a good sign. It meant the missile was an EMP, an electromagnetic pulse. It also meant the gunship didn't want to kill everyone on board. They wanted survivors. His thoughts went back to the compound. Why would they want Kris that badly? The risks they were taking were astronomical.

The transport bucked and turned. Miller's best guess was that the pilots were trying to land the fucking thing on the small strip of land between the bottom of the cliff and the water. He wasn't a pilot, but even he knew the chances were slim to none. They were too high up and moving way too fast. As the top of the sand-colored cliff came into view, Miller realized his mistake. The pilots wanted to bring the transport down on the thin piece of land between the top of the cliff and the wall.

He didn't have time to think about it. The transport hit the top of the cliff hard and fast, not turning or slowing down. Instead, it launched back into the air and arced down. He floated in the temporary zero-g created by the downward arc, his world slowing to a crawl. Every heartbeat took seconds to complete.

He looked down and saw the fear written all over Kris's face, and smiled. *It'll be okay,* he thought. *You'll be fine.* None of the words were spoken out loud, but he still felt as though he was lying to her. There was no time to do anything else.

They plowed into the wall, peeling the side of the transport open like it was made of tissue paper. Miller felt himself sucked out. The air hit him, a solid wall of pressure, and his forward motion stopped. He felt something in his chest pop, a sudden release followed by stabbing pain. The ground rushed up to meet him. His world went black.

When Miller came to, he didn't remember the impact. Didn't remember where he was. He tried to move, but couldn't, and ended up just lifting his head. Even that small motion sent stabs of pain through him, and his vision blurred.

Huge chunks of fibercrete lay around him, and the air smelled stale and burnt. He'd gotten lucky, though. Less than a meter in any direction and he could have snapped his back landing on the rubble.

As his surroundings came into focus, he knew he couldn't rely on luck. You had to rely on yourself. Your skills. Your knowledge. He tried to push through the pain, levering himself onto his elbows, trying to stand before noticing the fibercrete and metal on his legs. Case in point.

He lay back down, his skin suddenly clammy. He could feel the fibercrete dust sticking, creating a shell around him. He fought against the fear starting to take over. Breathing became difficult, short small gasps that pulsed through his chest. Each intake shot pain through his ribs.

Miller concentrated on the pain, slowing each breath until the sharp jolts turned into long slow burns. He held on to the burn, refusing to let it go. It became his anchor to reality. He followed the pain until he was back in the transport wreckage.

Raising himself onto his elbows, Miller tried to pull his legs out from under the debris. The pain became his strength, and he tried to wiggle his legs.

When he finally stopped, exhausted by the effort, he realized he couldn't feel his legs anymore. There was no pain. Wondering if his legs were salvageable, he moved his toes and stopped. He had no way to tell if it was working or not. He wasn't going anywhere.

He wasn't going to be able to find Kris.

Through the hole in the wall, Miller watched the gunship grow larger.

SANTA BARBARA, LEVEL 1—SUNDAY, JUNE 11, 2141 10:19 A.M.

Cold enveloped me, a dark expanse of nothingness. Bright specks of light tumbled in the distance, breaking through the black veil. Stars shone like pieces of diamond. I closed my eyes and slowly opened them again. The stars came into focus, light reflecting off glass, lying in shattered constellations on the ground.

Something was running into my eyes. I reached up and tried to wipe it away. From somewhere far away, a voice said, "Head wounds always bleed like a bitch." It took me a few more minutes before I realized I had said it, and another to remember why.

My ears rang in the silence; the only sound cutting through the high-pitched whine was the noise of the transport's thrusters. I reached up to wipe more blood from my forehead, slowly shaking my head from side to side. That couldn't be right. The transport had crashed.

I tried to stand, but something was holding me down, gripping my thighs like a vice. I felt with my hands. The seatbelt. Something about it was funny, and I giggled. A seatbelt around my legs. That wasn't where it was supposed to be. I released the clasp and dropped to the floor. The safety glass ground under my hips, uncomfortable. Painful.

The back of my seat lay behind me. I twisted and pushed myself up, first to my knees until the world stopped spinning, then to my feet. Twisted composite and glass lay like so much garbage around me. Seats and cushions were scattered as far as I could see. Where were all the people?

Where was Ian?

The thought penetrated through the fog with laser focus, burning it away. Ian had been floating above the seat before our impact with the wall. I stumbled forward, forgetting I had no shoes. Glass cut into the soft skin as I spun. I ignored it. *Where was Ian?*

As I turned, the massive hole in the wall came into view, gaping and jagged. Bright sunlight streamed through it. In the distance, a bird floated on the wind, moving in closer.

Something was wrong with the bird; it was too big, and it hung in the sky. The sound of thrusters firing got louder and the bird flew closer and began to take shape. It was a gunship, moving toward the downed transport.

Ignore it, I told myself. *Ignore it and find Ian.*

I moved through the wreckage, parts of it smoldering, not feeling my feet anymore. All that mattered was him.

The first few times I saw a body, I ran, not caring what I was stepping on. Each time, it was a soldier or a medic, dead and mangled in the wreckage. The sunlight streaming through the hole fought with the Ambients, created twisted shadows and hidden spots. The last one I found was still alive, the black paint on his face smeared into streaks of white. When I saw he wasn't Ian, I helped him stand up and quickly moved away, leaving him to fend for himself. Ian first, then I'd come back.

I don't know how I found him. I was moving off to the side, deeper into the darkness, when I saw him. His face was white, his eyes closed. I couldn't breathe until I'd found his heartbeat, slow but steady under his t-shirt. At my touch, he opened his eyes and looked at me. Relief weakened my knees and I collapsed beside him. His lips moved. I leaned in closer, lowering my ear to his mouth.

"Go."

I got back up and started searching for wounds, ignoring his legs for now. Ignoring his words.

His hand grabbed my arm. I tried to pull away, but he held firm, refusing to let go. Pain flashed across his face.

"Go!" Louder this time.

"I . . . I can't. I won't."

"You have to. They want you."

He coughed and a drop of blood hung from his lips. I wiped it off.

"I'm not leaving you here," I said.

"You're no good to me captured, either." Another cough and some more blood. "I don't have a chance to get away. You do. You'll find me. You did last time."

Last time. Last time I'd almost gotten both of us killed. Last time I'd gotten lucky.

"I don't want to." I sounded like a petulant brat. I wiped at the tears streaming down my cheeks with the back of my hand.

"Do it because you love me as much as I love you."

He let go of my arm, pushing me away. I fell backward onto an upside-down seat, the hard plastic pressing into my back. Miller turned his head to the opening in the wall.

The gunship inserted itself into the hole left by the transport, landing at the edge.

"Run. Now. ACE will help you find me."

I stood and stumbled backward, farther into the darkness. Each step drove another spike into my heart. I fell twice more before turning and running forward, my mind numb.

At the first crack of a gunshot, I tripped and almost fell again. I scrambled for one of the support pillars and put my back against it, struggling to breathe and stay quiet at the same time.

At the second gunshot, I turned and peered around the pillar, my hands slipping across its slimy surface. Two silhouettes stood against the bright sunlight pouring through the hole. One pointed his gun at something in the rubble and waited. The other stooped over, pulling up a limp figure. Even from here I knew it was Ian. The silhouette lifted Ian over his shoulder and moved back to the gunship.

Another crack split the air, echoing in the close quarters.

My heart thudded in my chest. The bastards took Ian, and they were killing everyone else. Was it really me they were after, or had they found their prize?

A small quad-engine police drone flew over my head, rushing toward the site of the crash. I knew I had to move before the place was filled with them, but my legs wouldn't work. A sudden flash of light arced from the gunship and the drone crashed into the ground, becoming just another piece of wreckage.

From off to my left, I heard a muffled whimper. I scanned the silhouettes again. One had made it to the gunship, still carrying Ian. The other was at the far end of the crash site.

I couldn't get my breathing under control, but if there was someone out there, alive, I couldn't let them become another casualty. There was a chance I could save the person without being seen. Forcing my legs to obey, I left the pillar at a low crouch, winding between pieces of transport and fibercrete until I found her.

Pat lay huddled on the ground, her eyes squeezed tight and her hands pressed over her ears. She was slowly rocking her body on the ground from shoulder to shoulder. I took another glance at the advancing figures.

I only had a few moments before they broadened their search.

CHAPTER 4

WILLIAM CLARK QUIETLY closed the link on his comm unit and sighed, continuing his walk down the blue-carpeted hallway. His role in ACE had changed after Nigel had been killed last year. The number of assistant directors had stayed the same, meaning Nigel's workload had been transferred to everyone else, and William had gotten the bulk of it, including the Black Ops division. Which had been the goal, after all. Along with the change had been William's move from Nigel's old office on the top floor to his more comfortable one on the third. From there, the ceiling was something he could ignore, instead of something that punched him in the gut every time he looked out the window. It would get even better in the next few days as ACE completed its move to the new building on Level 6, though he wasn't happy with it. ACE worked better in the darkness of the lower levels.

Nigel, though he had been brought on shortly after William, hadn't been part of the core group—that had been only Jeremy and himself. What Nigel and the other assistant directors knew of ACE was exactly what they needed to know to get the job done. It was a tough position being in charge of the Black Ops and infiltration teams. Jeremy and William had needed a true believer to pull the deceit off. If Nigel had known the real purpose of ACE, he would never have signed up, and they would never have been able to get someone as dedicated as Nigel had been. When he had outlived his usefulness, Jeremy had arranged to get rid of him.

William and Jeremy had been the masterminds behind ACE, and as far as William knew, that was still the case. Since the beginning, ACE's *true* purpose—hurting the major corporations to help Jeremy advance up the corporate ladder—had aligned pretty well with what everyone thought ACE did, but since Jeremy's fall from grace, things were changing. And it looked like Jeremy was about to blow the carefully crafted cover they had built together.

In theory, that was Jeremy's right. He had come up with the whole thing, with William's help. But after so many years and so much hard work, it rubbed William the wrong way that he hadn't been included. And if William was being fair to himself, he'd started believing ACE was actually doing some good. It didn't help that Jeremy had drifted away in recent years, either.

They weren't as close as they had been. Once Jeremy had moved up through the ranks at Meridian, he no longer whispered secrets into William's ears as the sweat dried from their bodies. Jeremy had changed. Slowly at first, almost imperceptibly. But he would do whatever it took to gain an advantage, and that included sleeping with anyone, and their husbands or wives if necessary. Back then, William had been blind to everything.

What they'd had together was special. It wasn't about rank or privilege. It wasn't about climbing the corporate ladder. For a while, William had believed Jeremy loved him, had needed him. He still held on to that hope, though lately it had seemed to be a one-way street. It didn't matter. When all this was over, when Jeremy reached the pinnacle, when he was ready to call it a day and rest, William would be there waiting. They would spend the end of their years together in peace.

William sighed again. He knew it was a dream, but he clung to it nonetheless. Everyone was allowed a secret weakness or two, as long as it remained just that. A secret. One of his was Jeremy, and the other was ACE.

This time, Jeremy may have stepped too far. Screw that, he *did* go too far. If he had at least brought William in, there may have been a clear path out of this mess. He was pretty sure he could credit the loss of the training facility to a corporate attack, he was supposed to be the one with all the information anyway. Or maybe the insurgents that had been getting stronger and more brazen, even if they were theoretically on the same side. They had both become an easy excuse as the threat of war moved closer. Either way, it would make him look incompetent, but right now, he couldn't see another way out.

William tapped on the nondescript door and waited. It was never a good idea to barge in on Jeremy. He heard a chair scrape across the floor, followed by a faint "Come in." William opened the door and waited to be asked before he sat.

The delay gave him an opportunity to study Jeremy, and William noted he looked older. Over the last year, gray had replaced almost all of the color in Jeremy's hair, adding years to his image. The ultra-correct posture was still there—ramrod-straight back, pulled-back shoulders. But the lines around his eyes were deeper, and he seemed tired. More tired than William had ever seen. With the movement of a hand, Jeremy indicated one of the chairs in front of the small, worn desk. William took it.

Jeremy smiled.

"You look tired," William said. "Are you getting enough sleep? Is there anything I can do to help?"

William held back a wince, knowing Jeremy saw it anyway. It went completely against what he had planned to say, but seeing Jeremy like this made his heart break.

There was a flash of anger in Jeremy's eyes before he answered, even though the smile never wavered. William wasn't sure if the anger was from the question or William's reaction.

"Of course I'm fine. As fine as I can be living down here. I don't know how you people do it."

You people. Jeremy was definitely in one of his moods. This would not be an easy conversation. William hesitated, giving Jeremy a chance to talk again.

"You came here for a reason, Will. Let's get it over with. I have a lot of work to do."

William had the distinct impression that Jeremy knew exactly why he was there. It didn't surprise him. You didn't get to be where Jeremy was—where he used to be—by being stupid.

"One of our training compounds in Canada has been hit," William said. "Knowing who was there, I was wondering if . . ."

Jeremy shifted on his hard wooden chair. It didn't indicate he was uncomfortable; it was more like he was readying himself for battle.

"What is your question?" Jeremy asked, looking directly into William's eyes.

Now it was William's turn to shift in his seat. The move didn't convey the same readiness. "Did you know anything about it?"

"Next time, don't hesitate." Jeremy continued to stare before he replied in a defiant tone. "Yes, it was me."

"But why? Why without at least letting me know? We could have waited. She would have been out in another couple of weeks. If you couldn't wait, we could have at least saved the facility."

"Why?" Jeremy surged to his feet, his thighs hitting the small desk and throwing it forward onto William's lap. "Why? I've been sitting in this hellhole for a year, everything I've worked for destroyed. A war that *I* should have been in control of beginning above us, and all I have is this tiny room and a tiny shitty desk to sit behind, hiding like a common criminal. All of it taken away from me by that damn courier. And you have the balls to sit there and ask me *why?*"

"I know the reasons you want her," William said, pushing the desk back onto its legs. "What I don't know is why now? You've waited almost a year, and there were only a few weeks to go before she was back here. Now we've lost one of our prime facilities. Some of our recruits are dead. Recruits who would have been able to help you. I—"

"You what?" Jeremy interrupted. "You had everything you worked for taken away? Look at me, I'm sixty-two years old. I gave the best years of my life to get to where I was." He slumped against the wall, a rare sign of weakness. "I'm tired and I'm angry, and I just don't give a shit anymore. The corporations can have their little war without me. With any luck, they'll ruin themselves," he paused, drawing in a steadying breath and standing straight again. "I can't get back what I lost, but I can hurt the ones that ruined my plans."

"They were our plans, remember?" William almost whispered the words.

Jeremy's features softened and he sat back into his chair, the desk still closer to William. Jeremy rubbed his eyes, another sign of weakness William rarely saw. "Of course I remember," he said softly. "How could I forget? Those were good days."

"They were. They still can be." William sat straighter, trying to strengthen his resolve. He wanted to hold Jeremy. Cradle him until all his anger, all his worries, melted away.

Now was not the time.

"But right now, we have a situation on our hands," William said. "You didn't get Kris, and now she's headed back here with what's left of the facility's complement. She's with Miller, which makes the task even more difficult."

Jeremy looked into William's eyes. "It will be even worse than that."

SANTA BARBARA, LEVEL 1—SUNDAY, JUNE 11, 2141 10:23 A.M.

I crouched beside Pat as she whimpered, not daring to touch her in case it made her scream or shout. From what I could see, she didn't look hurt. I glanced back at the men from the gunship, hoping for a glimpse of Ian. He was thrown into the gunship like a bag of garbage. My face flushed and my calves twitched, aching to launch me toward them. It took everything I had not to run back, not to get him off the ship and back into my arms. But I knew there wasn't anything I could do against armed soldiers. I didn't even have a knife to protect me.

Some of the men were still moving in the wreckage near the hole in the wall.

I focused my attention on Pat, my head swirling in a fog. Her shirt was wet with sweat. She lay in a small depression, trembling. Every gunshot that echoed through the level sent her body into spasms.

I knew we couldn't stay here. The search would expand, and it wouldn't be long before they were close enough to find us. I reached out and brushed her shoulder. Pat's eyes snapped open and she let out a cry that I quickly muffled with my hand. She struggled against me, kicking me in the ribs before I let go. It wasn't a hard hit, but it took me by surprise. The men were expanding their circle, killing anyone they found alive. We had to leave. Pat had helped me through some tough times. Now it was my turn to help her.

"Pat, it's me, Kris," I whispered as I lightly stroked her cheek. "We need to move. They're getting closer. We don't have time to wait."

Somewhere in the depth of her eyes, through all the suffering and memories, I thought I saw something, some flicker of recognition. I kept stroking her cheek, keeping my voice as calm and quiet as I could, hiding the fear that threatened to engulf me. She clenched her eyes and drew in a deep breath. Almost immediately the trembling stopped. When she opened them again, I could still see her memories, full of pain and fear, flashing behind them.

But through that, I also saw Pat.

At the next gunshot, she flinched violently, but kept her focus on my face. The sound was way too close. I peeked over the top of the rubble and saw that the soldiers had almost reached us. I could smell the gunpowder from their weapons.

"We have to go." I couldn't keep the edge of panic out of my voice this time.

With a barely perceptible nod, Pat struggled to her knees. I didn't wait before turning my back on her and crawling over to the support pillar. The sounds of Pat following kept me going. When I reached the pillar, she was right behind me, already using the support to pull herself to her feet. I could tell she was exhausted. Her legs shuddered and she leaned against the pillar, but I knew we couldn't stop to rest. We had to keep going. I hoped she felt the same. A row of blurry houses stood across a small open area. I blinked to try to bring them into focus.

I kept the pillar between us and the gunship as best I could.

Right now I was more scared of them than anything else on Level 1. I was pretty sure this was Level 1. It had the low-quality Ambients, poor substitutes for light from the actual sun, and the incessant stench. When you lived down here, you just got used to it. The ceiling wasn't as low as I was used to, but everything else fit. Under the smell of recycled air and filth was something else, a strange chemical undertone that burned my throat when I breathed.

I'd never been anywhere near this part of San Angeles, but I imagined Level 1 was Level 1 no matter where you were. Even with the higher ceilings, I didn't remember it feeling this claustrophobic.

Movement to my left froze me in my tracks before I had the sense to drop to the ground. Pat blindly followed suit. Someone was running away from the crash site. Running through open ground in clear view of the soldiers. Two gunshots rang out, and a puff of dirt flew up from the runner's feet. The runner stole a quick glance over her shoulder, and I recognized Janice before she turned a corner.

One of the soldiers ran after her, slowing as he reached the houses. He held his gun around the corner and sprayed the street with bullets. Blood pounded in my temples. If Janice was still there, it would be a miracle if she was alive. The soldier turned the corner and disappeared from view.

Getting out of here and onto a higher Level was the first order of business. I had no fucking idea where an up-ramp was. For all I knew, I was walking away from the closest one. It didn't matter. I wasn't going anywhere near the soldier following Janice. She was on her own.

Once we found a way up, the next step would be to get in touch with ACE. With their resources, finding Ian should be fairly straightforward. He was the only one the soldiers had taken, so it was obvious, to me at least, that they wanted to keep him alive. My stomach dropped. What if I was wrong? I couldn't be. I *had* to be right.

One thing ACE had taught us was that we always stood up for our own. Always. And Ian was one of our best. There was no way ACE would want to lose him.

Another thought popped into my head. If it wasn't Ian the men from the gunship wanted, if it was me, I'd have to be careful. If ACE was forced to make a choice between us, I would be on the losing end. Ian was a more valuable asset to ACE than I was. I would much rather we both came out winners. Though if I was given the choice, I knew what I would do.

Once we were far enough away from the crash site, I sped up, no longer worried about being seen by the men. I put an arm around Pat to help her keep up. Her entire body tensed, and I immediately let go again. We had to pick up our pace, and she kept slowing down and then jogging to catch up again. We needed to stick together. Two individuals walking on Level 1 were more likely to be attacked than a team. Or at least the semblance of one. I slowed down, allowing her to keep up. We had to find someplace for her to rest.

Each step ground more Level 1 filth into my feet. They didn't hurt anymore. Much, anyway. The caked-on blood and dirt had formed a shell over my soles, which seemed to help a bit. I'd have to take care of them sooner rather than later, or I'd end up with amputated stumps. Right now, we had to keep moving. I hid my limp from Pat as best I could.

Even with the stench and the Ambients I felt I could almost touch, this wasn't the Level 1 I knew. Before the walls had gone up, this part of Santa Barbara must have been high class. The streets were wide, and what was left of the original buildings looked like they had once been majestic homes.

It made me uncomfortable. I was used to the old concrete and chopped-off buildings. The openness made me feel exposed and on edge. Going against everything I'd learned, I stayed in the middle of the street, keeping an eye on the garbage-strewn patches of dirt in front of the houses. This way, if someone jumped out at us, we'd have time to run. The place felt empty, deserted. Wrong. Where were the people?

The feeling of something being wrong made me change my mind. I veered toward the closest house. If it was deserted, we would be able to hide there, at least until Pat got better. It was getting harder to keep her on her feet. She kept stumbling over them, walking as if she'd had too much to drink. My headache and eyesight were getting worse as well.

The house's door, cracked and faded red in a dirty white frame, stood open on broken hinges. What used to be a brick facade hung from the walls in pieces. Dried strips of glue still clung to the building's exterior where the bricks used to be. The floor by the entrance hadn't been disturbed in years. Layers of dust and grit covered everything. We walked in, and with each step a thick cloud rose into the air, threatening to choke us before settling back to the floor. This would have to do.

I helped Pat into a corner and went back to the door, working to close it. The first push only flexed the top portion. The bottom was jammed against the buckled subfloor. Someone had removed the hardwood long ago. I tried harder and the bottom corner dragged a few centimeters. When I tried again, I lifted the door onto its single hinge and shut it the best I could. If anyone got inside, they would see our footprints, but by then it wouldn't matter. We weren't in any condition to fight.

Pat sat in the corner, her head resting on her arms, her eyes open and staring at the floor. I slid my back against the wall, suddenly exhausted, and lowered myself to the ground beside her. More dust rose into the slimy air, and I breathed it in, forcing back a sneeze.

After a few minutes, I reached out and gently touched Pat's

hand. She didn't jerk away; instead she grabbed on, as though she would fall into the earth without me grounding her.

Pat fell into a fitful sleep. I eased my fingers from her grasp and, fighting through the pain in my head, crept to the glassless front windows, peeking through. The streets were quiet. Too quiet. After the first police drone was destroyed, I'd expected more to follow, but even they didn't want to be here.

I went back to Pat and used a nail to start a tear in my shirt. I ripped off the bottom, leaving my midriff bare, and used the material to wrap my feet. It wasn't much, but it was better than nothing. They'd started bleeding again, and when I tied the knot to hold the strip of cloth on, the fresh pain made me gasp.

Pat groaned in her sleep. Her face was wet with fresh sweat and her arms and legs twitched as though she was trying to run.

This was as far as we would get for a while.

＝＝＝＝＝

LOS ANGELES, LEVEL 7—SUNDAY, JUNE 11, 2141 9:15 A.M.

By the time the hold doors were opened, Bryson had already squirmed under the luggage, hiding the best he could. No amount of planning could help him get out of the shuttle; it all depended on the ground crew. Listening to other transports land and take off through the open door, it felt like he waited forever, but it couldn't have been more than a minute before he realized no one was going to walk in on him. He didn't know how much time he had before they came to empty the hold, but lying here shivering wasn't going to get him away safely. He dug himself out and rushed to the door, stumbling over the uneven footing.

The first thing Bryson noticed was the terminal. From the out-side, it looked like the Los Angeles shuttle port. At least he'd made it to somewhere he knew. San Angeles was a big city. Big enough to get lost in. The second was the smell of shuttle fuel with a faint hint of the ocean underneath it. It had been a long time since he had smelled the ocean, and even the faint scent of it brought back memories of the last time he'd landed here. He'd just finished defending his thesis and was coming back from a celebratory holiday. That time, he had been on a stretcher with a straw sticking out of his throat, breathing through the tiny hole. He'd been eating in the mess on a transport coming back from Mars and choked on his food. Bryson was told that a complete stranger had cut into his throat and inserted the straw, saving his life. His only really clear memory had been how it had whistled at each breath. Back then, he had believed he was going to die. Looking back, Bryson realized it sounded pretty stupid. He didn't even have a scar to show for it.

This arrival scared him more.

Bryson glanced around the door, trying to get a glimpse of what was happening outside. In the distance, a truck with a conveyor belt was driving across the tarmac with some ground crew. They were busy chatting and didn't look toward him at all. This could be his only window for getting off the shuttle. He looked toward the nose of the shuttle and saw a stairwell leading up to the passenger ramp. Bryson jumped down, running to the door. It opened with no alarms. Maybe all the security was geared to keep people from getting to the tarmac, rather than keeping them away from the passenger areas.

The door opened to a short staircase. He climbed them to the top and exited onto carpeted floor. The shuttle's passengers walked past him, carrying whatever they'd brought on board, not even giving him a second glance. The stored luggage would be picked up on a carousel on the main floor. He blended in with the moving line and entered the shuttle port. As soon as he merged with the general traffic heading for the moving walkways, he felt more relaxed.

Skipping the first walkway, he moved to the wall and walked past the windows overlooking the tarmac. Outside, the sun shone down, creating waves of heat shimmering just above the ground. A shuttle roared down the runway, and he stopped to watch it climb into the clear blue sky. Now that he was here, it was time to get lost.

If Kadokawa had noticed him missing, Earthside security at the airport would have been swarming everywhere, searching for him. Or would they? This was SoCal territory. Would Kadokawa really want to alert SoCal that their pride and joy was free and ready to be stolen? He doubted it. Instead, they would most likely alert their own private forces. They would be waiting outside the secure area of the shuttle port, looking for someone that matched his description.

He wished he'd had a chance to bring some sort of disguise, but that would have been too risky.

There wasn't much he could do beyond the basics. There were a few shops between here and the exits. He would buy a stupid I ♥ LA t-shirt and a ball cap. At least at first glance, he would look different than he had in orbit.

The first thing he did was buy a disposable comm unit. Once it was activated, he transferred all the money he had onto it and threw away his old one. When Kadokawa started looking for him, they'd probably find the initial transaction, but his new comm unit should be untraceable. It would give them a place to start, though. He visited a couple of other stores, never buying too much from any single one, and headed for the exit.

When he finally walked out, he looked at least a little different than when he had arrived. Bryson still kept looking for signs that Kadokawa was on the hunt for him. He didn't see anything. Either his new clothes were helping or they hadn't realized he was missing. Yet.

He found a cab to take him to the nearest Level 5 down-ramp.

It dropped him off in front of a bed-and-breakfast place used by tourists. The cab driver didn't comment on his lack of luggage.

Alone again, Bryson stuck his hand in his pocket, fishing for the memory chip. Panic took his breath away when he couldn't find it, believing he had lost it before his fingers found the tiny device buried in lint. He breathed a sigh of relief and started the walk to the down-ramp itself.

At first, he'd considered calling some old friends from university, but he pushed that thought away almost immediately. If Kadokawa was willing to hurt his staff, what would they do to a friend that had helped him? Whatever it was, it wasn't worth the risk. No one else would get hurt because of what he did, or didn't, do. Not if he could help it.

When moving between Levels 5 and 6, security was only tight in one direction—going up. Getting down was always easy. SoCal must have figured if you were willing to go down, more power to you. If you were trying to get up, they would make sure you actually belonged.

The ramp exited on the edge of McConnell Park, and Bryson turned into it, following the gravel path past the scummy pond that smelled oddly sour to a bench near the statues. He lowered himself onto the bench and sat staring at the people walking past.

Time to find a place to hole up before he decided where to run next.

SANTA BARBARA, LEVEL 1—SUNDAY, JUNE 11, 2141 11:42 A.M.

I sat there for over an hour while Pat slept. My head started bleeding again, and my brain throbbed. I started falling asleep once or twice myself, but I didn't think that would be a good idea; we needed someone to stay on watch. I couldn't bring myself to wake Pat up and get us out of Level 1. Not after what she'd been through this morning. Besides, it gave me time to think. No matter which way I looked at it, we were in a bad spot. Level 1 was bad enough to start, but Level 1 in an unknown part of the city with people hunting for me made it worse.

The only thing I had to draw on were my memories from a year ago, and for all I knew, downtown Los Angeles had a whole different set of rules than Santa Barbara suburbia.

We hadn't been completely cut off from the world at boot camp either; news still trickled in at least once a week. From various reports, I knew a lot of law enforcement had been drafted in preparation for war. My guess was SoCal took them from the lower levels. Our corporate masters wouldn't want to inconvenience their lifestyle too much. That meant the gangs could have complete control down here.

By the time Pat finally started to stir, I was getting pretty antsy. I couldn't sit still for too long before I started pacing between the window and the door. I even took a tour of the house. This place was big. It used to be pretty fancy, but everything of value had been gutted. When you were desperate, even a meter of copper wiring was enough to get some food into you.

The constant movement helped me a bit. Just sitting there, I could feel my muscles start to stiffen up. My neck was so bad that I could barely turn my head to the right, and my shoulders ached every time I moved my arms. A massive headache had formed right under where I had hit my head during the crash, and at times my vision went blurry.

When Pat woke up, she seemed more embarrassed than anything else. I started talking about leaving, and she jumped on the idea like a rabid dog. She made it to the door before I had left the window.

The view out the window hadn't changed. The Ambients were still the same. There was a brighter area, back where the transport had crashed. Way brighter than what a hole in the wall would create. Crews must have been out looking at the damage already. We were okay, though . . . there was no reason for any of them to wander this far.

Pat dragged the door across the floor as she pulled it open. We left the house and walked across what used to be a lawn, but was now a dry patch of barren dirt. If Pat noticed my feet wrapped in scraps of t-shirt, she didn't say anything.

Ahead of us, the neighborhood got darker. A lone Ambient flickered, creating brooding shadows that crept across the street and writhed up and down the sidewalks. I slowed down. If I had known the area, I'd be able to go around, but I hadn't seen a cross street since we started walking. The pain in my feet surged just thinking about it.

We could always turn back, head in the other direction. But that would get us close to the crash site again. Even with all the bright lights and added security, the worst of the worst would converge on the site. Including the police.

With that thought came the idea that maybe it was a good thing. If everyone went to the crash, the chances of meeting someone here dropped. Any local gangs may have even left the ramp. I sucked in a breath and moved on. It was a chance we were going to have to take. Pat stayed quiet, following me into the gloom.

As soon as we entered the dead zone, I could see the light on the other side, and right after that what looked like an up-ramp. I wanted to run, to get there as fast as I could. Instead I slowed and stopped behind another pillar. Ramps were the most dangerous places on Level 1. Pat and I stood and waited in the dark.

A few minutes later, we still hadn't caught sign of any movement.

There could have been a hundred gang members between us and the ramp. The flickering light could have been hiding anything. At least it helped as much as hindered us. It was time.

I moved away from the pillar, Pat following close behind, angling toward the decrepit houses. I felt safer here, where I could walk next to the house walls, with their peeling paint and rotting wooden exteriors. I fell into my old pattern, the one I'd always used back home. I moved along the wall, ducking under the gaping windows, the glass long since broken or stolen, and dashed past doorways and the gaps between the houses. At every house corner, I stopped and watched, looking for telltale signs of someone guarding the ramp.

By the time I reached the edge of the darkness, I was only about thirty meters from the up-ramp. It was lit up like a Level 4 mall, every feature casting a short, sharp shadow on the cracked road. I forgot about my shoeless feet, forgot about the crash. Forgot about Ian. My heart pounded in my chest. Once I made it up the ramp, I could start thinking again. But now, right now, I had one fucking goal.

Looking back at Pat, I could see that the ramp worried her as well. I told her to wait until I'd reached it before following me. If someone was watching, they'd think there was only one of us. That could give us an advantage. Anyone guarding the ramp would attack one or two people walking up. So a hidden protector could add an element of surprise, giving us the upper hand. With one more quick scan of the area, I leaped away from the wall and ran full tilt, never slowing, never looking back.

I swerved around the ramp's barriers. No one would be hiding on the other side—they'd be visible from the ramp itself. My feet pounded on the cold surface, sending sparks of pain from my feet into my calves.

Someone slammed into my back, wrapping their arms around my chest. I tumbled forward.

The ramp rushed toward my face. In the split second before I reacted, I knew this was going to hurt. I reached for the ground, twisting my body into a roll, and landed on my side. The vise-like grip around my chest loosened. My head impacted the ramp. The world lit up as lightning flashed through the sky.

It took a few seconds to get enough of my wits back to scramble away. My knees scraped along the ramp as I tried to rush higher. A groan behind me made me stop and turn. The person who had attacked me was huge. I could see muscles stretching the back of their shirt. My fuzzy brain slowly registered the fact. *The back of their shirt.* This might be my only chance. I pushed off the ramp, aiming my shoulder for the back of their knees. With our size difference, my best bet was to bring them down fast and hard.

That's when I saw the pink socks—blurry flashes as I tried to focus my eyes.

The smallest moment of distraction can get you killed. That's what my instructors had told me. It looked like I was about to put their warning into practice.

The pink socks stepped sideways and I flew past them, diving lower onto the ramp. A foot rushed up to meet me as I passed, and missed.

I surged back to my feet, the city spinning around me, and faced the girl. She wasn't just huge, she was gargantuan. Standing above me on the ramp, she towered over me. A split second before she jumped, her body tensed, and each muscle stood out on its own, like it was sculpted out of marble. She charged.

There was no way someone my size was going to meet that head on. Not even if there were three of me. I turned and ran, aiming for the darkness of Level 1. My vision blurred and I almost tripped.

One thing I'd learned about size—usually the bigger you were, the slower you were. I'd only met one person who broke that rule, and thank god we'd been on the same side. She'd taught us three months of the most brutal fighting I'd ever seen.

I staggered to where the wall of the ramp dwindled into a low barrier, originally designed to keep vehicles from driving off the ramp before they reached the bottom. I leaped over it, keeping a hand on the top to stop myself from sliding down the steep slope on the other side. This one felt like it had been grass, once. Now it was just a slippery dirt incline.

I dug in my toes and ducked below the barrier, hoping it looked like I had slid down the slope. The girl stopped at the edge, only centimeters from where I was, and leaned over to search the bottom of the hill. Before she could register that I was right there, I jumped, wrapping my arms around her neck. I put my feet on top of the barricade and used it to lever her over the edge. Instead of using the barrier to keep her balance, the girl grabbed for my hands. I heaved, and her body rotated, her center of mass hitting the critical point.

She let go of me, trying to brace herself against the barricade, but it was too late. Nature and gravity had kicked in to help me. My feet slid down the barrier. As they did, I pulled her head close to my chest with everything I had. She flipped over the low wall, her head barely landing on me as her feet flew in an arc overhead. I let go, feeling myself starting to slide headfirst down the incline, grabbing for anything that could help me.

Her back hit the ground and I heard her breath whoosh out. She flipped again, rolling head over heels down the steep grade. I slid another meter before friction managed to stop me. Carefully rolling over, I got to my hands and feet, my toes digging into the hard-packed dirt, searching for traction. Centimeter by centimeter, I clawed my way back to the barrier and climbed over it.

Looking back down, I saw her body crumpled at the bottom. Her neck was bent at an awkward angle. I knew what all my training had been geared toward. I knew before I'd started that killing would be part of the job. Ian had told me as much. What took me by surprise was the lack of remorse I felt. The lack of anything. It had been me or her. Only one of us was going to walk away. Today was my turn.

I turned to face uphill. It was time to get out of this place. Time to steal a car. I tried to move my feet but couldn't. Looking down, I was surprised to find myself on my knees. When had I done that? The ramp spun around me and I fell forward, my cheek landing on the rough ground. Drawing a breath, I choked on dust and dirt.

LOS ANGELES, LEVEL 2—SUNDAY, JUNE 11, 2141 10:31 A.M.

Kai walked to the back of his restaurant and looked around the alley before unlocking the door. Level 2 Chinatown wasn't bad, but you could never be too careful. No one was in the alley, and he slipped inside the restaurant, quickly locking the entrance behind him before turning on the lights. The familiar smells of used oil and spices filled the air, with only a hint of antiseptic cleaner. He moved into the small kitchen, away from the medicinal scent and breathed in deeply. This was where he was most comfortable.

He went back to the storeroom, maneuvering around Kris's motorcycle to get to the electrical panel. He flipped the switches and heard the fans in the kitchen start up. It was the same thing he did every morning. It took a while for the woks to get to an even temperature.

From the cooler, he grabbed the last of the manufactured chuck steak and chicken thighs—cheap cuts, but it was all he could do to get even that. To supplement the meat, he pulled out some extra firm tofu.

The comm unit on the wall started ringing, but he ignored it. He never served food before noon, and he needed the time to prep. Anyone needing his other services would call his personal comm unit. He grabbed his apron off the wall, still dirty and used from yesterday . . . and the day before that.

Before starting, he turned on the vid screen and sharpened his knife. He'd barely gotten the first chicken coarsely chopped before the video stream grabbed his attention. A few seconds later, the knife slipped from his fingers and clattered from the cutting board to the floor.

He drew in a quick, sharp breath and felt light-headed. They'd done it. They had *actually* done it. Years ago the insurgents had planned to blow a hole in the wall and get some people outside, hopefully take out a desalinization plant and climb up the empty water pipes. They'd tossed out the idea as too dangerous. A knot grew in his chest, and he found it hard to breathe.

The image on the screen showed a hole in the Level 1 wall by Santa Barbara. Sunlight streamed in, casting its warm glow on ground that hadn't felt it in generations. Dust still obscured most of the damage, but he could see that some of the support pillars had buckled.

At least the insurgents had the common sense to do it where no one lived. That part of Santa Barbara had been high-end property before the city went up. With the rich moving to higher levels, the criminals had moved in. Soon no one traveled there anymore. When they discovered somebody had been using the area as a chemical dump, everyone left had moved out. SoCal never bothered cleaning it up. It was only Level 1, after all. When the fumes began to permeate the Level 2 air above it, SoCal just evacuated that area as well. That place was a ghost town.

Kai picked up the knife and walked to the sink. He let the water dribble out as he washed and rinsed the blade. He wiped his hands on his apron and grabbed the comm unit from his pocket, dialing a number he'd memorized years before. It rang once before being picked up.

"Yes."

"We agreed it would not be done, Jack," Kai said.

"I have no idea what you're talking about, old man."

"Turn on your vid screen. Pick a news channel. Any one." Kai heard papers shuffling and a cough on the other end of the line followed by a low whistle.

"Looks like someone else had the same idea."

"You did not do this?" Kai asked.

"Nah. We haven't been able to get enough explosives. The damn war may be making it easier for us to get stuff, but it's also taking a lot of it away."

So, they *had* been thinking about it. "It is difficult for everyone." Kai couldn't keep the sarcasm out of his voice.

After a slight pause, the man on the other end continued. "Yeah, well, this wasn't us. You know we would have told you about something this big. We work too well together to fuck up our arrangement."

It was Kai's turn to pause. What Jack had said was true. With Kai's analytical skills and the insurgents' seemingly endless supply of people, they had managed to achieve far more in the last year than he had in his entire career with ACE. Lately though, the only thing the insurgents had used him for was his medical training, something that had lapsed during his time with ACE.

The announcer's voice broke through his thoughts.

"A small unscheduled transport apparently lost control and flew into the wall near Santa Barbara. At this point, SoCal is blaming the accident on pilot error. Police should be in the area soon to search the

wreckage, but it is believed everyone on board died in the crash. Citizens are encouraged to stay away."

Kai tuned it out again. "Did you get that?"

"Yeah. Man, I wish we'd thought of that. A transport that size is easier to get hold of than explosives. 'Course, we would have had to get to Level 7 and find a pilot."

"Dream on," Kai said. "Now that the work has been done for us, we should at least follow through. Get your team together and get them through that hole before the place is so protected even a rat wouldn't make it out."

"I thought you said it was too dangerous."

"The dangerous part has been done. Who knows what has happened to the structural integrity of the city? That does not mean we cannot take advantage of it."

"It'll take some time. We weren't prepared."

Kai glanced at the vid screen and saw some drones flying across the ceiling. "Too bad. I would say you have maybe ten minutes. Some of you will not make it."

"Shit."

The connection went dead without anything else being said.

Kai flipped to a different feed and a grainy picture came on the screen. Pirate vid streams were illegal and required special equipment. Kai had had his installed years ago. The images showed a shaky picture, obviously taken by someone running. The view changed to the inside of an abandoned house and feet pounding up rotten stairs. The camera stabilized to an overview of the crash. From this angle, he could see the wreckage and bodies strewn over the ground.

Kai went back to the cutting board to finish the chicken and cut up the chuck. He kept most of his attention on the vid screen. If they were lucky, one of the pipes feeding desalinated water up to Level 6 or 7 had been ruptured. Anyone who made it out could use the maintenance ladder inside the pipe to climb up.

Was this an accident, or had the war suddenly gotten a lot closer? The city had managed to escape being directly affected so far, but if the last corporate war had been any indication, nothing was safe.

No one was calling it a corporate war yet, but it was only a matter of time.

He focused on the vid screen, still showing the crash site. Small drones filled the airspace, pausing to shine their lights on the rubble before moving on. Even with the distance of the news cameras, Kai thought he saw shadows darting near the walls. That had to be Jack's people, the insurgents, trying to get out through the hole. Jack could move fast when he needed to. The vid shifted focus onto a drone zooming toward the motion. The drone fired its weapon.

Kai sighed. They'd be lucky if any of them made it. He would have to get prepared for the incoming wounded. He'd dropped out of med school to get away from shit like this.

CHAPTER 5

UNKNOWN

WHEN KRIS LEFT, Miller had relaxed. She was his girl, and with her out there, he knew he would have a better chance of getting out of this. Even if it all ended badly, at least she would be safe. It was the last thought in his head as a figure dressed all in black blocked the light coming from the hole in the wall. As he felt a needle pierce his neck under his jaw. As his world slipped into oblivion.

Vibration. The sound of tires on a bumpy road. They were the first things he noticed. Miller groaned and tried to roll over, his body aching. Straps held him down. He felt another sharp jab in his neck and faded away again.

Cold. Cold and still. His shoulders ached, something pulled at his wrists, digging in, cutting off circulation to his hands. He tried to stand, but his legs collapsed under him, sending more sharp jabs

into his wrists. His legs hurt from being trapped under the pillar, but
he didn't feel the sharp pain of a break.

Miller struggled to open his eyes. The room was black, the only
light coming from under a door to his left. He forced himself to relax,
looking at the darkest corner until his eyes adjusted. It wasn't much,
but it would have to do. He tried to stand again, pushing his back up
against a smooth wall. His legs shook from the strain until he was
able to lock his knees. Blood rushed into his hands in a painful flood
and he gasped, his voice echoing in the room.

He couldn't move beyond that. His feet were held the same as
his hands. He couldn't move them more than a few centimeters to
either side. The backs of his hands felt the wall, searching for something, anything, that he could use. He duplicated the search with his
heels, finding something that felt like a rubberized baseboard. The
kind of stuff they used in cheap offices. Useless to him. He still
couldn't see anything, so he used his nose, drawing in a huge breath.
The only scent he picked up was water.

The limited light flickered. Two gray shadows blocked the light
from under the door. Feet. They looked too faint to be standing
close. Was it a guard? Someone coming to check on him? Miller
thought of yelling before deciding to remain quiet. The longer they
left him alone, the more of a chance he had of finding something,
anything to help him get out.

His fingers reached for his restraints. They weren't hard or cold,
so not metal. Definitely not rope either. They were flat, and their
surface felt slick under his fingers. Not wide enough for a seatbelt,
but some sort of webbing. He couldn't feel the knot; it was too close
to his wrist. Without knowing what kind of knot they'd used, anything he did might just make the damn thing tighter.

Miller stood as long as he could, watching the shadows move
under the door until his strength gave out. The straps around his

wrists jerked his shoulders painfully, and he slipped into a dark world between consciousness and blackness.

―――――

SANTA BARBARA, LEVEL 2—SUNDAY, JUNE 11, 2141 11:52 A.M.

Pat waited while Kris ran to the ramp. This morning, as the memories had hurtled through Pat's head, Kris had remained cool and collected, finding them both a place where they could rest and hide until the tempest of emotions subsided. Pat still wasn't over it, but she knew staying on Level 1 wasn't a good idea. When Kris had told her to wait in the dark until they knew the ramp was clear, Pat had taken the opportunity to muddle through her thoughts. She closed her eyes and breathed deep, trying to wash the flashbacks away.

It seldom worked, but her therapist had told her to try. The therapist had spent the first six months with her at the compound. She wished he was here with her now.

She opened her eyes in time to see Kris duck behind the up-ramp's barrier. It took a second to figure out why. Another figure rushed to the wall and leaned over to see where Kris had gone.

Pat surged to her feet, anger flowing through her like a blast furnace, and ran to the ramp. The fight was over before she was halfway there. Kris had pulled herself back over the barrier and turned, staring down the other side. Blood ran down her face, turning her shirt red. As Pat got closer, she could see the deep red spreading.

The memories threatened to plunge Pat back into her own hell.

Kris teetered on her feet, falling to her knees and swaying before collapsing forward. Pat pushed away the horrors threatening her vision, fighting the narrowing field of view, and ran faster.

Kris hit the ground.

Pat reached Kris's side, her lungs aching from the sprint and the taste of chemicals on her tongue. There was more blood this close. Her world filled with the sound of gunfire. Fear reached its icy fingers into her chest, sucking the life from her.

Pat ducked, hearing a grenade fly over her head. Her partner lay at her feet, his life bleeding out onto the concrete. The air smelled of burned flesh and death. Bullets ricocheted off the walls around them and Pat dropped, her body covering as much of her partner's as she could manage.

A scream punctured the air, small, high-pitched. A child. The sound of tiny feet running. A bundle of cloth leaped through the busted doorway, moving toward her. Pat lifted her head.

The screaming stopped.

Beneath Pat, her dead partner shifted, pushing Pat to the side. Her breath came out in small gasps, her chest jerking with each inhale.

It wasn't her partner lying on the ground; it was Kris. And Kris wasn't dead. Pat scanned the area, her eyes twitching at noises that still echoed through her memories. She squeezed her eyes tight, pressing her hands to her ears.

This wasn't real. There wasn't any gunfire. There weren't trained soldiers hiding, waiting for their chance to kill her.

Something pounded Pat's leg. Not painful, but insistent. Different. It didn't belong. She opened her eyes and looked down. Kris hit her leg again and again. Each impact landed with less power behind it.

Kris!

Pat looked down the empty ramp, the Ambients in the distance still flickering in the dark. Kris's eyes slowly closed and then opened again, staring at her.

Things came back. The transport crash, the fitful sleep filled with nightmares, the walk to the ramp. Pat forced herself into the present and helped Kris to her feet, taking most of the weight. In her head, she whispered the litany: *not this shit again, not this shit again.*

They needed to get off of Level 1. Kris needed to be looked at.

Pat moved up the ramp, almost dragging Kris along with her.

A few steps behind, from the flickering darkness, a child screamed, abruptly cut short.

Pat flinched and struggled to put one foot in front of the other.

Level 2 was almost as empty as Level 1, but the sounds were different. Pat could hear cars moving off to the left, and she swerved that way. Kris had become dead weight, no longer even trying to take steps. They weren't going to get far.

She ducked into an alley, moving far enough into it that the Ambients barely touched the walls. Pat moved to a small depression and lowered Kris into it. It took her only a few minutes to cover Kris in garbage.

"I'll be back soon," she whispered.

It would be easier getting a car if she wasn't carrying Kris. Once she had one, she'd come back, and they'd find a way to contact ACE. She grabbed a chunk of fibercrete from the ground and hid it under her shirt before leaving. The sharp texture of the fibercrete made her feel hopeless, but she fought it off.

———

UNKNOWN

Miller woke to a gentle hand on his cheek, brushing the lace pattern of scars. A bright light shone into his eyes, blinding him from what was in the room. Two pairs of hands grabbed him and jerked him to his feet.

"Gentle. You will always treat Mr. Miller with care."

The hands loosened their grip slightly, and Miller swayed on his feet. He squinted past the light, barely seeing a vague outline of a person. He had heard that voice before. Who the hell was it? Somewhere in the corners of his mind, he knew he should be fighting back, knew he should be feeling the rush of adrenaline and fear. Instead, he just felt numb.

With his weight off his arms, Miller once again endured the painful rush of blood back into his hands. This time he made no sound. He felt the webbing holding his hands and feet loosen, and the unseen men moved him away from the wall. Miller twisted to see who they were, but the light shifted to point directly into his eyes again. They'd attached it to his head, effectively blinding him no matter which way he looked.

The hands lifted him off his feet, and he tried to twist out of their grip. The time he had spent tied to the wall robbed him of his strength. He was placed on a frame leaning against the wall, the hands pushing him into position as though he were a small child. He was stripped and tied to it, his hands and feet pulled to the corners of the frame. He felt the webbing tighten as they were tied back down.

The rack behind him wasn't solid. It almost felt like a lattice of thick wires woven together. Someone gave the rack a quick shake, and Miller's shoulders screamed in agony as they twisted in their sockets.

He heard footsteps walking back to where he thought the door was, muffled by a thin layer of carpet on fibercrete. Two sets of feet in rubber-soled shoes. When the confirming snick of a door closing echoed across the room, he risked a glance up into the light again.

His glance froze at the briefcase near his feet, just at the edge of the blinding light. He'd seen it before. It was something he wasn't able to forget. The last time he'd seen it, he'd been in a limousine, his hands zip-tied behind his back and a psychopath sitting beside him. A roar of panic broke through the numbness. The owner of the voice clicked in his head, and an involuntary whimper escaped Miller's lips.

"You do remember. Good!" said Jeremy, stifling a laugh. "I was afraid I would have to begin right at the start, but I see our last—interrupted—session left its mark on you."

Miller heard footsteps move across the floor again. Hard shoes this time, ones that hit the floor with each step and reverberated in the empty room. Dress shoes. Useless in anything but an office.

A band was removed from around his head, and the blinding light stopped burning into his retinas, replaced by small overhead ones that pushed away the shadows. Miller tore his gaze away from the briefcase and focused on Jeremy. Black spots danced in front of his eyes.

"Did you ever think," Jeremy asked, "that we would be together in a room again? You and me, duplicating our earlier efforts to become friends?"

When Miller didn't answer, Jeremy bent over to pick up his briefcase and moved it to a table against the near wall. When he came back, he stood a meter in front of Miller and smiled.

"We won't be needing that right away." Miller sagged back against the mesh table he'd been tied to. Jeremy's smile got bigger. "But we'll get to it. You and I will become very close friends before this is over. In fact, we'll be sharing one of the most intimate things two men can share. We'll both have front row seats when your bitch cries out to me, wanting me to end it all. We won't, of course, you and I. We'll both be having too much fun. I'm sure that, working together, we'll be able to bring her to that point more than once."

Miller's jaw clenched until he thought his teeth would snap. Adrenaline pushed the last of the drugs from his system. He struggled against his restraints, forcing his body to its limits as he tried to reach out and grab Jeremy's scrawny neck. His left shoulder popped, and a scream tore from his throat.

"Tsk, tsk. It won't do to have you damage yourself that way. It takes away from my own pleasure . . . and that's really why we are here, isn't it?"

Before Miller could try to answer, Jeremy picked a hose off the floor and turned it on, spraying Miller in a wash of water so cold it felt as though it was burning.

"It really is only by chance that you're here. Once I found out you were in the crash, I instructed my men to bring you in as well. If you were alive. Now I'll have something to do while we wait for Kris. Why don't we start with something a little coarser this time? Something that hurts you, and gives me great satisfaction." Jeremy stepped into a pair of rubber boots and pulled on long rubber gloves. He moved toward Miller. From the back wall, he connected a power cable to the metal mesh of the table. Lifting another cable from the floor, he quickly clamped a wet sponge to the end of it and flicked a switch.

"The rack you're strapped to is a backdrop to the parrilla. A very old, but very effective way to get information. I had this one built specially for you." When the sponge touched Miller's arm, he jerked and stiffened, his back arching off the mesh. "It's very high voltage and low current, so there's less chance of killing you before I've had my fun." He touched the sponge to Miller again, and a scream tore from his throat. Jeremy took a step back and flipped the switch off before placing the cable and sponge back on the floor.

"It won't do to have you screaming too loudly. I've had an aversion to loud noises recently, ever since I was hit with the dart in the safe house. They say it'll go away in time, but for now . . ."

Jeremy grabbed a knotted cloth from the table where his tools sat, still in the closed briefcase, and jammed the knot into Miller's mouth before tying it around the back of his head. Miller barely moved, his chin resting on his chest.

When Jeremy was done, he picked up the sponge-tipped cable again and flipped the power switch back on.

Miller didn't know how long he was there. He wasn't asked any questions. He wasn't grilled for any ACE secrets. Jeremy just tortured him for fun. When Miller passed out, Jeremy poured cold water on him until he came to so that the process could be started again.

Electrocute, revive, repeat.

Electrocute, revive, repeat.

———

SANTA BARBARA, LEVEL 2—SUNDAY, JUNE 11, 2141 12:22 P.M.

The sound of traffic and people, of a busy city, increased as Pat continued to head west. Ahead lay a street, cars and bikes, pedestrians walking along as though nothing in the world had changed. She stood only a few meters from the bustling flow, yet no one looked in her direction. The street and sidewalk around her were empty, as though someone had drawn an invisible line that no one was allowed to cross. The feeling of not existing, not needing to interact with others felt like euphoria. Pat fought it off—she had Kris to worry about.

She took a second to make herself more presentable, running her fingers through her hair and wiping her face on the sleeve of her shirt. She removed the apron she'd worn all day and tossed it into the gutter. Underneath, her clothes were almost clean. It would have to do. Pat walked forward and, with a shudder, merged with the foot traffic.

Small shops and businesses lined the street. Each one had

barred windows and shutters that slid down at night. The people around her looked tired and almost as dirty as she was. The cars that drove past held a better collection of society. People who didn't live here and wouldn't stop for anything, just getting from point A to point B.

Pat crossed the busy street, dodging between the traffic, hoping to move deeper into civilization. The chances of finding a car were better if people felt safer. Several blocks later, a three-story office tower stood on the corner. A small parking lot sat beside it, surrounded by two-meter-high fences and patrolled by security.

It was too busy and too well protected for her to get in easily. But if it was all she could find, then it would have to do. She walked past the lot, watching the security out of the corner of her eye. They ignored her, standing around a small booth at the gate. With only one way out and the security, she decided against it and moved on. The gate slammed shut and Pat flinched, fighting the urge to duck.

She'd have to be careful. Pat had left her comm unit back at the compound, and without it, she had no way to change or hide her tracker ID. If she was caught and her ID was scanned, she wouldn't be able to hide. Not until she'd found a way to contact ACE.

A few blocks later the perfect opportunity showed up. A large retail mall made of individual small prefab buildings. The lot was about half full of cars, and more were pulling in as she watched. The Ambients were ultrabright here, but she couldn't see any security or cameras. Everyone must have been hoping the quantity of people moving around would stop most car thieves.

Pat wasn't like most thieves. She wasn't here for a quick thrill ride or to make a buck. She had to get Kris back to ACE. They could get her to a doctor.

She walked up to a car that had just pulled into the lot. The woman had parked the old car between two trucks and then run off toward the buildings. It took Pat only a second to get in. Most of the safety glass shattered on the rear seat when she slammed the fiber-crete into it. Pat reached around and unlocked the driver's door. This thing was too old and beat up to have more than a rudimentary on-board navigation system. With some luck, it wouldn't have any anti-theft or tracking systems.

A couple of minutes of fiddling with the computer under the dash, and Pat had the car running. The batteries had under a half charge in them. It would have to be enough to get them closer to Los Angeles and ACE headquarters. Pat didn't think Kris had the time to wait while it recharged.

She drove the car out of the lot, keeping an eye on the rearview mirror. She didn't want the owner to come out and see her driving away.

Pat got some strange looks when she drove across the busy street back into no man's land, but once she was there, everyone went back to pretending she didn't exist. There was some strange stuff going on in Santa Barbara. Something she'd have to tell ACE about and have them look into.

Pat backed the car into the alley and got out. She moved to the pile she'd hidden Kris under, her blood pounding in her ears. The pile had been moved. She fished through what was there and came up empty.

Kris was gone.

CHAPTER 6

LOS ANGELES, LEVEL 4—SUNDAY, JUNE 11, 2141 12:22 P.M.

A KNOCK ON THE DOOR brought Jeremy back to the real world. He had been watching the displays on the walls and had let his mind wander back to the previous year.

Back then, he had been in control of everything. He'd had an army that was willing to go to war for him, a president who had given him carte blanche to build a superweapon, and a plan to use it all to make himself one of the most powerful men in the world.

Now, Meridian was gone. Kadokawa had swooped in and taken it all. No one had come to their rescue. No one had answered the president's call for help when the attack began. And when it was obvious they had no chance of winning, the damn president had caved, opening the door as wide as he could to let the bastards in. It had taken all of three days.

They'd killed the president before calling in the rest of the board to show them what they'd done. Jeremy hadn't been there. He'd left the day before the attack started.

There was another quiet knock on the door, and Jeremy pulled his attention away from the displays, switched them away from viewing the sparse data he was able to gather on the brewing war, and answered.

"Come in."

William walked through the door, closing it gently behind him. "You've heard about the transport?"

"Yes."

"What do you plan to do now? You've destroyed part of the city, brought unwanted media attention to what you're doing—"

"What's your point?" Jeremy asked.

"My point?" William's voice rose in anger. "You left behind enough bodies with bullets in them to feed the vids for a week. Good people, *our* people. And you want to know what my point is? You've managed to do more damage to ACE in a day than the corporations have been able to in years."

"It's mine to destroy."

This time when William replied, he didn't bother to hide how he felt. "Are you really that egotistical? *We* started ACE. Together. It's no longer yours or mine. We created a force that would hurt the major corporations so that Meridian, so you, could rise to power. We brought in people who would help us do that. People who didn't and still don't know who was behind it all. Do you really think we can tell them to stop what they're doing?"

"Everyone can be dealt with, in one way or the other."

"Listen to yourself, Jeremy. Did you hear what you just said? Am I just someone who can be dealt with? Maybe by someone you hired to point a gun at me?"

"It would never come to that."

"Never come to that? Are you sure? Where do you draw the line?"

Jeremy took a step closer to William, his face flushed red. "I don't draw the line. I *am* the line. You have no idea what the bitch did to me. She destroyed everything I worked for, everything *we* worked for. I should be up there. I should be fighting the war with armies at my command. Instead I'm down here, watching everything on a screen. Watching some of the smaller corporations make moves Meridian was prepared to take. I could have controlled it all."

"And you blame the courier?"

"Yes." Jeremy took a breath and stepped back again, putting more space between himself and William. "Yes, I do. She was a throwaway. Someone to deliver the plans to Kadokawa before we killed Gorō. She was the linchpin that would turn the big three against each other."

"She was a courier, nothing more."

"I'll kill her for what she did."

William sighed and rested his hand on the doorknob. "You made her, Jeremy. Can you truly hate something you made? Hate it so much that you're willing to destroy *everything* else?"

SANTA BARBARA, LEVEL 2—SUNDAY, JUNE 11, 2141 12:23 P.M.

My world was warm. Dark. I had no sense of space or time. Where was I? I wasn't sure it mattered. There was some sort of weight pressing me into the ground, but I didn't care. I settled into the dark, embracing it. Letting it embrace me.

Pain lanced through my head, and the darkness was replaced with a blinding flash of light. I turned to get away from it and the weight on top of me shifted, feeling heavier. The oppressive odor of sewage filled my nose.

Some part of my brain knew I should be scared, and for a moment my heartbeat raced. Blood thundered in my head. I lay still until it stopped. It was warm in here. Wherever here was.

I slowly became aware of a beat. Steady. Harsh. It invaded my warmth. My space became hard and unforgiving. I shifted again, and the pain in my head returned. This time it didn't go away, pounding in time to the bass beat from some distant music.

I had to make it stop.

I opened my eyes. The world refused to come into focus. A wall swam into view over me, reaching up to a ceiling. I must be indoors. No, that couldn't be right. I blinked and my vision blurred more. All at once I felt trapped, confined. I had to get out. Dust fell into my eyes as I struggled to get out from under whatever was on top of me. I blinked, trying to clear them. Tears ran down my nose and temple. Bile rose in my gut and I squeezed my eyes tight, bringing another wave of pain.

The weight on top of me lessened and I flailed harder. It felt like I was pushing through water. My hands were heavy, and each movement hurt. I finally felt fresh air on my face and opened my eyes again. Everything still swam in huge undulating waves. I reached for something solid to hold on to. My hands whipped through the air, hitting things I couldn't see, never reaching their intended goal.

Rolling over, I finally got my knees under me. Even the ground curled gently beneath me. It felt as though I stayed that way for minutes, trying to get my breathing under control. I pulled myself to my feet, a wall magically appearing before me, solid enough for me to use. I swayed and felt myself falling again. My shoulder hit the wall first, followed by my skull. The throbbing in my head increased, still keeping time with the damn music.

Shuffling toward the noise, my right hand found the wall. The damn thing kept moving away from me. I shuffled closer, gently leaning my shoulder against it, and stumbled forward.

The wall vanished. I lurched and almost fell before catching myself. Swaying on my feet, I heard noise from the right. My body turned and followed the sound before my head caught up. The sidewalk moved under me in great groundswells. I shivered, suddenly cold, and jammed my hands into my pockets. My fingers found Oscar of their own accord, and my world came into focus. Where was I? Where was Pat? The sidewalk buckled in front of me and I almost tripped. Oscar slipped from my grasp, nestling deep into my pocket once again.

Time was as fluid as the street. At one point, I found myself sitting on the curb, leaning my head against a cold metal signpost, letting the chill sink into my skin. I fought nausea at every step, eventually dry heaving in an open doorway. The music got louder.

The steady beat was joined by screaming guitars. Occasionally, a voice broke through, sounding like fingers on a chalkboard. I turned down a smaller street. Lights flickered off the ceiling: red, then orange and green and blue. I could hear people chanting, their rhythm matching the music.

I turned a corner and saw them, their fists pumping the air, their bodies swaying together, merging into a living organism. Lights flashed in my eyes and I squeezed them tight, almost immediately losing my balance and careening across the street.

Arms caught me, stopping me from driving into a wall at top speed. Why couldn't the world stop spinning and come back into focus?

"Whatcha on, girl?"

I turned and stared dumbly at the woman that stopped me.

"I said, whatcha on? Looks like someone hit ya in the head pretty good. You just trying to dull the pain, huh?"

"Imma no on antin." I couldn't get my mouth around the words.

"You got any more on ya?" The hands went from being supportive to searching, digging into the pockets of my pants and moving to the waistband.

I jerked away, tripping over my own feet and landing on the rough street. The hands followed me.

"Where ya hiding it? That shit looks good."

"Lea me alo." I rolled away, kicking out at the hands.

"Fuck, girl, that hurt. If you don't have any to share, just say so."

Light from the concert played across the ceiling. I rolled onto my side and dry heaved again.

"On second thought, that shit don't look so good. Keep it."

When she left, the only thing that remained was the pounding in my ears. I struggled to my feet. I had to stop the music. I weaved over to the crowd, pushing my way through the mass of bodies.

More hands grabbed me, lifting me off my feet. I was on top of the crowd, hands pushing me wherever they could. I was rolled onto my stomach, hands grabbing, clutching at me, constantly being maneuvered closer to the stage. The hands slipped, and I almost fell before they caught me again.

Then it was as though the crowd gave up. I dropped to the ground, feet milling centimeters from my head. I grabbed at someone, hauling myself back upright. The mass of humanity squeezed back together, keeping me on my feet. I felt trapped. Unable to move. I had to—

The music stopped.

The horde let out a low-pitched shout that climbed into a crescendo. They crashed forward, pushing me along with them. My feet dragged. The only thing keeping me standing was the crush of bodies.

As if on cue, the music started again, the bass beat hammering my temples. The lead singer screamed at the top of his lungs.

I reached the front of the crowd. The stage was bathed in red light. On the stage behind the drummer stood a horned beast, its mouth open, sharp white teeth guarding a pink tongue. Its eyes glowed icy blue.

Without a doubt, I knew that he was the cause of the pain in my head. It was his fault I couldn't see, his fault I felt weak and confused. His fault.

Everyone around me was jumping up and down to the beat. The monster on the stage ran forward, screaming at everyone to go higher. Two people in front of me leaped into each other and fell back, creating a gap in the wall of bodies. I stepped forward, only thirty centimeters from the stage. The creature stopped his gyrating in front of me and leaned forward. I could see a microphone taped to its jaw. Laughter filled the air, the guitars and drums merging with it, taunting me, ridiculing me, threatening me.

The creature reached a hand out to me, palm up. Tattooed on the palm was single, unblinking eye. I grabbed the hand, letting it pull me closer to the stage.

The monster's mouth contorted into a sneer. I swung with my free hand, using the creature's grip as a pivot point, and drove my fist into its gaping maw. My hand went through as though its teeth were made of paper-mache. The laughter turned into a scream of rage and I was let go.

The music stopped.

I melted back into the crowd, falling into warm water filled with bodies. The real screaming started then. Onstage, the monster was trying to pull off its head. The band members yanked cords out of amplifiers, scurrying like rats around a hungry beast. The stage, two flatbed trucks parked back-to-back, separated and sped away.

Overhead, police drones filled the sky. The crowd flowed away from the stage, carrying me with them. People fell and were trampled. I tripped over a leg, barely catching myself on the person beside me.

I don't know how long I ran, or where I ran to. Ambients flashed overhead, dim and flickering. I ran until I couldn't hear the drones anymore. I ran until my legs couldn't hold me up. I ran until I fell, quivering, into a dark alley.

SANTA BARBARA, LEVEL 2—SUNDAY, JUNE 11, 2141 12:30 P.M.

Pat stared at the empty alley. Where the hell could Kris have gone? Kris had been so out of it, it was a wonder she had been able to get out of the alley at all.

She should never have left Kris alone. The city—hell even just this one part of it—was so massive that it would be a miracle to find anyone. Her mouth went dry and she shook her head slowly, staring at the spot where Kris was supposed to be.

Pat jerked at the piercing squeal of hyper metal music, pressing her back into the building's wall and closing her eyes. The sound ripped through air like a dull knife cutting meat, shredding everything it touched. Pat forced herself to stand in the middle of the alley and looked toward the noise. Could Kris have gone that way?

The music stopped, and the sound of screaming replaced it.

Shit, she couldn't have.

With that thought, Pat got back into the stolen car and sped toward the noise. A few blocks later, she stopped. There was no way she could move without running over someone.

Police drones hugged the ceiling over her head. Occasionally, one would swoop down and hover over the crowd. Pat knew they were scanning identities. If Kris was anywhere in there, she was in big trouble.

Pat backed the car down the street, turning into a gap between two empty, hulking buildings, and turned the car off. She'd heard about these concerts, even used one when she was on the job. They were highly illegal, and always held in desolate sections of Level 2.

You could get almost anything at these events, including dead if you weren't careful. Kris had been really out of it when Pat had left her in the alley. Head injuries like that weren't something you took lightly. Had Kris been able to get up by herself, or had someone found her?

No, that couldn't be it. Pat had done a pretty good job of hiding her. If someone had taken Kris away, they would have to know she was in there in the first place. Unlikely.

That meant Kris had to have wandered off on her own. Did she think Pat had abandoned her, or was the injury so severe that she didn't know what was going on?

Pat banged the steering wheel in frustration.

Outside the car, the occasional straggler wandered past her parking space. Most of the drones had left, leaving only a few behind to make sure the illegal concert didn't start again. Pat knew that no ground forces would be coming in. For one thing, most of the law enforcement on the lower levels had been thinned out to supply able bodies for the war that was coming. Even if that wasn't the case, the police wouldn't come. The cost of sending in ground forces, arresting people, and putting them in jail was just too high. All they needed to do was break up the party.

With the last of the stragglers, Pat decided it was time to move. She started the car and drove slowly to where the concert had been. When she saw the first body, a young man with a long bushy beard, she pulled over again. Looking up the street, she saw at least a dozen bodies, trampled and crushed when the mob ran away. The police might not come, but the coroner would. She figured she had maybe ten minutes.

Fighting the almost irresistible urge to run, she got out of the car and slowly approached the second body, switching to the third before she even got close. The air was filled with the smell of illegal drugs and the street was littered with used patches and empty pill packets. A few minutes later she had finished her scan. She flushed with relief. A feeling that was quickly replaced by fear. If Kris wasn't here, if she hadn't been here—

Pat shoved the thought from her mind. She could feel the PTSD tickling at the corners of her brain. She couldn't let it take control. She had a friend that needed her.

With that thought, Pat got back in the car and drove away. A block later, two dark blue vans drove past her, heading to the illicit concert site.

Searching randomly wasn't going to help. Pat pulled up a street map on the car's comm unit and plotted a grid pattern. There were some smaller streets and alleys in there that she'd have to search on foot.

Pat checked the car's clock. She'd left Kris at about noon, and she'd gotten back around a half hour later. That meant Kris couldn't have gotten far. At best, a person could go four, maybe five kilometers in that time. Faster if they were running, which Kris wouldn't be able to do. That made for a sixteen square kilometer search area.

She drove back to the alley she had left Kris in and started the pattern from the center.

It took the better part of an hour to finally find her. Pat had gone down so many streets, dug through so many piles of garbage, that she was sure Kris was lost for good. Each time Pat saw a pair of legs or someone slumped against a wall, her heart raced until she got close enough to realize it wasn't Kris.

The last time was no different. Pat spotted a foot sticking out from an alley. As she got closer, a leg came into view, and then the shadow of someone lying against the wall. Pat got out of the car, preparing for another failure. When she was close enough to recognize Kris's shirt-wrapped feet, she sprinted forward, dropping to her knees on the rough concrete.

Pat placed her fingers on Kris's neck, feeling for a pulse. It was there, slow and steady, but shallow. Pat turned Kris's head and looked at where it had been damaged.

The blood had dried. From the looks of it, the wound had broken open and dried at least a couple of times. Pat hoped the blood made it look worse than it really was. Gently, she lifted Kris and carried her to the waiting car.

Now that they were together again, it was time to get in touch with ACE. The only way Pat knew how to do that was to get back to Los Angeles and find a secure comm unit.

―――――

LOS ANGELES, LEVEL 4—SUNDAY, JUNE 11, 2141 9:07 P.M.

The hotel was bad, even for Level 4. They called it the Hotel Ruby, but it was really just a cheap two-story motel with a bar at the front. They'd painted the fibercrete a lurid purpley-red color. When Bryson walked in, they had a room available. He prepaid for two nights using his new comm unit.

The room had a couple of queen-size beds sitting on worn blue indoor/outdoor carpet and a small viewscreen mounted on the wall. The remote didn't work, so he'd had to call down for a new one. The room smelled like detergent and disinfectant, which was why the mold on the bathroom walls came as a surprise. Still, it had warm running water, and the shower floor appeared clean enough to stand in with bare feet. The manager had given him the regular spiel about using too much water, but since there wasn't any rationing in effect, he'd just be billed for whatever he used. The idea of rationing took him by surprise. It was something he hadn't needed to think about for the last decade. The Sat City always had plenty of water.

The view out the window was almost as bad as the inside. Across the short driveway leading to the hotel's gated parking was a three-story building covered in a fake brick facade. It had no windows, only gaping holes with bright orange tarps hanging on the inside like cheap curtains. Bryson figured he would be hearing construction noises in the morning. Hopefully they wouldn't start too early. He closed the curtains and turned on the viewscreen to a news station, muting the sound. Images of military vehicles driving on one of the lower levels flashed across the screen. He ignored them. He had more important issues.

He knew he had to start making decisions. Walking out on Kadokawa and making it down to Earth was the first part of the plan. That part had been risky enough that he hadn't thought he had a hope in hell of making it. It was pure luck he had landed in Los Angeles, really. At least he was familiar with the area. If they'd put down on the Nippon Islands, he would have been in big trouble.

Bryson snorted. He had a fucking PhD in Physics from Harvard, with a thesis on quantum teleportation, and when his life depended on it he counted on dumb luck. There *was* something almost majestic about it, he supposed . . . relying on the indeterminacy of the universe to get him where he needed to be. If he had his computers, he could probably find a Paterek algorithm that—

A shadow crossed the curtain, moving toward the stairs that lead to the driveway. Someone was on the balcony outside his door. Bryson froze, his blood racing to his head, flushing his face with heat. All thoughts of computers and his labs vanished. His first instinct was to duck, to hide behind the bed, before common sense kicked in. For all he knew, they were just going down to the hotel bar. Not only were his curtains closed on the balcony window, but Kadokawa, even if they knew he was gone by now, couldn't have any idea where he was. He was safe.

Bryson forced himself to calm down, splashing cold water on his face before getting back to planning.

He thought about going to see his dad on Level 6, but he had no idea if security would let him up there. They'd had a major falling out when Bryson joined Meridian. He didn't know what his dad had expected. A physics doctorate didn't give you too many choices. You ended up either teaching or being hired by one of the corporations, and he wasn't the teaching kind of guy. Besides, Meridian had been small compared to the others.

His dad had always been against them. Not Meridian in particular, but all corporations in general. He thought they were evil, the downfall of society. He blamed them for everything from the water shortages to the high prices of the drugs some of his patients needed. Hell, some of his patients on the lower levels couldn't afford the medication he prescribed, and good ol' Doc Searls would buy what they needed for them. Usually by overcharging the patients that could afford it, but not always. It was tough to get ahead in the world when most of your income went out the window.

Bryson didn't want to fall into that trap. He was looking after numero uno and no one else. He'd always been that way, really, even as a kid. His dad had told him that would change when he got married and had kids of his own. Bryson snorted. Who had the time for that? And who would be dumb enough to bring kids into a world that was already falling apart?

They had never really understood each other's points of view, so going back to his dad on his hands and knees was out. Oh, the good doctor wouldn't say anything. That wasn't his style after all. But Bryson couldn't find it in himself to do it.

San Angeles wouldn't be a bad place to stay. The Kadokawa presence was small, just a few offices in the major centers like Los Angeles and San Francisco. Maybe he could head north, maybe get to Santa Maria or Monterey.

Now that was an idea. Monterey had always appealed to him. A good jazz scene. He'd played the saxophone all through school, only stopping when he got to university. The place had pretty good weather, though that didn't matter too much below Level 6. There wasn't a shuttle port, so they wouldn't expect him there. He could forget about physics, forget about quantum anything. Maybe pick up the sax again, get better at it. Math and music were supposed to use the same part of the brain. There was no reason he couldn't go pro, except for the exposure it would give him. Lying low would be the rule for the rest of his life. All right, then. Destination chosen. Bryson felt the excitement start to bubble in his chest.

Now how to get there? Renting a car was out. They would want some sort of identification, and that would be something Kadokawa could trace. A bus ticket might work, under an assumed name and using the comm unit he'd purchased at the airport to pay for it. Hitchhiking would be even better.

With the decision made, he started to feel hungry. He doubted the hotel had any sort of room service, and with the condition of the place, he wasn't sure he would want to try it anyway. That also ruled out the bar. If he remembered correctly, there was some sort of craft beer place up the street. He'd head there and get a burger. Those places always had a good menu.

Bryson grabbed his jacket off the bed by the window and opened the door. He looked over the railing to the driveway. Except for a couple cars, it was empty. He closed the door behind him, double-checking his back pocket for the key, and went down the stairs. The gate at the bottom opened to the driveway between the buildings, squealing a bit as it swung open. He would need his room key to get back through it. Habit made him reach into his back pocket again to check for the key.

A few cars drove on the street, and the sidewalk had people on it, though it was nowhere near busy. As far as he was concerned, it was just enough people for him to blend in, and not so many that someone could sneak up on him.

The craft beer place was where he remembered it. The sign on the door said The Lab Gastropub. Bryson smiled. The interior wasn't like the lab he had left behind, but it had enough chrome and white countertop to make him feel at home, and the smell of food that wafted from the open door set his mouth watering. They wouldn't have real beef, but right now it didn't matter. He slid into a booth and waited for the serving staff, ordering off the menu when they came.

An hour later, Bryson had finished off a great burger, leaving the bun on the plate as he always did. He'd washed it down with a couple of beers. The menu said the beer was made with ten percent real hops. It wasn't bad, but it tasted like they had added extra sugar to speed up the fermentation process.

By the time he walked back through the doors, the streets were empty of foot traffic and only the occasional car zipped past. He flipped up the collar of his jacket and headed back toward the hotel, watching its garish light flicker and dim. The place was definitely a dive. He would stay here tonight and find a new place tomorrow, start his journey to a new life in Monterey.

He had just turned into the hotel's driveway when a fist smashed into his cheek, cutting it open. Bryson stumbled backward, and rough hands grabbed his jacket, pulling him deeper into the shadow. Another punch in the gut drove him to his knees before he toppled face-first onto the driveway. He didn't feel the impact.

One thought raced through his head. *They found me!*

It was only as he was being dragged farther into the dark driveway by his hotel that the thought of fighting back entered his head. He twisted violently, breaking the grasp of the person holding his feet. The move placed him on his side, and he stared at the silhouette of the person above him as a boot impacted his ribs. Pain flowed through him this time. Another swift kick landed on his back as he squirmed into a fetal position.

The attack stopped as quickly as it had started. Hands tore off his jacket and reached into his pockets, pulling out whatever they found. What felt like minutes later, but could only have been a few seconds, the sound of feet pounding the pavement echoed in the drive. His attacker left him lying in the dirt and grime of the city.

Bryson didn't dare move. As he lay there, the searing pain in his ribs and back met up with the new one coming from his knees. His face still felt numb.

It wasn't them. It wasn't Kadokawa. The realization slowly seeped into his brain and he uncurled. Of course it couldn't be them. How would they have found him? He had been mugged! Dammit, how could he have been so stupid?

He pushed himself to his feet and leaned against the building under construction. Across the alley, only a couple of meters away, the locked gate to his room reflected the beam from an overhead spotlight. Where he stood, it was as close to pitch black as you could get in the city. He shoved off the wall and careened over to the gate, grabbing the handle to pull it open. It was locked.

With painstaking care, he moved his arm to reach into his back pocket. The key card was gone. He let go of the support the gate provided and stumbled back to the brick facade building. At his feet lay the key card for his room and the gate. He stared at it, not quite sure whether, if he reached down to get it, he would ever be able to stand back up.

The short walk back was more painful the second time. He unlocked the gate and swung it open. The squeal of the hinges barely pushed through the haze of pain that enveloped him. He stared at the flight of stairs.

It felt as though a lifetime had passed before he reached his room. Each step was agony, each breath made it feel like his ribs were stabbing through his chest. He ended up breathing through his mouth as his nose clogged with thickening blood. With the room door safely closed and locked behind him, he lay on the bed, not caring how much blood seeped into the sheets.

The Ambients shone through the curtained window before he woke up and moved into the bathroom.

LOS ANGELES, LEVEL 4—SUNDAY, JUNE 11, 2141 10:02 P.M.

William caught Jeremy as he was leaving his office. The door had barely closed as William rounded the corner. He smiled to himself. His timing had been perfect. At least he hadn't been hanging around the hallway like a high school kid waiting for his crush. Those days were long gone.

He wasn't quite sure what his feelings for Jeremy were anymore. Though he was pretty sure there was still love, he didn't know if it was the same as before, or even salvageable. That's what he was here for, to find out if what they'd had was worth saving.

He was through playing games. There would be no skulking in hallways, no more long nights wondering what had gone wrong, where he had made his mistake. In fact, over the last little while, he'd come to the conclusion that it wasn't his fault at all. Jeremy had changed. The loss of his position at Meridian, his obsession with that damn girl. They had replaced just about everything Jeremy had cared for. He had always been ruthless, but he had never been so mean, so insular. It was as if everything that made Jeremy human had been stripped away. William hoped it was still in there, and if it was, he would try to find a way to bring the real Jeremy back.

And now it was time.

He smiled at Jeremy, tucking a folder under his arm. "Jeremy! Heading home for the day?"

"I still have a couple of . . . things I need to take care of . . ."

William held back a groan. This wasn't going as he had planned. "If it doesn't take long, maybe I could join you. When we're done, we could grab a drink down at Stacey's?" He couldn't keep it from sounding like a question.

Stacey's was where they had first met. They'd had a small meal— Jeremy had had the lightly breaded halibut with asparagus spears and herbed potatoes. The fish was from one of the farms on Level 5; you'd have to go up to Level 7 to get the real thing. He couldn't re- member what he'd eaten.

"If you haven't had dinner, we could get the halibut."

Jeremy stopped walking and stared at William. For a moment, William thought he had a chance. The look in Jeremy's eyes soft- ened, and the old Jeremy stood in the hallway.

"I'd love to, but I really don't know how long this is going take."

The new Jeremy came back with an abruptness that shocked William.

"I . . . I could still join you?" he almost cringed at the hesitation in his voice.

Jeremy started to walk away, and William followed, eventually catching up and walking beside him. He hadn't said yes, but then again, he hadn't said no either.

"I don't think you'll enjoy this," Jeremy said.

"How bad could it be?"

Jeremy walked in silence for a while, taking the stairs down. When they went past the first-floor exit, William tensed. There wasn't much in the basement, just storage and empty rooms. When they went down one more floor and the walls changed from a smooth white to unpainted rough fibercrete, he started to regret his decision.

"I have someone from the transport this morning," Jeremy said.

William stopped. "A survivor? You said everything was taken care of. I thought you meant . . ." He jogged a bit to catch back up to Jeremy.

"That's part of your problem. You think too much without digging to get the real facts. There were four survivors. Unfortunately, I only managed to get one."

William pretended he couldn't hear the edge of contempt that crept into Jeremy's voice. "So, who is it? Are they hurt?"

"Not as much as they will be." Jeremy paused as if giving William a chance to say something. "I've got Ian Miller."

This time when William stopped, he grabbed Jeremy's arm to stop him as well. "We can't let him see you. He can't know you're part of ACE."

Jeremy pried his arm away. "If that's the way you feel, then maybe it's you he shouldn't see. We've already had a short session, and he has no idea where he is."

At the words "short session," the dread in William's chest blossomed. His next words came out short and chopped as he struggled to regain control of his breathing. "What do you mean?"

"Last year, you and the courier stopped me from finishing my job with Miller. I went to a lot of effort to get him." Jeremy continued walking. "Once I found out Miller was at the compound, I decided I wanted him as well. Imagine my excitement on discovering he survived the crash. He killed one of my best agents last year. An act like that can't go unpunished."

"Miller is the best operative we've got. You need to let him go. *We* still need him."

Jeremy paused midstride and turned to face William. "You still haven't figured it out yet, have you? I created ACE to help *me*. Now that I've been temporarily reassigned, ACE has outlived its usefulness. Besides, ACE is mine to create and destroy as I see fit."

"No it's not." William pulled strength from a reserve he didn't realize he had when facing Jeremy. "ACE is ours. We built it together. And over the years, we've shared what we've built with the other directors. ACE isn't yours or mine. It's bigger than that. Much bigger."

"I think that's where you and I will always disagree. ACE was built to get me to where I wanted to be. *That* was its sole purpose. *My* sole purpose."

William started thinking fast. "Then why destroy it? I mean, sure, Meridian is gone, but there's always another corporation to—"

"Another?" Jeremy interrupted. "Another? There are no others. There's no one that would dare to bring me on. Sure, maybe as a janitor, but that's it."

"Then we can leave," William said. For the second time, he saw Jeremy slouch and lean against the wall. "ACE is big enough to continue doing its job as a corporate watchdog and environmental organization. They don't need us. We can release Miller somewhere, he'll never trace the facility's attack and his capture back to ACE. We still have that place in St. Thomas. White sand, blue water. We can leave tonight and wake up to the fresh salt air tomorrow morning." He reached out and touched Jeremy's hand, grabbing hold of his long, slender fingers. "Come on, let's go. Leave all this crap behind."

Jeremy stood up straight and squeezed William's hand back before gently pulling away. When he answered, his voice was soft. "I'd like that. I really would. But I have to finish this first. If I don't, it will eat at me every day so much, you'll want to be rid of me before too long."

William sighed, his opportunity to get out of the whole thing disappearing from his grasp with each word Jeremy spoke. "Okay." He didn't have any fight left in him.

When Jeremy continued down the stairs, William followed a few paces behind. No matter what happened, as soon as Miller saw him, the asset would be gone. And if by some fluke he wasn't, ACE sure as hell was. Maybe it was time.

They left the staircase and walked down a short hallway. When it ended at a perpendicular hallway, they turned the corner. The hall dead-ended at a door with a crossbeam holding it locked. Jeremy lifted the beam and leaned it against the wall. He walked in without looking back at William, his perfect posture and angry demeanor returned.

William hesitated before following him in, not quite sure why he did.

The room felt empty. It looked like at one time it had been commercial office space, with carpet on the floor and rubberized baseboard. Why anyone would have set up an office down here was beyond him. On the right wall, huge hooks had been drilled through the drywall into the surrounding fibercrete: two near the roof and two near the floor. The stench of released body fluids hit him before he took another step in.

What caught his attention was the figure at the far end of the room.

Miller was shackled tightly to a wire frame. He was naked, burn marks up and down his arms and thighs. Feces and urine had run down his legs, pooling on the floor. Attached to the mesh was a wire that fed into a box plugged into the wall. He knew what it was. He'd been in charge of Black Ops long enough to know that sometimes special *inducement* was needed to make someone cooperative. Beside the rack stood a stainless steel table.

When the door clicked shut, Miller struggled to stand straight in his restraints. Jeremy walked to the box and flicked it on, filling the room with a soft hum. Miller stared at William, the realization slowly dawning on his face. William wondered if it was worse than what was about to happen, knowing that the company you worked for, that you were willing to give your life for, was just a sham.

Jeremy continued as though he and Miller were the only people in the room. He picked a hose off the floor and turned a torrent of water at Miller, changing the carpet at his feet into a fetid lake. When Miller was soaked, Jeremy pulled on a pair of rubber boots and gloves and picked up the second wire coming from the box.

"At first, I thought I could use you to get Kris, but I really don't need to, do I? You know that now, don't you?" Jeremy asked. "She'll come to me; it's what we trained her to do. She'll come home like a good little girl."

Miller fought against his restraints. William was sure that if he got loose, he would tear Jeremy's heart out with his bare hands.

"This," Jeremy said, waving his hand at the rack, "is for Abby. You remember her, don't you? She was my best asset, and you killed her protecting that little courier of yours. I'll consider this practice for when Kris takes your place." Jeremy rubbed the second wire across the mesh, creating a shower of sparks. Miller's body jerked against the shackles and a scream tore from his throat. Jeremy laughed, and then, as if realizing William was still in the room, abruptly stopped.

William stayed for a while as Jeremy tortured Miller, watching what had become a complete stranger torture someone he had worked with for the last year. This wasn't the Jeremy he remembered. He left, closing the door softly behind him. He wasn't sure Jeremy even noticed.

Seeing Miller strung up and helpless, tortured for Jeremy's amusement, tore at him like barbed wire. He would do whatever he could to keep Kris from ending up in the same place Miller was. And he'd have to come up with a way to stop Jeremy from destroying ACE.

CHAPTER 7

KRIS HAD COME TO during the car ride. At first, she just stared out the window and screamed, as if the movement of the car was the most painful thing she had ever had to endure. Pat drove into a parking lot and stopped, pulling Kris into her arms until the screaming had quieted and the shaking had subsided a little. They stayed that way for almost half an hour.

Eventually Kris pushed away and put her back to the car door. Her sweat-soaked hair clung to her scalp, making her look gaunt. Her eyes were out of focus, and when Pat took a closer look, one pupil was bigger than the other. They had to get some help really quick.

Through the mumbles and slurred words, she had managed to pick up a few phrases repeated over and over again. The name Carl, and a place in Level 2 Los Angeles called Northern Dragon something. Pat knew where to go. The name Kris said was wrong, but everything else pointed to Level 2 Chinatown. From their conversations at the compound, Pat knew Kris had grown up there before her parents died and moved back as soon as she could. Her friend, Kai, had a take-out restaurant in the heart of Chinatown.

Without any immediate way to contact ACE, it could be a while before they would be able to get any help. She'd have to try and take care of Kris herself. Her comm unit was still at the compound, and without one, she couldn't use her outdated contact number to try to get in touch with ACE. She was hoping Kai would be of some use. Kris obviously trusted him, and that was good enough for now. It had to be.

Pat parked outside of the restaurant for about fifteen minutes, not expecting anyone to be inside at this hour. Even though all the lights were off, she thought she saw a faint glow from behind the counter, and maybe someone moving around. What were the chances this guy would be in the building at this time of night? Maybe he lived there?

Pat started the car and drove around the back. She pulled in close to the wall and crawled into the back seat to get out. Kris was still leaning against the car door, and when Pat opened it, she had to catch Kris before she slid out and hit the ground.

Kris had always been small, but as Pat carried her to the back door, it felt as though she was carrying a child. She kicked at the steel-clad door. No sound came from inside. Could she have been wrong? Could the place actually be empty? If it was, she would have to revert to plan two. Kris wasn't going to make it through the night without medical attention.

In the dark, Pat noticed an eyehole in the door. She kicked savagely at the steel and took a step back, angling Kris's face so it could be seen. The door swung open immediately and an old man beckoned them into the soft, warm light. Pat strode through without hesitating. The door slammed shut and the old man pushed past her and lifted a brightly colored curtain into a side room. The light in the hallway increased.

"In here. Put her on the table . . ." He paused. "Gently."

The curtain swung shut and he was gone. Pat placed Kris on the table, pushing everything that was on it onto the floor. She leaned over and lifted Kris's eyelids one at a time. One pupil was still bigger than the other. She wished she had a flashlight to check for responsiveness.

The curtain opened again, and the old man pushed her out of the way before placing some equipment on the table beside Kris. Pat hadn't been in too many hospitals, but it looked like pretty high-end stuff. Who the hell was this guy?

"Are you Kai?"

The old man answered without looking up. "I am Kai. Now stop asking questions and get me some hot water from the front. Do not turn on any lights."

The urgency in his voice made Pat jump to his command. Before she left the room, she turned back to tell him about Kris's pupils, but he was already shining a light into her eyes. Pat left the room, moving around the small kitchen with only the dimmed Ambients shining through the plate glass windows to guide her. Where the hell did he keep his pots?

From the back of the restaurant she heard Kai yelling. "Not too hot, and bring back clean towels. Bottom shelf, under sink."

The towels were easy, the hot water wasn't. Pat left the tap running for at least a full minute before the water even started getting warm, ignoring the extravagant use of water. The pots were lined up over the row of woks, and she grabbed the biggest one she could find, filling it almost to the top. She stuffed the towels under her arm and carried the water back.

"Here, put it here." Kai had moved a desk from the corner of the room to the table, right beside Kris's head. Once Pat had put down the water and towels, he commanded her to get another pot of hot water ready.

By the time she came back, a lot quicker than she had with the first pot, Kai had already started cleaning the dried blood from Kris's head. He ignored what had accumulated on her face and body, moving directly to where the ramp had impacted. Fifteen minutes later, the wound was clean enough for him to see the damage.

"This is not good," he said. "Not good at all. She has lost a lot of blood. Go across hall and bring me some syntho. Quickly now." He was already inserting a needle into Kris's arm.

Pat floundered backward, her back hitting the doorframe beside the curtain. Her arms were crossed, hands covering the tender flesh in the crook of her elbows, rubbing the skin in a pinching motion. She curled around the doorframe and stood alone in the dark, her eyes closed, until she got herself back under control.

Finally able to move, she stepped into the storage room across the hall and grabbed a handful of syntho. What kind of restaurant owner kept synthetic blood in the back of his store? Maybe they'd gotten lucky. Maybe Kris had led them right back to ACE. It was too good to be true.

When she got back to Kris's side, the old man grabbed the bags from her and hooked one up right away. He handed it back to Pat, indicating she should hold it above her head.

"Do not move," he said, turning back to Kris. "Too much blood on the brain. She is bleeding internally as well. What did you do to her?"

He rolled Kris onto her side, bringing the wound into full view of the light. Surprisingly, it didn't look as bad as Pat had thought it would.

Pat started to deny she had done anything, but Kai just shushed her.

"No time. Too much chitchat distracting."

This guy better know what he was doing. He was starting to piss her off.

He turned his attention back to Kris and moved one of the machines he had brought with him closer to her head. He attached it to just below the impact point, pressing it hard into her scalp, and toggled a switch. Lights flickered on the machine's surface, and a tiny readout displayed text in a never-ending stream. Pat couldn't read any of it; Japanese was not one of her languages.

As the machine did its work, Kai sealed the wound before moving his attention to the rest of Kris. Pat shifted the bag of syntho to her other arm and shook out the numbness as she watched.

The rest of Kris's injuries, besides her feet, were minor. Some road rash on her hands and knees from when she'd hit the ground. He cut the back of her shirt open, exposing a giant purple bruise on her back. The bruise even came through the burn scar between her shoulder blades.

Kris had talked about what happened to her during their long conversations at the compound, but Pat had never seen the damage that had been done. Why Kris still had the scar was anybody's guess, since it didn't look deep enough to be unremovable. Not like her own. Kris had never talked about the reason for keeping it. Kai let out a long, low breath, and Pat had to agree. The skin had literally melted around the black box, and when they'd removed it, they had pulled a fair amount of skin with it. What was left had been stretched over the wound to close it.

Kai stopped his examination long enough to switch bags of syntho, telling Pat to keep holding it. He picked up a device shaped like a gun. On its barrel, "Yannis-Burke Regenerator" was printed in large yellow letters. He turned his attention to the road rashes. A few minutes later, the rashes were gone, and fine white and pink skin was left behind. Pat knew from experience that in a few hours even that would be gone, and the skin color would match.

When he turned his attention to Kris's back, Pat switched hands again. As Kai poked and prodded at the bruise, she looked around the small room, unable to look at the burn scar again. At first glance, it was just an office, but as she looked closer, she saw things that were out of place. There was a map still on the desk. It showed the outer wall near where the transport had crashed. The odd thing was that it also showed what was outside the wall, in amazing detail. The desalinization plants that brought fresh water into the city were clearly marked, as well as where the pipes entered the wall. Along with them were the sewage plant dumps. Once the city cleaned the raw sewage, it dumped what was left back into the oceans. Anything that remained was turned into fertilizer for the farms on Level 5 and Level 7.

Overall, it was a fairly decent system when it was first built. Unfortunately, the city had grown larger and quicker than the original designers had thought. Now the desal and the sewage plants weren't big enough to handle the millions of people that lived here. SoCal was slowly refurbing the old plants, but they'd stopped a few years ago, once the Level 6 and 7 people had stopped complaining. Who cared about the little guys below that? They didn't.

When Pat turned back, Kris's back was a bright red mass of fresh blood and skin. What the hell had the old man done? With her spare hand, she jerked the Yannis-Burke regenerator from his hands shoved him farther from the table.

"What the fuck are you doing?" she screamed.

With surprising fury, the old man came back to the table and shoved Pat back, forcing her to sit on the desk.

"I am helping old friend. I do not know you, so I will not be helping you, and you will need it if you touch me again."

Pat looked down at Kris's back again. "She wanted to keep that scar, as a reminder."

The old man seemed surprised. "A reminder of what? The pain it caused? The loss she went through when she got it?"

"I have no idea why. I just know she wanted to keep it."

"Well. Maybe you should tell me sooner, eh? Maybe then old Kai does not do something she doesn't want."

"How was I—"

Kai turned his back on her and looked at the machine attached to Kris's head. "She is doing better now. We keep machine on until morning." He glanced back at Pat. "Keep syntho held high."

"I can't keep this up all night."

Kai left the room, coming back almost right away with a coatrack. "No need to. Hook it up here."

"You had that the whole time?"

Kai just shrugged, and Pat thought she saw a humorous gleam in his eye.

"I did not know you. Had to keep your hands busy."

Pat almost laughed. "And you trust me now?"

He placed some moist bandages over Kris's back, and without turning to face Pat he said, "Anyone that cares about Kris as much as you just did, I do. Help me clean up." He picked up the bloodied towels. "You take water. Pots too heavy for an old man like me."

With that he left the room, making sure the towels didn't touch the curtain hanging over the doorway. Pat picked up a pot and followed him.

"You look tired," he said. "After you get next pot, there is cot where you got syntho. Lie down. Sleep. I keep eye on Kris and look at her feet."

Pat decided she would stay up with Kris as well, but by the time she had poured the second pot of bloody water down the drain and given the sink a quick wipe, she felt as tired as the old man said she looked.

She walked back down the hall, sticking her head into the curtained office. Kai was sitting by the table, one of Kris's hands in his, singing softly under his breath. There wasn't anything she could do by staying awake.

She let the curtain fall back into place and found the cot, falling asleep almost instantly.

UNKNOWN

Miller hung from his wrist straps against the parrilla. He felt as though he'd been beaten with a shovel for days. Twice during the session he had woken up to the sound of a defibrillator charging and Jeremy's smiling face looking at him.

Each time was the same. Jeremy would put the unit away saying, "We almost lost you that time. Can't have that happening this soon."

He'd offer Miller some juice, and once Miller had gotten a couple of sips it would be yanked away and spilled on the already wet carpet with a sad "Oops."

Miller had recognized the man by the door. It was hard not to. William Clark had become his boss when Nigel had been killed. It was obvious that William wasn't comfortable being here. Every time Jeremy's back faced him, William lowered his eyes, not wanting to look at Miller. William had always been queasy, even asking Miller to make his reports somewhat less detailed. What he couldn't figure out was what the hell the guy was doing here.

It was obvious what Jeremy wanted. Most of this was just fun for him.

But William being in the same room was a shock, and Miller couldn't figure out what the connection was. How long had they been working together? Or was William just an unwilling pawn in one of Jeremy's games?

Jeremy had left him shackled to the mesh again. He had turned off the machine, and relief flooded over Miller like a dousing of cold water. Then Jeremy turned it back on and given Miller one more jolt. He didn't remember Jeremy leaving.

When Miller opened his eyes again, the room was dark, with just the strip of light coming from under the door. He wasn't going to survive another session. Not at this rate. His heart would stop again, and Jeremy wouldn't be able to bring him back. It would be the end. The teasing sips of fruit juice Jeremy offered did little to sustain Miller. He needed more, and the only two items in the room were an unopened bottle of juice on the table beside him and what had been poured onto the floor.

Miller could almost smell the sugars in the juice from where he was. His body's need for it overrode the stench coming from the pool at his feet. He'd even suck that out of the carpet if he thought it would help sustain him through Jeremy's next visit.

He looked up over his shoulder to where the mesh frame leaned against the wall. The corner had worn through the drywall and started gouging into the fibercrete behind it. He didn't remember much from when the electricity had been applied to his body, but his imagination helped him figure out what had happened. As his body spasmed, the frame had shifted back and forth.

The movement of the frame gave him an idea.

If he could get enough momentum and throw his body forward

with enough force, he might be able to topple the mesh rack. The landing would hurt. A lot. But it was better than waiting here for Jeremy to come back. Once Miller's weight was off the straps holding his hands, he might have a chance to get them free.

Miller pressed his back into the mesh as far as he could, and then jerked forward. He didn't feel any change, but he thought he heard the frame fall back against the wall. He did it a couple of more times before looking back up.

The corner of the frame had definitely moved. He had no idea how far away from the wall he was getting, and he knew he didn't have the strength to try too many more times. He could feel the fresh blood seep down his arms from the reopened cuts where the tethers held him in.

After resting a few minutes, he tried again. Something shifted this time, he felt it. He held his breath and threw his body forward once more. His shoulder popped, and he held back a scream of pain. The mesh rack teetered, not falling back against the wall. He leaned forward, and the rack came to rest on its edge, balancing on the narrow metal frame. Miller didn't dare move.

Time slowed to a crawl. He held his back arched and his head pressed forward for as long as he could. The pain in his shoulder dulled to a persistent throb, until he accidentally moved. He could feel the searing pain all the way down to his feet.

Eventually he knew he couldn't hold his position any longer. He slowly let his body relax, feeling the frame shifting under him. It stayed balanced on its edge, and he hung from one arm, trying to take his weight off the other. There was more pain to come.

When his arm couldn't take the stress anymore, he shifted his weight to his feet and braced himself. He threw his body forward again and the rack toppled, gaining speed as it went. Miller quickly turned his head to the side. A broken nose wasn't going help his situation any.

The frame stopped abruptly, throwing Miller down. His shoulder tore and his face, the back of his head pressed tightly to the mesh, stopped just above the carpeted floor. The pain went away as he faded into blackness.

Time stood still. Miller opened his eyes to pure black. He could almost taste the juice mixed with water just below his face. Something had stopped the frame from hitting the floor. He had no idea what it was, but it had saved him. He craned his neck forward until his shoulder couldn't take the pain anymore. A different blackness pushed into his brain. Miller fought against it, straining harder. His shoulder dropped, but he still couldn't reach the floor.

This wasn't working. Miller relaxed, and his hips settled onto the carpet. He couldn't be more than 15 centimeters off the ground. He moved his weight onto his good shoulder and wiggled. The frame moved. He wiggled some more, and without warning, crashed into the floor. He lay there, praying for the stabbing pain in his shoulder to go away. When it didn't, he turned his head and began sucking the liquid out of the carpet.

He didn't get much, but he could feel the sugars, even diluted, course through his blood. He felt more alert than he had since the transport crash. Even the pain from his shoulder almost faded into the background. When his patch of carpet dried up, he jerked his body to the side and found a new patch. He was still tied up, but so far, this was a big improvement.

He laughed quietly to himself. He'd never thought being tied down and lying in his own excrement would be an improvement.

LOS ANGELES, LEVEL 2—MONDAY, JUNE 12, 2141 11:57 A.M.

I opened my eyes to the sound of harsh humming right beside my ear. Blinking as the room slowly came into focus, I saw an office-style drop ceiling. The supporting bars had shifted over time, and it looked like some of the stained tiles were being held in place by sheer willpower.

Smell came back next, and I breathed deeply. Hot grease and ginger sauce. I closed my eyes again and smiled. I must be dreaming. Nothing brought back memories of Chinatown like the ginger chicken at Kai's restaurant. The scrape of a chair across the floor brought me back to full wakefulness, and with it the sensation of burning mixed with itching across my back.

I tried to turn my head, but couldn't. Something was stuck to the side of it. I reached up and my hand got caught in plastic tubing full of almost clear liquid. I wrapped my fingers around it and gave it a gentle tug.

"No. You need to leave that in. You do not need syntho anymore, but you still need sustenance. A bit of painkiller does not hurt either."

I tried to turn my head again and stopped short. This time a dull clunking noise came at the same time. I let go of the tubing to reach for my head.

"That too is a no. Let the machine do its job. It will be done soon enough."

I flicked my eyes toward the source of the voice. It was so familiar. So relaxing. When the name of its owner popped into my head, I gasped. "Kai?"

"And who else would nurse you back to health, eh?"

"Kai! Where am I? Why can't I move my head? What's—" A wave of nausea swept through me, and what used to be the comforting smells of the restaurant turned sour. Kai whisked a small bowl into my hands.

"One question at a time. Old Kai cannot follow more than that. I will start with the first. You are in the restaurant. In my office. Safe."

"How?"

"Ahh, now you change the question on old Kai, to confuse him. Let me answer both of them then. You cannot move your head because I have attached a ventriculostomy machine to it. It relieves pressure and tries to fix any damage."

With those words, memories flooded my brain. I . . . we had been attacked on the up-ramp, trying to get out of Level 1. The girl had been big. Strong. I remember I had been losing before I got the girl close to the ramp wall. After that, nothing. Until I woke up here. By the sound of it, I must have banged up my head pretty good. I opened my mouth to talk again.

"As for the how," Kai said, "your friend Pat brought you in. You had quite the night, though I doubt you will remember too much of it. Not right away." He paused as though carefully measuring his next words. "I did not know you liked hyper metal music."

More memories came back. Fragmented and incomplete. I remembered the pounding beat of drums. An image of a beast came through, and I shied away from it.

"How long have I been here?" I asked.

"Almost ten hours now. You are recovering well. The medication in the IV and the ventriculostomy machine are working well together. You should be able to sit up shortly."

As if on cue, something beside me beeped, and Kai moved into my field of vision. When he saw me looking at him, a smile creased his wrinkled cheeks. "It is good to see you awake. I was not sure you would make it for a while."

"It's good to see you as well. I missed you." Just saying the words made me realize how true they were. Seeing Kai again felt like coming home. I covered up my emotions with a quick "I missed your ginger chicken." My stomach churned again.

"Well, we will see what we can do about that, but not now. Let me get this thing off you, and you can sit up and sip some water."

My head jerked, and with it came a sense of freedom. It no longer felt like a weight was attached to me. Almost immediately I felt a slight pressure pushing my head to the side.

"There is leakage, but that is normal. You lie here for a while, and hold this tight." Kai grabbed my hand and moved it to a cloth on the side of my head. "I go wake up your friend Pat. She will be happy to see you."

Kai left me holding the cloth. I followed him with my eyes until he disappeared behind a curtain. From another room I heard quiet whispering followed by the sound of feet pounding on the floor. The curtain was swept aside and Pat ran through. She barely had time to stop before she reached me.

Her hands grabbed my shoulders and she looked steadily into my eyes, worry written all over her face. She must have been happy with what she saw. She let go.

"How do you feel?" she asked.

"Good. Sore. I have a headache, and my back feels like a thousand ants are crawling through my skin." Another wave of nausea hit me, and I swallowed hard. I didn't want to talk about that.

"We will talk about your back later." Kai's voice came from the doorway. "The headache is normal. It should go away in the next few days. Most people can get back to their normal lives only a few hours after machine does its work."

"Normal life?" I laughed and the pounding in my head increased. "I haven't had a normal life in a year. I think I've forgotten what that is."

Pat joined in the laughter. "I think you'll be just fine."

With that, Kai shouldered in and moved my hand from the towel. He gently pulled it away and examined my head. The towel didn't come back. I knew something was wrong, though. The look in Pat's eyes spoke volumes.

"What's wrong?" Panic entered my voice.

Kai reached over and patted my cheek. "Nothing is wrong. I think she is surprised by the bald spot. The machine shaved off a patch so it could get to work."

Pat's gaze flicked between my eyes and the wound on my head.

"That's not it, Kai. Pat? Tell me."

"It . . . it looks really bad, that's all."

Kai threw Pat a nasty look.

"Is that normal?" I asked.

Kai nodded his head. "It is. In a few hours, it will be almost healed, and you will have hair growing back. By tomorrow, you need a haircut."

With Kai's words, the panic I was feeling subsided. I could see Pat nodding as well, as though the magic was happening right before her eyes.

"Now, what about my back?"

Kai turned, pretending to clean up the desk next to me.

Pat answered for him. "You got into a bit of trouble while I went looking for a car. I guess you got in another fight or something. Your hands and knees were all bloody, and you had a massive bruise on your upper back. Kai . . . we were worried you might have had some spinal damage, so Kai went in and cleaned it up. He . . . I mean you're okay, but he . . . well, he got rid of your scar."

A second wave of relief flooded through me. "Is that all? Thank god. The way you were going on, I thought maybe he had to regrow my spine."

Kai turned back to face me. "You have enough spine for both of us, I think. I am sorry, if I knew you wanted to keep it . . ."

"No. It's been bothering me for months. I've been thinking of getting rid of it, I just didn't know how. I guess my records will have to be changed again. ACE can take care of that."

The look on Kai's face transformed to one of sadness. Without a word, he spun around and left the room, the curtain falling in behind him.

I stared at the swaying curtain. Did I say something wrong?

"Who is this guy?" asked Pat.

"A friend. Could you see what's wrong?"

Pat looked like she wanted to talk more, but instead she pulled the blanket higher up my chest and tucked it in. "You wait here until the doctor says you can get up. I'll go talk to him for you."

After she left, I tried to piece my memories back together. This morning—*yesterday* morning—I'd been rock climbing when the compound came under attack. We'd all escaped on a transport. Ian had been there.

I almost sat up, but the pounding headache and my churning stomach stopped me. Ian! I remembered the sound of the gunshots as the men killed anyone who had survived. I remembered watching from behind a pillar as they jabbed something into Ian's neck and dragged him into the gunship.

I remembered almost everything until the attack on the ramp; the stay in the abandoned house, the run through the darkness. After that, it was all fragmented. I looked around the room, a cold hand reaching its fingers into my chest. Where was I? What had happened? Those memories flooded back as quickly as they had left me. Was this normal?

Outside the curtain I heard voices raised in an argument. Pat's voice rose to the top.

"You'll do nothing of the sort. If I don't believe you, neither will she."

They both charged into the room, the looks on their faces changing from anger to chagrin when they saw me staring. Kai reached up to a coat rack beside me and turned a wheel on one of the hoses still pumping fluids into my arm.

Warmth rushed through my veins, and I closed my eyes. There was something I wanted to ask him, but I couldn't remember what it was.

LOS ANGELES, LEVEL 2—MONDAY, JUNE 12, 2141 12:05 P.M.

Kai turned to Pat. "You need to keep your voice down. Whether we agree or not, Kris is not ready yet. Give her another hour or two, and maybe—*maybe*—she will be able to listen. Chances are she is still experiencing short-term memory loss with flashes of remembering."

"Me? You're the one that brought it up."

"I did not. When Kris brought up ACE, I left room. You followed me out and questioned me like I was criminal."

At those words, Pat went quiet before she responded. "You're right. I'm sorry." She turned to Kris. "Will she . . . will she have any permanent damage?"

Kai moved to the ventriculostomy machine and stared at the screen, scrolling backward and forward through the text. "All the readings look good. She will probably have a full recovery, except for maybe the memories between the injury and when we attached her to this." He waved at the machine. "Even that may come back, but it will probably always be spotty."

"You sound like you've had experience with this."

Kai leaned in closer to Pat and parted his hair just above his temple. A small patch of skin, no more than five millimeters across, remained a puckered scar. "Some mornings I wake up, and every-thing that happened is there. Then it fades like bad dream. I have spent years writing down my memory fragments. I got enough a long while back to know what happened. Any new memories that come back just reinforce what I know."

"And what's that?"

"I believe ACE is wrong. Evil. They are not what they say, or who they portray themselves to be. Their goal is not to get control back from the corporations. It is not to bring back a natural equilibrium to the planet."

Pat moved farther away, stealing a glance at Kris asleep on the table. "Then what the hell is it? And how come you're the only one who thinks so?"

"Ah." Kai sat down in his office chair. "I am not the only one who thinks so. There are many, and they are getting stronger every day. Back when I lost my memories, I thought there were only three of us who felt something was wrong. Together we quietly gathered infor-mation, combined reports from different agencies, until the whole image came together."

Kai slouched deeper into his chair. "That was when we were caught. By ACE. The three of us met one last time, hoping we would find something to prove we were wrong. We scoured our notes, re-read transcripts and data feeds. We found nothing. I guess we knew we would not. On the way home, we were attacked. They shot Kris's mother right away. She dropped right in front of us. I ran as fast as I could. I was not a front line guy, not like you were . . . like Kris was planning to be. Her dad stayed behind. From what I have read since then, they were not very kind to him.

"A couple of them chased me. I had already turned my tracker off, but it did not seem to matter. If I hid, they walked right up to me. If I ran, they were always right behind me. They shot me just before I reach the Level 2 up-ramp. I still do not know where they were. I remember feeling my face pinch, and a seeing huge wave of light. The next thing I knew, I was in a bed, that thing attached to my head, surrounded by strangers.

"I still have headaches. Sometimes I think I can feel the bullet moving around, mushing up more of my brain. One of these days, it will finish the job. Until that day comes, I will spend every bit of energy I have on reducing ACE's control. I will keep hunting for information, until I have enough to prove what I know."

"And what's that?" Pat asked in a soft voice.

Kai sighed and stood, staring down at Kris. "That ACE is just a cover for what was once Meridian. That its only purpose is to weaken the other corporations, so Meridian could rise to the top."

"And that's a bad thing? Weakening the other corporations?"

"No. And Kris's mother and father agreed with old Kai on that. We would continue to do our jobs. Keep ACE's secret. Despite what we thought their end goal was, ACE was doing more to help this planet than anyone else. All of ACE can't be bad . . . we were not. Maybe it is just a few idiots at the top?"

"So what changed your mind?"

Kai looked up from Kris and stared at Pat, his eyes flashing in anger. "When they decided that killing us was the answer. When they shot my best friend's wife in the streets. When they beat my friend so bad there was not much left to identify." In a softer voice, he continued. "When I ran away and left them to die. When I survive instead of them."

Kai went back to looking at Kris's sleeping face. "You are so young. Too young to be pulled into the middle of this. But it is too late, is it not? You were part of it the day you were born. My only wish now is that you come out of it better than they did. I could not bear to lose you, too."

Pat pulled aside the curtain to the hallway before speaking over her shoulder. "I don't believe you, old man. ACE has done more for me than my own family did. I owe them everything."

"You owe them your post-traumatic stress?"

Pat looked surprised. "How did you know?"

"When you sleep, you talk. I heard it from here. Your demons live within you."

Pat's face flushed and she gripped the curtain in a fist. "I've slept alone in my kitchen for so long, I'd forgotten I did that."

"Old Kai will not tell anyone. Just as we would not have told anyone about ACE and Meridian. You have my word on that."

"Thanks." She took a step and paused. "I still don't believe you about ACE."

"You do not have to. And neither does she. But she has to know. I will tell her when she wakes up."

"It's your choice, but I know she feels the same way I do. ACE saved her from Meridian last summer. They took her in and trained her."

"They turned her into a killer."

"They brought her into a family she never had. If you tell her, she may never talk to you again."

Kai's shoulders slumped. "That is risk I have to take. I cannot go on lying to her anymore, pretending I barely knew her parents. She, of all people, deserves to know the truth."

"The choice is yours to make, old man. You're the only one that can weigh the risks with the benefits."

Pat pushed through the curtain. Kai heard the back door of the restaurant open and close. He went into the hallway and locked the door behind her.

LOS ANGELES, LEVEL 2—MONDAY, JUNE 12, 2141 12:45 P.M.

I woke up groggy, but this time my memories came back in a flood. I turned my head experimentally, testing to see if the machine was hooked up again. It wasn't. The feeling in my back had turned into a slight itch. I wasn't sure what Kai had done to get rid of the scar, but I figured it was better if I didn't scratch it just yet.

I slowly raised myself into a sitting position and swung my legs off the side of the . . . table? I realized I wasn't even in a bed. That might explain why just about every part of me hurt. Then again, the fight and the crash couldn't have helped, not if I'd ended up here, like this. I still didn't remember anything between the fight and when I'd woken up the first time. I didn't even know when that had been. How long had I been out this time? It had been long enough for my stomach to settle.

When I leaned forward, my shirt fell off my back, billowing around me. It had been cut almost to the collar. I straightened and slid off the table. Kai had left a jacket over his office chair, and I put it on. It fit almost perfectly. It was then I realized my feet had been cleaned. I lifted one to look at the sole and saw soft, pink skin. All the calluses I'd earned climbing, running the foothills, and training were gone.

A curtain hung over the doorway. I pulled it aside and slipped past it, walking toward the sounds of cooking coming from the front of the restaurant. The smell of the hot oil made my stomach flip. The second I entered the kitchen Kai turned to me.

"Stay in the back area. We do not want anyone to see you through the windows."

I took a step back into the shadowed hallway and stopped, looking out at the Chinatown streets. It hit me then that I had come back home.

"Go. I bring you something to eat."

I turned and headed back. Another doorway stood opposite the curtain, and I walked through it. The first thing I noticed was a large object against the far wall. I pulled the blanket off of it. Underneath was my bike. It was cleaner than when I had brought it here, almost shining under the dim light in the room. On the seat lay my jacket. The scuffs had been patched, and it almost looked better than the day I had bought it. I flipped it over. The combination stun gun/taser was nestled into the small of the jacket's back, stuck to the velcro. The jacket itself had been rewired, getting a charge from the wall instead of from the air. The chargers had broken last year, and the wiring must have been Kai's way of keeping the jacking working. Both the jacket and taser were fully charged, ready if I needed them.

Hung over one of the bike's mirrors was the helmet. Flat black and still brand new. I lifted it up and held it in my hands, remembering the day Ian had given it to me. The day we had our first kiss. He'd been shy back then. So hesitant. My vision blurred, and I blinked the tears away.

Now he was gone. I had no idea who had stolen him from me, I had no idea where was he was. All I knew was that he was still alive, and I was going to get him back. Nothing was going to stop me from doing it.

First I had to get in touch with ACE. That was going to be difficult. I'd never been in the field, and they hadn't taught us how to reach them if we somehow became separated. Why would a recruit in a remote site need that? I was hoping Pat had some way to contact them. Being in the field was what she used to do. It wasn't the reason I had pulled her from the crash site, but it was a good bit of luck that I'd found her.

I heard footsteps coming from the kitchen and quickly put the helmet back on the mirror before wiping my eyes. No one had to know I'd been crying. Not even Kai. He walked in carrying a steaming plate of food.

"Old Kai knew he would find you in here," he said. "But there is no place to sit and eat. Come, you go back in the office and sit. I brought your favorite, ginger chicken. Other customer order it, but he can wait for my Kris."

I followed him back to the other room. He cleared a spot from the desk and put the food down before pulling the chair closer.

"You sit and eat. Get strong again, eh?"

Impulsively, I reached out and pulled him into a hug. His arms were stronger than they looked, and he returned the hug with a ferocity I didn't expect. When I pulled away, he turned and walked out, but not before I saw the tears in his eyes. Damn old man.

Kai and I had been friends a long time, but I had never done anything like that before. And I had never seen him anything other than cheery and happy.

The smell of the chicken drew me back to the desk. I sat in the chair and pulled the jacket tighter before picking up the plastic knife and fork. I dug in. The chicken tasted off, as though the meat had gone bad. I gagged and spit it out. The plain white rice was perfect, and I ate it as though I hadn't eaten in weeks.

There was a loud bang at the back door, and I stopped eating. Kai mumbled something under his breath and unlocked the door. A draft made the curtain move and the breeze slid under my jacket and up my bare back. I was going to have to do something about the shirt. I heard the door close, and Pat walked into the room. I stood up to say hi, and she swooped in, grabbing me into her arms and hugging me. It was, apparently, a hugging type of day.

Pat let me go as Kai walked in with another plate of food. He put it down on the desk and pulled a comm unit out of his pocket, handing it silently to Pat. She took it, grunting thanks when she found the

ACE app to manipulate her tracker ID. Kai picked up the dirty dishes without saying anything about the uneaten ginger chicken and left again. She watched him the entire time. I could sense there was something going on between them, and I didn't think it was good. Pat sat down and shoveled some rice in her mouth before she spoke.

"Has Kai had a chance to talk to you yet?" she asked.

"No, why?"

"Nothing, just wondering." She obviously changed the subject. "You were in pretty bad shape last night. I didn't know if you were going to make it."

"Why did you bring me here?"

"You were lucid enough in the car to tell me to. I almost went to a hospital once I figured out how serious it was, but if I had, I knew you'd be as dead as the others on the transport."

"All except Ian."

"Right, and Janice." Pat paused. "Why did you say to come here?"

"I don't even remember telling you to."

"Yeah, well. It worked. Did you see the room across the hall?"

"Yup!" I grinned from ear to ear. "My bike's there, and the rest of my gear. I'm back home."

"Your bike? I didn't notice it," Pat said. "I'm talking about the shelves. They're not filled with restaurant supplies. This guy's got enough stuff back there to supply a small hospital."

"I didn't see that."

"Then how did you know to come here?"

"I don't know. Kai's always helped me when I needed it, I guess."

"When he started pulling out all the equipment, I thought you had led me to an ACE medical facility." She looked down at her plate of food, concern written all over her face. "That's not what this is though."

"What is it then?" What had Kai gotten himself into?

"I don't know yet, and I don't want to know. He's earned my trust enough that I'll never tell anyone what's here." Pat shoveled more food into her mouth. "Once you're ready to go, we'll leave and look for Miller. I tried contacting ACE already, but I didn't get through. The number I have is pretty old. We'll find some other way, and get some help in figuring out where he is."

Behind us, Kai spoke up. "You know I do not think that is a good idea."

I jumped. I hadn't heard him come into the room.

"Not now, Kai," Pat warned.

"It has never been the right time, and so I do it now."

I moved so I could see both of them at the same time. "Not now what? What is it you want to tell me?"

Pat stood up, an edge to her voice. "Not now, Kai."

"Sit down, Pat," I said. It came out almost like an order, and with a surprised look she dropped back into the chair. "I'm not just a street kid anymore. I'm not a simple courier relying on luck to get through things." I turned to Kai. "For the last year, I've been in training. I'd better be able to deal with shit, but I can't if I don't know what it is."

Kai wrung his hands, looking even more like an old man from the old country. He glanced at Pat and then stared back at the ground. "I know where you have been, and what you think you are now. But I—"

"You know? Did Pat tell you?"

"She did not need to." Kai moved closer and reached for my hands. "There are things I need to tell you. Things you need to know. Please, can we talk alone?"

I gently pulled my hands away. "Whatever you need to say to me, Pat can hear as well. I trust her with my life." I already had.

Kai sighed and looked around the room before he started talking, as though he needed to find something to ground himself. He started with his ideas about ACE. I didn't believe any of it. There was no way Ian could have been suckered into working for them if they were that corrupt. It was when he told me why he thought it that I started feeling lost; when he said how he knew my parents, that he'd worked with them.

At first I felt empty, then the anger and confusion set in. All these years, all the time we'd known each other, and he'd never told me about my mom and dad. The anger turned to betrayal and pain. The Kai I had trusted, had believed in, had been lying to me.

Kai stepped toward me again. I brushed past him and ran for my bike.

By the time I'd switched jackets and maneuvered the bike into the hallway, Pat was already holding the back door open. Kai stood by the curtain.

"Kris," he said. "Kris, I—"

"Leave me alone!" I pushed the bike out the door and Pat slammed it shut behind me. I needed time. Pat jumped on the back of the bike before I took off.

CHAPTER 8

ONE HABIT WILLIAM had taken from Nigel was pacing when he had big problems to think or worry about. He stood from behind his desk and began the circuit of his office: first the corner desk, then to the viewscreen, the door, the credenza, and back to the desk. Repeat as often as necessary.

Today he was pacing because of Jeremy. Last night had made him sick to his stomach. It wasn't the torture. Not really. He had read enough field reports to know it could get a whole lot worse than that. But what the reports didn't show was how much the person doing the torturing enjoyed it. How, when the person being tortured was revived or held out a little bit longer than the last time, they thrilled at it. Jeremy had grinned and laughed.

The reports didn't talk about how the human body reacted.

It didn't help that the person being tortured was Miller. William stopped in his tracks, hit by the sudden realization that the last time he had seen Miller, they had been right in this office. Miller on the couch by the credenza, him sitting behind his desk. Miller had asked for a few days off. He'd wanted to fly north to surprise his girlfriend, the courier. It was William's permission that had gotten Miller into this mess.

William resumed his pacing. Whatever the reason, he had stayed with Jeremy and Miller far too long last night, but he didn't stay until the bitter end. By the time he'd left, Miller had raw electrical burns up and down his body. He left after the first time Miller had died and been brought back. How his heart was able to take being revived time and time again was a mystery. William wasn't sure his own weak ticker would have made it.

And still, Miller had never begged Jeremy to stop. He had screamed and cursed and shouted, but had never once begged.

William was disgusted by what he had seen. It was a part of Jeremy he never knew existed, and he didn't like it.

It was too late for Miller now. If he survived, he would be a changed man. How could you go through that torture and not be changed? The sad truth was Miller wouldn't survive. He couldn't. Just seeing William in the same room as Jeremy meant he knew enough that he had to be killed. William didn't think he'd have to worry about that; Jeremy would take care of it.

He could bring in Kris, that might at least stop Miller's pain. They had worked too closely together for William to want the torture to continue. He owed at least that much to the man, after all he had done for ACE. But he couldn't just hand Kris over either, knowing she would be tortured the same way.

It would help to find out if she knew about the tie between Jeremy and ACE. William didn't think so. There hadn't been even a whisper of it since that incident four or five years ago, and that was only with Meridian, not Jeremy specifically. Jeremy had taken care of that leak. Two bodies found, killed by a gang, and a suicide of an old Chinese guy. It barely even made the vids. Besides, Kris saw Jeremy get shot, and William had done everything he could to build the story of Jeremy's death.

When Kris had been pulled into the mess last year and Nigel had recruited the girl, it created a sense of symmetry for William, a sense of trying to make things right. He'd followed through on Nigel's plans for her.

That was before William knew Jeremy was involved. By the time he found out, plans were already in motion. ACE had captured the mole without knowing who he was feeding information to. Once William discovered that, it changed everything.

After Kris had explained to him who had Miller, William had to do something. ACE had a cover to protect, and Miller was a valuable asset. He'd instructed the team to capture Jeremy, not kill him. When William had heard the shot fired over the radio, he had panicked for the few seconds it took the team leader to report back. Kris and Miller were safe. Jeremy was out cold, a dart with an almost instantaneous paralytic buried in his shoulder.

At that point, Miller and Kris had no reason to put Jeremy and ACE together. Neither did the extraction team. As far as they knew, Jeremy was delivered and moved to a safe location for interrogation. In reality, William had waited until the paralytic had worn off, and they'd both moved on from there. That was one nice thing about compartmentalization. Without it, William was sure he wouldn't have gotten away with it.

He almost wished Jeremy had been killed that night. It would have changed what was happening today.

Now, he had to find Kris and then figure out what to do with her. He would probably have to have her killed. She was too involved in this mess, and ACE was too important to leave loose threads. He wished there could be a better way, but he just couldn't see it. Even if he could find a way without getting rid of her, what would happen if Jeremy found her? At least this way he could guarantee there would be no pain.

Inspiration hit, and he went to his desk. He'd received a report this morning on the compound's attack and the subsequent crash of the transport. One of the passengers, a trainee at the camp, had managed to escape. When she finally found a way to report back in, she didn't make it sound good for Kris.

He could work with that. It was a place to start anyway. Janice's hatred toward Kris would be the motivator he needed, and when the job was done, Janice would be eliminated as well. They'd both volunteered to give their lives for ACE, and what was more important than keeping the company alive?

It would be a simple task to convince Janice that Kris was actually a mole from SoCal, sent in to find out how ACE trained its operatives, and then destroy the training compound. William sat down and pulled up Janice's profile on the viewscreen. The more he read on her, the more he was sure this would work.

He placed an order to have Janice brought to his office. Now he needed a team to find Kris.

The comm unit on his desk beeped and he picked it up. "Yes?"

"Sir, I have a contact on an expired safe line."

"Yes?"

"Sir, it's a retired operative, Pat Nelson, and a trainee by the name of Kris Merrill. They—"

William couldn't believe his luck. He knew Kris and Janice had gotten away alive, but to have the cook with Kris made things easier. And harder.

"Excellent. Arrange a meet at the old Pasadena greenhouses on

Level 5. The ones that burned down last year. Tell them we'll arrange a pickup in a couple of hours."

"Yes, sir."

"And I sent out an order to bring in the other survivor from the transport accident. Please get that expedited. I want her in my office within the half hour."

"Yes, sir."

William smiled. He loved it when everything kind of clicked and it all worked out. The end result of this whole exercise would be the loss of four people: Miller, Kris, the cook, and Janice. There wasn't much he could do for Miller, but he would make Kris's death as quick as possible. Janice would take care of the cook and Kris, and he would get rid of Janice.

With Jeremy's obsessions out of the way, there was a chance he could save ACE and all the good it had done. Then he would have to figure out what to do with Jeremy.

———

LOS ANGELES, LEVEL 2—MONDAY, JUNE 12, 2141 1:07 P.M.

Kai bustled around his kitchen, cleaning up after the lunch rush—if you could call it that. He normally just did a cursory wipe here and there, waiting until after dinner before he did a thorough job. But he had found, over the years of owning the restaurant, that cleaning it was therapeutic. Today he needed it. He couldn't get Kris's reaction when he told her the truth, or most of it anyway, out of his mind. He knew she would take it hard, but he hadn't expected her to leave. And he hadn't even told her about running away when they were attacked. Not yet.

As he started pulling the air cleaners from the vents above the woks, he knew he was in trouble. This was his inner self telling him he had really screwed up. Whoever said the truth shall set you free never had to deal with the real fallout. Kai was sure of that.

After the kitchen was spotless, Kai moved into the back room. It was still a mess from Kris's surgery. He picked up the last of the blood-soaked towels and dumped them in the sink. Even though the blood had dried, it would come out. He'd used the towels enough to know that.

When the comm unit rang, breaking the silence that enveloped the restaurant, Kai jumped. He reached into his pocket, his heart racing, and picked it up.

"Kris?" he asked.

"I don't know who Kris is, but we're bringing someone in."

Kai sighed. He didn't want to deal with any of Jack's problems right now. "Can you find someone else?"

"Too late for that. We were lucky to find this one, and there was no way we were going to use a local doc. We're almost there."

Kai sighed again before the choice of words sunk in. "We? Are you coming in as well?"

"Yeah, we need to talk. Figure out where to go from here."

"We have already talked about it. Get whoever made it through the hole in the wall into those pipes and up to Level 6 or 7."

"We'll talk later. After you fix this poor bugger up."

"But I—"

A knock sounded on the back door, five sharp quick raps and two bangs with a foot. Kai hung up and ran to the back, opening the door. Two men carried in the body of a boy, no older than twelve.

"Same place?" asked Jack.

Kai nodded. He couldn't stop looking at the boy's face. "You sent in someone this young?"

"I told you we weren't prepared. We needed smaller people. Those pipes get pretty damn tight."

Kai pushed Jack out of the way and walked to the boy. Bullets had torn through his shirt, and blood seeped from the wounds. If anything major was hit, he wouldn't make it.

He cut the shirt away, yelling for syntho and equipment. Jack and the other man scrambled for the storage room. Before the curtain had settled in the doorway, the boy stopped breathing. Kai climbed on the table, giving CPR. By the time the men came back, he was almost ready to give up. Each chest compression squeezed more blood from the bullet holes. He tried for a few more minutes before getting off the table and leaving the room. When he walked back to his office, his hands washed and scrubbed, the only thing left to indicate a body had been in the room was a pool of blood on the table. Jack was alone.

Jack fell into the chair, his head resting in his hands.

"I didn't want to send him, you know. I didn't want to send any of them. Everyone else was gone. Fredericks is in San Francisco and Carver is in San Diego. I had to send what I had, didn't I? I couldn't lose the opportunity handed to me. Could I?"

Kai grabbed one of the remaining clean towels and wiped the blood from the table, smearing it over the smooth surface. He'd have to do a real clean with disinfectant. But not now. "What do you want me to say? You send kids to blow up water distribution plants, and kids come back hurt or dead. You made your choice."

Kai got no response.

"How many you send in?" Kai asked.

"Seventeen. Eleven from the original team, and six kids. They were just fucking kids. They should be playing games, or teasing their brothers and sisters. They shouldn't have to do this kind of work."

"They did not until you sent them."

"*I* sent them? I might have given the final order, but SoCal sent them in. Kadokawa sent them in. Fucking IBC sent them in." Jack had lurched to his feet and was yelling at the top of his lungs.

"That is not the way it works," Kai said, ignoring the anger directed at him. "You need to take responsibility. That is what a leader does."

"I won't, not for this one. Not for any of them."

Kai heard the hitch in his voice. "How many?"

Jack fell back into his chair, a defeated expression on his face, but his voice was defiant. He waved at the empty table. "With this one, we lost fourteen."

The numbers floored Kai, and he leaned against the table, balling the towel into a tight bundle. "The kids?" he asked.

"From what we can see, two made it with Albert."

"From what you can see?"

"Albert and the two kids are the only ones who reported in. The rest we can't find."

Kai forced the dead from his mind with difficulty. There wasn't anything he could do for them now. "When does Albert start?"

"They're already in. Repair crews have started fixing the wall and the pipe. A lot of Levels 1 and 2 in Santa Barbara are on water shortage rations. It's going to be tough for them."

"Yes it will. How long until they get above Level 5?"

"We don't know. Once they got in the pipes we lost communication."

"And when they get there? What are kids going to do?"

"Albert's made it. He'll take over until we can set up better communications. The kids will be all right. Maybe even have less of a chance of being caught."

Kai mulled it over. Children had no place in war. "You should not have used kids."

"You think I had a choice?"

"There is always a choice," Kai said. "How will we know when they get there?"

"Simple. They blow the water distribution station, since they're inside it already. Let those bastards have a taste of their own medicine."

"SoCal will know how they got there after that."

"Albert knows. They'll be careful."

As Kai cleaned the last of the office space, he thought, *They had better be.*

UNKNOWN

Miller shifted his weight. His best guess was that he had been lying here for four or five hours. He had fought off sleep, for the most part. When he had dozed off, it was as though his brain gave him a swift kick, and he jerked awake.

He spent that time twisting and turning his legs any way he could. With the weight of his body off the ties, he could almost get them free. It wouldn't be much, but it would be a start.

The stench of the room had become simple background noise, no longer bothering him or making him gag. He'd almost thrown up everything he'd worked so hard to suck out of the carpet.

Jeremy kept talking about Kris, what he would do to her when he had her. Miller was a sideshow, the warm-up for when Jeremy finally got his claws into her.

Until this last session, he'd still held out hope that Kris and ACE would figure out where he was and come and get him. That hope, the last thread to life Miller held on to, had disappeared when William walked in. William had watched, never saying anything. Never doing anything. The question Miller couldn't answer was whether just William and Jeremy were working together, or if the bastards had compromised all of ACE. Maybe it didn't matter. William was the leader of Black Ops. He contributed the information the rest of ACE saw.

With that thought, Miller's left leg finally popped free of the restraint holding it to the mesh frame. Miller gave himself a moment to relax, letting his leg lie flat, enjoying the pain of blood flowing back into his foot. The pain meant the damn thing was still viable. That he wouldn't end up a cripple for the rest of his life. That was one of his worst nightmares.

Miller woke with another start. He was falling asleep more often. How long had he been out this time? He moved his foot to the tether on the other leg and starting humming a song. He laughed when he recognized it. An oldie but a goodie. "Stuck in the Middle with You" by Stealer's Wheel. It was a song from way back. Before he was born. Before his grandparents were born. He had heard it when he was a kid. The last time he'd been tied up.

The night his home had been broken into, and his parents had been killed.

"I made it out of that alive, I'm going to fucking make it out of this."

His voice startled him. It was hoarse and dry. Weak. The only way he was going to make it out of this was if he got out of the damn ties. He doubled his efforts on his other leg. It seemed easier with the help of his freed foot.

When he finally got it out, he suffered the pain of the blood rushing back into his foot again, giving it a few minutes more before trying anything else. He wiggled his toes, pretty sure he could feel them moving. He was doubly glad the frame had fallen forward. He'd managed to get some sustenance, and now he'd be able to at least try to stand up. If the frame had slid down the wall instead, placing him on his back, there would have been no hope for him. He would probably have been unconscious already.

Slowly, Miller lifted a knee, getting it under his belly. His shoulder cried out with every movement. By the time he managed to get his other knee under him, he was covered in sweat. Liquid his body couldn't afford to lose. Even with just his knees up, the bands holding his wrists loosened.

Miller walked on his knees, holding the frame off the ground, until he reached a wall. He lifted the top edge of the frame as high as he could, bracing it against the wall, and shuffled forward some more. Using the contact to keep stable, he moved to get a foot under him and pushed. The frame slid. He brought his second foot under him and abruptly teetered backward. His legs struggled to keep pace and he leaned forward, slamming the frame back into the wall in front of him.

Searing pain from his shoulder threatened to take over again. Miller fought it as best he could, thinking of Kris. Of how she was worried and searching for him. Of how much danger she was in from William or ACE. Or both. People she trusted. His breathing slowed and he regained control. He could still feel his heart pounding, threatening to explode through his chest. He almost laughed. At least his heart was still trying.

Getting his hands free was the next task. It wasn't going to be fun. With the frame balanced on his back, Miller crabbed over to the table. He found it when his head hit the edge, sending a shower of sparks across his vision. He backed up and rested the frame on the tabletop. The second the table had most of the frame's weight, he felt his torn shoulder cry out in protest. He braced himself, and threw his body under the table.

Miller's shoulder popped and he screamed. Pain lanced through his chest and back, hammering at the back of his head. He didn't care that new tears dropped from his face onto the carpeted floor. All he knew was that it had worked. His hand pulled free from the tie, laying twisted almost palm down on the floor. It felt like he may have dislocated his elbow as well.

He struggled back to his feet, trying to cradle his arm in the crook made between his legs and his waist. Each step made him cry out again. He finally moved his shoulder to the table and used his body to throw his arm on top of it. Before he could think about it too much, he dropped down to his knees. He felt his shoulder pop back into place. He couldn't fight the pain any longer. This time he welcomed the dark, no longer trying to hide from it. The blackness swept some of the pain away, but refused to take him. He lay on the floor, the pain in his shoulder slowly subsiding into a dull throb that kept time with his heartbeat.

Miller sucked in a breath, spitting out the crud that came in with it. He had ended up back by the wall. He moved, and his shoulder flared again, nowhere near as bad as it had been. He knew he'd done more than just dislocate it, but at least it was back in place and he could move it again. He struggled back to his feet, pushing the wire frame off of his back.

His elbow still hurt, but it no longer felt like he'd dislocated it. A few tentative moves later, he was pretty sure it was usable. When he finally got out of this, he wouldn't be able to use his arm for weeks. With his hand, he removed the tether from his other arm easily.

Now that he was free he stumbled back to the table. He knew Jeremy had left a bottle of juice on it, but it wasn't there anymore. He finally found it by crawling on his hands and knees in the dark. Bracing the bottle between his injured arm and his waist, he popped off the cap, wasting half of the juice on the floor. He grabbed what was left and guzzled it down.

He felt so tired, even the sugar didn't help. But now that he was free, he couldn't stop. He had to get out. At least there wasn't a guard at the door. If there had been, he would have come in when Miller had screamed.

Finding his clothes proved to be pointless. Miller searched the entire room, crawling through and around everything in his way. They weren't here. He tried to relieve some of the pressure on his shoulder and elbow by cradling one arm in the other, and shambled through the dark toward the fine white line under the door. He searched for the knob. When he found it, he held his breath and twisted, feeling the door unlatch. A flood of relief poured through him. He rested his head on the door and pushed.

It didn't move, and Miller's hope died.

LOS ANGELES, LEVEL 2—MONDAY, JUNE 12, 2141 1:12 P.M.

I rode down the back alleys of Chinatown, not wanting to hit the major streets. At every intersection I was careful to check and make sure we weren't being followed.

How could Kai do that to me? How could he pretend to be my friend for so long, and not tell me the truth?

Pat hung on for dear life on the back of the bike, squished between the carryall and me. With every bump, I was pushed closer to the handlebars. Every once in a while I shoved back, and she grunted when she made contact with the carryall.

We'd been riding for a half an hour and were well outside of Chinatown before Pat tapped me on the shoulder and pointed to a parking lot. I slowed down and slipped in between two cars.

I got off the bike and slid my helmet over the mirror before turning around. Pat looked like she'd had a rough ride. Tear tracks ran from the corner of her eyes to her temples. I had the lid protecting me from the wind generated by riding fast. I was so upset that I hadn't thought about Pat at all. Instead of ducking behind me, she'd obviously been keeping a lookout for us. It was comforting to know someone had my back.

Kai had rattled me more than I thought possible. Why had he picked now to tell me? Had the lie been too much for him, or did he have another reason?

Pat let me simmer for a few minutes before she started talking.

"Kai told me the same things while you were still out," she said.

"He told you how he knew my mom and dad before he told me?"

"Well, I . . . umm . . ."

I changed the subject. "What about what he said about ACE? Do you think he's right?"

"No. Do you?"

"I don't know. It feels like I don't know anything anymore." I leaned against the motorcycle's seat, filled with doubt about everything that had happened in the last year.

The chill of Level 2 seeped into my bones, and they ached with the ferocity of a Canadian winter. Most of it was probably still from yesterday. I pulled my jacket tighter around me and started shivering. Pat moved to grab me in a hug, wrapping her arms around me, willing the cold and pain away. I eventually stopped shivering, but the ache in my head had tripled.

"We need to get you someplace to rest," Pat said. "We shouldn't have left Kai's place yet. You're still not well."

I tensed and took a half step away from her. "I'm fine. I just couldn't stay there. It was . . . I'm not going back. Not yet."

Pat reached out a hand to me again, resting it on my shoulder. "I know. Is there any other place we can go?"

I thought about it. My old place above the Lee Fish Market had probably been rented out the day I left. No way was Pat going to fit into my hole on Level 1, not even through the pipe between the two buildings. The only place I could think of was my aunt and uncle's apartment, and there was no fucking way I was going back there. Ever. Even the thought of it made my skin crawl.

"No," was all I said.

"Okay. I don't have enough cash on this comm unit to pay for a hotel, so that's out." She paused, thinking. "My comm contact with ACE doesn't work anymore. I tried while you were sleeping, and there was no answer."

"Did you try it again? If it's not disconnected, maybe there was no one there."

"It's an—it was—an ACE Black Ops contact number. It should be manned twenty-four hours a day."

"Try again," I said.

Pat shrugged and pulled the comm unit from her pocket, dialing a number from memory. I memorized the unlock code and number she used. A voice answered before she'd lifted the comm unit to her ear.

"Pat Nelson, wun fower alpha golf fiver seven." She paused. "Deactivated. Non-secured connection."

The look on her face changed from concern to relief. She tossed me a quick smile.

"We were on the crashed transport." Another pause. "Kris Merrill and myself. We saw Janice Robertson running in the opposite direction, but weren't able to follow her."

A minute later, Pat hung up.

"That was ACE?" I asked. "What did they say?"

"We've arranged a meet. They're obviously a bit nervous. Considering the circumstances, I'm not surprised. We need to be on Level 5 at the Pasadena greenhouses. Do you know where that is?"

I'd heard of Pasadena, but it had been outside of my delivery area when I was a courier. I could aim in the general direction, but didn't know exactly where to go.

"There's greenhouses on Level 5?"

Pat laughed. "I can guide you."

I would have used the navigation system in the helmet to get us there, but I knew that as soon as it touched the net, we had a chance of being tracked. That was too big a risk with everything that had happened.

"We have some time anyway," she said. "The meet isn't for another couple of hours."

"Why the wait?"

"Like I said, they're nervous. They have a right to be cautious. We need to let them get everything in place."

Pat's words brought back lessons from the compound. If at all possible, get the lay of the land and the upper hand before any meet. We didn't need to do that now though, ACE was family. It still felt wrong not to.

"We'll get there a bit early and do our own scouting. Never walk in unprepared," Pat said.

I felt better knowing she thought the same. I swung my leg over the seat of the bike and started the motor. "I don't want to stay in Chinatown, or on Level 2 anyway," I said. "The ceilings are so low."

Pat climbed up behind me. "Okay. A bit slower this time, if you don't mind. Unless you've got a spare helmet someplace."

I grinned into my helmet and drove away, heading for an up-ramp, my head feeling every bump in the road.

CHAPTER 9

BRYSON CHECKED HIMSELF in the mirror. His face had already mottled with bruises, and dried blood had run down his cheek from his cut, soaking his shirt in rivulets that made it halfway down his chest. Without warning, the world got fuzzy and tilted. He grabbed the sink to balance himself until he had enough control to sit on the edge of the bathtub.

Slowly, he raised his hands to his shirt buttons and fought through the dried blood to get them undone. His muscles had stiffened as he'd slept, and each time he moved to the next button they protested. By the time he had the whole shirt undone, he was hurting pretty bad. His tolerance for pain had always been low.

Once he had his breathing as under control as he thought he could get it, he forced himself to stand in front of the mirror again. He pulled the shirt off his shoulders and examined his chest. A bruise had formed at the bottom of his ribcage. He sucked in a deep breath and let it out again. Now that he'd seen it, it didn't seem so bad. The only blood seemed to have come from his head. Bryson gingerly fingered the bruise, searching for broken ribs. He had no idea what he was looking for, but since there was no sharp jab, he figured he was okay.

He turned and twisted to look at his back. That sent a new wave of pain through him, but this time he just took it. His back looked about the same. The bruise was a bit higher, just over his kidney, but didn't seem to be as bad as the front. The edges were already turning a sickly yellow from the blue-black of the center.

Bryson stripped down, pausing as his pants pulled away from his knees. He filled the sink with the hottest water possible and threw in his shirt, taking one more look in the mirror before stepping into the tub. It could have been worse.

The shower stung, but relaxed all his muscles. Once he'd gotten most of the blood off his face, he pulled the plunger and let the tub fill almost to the top. He didn't even think about how much water he was using, or what it would cost him. It was never an issue in orbit. Lowering himself in, he lay in the hot water, letting it work its magic.

When he woke up, the water was cold and his skin had crinkled from being immersed. The water had turned a light shade of pink. He controlled a shiver, draining the tub halfway before filling it up with hot water again. This time, he stayed awake, eventually sinking his head below the surface. The twinge in his cheek was sharp and short.

He held his breath as long as he could before coming back up, sucking in a lungful of air, and lowering himself in again. He stayed down less than twenty seconds before he burst out of the tub, throwing water on the bathroom floor.

How could he have been so stupid? The damn memory chip.

What if the mugger had taken the memory chip? He reached for his pants and jammed his hand into the pocket, feeling the seam before turning the whole thing inside out. His heart lurched in his chest and he shivered in the cool air. Bryson searched the other front pocket the same way.

A hole opened inside him. It was gone. The bastard had taken it. What did a lowlife mugger think he would do with a memory chip, and an encrypted one at that? Bryson got out of the tub and walked, dripping, to the bed in a daze. Panic welled in the hole in his chest, rising until his ears filled with steady rush of pumping blood.

He'd lost everything. Years of work. The solution to the problem. What if the mugger knew what it was? What if he sold it to the highest bidder?

A knock on the door jolted Bryson back to his feet.

"Housekeeping."

The door clicked and started to open.

"No! No, I'm still in here. Come back later."

The door closed faster than it had opened.

A memory from the night before flashed through his mind. His room key. He'd found it on the ground last night. What if the memory chip had been discarded the same way? He limped back to the bathroom as fast as he could and pulled his pants back on.

The room key was still on the bed. Bending over to get it reminded Bryson to go slower, to take it easy. His beating heart told him to hurry up. He left the room, making sure the door was locked behind him, and took the stairs as quickly as he could, using the banister for support.

Cars had been through the driveway since he'd been mugged. Tire tracks ran through the small pool of blood where he'd split open his cheek, almost erasing its existence. He got down on his hands and knees. It had to be here.

A glint closer to the main street got his attention. He crawled over to it and brushed construction sand away from it. The memory chip. He picked it up with shaking fingers and lightly blew the remaining road dust off of it. It didn't appear to be damaged. He'd have to find some way to read it before he knew for sure. Bryson sat on the driveway, his back to the brick facade, and held the chip in his fist.

When he opened his eyes, the hotel manager was leaning over him, a scowl on his face.

"Get out of here. We don't allow bums on our property." He kicked Bryson's foot.

Bryson slid his back up the wall, the fake brick scraping his skin. The manager stared at his face and bruised chest.

"Christ. Are you okay?" the manager asked.

Bryson shook his head and headed for the gate.

"Hey! You can't go in there."

He held up his room card, unlocked the gate, and plodded up the stairs. He didn't look back until his room door was once again locked behind him.

He'd attracted too much attention.

LOS ANGELES, LEVEL 4—MONDAY, JUNE 12, 2141 1:13 P.M.

William closed the link on the comm unit. He had a plan to put together. At least he'd given himself a few hours to figure it out.

He fell into his chair and stared out the window over the city. In the streets below, people went on with their lives. They were walking, talking, eating. Making love to the people who mattered the most. He envied their simplicity.

He had been in similar situations before. Well, not exactly the same. He'd never had to decide what he was going to do with his own people. Not this way. Ordering someone's death when you didn't know them was remarkably easier than ordering the death of someone you did. Especially when two of them were Miller and Kris. He had worked closely with Miller recently, and that connection had created a bond he hadn't realized was there. How many times had he listened to Miller talk about Kris? Enough to care about the both of them. Maybe too much.

Having to make the same decision twice in as many days didn't make it any easier. He paused. Not just twice, but four times. There was Janice, and since the damn cook was still with Kris, he'd have to get rid of her as well. Four casualties to keep ACE's secrets. He knew it was a fair trade, no matter how much it hurt.

Originally, he had wanted to keep Janice, but he had to tie up all the loose ends. There couldn't be any trail left for Jeremy to follow. If Jeremy discovered what he had done to stop his plans and save ACE . . . he didn't want to think about it.

The one thing he could console himself with was the thought that at least Kris wouldn't go through Miller's hell. She wouldn't die only to be brought back from the edge so she could be tortured again. There was no point to it, no end goal. Except for Jeremy's twisted sense of satisfaction.

William was well beyond caring about that.

Janice was the best way to take them out. He had a full contingent of people capable of doing it, but that would trace back to him too easily. One order from him on the records, and Jeremy would know. The thought didn't sit easily.

William forced his mind back to Kris. The timing would have to be perfect, as would the execution. William chuckled. A double entendre.

He always fell back to nervous laughter when he was under stress.

He would have to be seen as trying to get Kris, to bring her back into the fold, so to speak. Jeremy couldn't find out what William was actually planning.

The comm unit rang again, startling William from his reverie. He answered. "Yes."

"We have a positive position on Bryson Searls, sir."

William immediately straightened his back and swiveled to face his desk again. They'd only learned Bryson had escaped from Kadokawa control a short while ago.

"Where?"

"Right here on Level 4 Los Angeles, sir, by the Hotel Ruby. He just started moving. It seems he has an active tracker."

"Good. Good. Keep watching him. Place a set of eyes on him in case he alters his tracker. Keep me informed." He closed the connection. ACE made it a habit to keep track of employees' families, you never knew where a weakness would show up that could be exploited by the corporations. Bryson's distance from his dad ended up being a good thing. If they were close, there was no doubt that Bryson's tracker would have been disabled.

This was getting better. Jeremy would be pretty pissed that Kris was dead, but William would have a built-in scapegoat in Janice. Since he would be there to bring Kris in, he would get rid of Janice himself. Bringing in Searls, the creator of the quantum jump drive, would be a bonus.

He picked up the comm unit again.

"I need a small team for a pickup and extraction. Have them meet me in my office in forty-five minutes." He disconnected without waiting for a reply. They'd plan for an extraction tonight, when there were fewer people to witness it.

He would explain what he wanted from Janice when she arrived, and have her out the door before the extraction team came in.

LOS ANGELES, LEVEL 2—MONDAY, JUNE 12, 2141 1:30 P.M.

Kai sat slumped in his chair in the back office, staring at the table Kris and the young boy had both lain on without actually seeing it. He had saved one life today but lost two people. Kris leaving had created a hole in his life that he hadn't felt in years. He hadn't realized, hadn't admitted to himself, how much Kris had filled the spot left by her parents.

It really should have been him who died that night. A strong man, a wise man, would have stayed and let the ones with the young kid at home get away. Kai's own children had already had young ones of their own. Some Kris's age. He would have been missed, but no children would have been left without parents. He couldn't remember what he had been thinking back then. All he remembered now was that he'd run and left his two best friends to die.

And now he had lost their daughter. She had grown up too fast, but had done well. Although he had never directly interfered in her life, he had always kept tabs on her.

Her invisible guardian angel.

When she'd joined ACE, he'd fretted for months before coming to the realization the training would help her. As long as he could get her out of their grasp when she was done.

Now she was heading into danger because of ACE. Into a situation that could get her killed, and he was sitting in his office. History was repeating itself.

He jumped up, throwing the chair against the wall. It wasn't going to happen again. He couldn't let it. He wouldn't.

Kai reached for the comm unit, picking it up just as it rang. "Hello."

"Turn on the news." He recognized the voice right away. Jack.

Walking to the front of the restaurant, Kai started talking. "I need a favor. I need to find someone who does not wish to be found." He wished he had given Pat a comm unit that could be tracked.

There was a pause at the other end. "Turn on your vid screen, then we'll talk."

Kai touched the screen and it came to life. A building spewed smoke into the air. It was somewhere on Level 6. He could tell by how the Ambients were in tracks to simulate the sun's motion, and from the height of the ceiling. Fans were already sucking smoke into the ventilation system, and drones filled the sky like gnats. The view switched to a news desk with a man sitting behind it. Words on the bottom of the screen said the building was a water distribution station. Kai turned up the volume.

"—SoCal officials are calling this a terrorist attack, the first on Earth since the corporations started fighting last year. Experts have been declaring the current skirmishes the start of another corporate war, and corporations around the globe have increased their security. The people of Earth learned after the first one that we couldn't survive another. The corporations obviously did not."

With those words, the sound abruptly cut off and the display turned blue with the text "Service Interruption" splayed across it. They stayed there for no more than fifteen seconds before the stream came back on. A woman sat behind the news desk this time.

"We apologize for the interruption." She glanced down at the screen embedded in her desk. "This just in. SoCal is calling this a Kadokawa attack. We have an official statement."

The screen switched, and another woman, standing in front of the SoCal offices on Level 7, came into view.

"We've just gotten off the comm with the President. He is calling this an act of war against all of the United States, not just against

San Angeles. No one has yet accepted the blame for this atrocity, and all leads are being diligently followed."

The news people didn't seem to know what was going on. Kai lifted the comm unit back to his ear. "The president is siding with SoCal?" he said to Jack.

Everyone knew the president was an IBC placement. If he was aligning with SoCal, the lines between the corporations were being drawn, and SoCal was with IBC.

"Yeah," Jack said. "Things are about to get real. At least they aren't blaming us yet."

Kai didn't care who got blamed. He cared about the losses that would result. "We started a war."

"No. We accelerated it. We knew this was going to happen, Kai. We planned it this way. Weaken the corporations and take back what rightfully belongs to the people."

Kai sighed. "I know. It is just—"

"Too late for worries now," Jack paused. "Shit, those guys move fast."

Kai looked at the screen again. They were back at the water transfer station, but something was different. There were no drones in the air. A banner exploded across the bottom of the screen. *Second water distribution station hit.*

They *were* moving fast.

The announcer came back on. "Strict water rationing measures are in place for Los Angeles, Levels 6 and 7. All residents are encouraged to stop watering their lawns. For those closest to the distribution sites, fill your tubs and any pots and pans you have before the neighborhood sites are drained.

"Water trucks will be arriving to supply the essentials to neighborhoods farther away." She glanced down at her screen again. "SoCal has extended the water rationing down through Level 1. They've already begun to send trucks to transfer water from the lower levels up to us."

Kai turned off the vid screen and cursed. "*Wŏ cào*. Things are escalating faster than we wanted."

"Yes. I wonder why."

"Who cares why? Are we prepared for it?"

"No. But we wouldn't have been later, either. We don't have the manpower to protect our water. They have control anyway. They control the desalinization plants."

Kai hung up and stared at the comm unit's blank screen, lost in thought. A truck rumbled down the street outside the restaurant, its giant plastic water container empty. It would come back full, giving to the upper levels what didn't belong to them. Things were moving too fast.

The insurgents had hit where it hurt the most, and they weren't prepared for the repercussions. There was supposed to be time. Time to rally the people to protect what was theirs. Time to . . . to . . . Kai closed his eyes and let out a slow breath. The insurgents had decided for everyone, and Kai had helped. It had been his plan originally, but it wasn't really supposed to happen. The transport crash in Santa Barbara had made it possible, and they'd moved forward. How many thousands would die? How many millions? The crew on Level 6 would move through San Angeles up to San Francisco, destroying every water distribution station they could on the way. They were already in motion, and there was no way Jack would stop them.

Kai swore again. He'd forgotten about Kris. He hit the call back on his comm unit and waited for an answer. There was a lot of stuff he could be blamed for, but Kris's death was not one he would allow.

LOS ANGELES, LEVEL 5—MONDAY, JUNE 12, 2141 3:00 P.M.

We rode past the greenhouses a few times before we figured everything looked normal. People walked the streets with kids and businesses were open to the public. There weren't too many places to hide, except maybe in the greenhouses themselves.

I'd seen green places before. Mom and Dad had put up a live tree at Christmas every year. It had been up when I'd grabbed Oscar from its branches as the police dragged me out the door when Mom and Dad had been killed. I'd seen the trees and grass on Level 7 and in Doc Searls' gated community on Level 6, but not like this. The best I'd ever seen was the compound in Kananaskis, with the mountains and the bright blue sky. It was beautiful even in the cold of winter.

This came close. Maybe it was just the greenhouses that stretched on for kilometers in this world of gray that made it seem that way.

Most of them were closed to the public. I yelled back at Pat, asking about them. She told me they were corporate owned, and supplied a huge quantity of fresh fruits and vegetables to people below Level 6. The two upper levels had their own food sources. Through the protective plastic I could see stacked rows of plants sitting in white troughs seemingly too small to hold them.

The open greenhouses were a glorious mixture of every shade of green I could imagine, speckled with masses of color. Even the air here was different. I could smell the moist soil, the leaves composting on the ground. One greenhouse in particular filled the air with a smell so sweet, I almost felt giddy. I hadn't thought anything in San Angeles could surprise me anymore. Not the way this did.

Scattered around the open greenhouses were small cafés and eateries, each one with tables and chairs outside, placed as close as possible to the greenery without actually being inside. Even here, the walls of the restaurants and a lot of the unused surfaces were flashing some sort of advertising. Eat here. Buy this.

I wished we had more time to walk around. One greenhouse was filled with tall birches, each trunk a straight white line leading from the ground to the leaves. People strolled down paths between the trunks, and a sign outside read "shinrin-yoku," with the Kadokawa logo imprinted underneath. We were past it before I could get a really good look inside. Pat pointed down a side street, and as I maneuvered between the traffic and pedestrians, I forgot to ask if she knew what it meant.

The farther we got from the greenhouses, the more confining the streets felt, until finally Pat indicated we should park. I found a spot in an empty lot, turned off the motor, and thumbed the lock.

"We're supposed to meet at the greenhouses that burned down last year," Pat said. "We can go a couple of streets over and walk up."

"Why did we park so far away?" I asked.

"Look, whoever wants you knew about the compound, and knew what transport we—"

I took a step back. "You're thinking Kai was right, that ACE is behind this."

"No. Absolutely not. Not knowingly anyway. What I'm saying is someone inside ACE may be feeding information to the wrong people, or they've tapped our communications. I used to get paid to be suspicious and cautious. I was good at it."

Everything she said made sense, though I still wouldn't have parked so far from the meeting point. If we needed to get away quick, we'd have to make it all the way back here first. Pat was more experienced than I was, and I let the decision stay without questioning it.

One thing ACE had pounded into us over and over again during training was to trust them and trust your partner. When you were in the field, they might be the only thing you could rely on. It felt *wrong* to question ACE, but I knew it was also smart.

What if communications were being intercepted, or worse, a mole was in place? I couldn't believe a mole had made it into ACE again. They had to have gotten a lot more careful after last year.

"I can't leave my bike here for too long," I said.

"ACE will have someone come and get it, and if everything goes wrong, we'll meet back here. Come on, we'll take the next street."

As we walked, Pat and I fell into the regular pattern of scanning the area and blending in with other foot traffic. This was just like a training simulation. I could do it. We crossed the street and went into a greenhouse. Roses grew in neat rows, each plant alive with vibrant flowers in every shade between deep red and white that I could imagine. The air was intoxicating. As we exited the other side, the space opened onto a grassy park with what remained of a burned-down greenhouse across from us.

A single man in a suit stood further down the street, out of place among the more casual dress of the other people. He turned slightly, and for a second I thought I recognized him before he moved behind a small group and disappeared from view. I couldn't remember from where. Movement inside the burned greenhouse drew my attention.

I elbowed Pat and slowed down. "That's Janice. From training."

I'd expected Pat to continue across the street. Instead she stopped, bending down to tie a shoelace that wasn't undone.

"What's wrong?"

"I didn't expect her here."

"Why not, if ACE is here to get us, then why not her as well?" I took another step, and Pat laid a hand on my shin.

"How did she contact ACE? We had an old number that was still in service, and even then it took a while."

"I don't know. Maybe when she was recruited, she found out how to contact them."

Pat lifted her hand in a brief wave. I turned and saw Janice smiling, making her way out of the burned structure. Was she trying to hide in there? I'd spotted her too easy for that.

Then I remembered the look Janice had given me back at the compound, just before she'd boarded the transport. It was starting to feel wrong to me as well.

"Should we leave?" I asked.

Before Pat could answer, Janice called out. "Come on," she said. "I'm supposed to bring you in."

At that, Pat stood and grabbed my arm, leaning close to whisper in my ear. "This isn't right. ACE doesn't send people who haven't finished training into the field."

"But it's just us. Maybe they brought Janice because we know her?"

"That's what has me worried."

I watched as Janice stopped on the sidewalk a few meters from us.

"Hey, Janice," Pat called. "You alone?"

"Nope. My partner's in the car around the corner. Come on, let's get you two home." She turned and walked down the sidewalk away from us. Away from the man in the suit. His name popped into my head. William. He'd recruited me. What would he being doing here, during what was supposed to be a routine pickup?

"This is wrong," Pat whispered. She placed herself between Janice and me and started jogging back to the rose greenhouse, pushing me ahead of her.

A single shot echoed through the park. Pat stumbled, and for a split second I thought the sound had triggered another episode. Instead, she tightened her grip and ran faster.

We raced into the rose garden. There wasn't any cover. People stared at us like we were abominations for destroying the tranquility of the place. Another gunshot rang out, and an older gentleman just a few paces in front of us fell. That's when the screaming started. We merged with the panicked crowd, losing ourselves in their midst.

Just before we were swallowed by the group, I looked back to where I thought I'd seen William. He still stood in the same spot. From this distance, I couldn't tell if the look on his face was one of shock or fear. Pat was right, something was wrong.

Once we were past the greenhouse and on the other side of the street, Pat stumbled, nearly falling. We emerged from the crowd, and I elbowed her into a recessed doorway. She slumped against the sidewall, staring into space, her body vibrating. I'd seen this before.

Pat reached out and pulled me close, leaning in to whisper in my ear. "Will . . . William—"

"Yeah, I saw him, too. Come on, we need to go." I reached around her and tried to lift. She weighed more than me, and we both fell back against the wall.

Pat pulled me close again. "Kai . . . right . . ."

She must have been bordering on delirious. Did she think William had sent Janice after us? If that was true, then ACE had to be as corrupt as Kai thought.

If Kai was right about ACE—

A car skidded to a stop on the street outside our recessed door, leaving two black marks on the road. I wheeled, ready to run. Pat slid to the ground and I stopped. I couldn't leave her. I shouldn't have left Ian, and I wasn't about to leave her. I knew firsthand what running away could mean.

The car door swung open and a man dressed in gang colors got out, leaving someone in the driver's seat. "Get in the car."

I didn't budge.

"Dammit, get in the car before they figure out where you are."

He reached for Pat, and I moved to stand between them, pushing his outstretched arms away.

"We need to move now. For fuck's sake, Kai sent us."

His words thumped into my brain. "Kai?"

"Yes, Kai. Now get out of the way."

I lurched onto the sidewalk and let him pick up Pat as though she was a rag doll. She screamed once, and he slapped a hand over her mouth. I followed when he tossed her in the back seat, gently pushing her to give me room. My hand came away bloody. The car was moving before he'd closed the door.

I hoped I hadn't just made a mistake.

CHAPTER 10

PAT SHIVERED IN THE BACK SEAT of the car. Her shirt was soaked through with sweat. Something outside banged and she started, pushing herself deeper into the seat. Someone touched her arm, and she jerked away, whimpering.

Gunfire echoed in her head. A scream of "grenade" cut through the noise and she hit the ground, sliding in the fibercrete grit. She sucked in a lung full of air and her chest spasmed, coughing out fine dust. Tears ran from her eyes. Her partner, Bobby, lay a meter ahead of her, hunched over in the open.

She grabbed the back of his armor and dragged him toward the shattered wall. He didn't help. Didn't resist. Bullets impacted the other side of the wall. Pat felt them puncture the old cinder block and stop before they reached the other side. Another grenade flew through the door, rolling to the far corner.

Pat ducked, covering her head with her arms. A loud bang drove her to the wall and a bright light flashed off the floor. Her ears rang. She stood, firing her gun at the doorway she had followed Bobby through. Lights flashed and the ringing in her ears increased to a high-pitched whine, blocking all other sound.

Her weapon emptied and she ducked, blindly reaching for another clip. The reek of bodies burned beyond recognition filled the room. Bullets flew over her head, ricocheting off the distant wall, throwing more dust into the choked air. Light pierced the gloom from the far wall, a rectangle that showed the only way out.

The bullets stopped, leaving only the ringing in her ears. A shadow blocked the light from the far door.

Somewhere in the distance, a child screamed, pulsing through to Pat's brain. She dropped, covering her partner's body with her own. His blood soaked through her fatigues. The sound of feet made her lift her head. A young girl, almost a baby, ran toward her, screaming as loud as she could.

The girl carried something. Small, hard, metallic looking. Another grenade! Pat blinked through the sparks dancing in front of her eyes. She raised her rifle and squeezed the trigger.

The girl dropped, the grenade rolling on the floor toward Pat. It stopped only a pace away from Bobby; the head of a doll, broken, dirty, the paint rubbed off the face in patches. Pat's control shattered. She stood, running toward the back door, leaving Bobby behind, jumping over the girl.

Pain flared through her back, and she collapsed. Underneath her, the girl moved. Pat fought through the pain, shifting into the fetal position. The young girl, dressed in filthy rags, huddled against her chest. Pat looked down, meeting the girl's eyes. She couldn't have been more than three years old. Scars latticed her arms and face and one eye was white and foggy. Pat's bullet had torn through her shoulder.

There were no tears. No more screams. The girl whispered a word. Pat twisted closer, her back shrieking.

"Pourquoi?" It was barely a whisper. "Pourquoi?"

Blackness closed in. Pat felt the girl pulled from her arms; heard a final sharp scream, cut short. Something fell to the ground beside her.

When she came to, the ground under her had turned from fiber-crete to cold plastic. It vibrated and rocked. A vehicle of some type. She opened her eyes and saw nothing. A blackness darker than the night. The vehicle stopped and she heard voices, jumbled, muted. A door opened and flooded the space with a bright light. Pat blinked and shaded her eyes.

She was alone.

Rough hands grabbed her, pulling her out, throwing her to the ground. Her back convulsed, engulfing her in a world of blood and death. The darkness came again.

A dim light, shining through a small grate in the door. Dirty water. Dry, crusty bread. Sometimes the door would open and she would be dragged out and beaten, or worse. Needle marks up and down both of her arms made them look like ground meat. Her brain turned into a pile of mush. Only one image stayed true. Only one sound stayed clear. Only one.

"Pourquoi?"

The next time she recognized where she was, the walls were white. Lights shone from the ceiling, blinding her until she got used to them. Machines beeped. People hustled by, always in a rush to go somewhere, be somewhere else.

Physical recovery took months. Mental recovery took over a year. Throughout the process, she was told they had won. People lived, thrived, had clean water. Fields were planted again. Things grew. They had won.

Hollow words.

The day they released her, the day ACE shipped her to the training compound, a young girl dressed in rags stood in the corner of her hospital room.

"Pourquoi?" she said.

<hr>

LOS ANGELES, LEVEL 2—MONDAY, JUNE 12, 2141 3:04 P.M.

I forced Pat onto her stomach in the back seat of the car as it sped down the ramp to Level 3. Every time the car took a corner, Pat let out a soft groan.

I lifted the back of her coat and shirt. There was a fair amount of blood, but the wound didn't look bad. Only a small scrape above her hip. I used a clean part of her shirt to dab at it, and fresh blood oozed from the gouge. Physically, she would be fine.

Pat slid to the car's floor and hugged her legs in a fetal position. I let her lie there. She had told me once that being in enclosed spaces sometimes calmed her down, at least enough for her to function a little.

The car sped around another corner, swaying on its suspension.

"Slow down. You'll attract attention," I said. Since when was I the expert?

"How do we know they're not following us?" the driver asked. He slowed down anyway.

"Just get us down to Level 2. I'll keep lookout."

The driver did as he was told. This guy was definitely not ACE, and with the edge of panic in his voice, I doubted he'd had any formal training. His partner in the passenger seat sat like he was made of fibercrete. I couldn't get a read on him at all.

The car turned a few more corners, doubling back on its track and driving in the opposite direction. There was hope for the driver after all. He hit the down-ramp for Level 2 at a normal speed and exited east of Chinatown. He started making a beeline for the restaurant.

"Don't go straight there, not yet. Give us a chance to make sure we didn't pick anyone up." *Give us some time to get Pat back to normal,* I thought.

The driver left the main road and drove around a neighborhood I didn't recognize. Gray buildings hugged the road, their windows just slits in the fibercrete, like a prison's.

Pat was coming out of it. Her eyes were still glazed over, but she wasn't jumping out of her skin every time I touched her. Once we got to Kai's, we'd have to figure out where to go from there, and I needed her to be aware of who and where she was for that.

I still didn't want to see Kai. Yes, he had been right. ACE wasn't what I'd thought it was. But there were too many secrets he had kept to himself. I wasn't ready. If I could have gone anywhere else, I would have.

ACE had tried to get rid of Pat and me, but I didn't understand why. Worse yet, why use Janice to get the job done? Janice and I had never gotten along too well, but she and Pat did. Yet Janice hadn't hesitated to pull the trigger.

Things just weren't making sense. If ACE was behind the compound attack and the transport crash, why now? Why not just a training accident? It would have been easy enough to arrange for one of those and cover it up.

Instead, they had risked a lot, and lost a lot, by attacking the compound. A whole crew of operatives almost finished their training. A year of effort. What if it wasn't ACE? What if it was just William? Pat and I had both seen him near the greenhouses. Had he been there to meet us, or to make sure Janice did her job?

None of it was making any sense.

Pat shifted on the floor and opened her eyes. From what I could tell, she still wasn't focusing on anything. But it had to be a good sign. I hoped it was. I wished I could talk to her about everything that had happened.

By the time we'd reached the outskirts of Chinatown, with its flickering neon signs and smells, I'd made a decision. I wasn't about to write ACE off. Not after what they had done for me and Ian. I needed to figure out where William was and what his plans were. That would require a one-on-one meeting. He might even know where Ian was. I was going to get some answers, even if I had to break into his office to do it.

And if I ever saw Janice again, I would kill her.

———

LOS ANGELES, LEVEL 2—MONDAY, JUNE 12, 2141 3:32 P.M.

Kai opened the door when the man knocked, five raps with his knuckles and two kicks to the bottom of the door. I could tell he'd done this before. Pat was between us. She was at least keeping herself on her feet, but she obviously didn't like us touching her. Every time she shifted her weight, or we had to change our grasp on her, she shuddered and squeezed her lips together. A moan slipped out once, but I didn't think the man heard it.

Kai took one look at Pat and stepped out of the way for us. "Put her in the storage room," he said.

The storage room had been rearranged. The cot had been moved to where the bike had been, making the room appear bigger. We lowered Pat down, and I pulled a blanket over her. She dragged it higher, burying her head under it.

"Do you want me to stay?" I didn't get an answer. "Do you want me to go?" Still no answer. I pushed Kai and the man ahead of me as I started to leave.

"Stay. Please." Pat's voice was strained, barely above a whisper.

I got rid of the men and went back to the cot, sitting on the cold floor. I put my head near hers and whispered, "I'll stay as long as you want me to." She didn't answer, but I thought I felt her relax into the bedding. I leaned against the side of the cot, slouching against its leg.

Minutes later, Pat fell into a fitful sleep. This was worse than what had happened in the house on Level 1. This time, she had lost all control, lost herself to the memories that had forced themselves to the surface.

At least mine stayed in my dreams. Hers were a reality that she fought every day. I knew then that I couldn't let her help me get Ian, at least not directly.

When Pat finally stopped tossing and turning in the cot, when she finally lay still, breathing deeply and evenly, I stood up. I ached all over from sitting for so long. My back popped when I straightened it.

I knew I could stay in here, using Pat as an excuse to not talk to Kai, but my hunger cut through that. He'd looked in on us once, and I just shook my head. He had backed away. I hadn't seen or heard from him since.

I walked to the open doorway and peered around the corner. The lights were off in the restaurant and hallway. I could see a bit shining from around the curtain covering the door to the office. I took a step. My foot nudged something on the floor. Kai had put water and food on a tray and left it just outside. I brought it back into the storage room.

The water was still a bit cold, and the food was a sandwich with chicken and some greens on it. I ate it as though I hadn't eaten in days, washing it down with the water. I put the second water and sandwich by the cot and walked back to the door.

What would I say to him? My stomach was in knots and I caught myself rubbing my hands together like I was trying to get some dirt off them. I stepped across the hall and moved the curtain aside. Kai sat in his chair, his upper body resting on the small desk. I could hear faint snores. The room was cold, colder than the storage room where Pat slept.

I remembered coming here, to the restaurant, after a long day, sitting at the only table at the front, with its two rickety plastic chairs. The sound and smells of meat and vegetables hitting hot oil. He'd sit with me, and we'd talk as though we were old friends. As though we'd known each other for our entire lives. I was fifteen the first time it happened. Now here we were, almost three years later, and a friendship that had felt so natural and so comforting now felt strained. Almost fake. But it was still there. I still cared.

I tiptoed in and grabbed an old blue blanket from the table, now cleared of any evidence that I had been there. Just the thought of it made my head hurt again. I ignored the feeling and shook out the blanket, walking toward Kai.

He moved when I put the blanket over his shoulders. I held my breath until he settled back down. He still didn't seem comfortable, but it was the best I could do.

As I walked back out the office, I heard him call my name.

"Kris?"

I turned. When had he started to look so old?

"Kris, I . . . I would like to talk about it."

"I don't know if that's a good idea right now." My insides churned in confusion.

"Now may be the only time we have. Things are changing, Kris. Things are going to get worse before they get better."

I took a step toward him. "What do you mean?"

"Later. First, we need to talk about us. About ACE. Your parents."

The last words were barely audible.

"You told me everything already."

"Almost everything. I need to tell you about that night. The night they died."

I stumbled, and the doorframe dug into my back. The pain in my head increased. "I don't know if I can do this." I wanted to know more, to learn how my mom and dad had been taken from me, but every part of me screamed out to run.

Kai pulled out an extra chair and sat waiting. The choice was mine, or at least I thought it was. I don't know what I was thinking. I could barely feel. I sat in the offered chair.

Tears streamed down Kai's wrinkled cheeks, and I heard how he ran the night my mom and dad were killed. How he had lived and they didn't. All I could think about was how I'd done the same to Ian.

———

LOS ANGELES, LEVEL 2—MONDAY, JUNE 12, 2141 4:07 P.M.

I left him there, with Pat in his care, grabbing her comm unit before walking out the back door and closing it softly behind me.

In the end, Kai and I had done similar things. I hadn't run, but I still left when Ian had told me to. No matter how many times I told myself that, I knew the truth. I had left him to die . . . or worse. I didn't want to think about it, didn't want to face the consequences of what I had done. Kai must have felt the same way then as I did now. Understanding that helped to heal the wound he had opened. Maybe he needed the same from me.

I'd never had time to mourn my parents. When they'd been killed I was taken to a halfway house, a ward of the state, sleeping in a room with a bunch of other kids. I didn't know anyone. The kids had left me alone, crying into my pillow. The adults only made sure I ate.

After that, I wasn't allowed to cry. My aunt and uncle told me to get over it, as though I had lost a favorite stuffed animal instead of my parents. They put me back into school right away, and I worked a bit to bring in money. Then the bad stuff started with my uncle.

When I ran away from them, I was too busy trying to stay alive to think about it. Eventually, everything was pushed into the not-so-little box in my brain, locked and secure where it couldn't hurt me.

My nightmares had opened the box a little when I slept, but Kai had ripped the lid right off, and everything gushed out at once. At the crest of the wave were Mom and Dad, and the old wounds opened as though they had never gone. I guess they hadn't.

I'm not sure how long I wandered the streets and alleys, stumbling across parking lots and through strip malls, not really aware of where or who I was, going through that box item by item. At some point, I realized I couldn't change what had happened. Yeah, it was fucked. Hell, I was fucked beyond belief, but it was too late for me to do anything about it.

I eventually shoved everything back into the box, back where it couldn't hurt me. But this time was different. This time, I didn't lock it, and the lid sat crookedly over the top. I had decided to go back in there one day. Soon. Not now. Now I had another problem to take care of. One I could change, or so I hoped.

Ian was somewhere out there. Maybe with ACE, maybe somewhere else. I was pretty sure I'd seen William back at the greenhouses, but I still didn't know if he was there to bring us in, or to make sure Janice did her job. I needed to talk to him. On my terms.

The moment I thought of the greenhouses, I yearned for them again. I wanted the smell of the grass and the trees, the dirt that they grew in. I needed it. Living in the Canadian wilderness for a year had given me something I didn't even know I wanted. And now, something I felt I couldn't live without.

I pulled myself from my dazed wandering. I wasn't quite sure where I was. The streets weren't familiar at all. I knew I hadn't taken a ramp, so I was still on Level 2. I needed wheels. My bike was on Level 5, and I had no idea how to get back up there to get it.

Two empty water trucks rattled by on the street behind me, and suddenly I knew. They would be my ticket up. I ran after them, eventually just following the sounds as they outpaced me. When I couldn't hear them anymore, I followed the sound of voices chanting.

The trucks had stopped by a local water distribution station. The first one was already being filled while the second waited patiently behind it. Outside the fence stood maybe fifty people. Some had signs, others just stood. They all yelled the same slogan in perfect sync.

Don't steal our water.

Police and military paced along the inside perimeter, with a bunch more manning the gate. They outnumbered the protesters. Just as I was thinking how odd that was, another busload of people arrived, and the numbers evened out.

The water trucks would be going back to Level 6 at least. They were, by a long shot, my best opportunity to get to Level 5 quickly. Watching the protest, I was pretty sure SoCal would start giving the trucks armed escorts soon, if they hadn't already. It was a risk I'd have to take.

I walked away from the crowds, back to where I had first seen the trucks. The streets here weren't wide. If the trucks took the same route back, I figured it was the best place for me to try to hitch a ride. I'd have to slow them down a bit first.

I fished through the garbage behind some squat gray apartment blocks, unpainted fibercrete, like all the others. Before long, I found a greasy bag and an empty bottle. I put the two together and sat on the sidewalk, my back against the apartments, and waited.

It took a long time before I heard the trucks again. They were a lot quieter this time, the weight of the water damping the bumps in the road from getting to the trucks themselves. I barely had time to stand up and walk to the middle of the road before they came into view.

I stopped and pretended to drink from the empty bottle. I veered to the left, overcorrected, and went right instead, moving almost to the curb. My next steps brought me back to the middle of the road. A drunkard's walk. I heard the lead truck's brakes kick in, and its air horns threatened to deafen me. Looking up, I squinted at the driver and tottered back to the curb, making sure to lurch backward once or twice so they were never sure where I would be.

The first truck accelerated past me, its electrics whining under the load. I teetered in front of the second truck before falling back near the curb again. The truck was going faster already, but with the massive weight it carried, it was still slow enough for me grab onto.

I took another fake swig from the bottle as it went past and lunged for the ladder that rose up the back of the storage tank, dropping the bottle in its bag in the middle of the road. My shoulder tweaked as it took the sudden stress before I was running at the same speed as the truck. The shoulder had bothered me ever since that delivery last year. I scampered up the ladder, lying flat on the top of the narrow catwalk that ran the length of the tank.

Now that I was on, I started worrying about getting off. The only time these guys would slow down was when they were going through Level 6 security. I wanted to be long gone by then.

As I clung to the tiny catwalk on top of the tank, a convoy of three empty water trucks passed us in the other direction. Two military vehicles escorted them. One stopped and turned around, racing ahead to lead us to Level 6.

―――――

LOS ANGELES, LEVEL 2—MONDAY, JUNE 12, 2141 4:50 P.M.

Kai paced around his small office, sometimes pushing aside the curtain in the doorway and storming to the kitchen in the front. Once there, he stared out the window, hoping to see Kris returning. After few minutes, he would stomp back to his office and start pacing again.

Pat cried out in her sleep, a forlorn sound full of fear. Kai ignored her and dropped into his chair. She had been doing it for a while. The first few times, he had rushed over to console her, to make sure everything was all right. Now, he just let her be. Nothing he had done had helped anyway. She had just moaned and rolled over, never waking up.

He'd considered opening for dinner, but once he'd found out the water had been turned off, he didn't bother. He could cook without the water. Everything was prepared and ready to go. What he couldn't do was clean up after. And somehow, he'd lost the will to cook. Maybe it had left with Kris.

His comm unit vibrated on the desk and he grabbed it.

"Kris?"

"No. Again." It was Jack. "Our guys on Level 6 seem to be moving pretty good. They didn't take out a main distribution point this time. I figure the security was too high. They hit a local substation on Level 7. Blew it to the ceiling."

"There is no ceiling on Level 7. Besides, the plan was to cripple them, not us," Kai responded. "SoCal is turning off water to the lower levels. I have not had any for quite a while."

"Anything they do can help us. You know that. I'm already hearing of protesters trying to tear down the fences around the water stations. The people are fighting back!"

"Against what? Police? Military? Unarmed civilians against people with guns. The plan was to start talking. Start equalizing the levels."

"You're an old man, Kai. Old and stupid. That may have been your plan, but it was never ours. I've already got teams out there. The protesters aren't as helpless as you think. We're building an army. SoCal will have to fight on two fronts now."

Kai slumped back into his chair. Had he been that blind?

"If I don't know you're with us, I won't be calling anymore," Jack said.

Kai sighed. "People—honest, hardworking, innocent people—will die."

"Yeah, war does that. But so will the scum that treat us like dogs."

The comm unit went quiet for a while.

"Are you with us, Kai, or are you out?"

The silence lasted a few seconds more. Kai felt a rush of heat course through him. Was this the way it was going to be? Never mind a corporate war, this was going to be a civil one as well. The armed against the defenseless. The rich against the poor.

"Keep me in the loop," he whispered into the comm unit. "Just keep me in the loop."

LOS ANGELES, LEVEL 5—MONDAY, JUNE 12, 2141 5:12 P.M.

The trucks labored up the ramp to Level 5 as it cut through the interlevel floor, the sloshing water in the tank below me making it wobble slightly on its suspension. I wanted to get off here, but if I did, there was no place to run. If I didn't fall under the tires of the water truck, I'd end up standing there, stuck with a fibercrete wall at my back.

I'd have to wait until the truck exited the ramp and go before the level roads allowed them to pick up speed.

I stayed where I was, clinging to the grating of the catwalk, feeling every bump in the road through my jacket and in my chest. I couldn't be here when we reached Level 6 security. That much I knew. I wouldn't have a chance to get away.

I gave Oscar a quick rub through my pocket for luck, and waited.

The sound of the lead truck changed as it left the ramp and entered level road. It was now or never. I threw myself over the right side of the truck, out of view of the driver, hanging from the catwalk by my fingertips. I was higher off the ground than I'd thought I would be, and I gripped the catwalk tighter.

The truck leveled off. I took one last look at the dual rear tires over the bulge of the tank and let go, trying to push off with my feet at the same time. I hit the ground flat on my back, pulling my legs in just before the rear wheels passed. Something in my chest burned, and I could hardly breathe.

I rolled onto my hands and knees, sucking in huge mouthfuls of air filled with dust thrown up by the passing vehicles, trying to cough and breathe at the same time. The burn in my chest bloomed into a deep pain. It took more than a few minutes before I was able to crawl away from the side of the road and lie down slowly on a dirt-covered boulevard.

As I lay there, two people walked by. The woman moved her bags to her other hand, farther away from me, and the man stepped in between us. I heard them mutter under their breath.

"Low-level trash. Why do they bother to come up here. They'll only be taken back."

They were gone before I moved again. Even here, below Level 6, I was still considered trash.

Struggling to my feet, I managed to get most of the road dust off of me, pulling in a breath and holding it before I dared move my arms to sweep the dust off. The pain flared at each movement, just above my bottom rib on the right side. I definitely did some damage when I jumped off the truck. I explored the area with my fingers, gently probing the bone, but I couldn't feel anything. The pain persisted. I gingerly zipped up my coat and walked away from the ramp.

I had to figure out where I was first, then find my way to the greenhouses. Ignoring the sharp pain as best I could, I walked until I found a drugstore and asked.

Luck had almost worked perfectly for me. Ian would have said there was no such thing as luck, but I'd managed to move north as I walked on Level 2, and the trucks had done a fair amount of work as well. The problem was, I'd gone past the greenhouses—too far east.

On the way out of the store, I managed to pocket an elastic wrapping bandage, telling myself I'd be back when I could pay for it. I moved into the lot behind the store, took off my jacket, and stretched the bandage over my ribs and back. The extra support seemed to help right away, with the added benefit of closing the cut Kai had made on the back of my shirt. I reached for my jacket and saw the taser; its casing had shattered and I could see the electronics inside. A board had cracked in half. I threw the weapon away in disgust, sending another jolt of fire into my ribs.

Following the instructions I'd gotten from the store employee, I crossed the street, heading to a major intersection only a few blocks away. From there, it was pretty much a straight run to the greenhouses, if a long one. Each step shot pain through my ribs. My pace was too slow. I wouldn't reach my bike before the Ambients had dimmed for the night. I figured I would try to hitch a ride somehow, otherwise it would take me hours to walk. No more water trucks for me, though.

I only had to wait about twenty minutes before someone stopped. The driver was an older lady wearing a dress that looked like it had gone out of fashion a decade ago, not that I knew anything about fashion. She was sweet and concerned. What was a young lady like me doing walking down the street trying to get a ride? Sure, this was Level 5, but sometimes people came up from Level 2 or even Level 1 to prey on girls walking alone. She went on for so long about it, I started thinking that maybe she was one of those people. The car was in too good a shape for that, though.

She apologized at least a thousand times that she couldn't take me all the way to the greenhouses. Her friends were expecting her, and she was already late.

When I got out of the car, I could smell the greenhouses. The air felt cleaner, and the noises of the city seemed to fade into the background. Ten minutes later, I saw the first garden, and my worries seemed to melt away.

I cut through the first public greenhouse to get to where Pat and I had left the bike. This one held large green bushes with yellow flowers and plants with purple and green leaves. The urge to stay, to sit for a while and just pretend I had a normal life, filled me. A bench nestled in a cranny created by roses climbing a trellis called out to me. The moment I stopped, I felt as though I was being watched. I couldn't see anybody. I left the greenhouse, heading toward my bike, keeping an eye out for anyone following me.

The bike battery still had a good charge. The ache in my ribs was getting worse. I needed someone to look at it, and the only doctor I knew was Doc Searls on Level 6. Getting there would be a hell of a risk, though. I started the bike and drove off, heading to Doc Searls' office. I knew he was ACE, that I shouldn't really trust him, but I had nowhere else to go.

I wasn't going back to Kai.

======

LOS ANGELES, LEVEL 5—MONDAY, JUNE 12, 2141 6:04 P.M.

The closer I get to the Level 6 up-ramp, the more I want to just run and hide. I swallow the dread that builds in me. We'd simulated doing this hundreds of times at the training compound—but this was real.

Normally, if they decided to not let you through, security would just turn you away and flag your name and ID in the computers so you couldn't get through somewhere else. This wasn't normal. The corporations were fighting, the people rebelling. It wasn't a great time to test my new skills.

I pulled over a block before the up-ramp and struggled to get Pat's comm unit from my pocket. The pain from my ribs hampered my movements. The code unlocked the comm unit and I started the app to change my tracker ID, picking the identification of a standard courier with Level 6 and 7 access. Stick with what you know.

The lineup for Level 6 was short. If it was much longer, I wasn't sure I would have been able to stick it out. It didn't give me much time to hide the fear and pain written all over my face. As I rode up to security, I could feel them scanning me, stripping away what I presented to them to find my true identity.

The questions were routine, just as we'd practiced. They took a quick look into the carryall and asked me why I dressed so badly. I convinced them I did it to blend in when I did lower level deliveries. Before I knew it, I was through. It had taken Ian longer to get past them last year when I was hiding under the rear seat.

I rode up the ramp, careful not to show how relieved I was. That would have to wait until I was farther away.

The ride to Doc Searls' gated community wasn't fun. Every bump in the road vibrated through my arms and into my ribs. I ended up leaning back and steering with my fingertips. It helped a bit, but when I needed to brake, I had to lean forward, and all my weight shifting made my ribs flare again.

Getting into the place was easier than I thought. Cars were going in and out in a fairly steady flow. All I needed was the right timing. A light blue family van had just finished entering the gate code when I accelerated. I rode through with my front tire even with their back one. The gate slammed shut behind me.

The driver of the car, a frustrated looking man with three kids in the back seat, didn't even notice I was there. The kids waved at me, and I waved back. I kept on going and passed him in the first block.

I ended up doing the same thing Ian had when we were here last year. I drove by the parking lot nice and slow, watching the building. Everything looked normal, but then it had last time as well. I pulled a U-turn at the next intersection and angled in, parking in the rear lot right next to the door. I didn't find an outlet to plug into, but my charge still wasn't too bad.

I waited until someone else, some guy in a suit and tie, walked through the entrance and then followed him. I wasn't sure I could have pulled the door open myself. I grabbed the elevator and went to the second floor. It opened to the reception area, as deserted as it had been last time I was here.

I heard a door shut down the left hallway, so I took it and listened at each examining room. A chair squeaked from the third one. I knocked and walked in.

"Hey, Doc," I said.

Doc Searls, old and a bit overweight, with thin wireframe glasses perched on the tip of his nose, looked up from his paperwork. "How did you . . ." His voice trailed off as the recognition sunk in. "Kris, isn't it?" He had worked on me last year when the black box had melted into my skin.

I nodded and closed the door behind me.

"How did you get in?" he asked. "The stairway doors lock automatically at five, and the elevator should refuse to open on this floor."

"The elevator." I sat in the only remaining chair and grimaced.

"I'll get them to fix that." He stood and came over to me. "I usually get a call when someone's coming in, is Miller with you?"

"I'm kinda off the record," I said, shaking my head.

He raised a single eyebrow and waited. I wasn't sure what I could tell him and what I couldn't. He was an ACE employee, and had been for a long time. Ian had trusted him, but could I?

Doc Searls stood and placed his hand on my shoulder, lifting my chin to look into my eyes. "Your secrets are safe with me. If ACE doesn't know you're here, then neither do I."

I don't know if it was the tone of his voice, or the look on his face, but I felt I had to talk to somebody that wasn't Kai or Pat. Someone that was . . . separate from everything that was happening. But I couldn't tell him everything.

By the time I finished giving him the highlights of how I'd gotten here, he was back in his seat playing with his pen. He stood again and motioned for me to get on the examining table. I took off my coat with his help.

"You took a hell of a risk coming here," he said, removing the elastic wrap and lifting my shirt to expose my ribs. He didn't ask why the shirt was cut open along the back. His probing fingers brought a sharp gasp from me. "It doesn't feel broken, but I'll have to do an X-ray to make sure. Come on, follow me."

I carefully slid off the table and grabbed my jacket, holding my billowing shirt close to my chest with the other hand.

"Leave it, we'll come back here."

Once he had me set up and left the room to take the X-ray, I almost panicked. I couldn't see him. Was he calling ACE? Was he turning me in? I struggled to maintain control.

He was back before I could decide to leave, no more than a few seconds later.

"Come on. We can see the X-ray on the viewscreen in my office."

As promised, we ended up back in the same examining room. It must have doubled as his office.

He touched the viewscreen and pulled up my image. "It looks like you have a hairline fracture from your impact. It's not completely broken. Sit down on the table and lift your shirt for me. I'll repair the fracture and wrap you back up. By tomorrow, you'll be as good as new. This will hurt a bit."

I did as he asked, and he ran a sterilization wand over my ribs before applying a cold gel. I jerked away, sending a new flare through my ribs. He turned his back and filled a syringe.

"This will heal the bone. I'll have to inject some behind the rib as well. That's the one that will hurt, so hold still. When I'm done, it'll feel warm for about ten minutes or so."

The pain of the needle was less than what I'd felt after my jump. When he was done he put a clean wrap around my ribs. I put my coat back on with his help.

"Anything else I can do while you're here?"

I hesitated before telling him about feeling sick almost every morning. I'd become so used to hiding it from everyone at the compound.

"Any fever at the same time? Pain or balance issues?"

I shook my head at each question.

Doc Searls thought for a while. "Have your periods stopped?"

I had to think back. "I don't know, maybe a month, a month and a half ago?"

"Hmm. Miller was on Vanspeterol, but nothing's perfect. I'll draw some blood and check your hCG levels. We should have an answer tomorrow morning . . . I don't have the equipment to test here."

Suddenly, I was more scared than I'd ever been.

"I don't know how to thank you," I said.

It was obvious he knew about Miller and I.

The doctor sat on the edge of his desk staring at me thoughtfully. "I do," he finally said. "I have a confession to make. ACE has been doing some—off—things lately. None of it directly affecting me, but I meet a lot of different people, all with different stories. Those stories add up to something being . . . something *having* gone wrong. There's a rot at the core of ACE. Has been since you came in here last year. I don't know what it is, but I don't trust it. Enough to keep what I'm about to tell you away from them." He leaned forward. "You owe me for what I did today. I'm asking for that favor to be repaid. Now."

"What do you mean a rot?" I didn't care what the favor was. I just wanted to know if I'd wasted the last year of my life. If I'd put my trust, my faith, in the wrong thing.

"You know what I mean. You've seen it. Your classmate turning on you. William in the area. The attack on a secret compound. You've put the pieces together. You're beginning to see what I've seen."

As he was talking, I nodded. Things weren't adding up, and hadn't been since I woke up yesterday. Now with Kai telling me what he knew, and Doc Searls basically confirming it, I was beginning to believe it as well.

"What's the favor?"

"My son, Bryson, is in Los Angeles, on Level 4. I want you to go get him and bring him to me on Level 5."

"That's it?" I asked.

"That's it."

It sounded too simple. "What's the catch?"

"Ah. The catch. Well. Kadokawa wants him."

"Why?"

"That I can't say. But they want him bad. A few of the other corporations may want him as well."

I sighed. What was he hiding from me, and why? I'd trusted him, but he couldn't do the same in return. "Do they know where he is?"

"We don't think so. But . . ."

"But?" My stomach twisted. This was sounding like a pretty big favor.

"His tracker is still active. By the time I knew about trackers, he was already gone, working for Meridian. I saw him briefly when Miller . . . when Miller saved his life. We never deactivated it. I didn't want to scare him, so I didn't tell him about it when he called. I just told him not to go outside."

Shit. That meant any corporation knew where Bryson was, and I might be walking into an all-out battle. "I don't know if I can do this. I—"

"We don't have anyone else. You know why I don't trust ACE. I've been trying to reach Miller, but . . ."

"Yeah. But." I thought about it for two seconds. "I'll do it, but you need to be here for me."

"What do you mean?"

"If . . ." I paused. "*When* I get Miller, he'll probably need medical attention. I need to know I can bring him to you."

Doc Searls didn't hesitate. "Of course you can. I owe him, and after this, I'll owe you as well."

So if I did this, not only would my favor be wiped clean, but the doc would owe me one. "Okay, where is he and do you have any blockers?"

Ten minutes later, I walked out of his office with a blocker and instructions on where I could find Bryson. I also got the address of his new offices on Level 5.

I charged the bike from my jacket before I left. I wanted to make sure I wouldn't run out of juice. The jacket was useless to me until I plugged it back in, but that was better than not being able to get away.

I left Doc's parking lot and turned left, back to the gates. I had a few kilometers to go before I got to Bryson.

CHAPTER 11

UNKNOWN

MILLER PULLED HIMSELF from his stupor when the door opened. How much time had passed since he had gotten free? How much time since he had realized there was no way out of this room? He had fallen in and out of consciousness, leaning against the wall beside the door. The drywall felt cold against his back, and he shivered.

During the long wait he had forced his mind to think, and it had worked for a while. Until it didn't. The first time he had jerked awake, he had convinced himself it was just a fluke. He crawled back to the water hose and drank his fill, before holding it over his head until he could hardly breathe. The cold water helped keep him awake for a while. The second time he fell asleep, he had realized he was fucked.

His shoulder hurt less, but he knew even if the door was open, he'd spent so long strapped to the wire frame that he no longer had the strength to get out. A child could have stopped him.

He blinked in the sudden light coming from the door. A tall silhouette blocked some of it. Jeremy.

"You surprise me, Miller. I can see why William is so fond of you, and why he is so upset with me. You must have been a formidable agent. Of course, I'd heard of you, heard of your exploits. And you did manage to take out Abby. But to see you here, off the parrilla, is astounding to say the least. If we had met under different circumstances, I'm sure we could have been . . . colleagues."

Miller just grunted and struggled to get to his feet. He almost made it when his legs gave way, and he collapsed back to the floor. The pain from landing on his shoulder threatened to send him spiraling back into oblivion. Miller fought it with everything he had, staring at Jeremy, feeling the hatred gather in his chest like a disease.

Jeremy stepped out of the doorway.

"Freedom lies outside that door," he said. "Would you like to see it? You have to get there yourself."

Miller knew it was a lie. He knew it in his heart, he knew it in his mind, yet his body betrayed him. His arms and legs moved of their own accord, dragging his carcass toward the bright rectangle of light, the carpet tearing flaps of skin from his burns.

"Here, let me help you stand, at least." Jeremy reached down and grabbed Miller's shoulder. His thumb dug in, and his fingers twisted. Miller screamed. "It looks like you've hurt it somehow. I don't understand it, really. I did everything I could to keep you comfortable." Jeremy laughed and straightened up. He pushed Miller away from the door with his foot and closed it.

Miller watched with half-closed eyes as Jeremy walked to the back of the room and put his rubber boots on. The sound of the metal rack being dragged across the floor sent Miller into a dizzy spiral of despair. He was pulled from it when Jeremy grabbed him under the arms and pulled him onto the rack, expertly tying him down. Miller lay on top of the mesh frame, more helpless than he was before.

Jeremy turned the hose on him, washing out the crud that had entered Miller's burns as he crawled around.

When he was done, he smiled and left the room.

LOS ANGELES, LEVEL 2—MONDAY, JUNE 12, 2141 6:11 P.M.

Pat rose out of her sleep like a drowning victim hauling herself out of a fast-moving river. For every breath of reality she pulled in, the current threatened to suck her beneath its whorling surface. Eventually she opened her eyes, images of a little girl still etched onto her retinas. Something kept pushing at her, urging her to get up. A low regular noise that rattled her brain.

She got out of the cot and leaned on the shelving units for support before making her way to the open doorway. She had no recollection of getting here, though she vaguely remembered Kris staying by her side.

The restaurant and hallway were dark, but a small sliver of light crept out from under the curtain to the office, or as Pat had started calling it, the operating room. She teetered across the hallway and pushed the curtain aside.

Kai was asleep in his chair, his head lolled back over the top. He was snoring, a long low gurgle followed by a snort that could wake the dead: the sound that had pulled Pat from her sleep. She walked around the chair and tapped Kai on the knee. He woke with a start, his mouth snapping shut in a loud click of teeth.

"Wha? Pat? Is Kris back?" He rubbed sleep from his eyes.

"I was just going to ask you where she was."

"I do not know. I . . . I told her everything I knew about her parents. I do not know if she believed me or not, but she left."

"Was she mad? Upset?"

"No," Kai said softly. "More sad. I am not sure how much she believed."

"Shit. Do we have any way of tracking her?"

Kai shook his head. "You know better than that. She has control of her tracker. If she does not want to be found, she will not be. Not that way. We might be able to track her by cameras in the city, but she is smarter than that."

Pat exhaled. It was all true. Not only did Kris have control of her tracker, she knew this part of the city like it was her own backyard. Hell, it was. Pat scraped her tongue with her teeth, the residue of sleep and nightmares coating it like the dirt on the streets. Her mouth felt chalky, and she couldn't swallow. "I could use some water."

Kai nodded and stood. "SoCal turned it back on for a while. I managed to fill most of my pots and pans."

"Turned it back on?"

Kai nodded again as he shuffled to the curtain. "There have been some attacks on water distribution stations on Levels 6 and 7. SoCal has been draining us dry, hauling our water up to those who can pay for it."

"And everyone's just standing by, letting it happen?"

"They were, for a while. Oh, they protested and threw rocks, but then the military came. Once that happened, people started getting guns. It has not been pretty."

Pat followed Kai out. He pulled the curtain across the door after them, leaving the hallway in darkness. "Some who have guns are not good people. If they know we are in here, they will assume we have food and water. We would not last a minute against guns."

In the semi darkness, Kai pulled a glass from the shelf and dipped it in a container. He handed the glass to Pat. The water was room temperature, tepid, but Pat didn't care.

"Can I have another one?" she asked.

Kai pulled the glass from her hand and filled it again. She drank it more slowly this time.

"Where did the guns come from?" SoCal didn't like weapons in the hands of ordinary citizens, and controlled what was out there.

"There is a group, they have been collecting weapons for a few years, waiting for a time they could use them."

"They're behind the attacks?"

Kai nodded in the dark.

"You work for them?"

Another quick nod.

"Use words dammit, I can barely see you."

Kai grabbed her hand and led her back to the office. "Yes," he said. "To both questions. ACE had killed the only people I knew. That I loved. I was angry at them. But even more at myself. I heard about the insurgents. This time I did my homework. These people are the real deal. No offices, no directors, and they have groups in almost every major city. I joined them, and we started throwing around stupid plans, things that would never work. The water stations were my idea, though I did not think they would be able to pull it off."

"And the guns?" Pat prompted.

"I did not know about those. Did not know they planned a civil war."

"They'll lose."

"I know that. You know that. They believe they have a chance, with the corporations fighting amongst themselves." Kai shook his head.

"So what do we do?"

"We sit. We wait for Kris. Pray that she makes it back to us."

"I don't know if I can do that."

Kai shrugged. "We do not have much choice. We do not know where she is."

LOS ANGELES, LEVEL 4—MONDAY, JUNE 12, 2141 6:28 P.M.

Bryson lay on the bed again, the memory chip still clutched in his fist and his entire body aching. He wasn't sure why he had called his dad. They hadn't really gotten along since Bryson had signed up with Meridian. Maybe it was what a son did when he had nowhere else to turn. Back to home. Back to family.

His dad had always said there had to be a better way, something better than the corporations. The thing was, there wasn't. Not for Bryson. No one had the cash flow he needed to continue his experiments. No one except the corporations, even a smaller one like Meridian. They had poured billions into his lab, and he had spent every penny, like a spoiled child eating candy on Halloween.

When Kadokawa had taken over, the money hadn't stopped. If anything, it had increased. But everything had changed. People started wanting to leave. They were refused. Communication with Earthside had stopped altogether. Wives weren't allowed to talk to husbands, nor sons to mothers. The lab had become a prison.

In the end, Bryson had realized his dad was right. The corporations wanted complete and absolute control, and they didn't care what it took to get it. Only now that he had finally escaped did Bryson realize that Meridian had done the same as Kadokawa. They hadn't been as forceful about it; no one had been hurt, as far as he knew, except for the test crew. Before that happened, Bryson wasn't sure he would have really cared, especially in the early years. He had his work. They all did, and they all immersed themselves in it so completely, they were blind to what was really happening.

When the three men from the first trip started showing Alzheimer's-like symptoms, Bryson had begun to wake up. By then it was too late.

He pushed himself to a sitting position and swung his legs over the bed. Every part of him ached. He wanted to step out and buy some painkillers, but even the thought of leaving the safety of his room sent a wave of fear through him. He didn't have any money anyway, the mugger had stolen his comm unit. Instead, he grabbed his water glass off the nightstand and slowly stood up.

The gate outside squeaked as it was opened. Normally, he could hear footsteps as people came up the stairs. If there was more than one, he could hear them talking through the thin glass in the window. This time he heard nothing.

He held his breath and stared at the door. Was that a flicker of shadow under the curtains? Had he heard the gate close again? Bryson shook his head. He was getting paranoid. Kadokawa had no idea where he was. Yesterday's attack had been a stupid mugging, nothing more. He had just been in the wrong place at the wrong time.

Bryson baby-stepped to the bathroom to fill his water glass, hunger gnawing at his gut. The door behind him burst open. Splintered wood flew across the room, stopping only when it hit the back wall. Bryson pivoted, his pain forgotten. Two men came through the door, guns drawn, faces hidden behind masks, dark eyes glittering in anticipation.

The cup slipped from his fingers. Bryson didn't feel the shards of glass hit his pants as it shattered on the floor.

They put away their guns, grabbing his arms and dragging him through the wrecked door. His back exploded in agony when his spine twisted. They didn't care.

The balcony was empty. The gate at the bottom of the stairs stood open. A black car was parked on the street, blocking the driveway's entrance. One of the men let go, heading down the stairs first. The second man gripped Bryson's arm tighter and pushed him ahead.

The gate squealed when it shut behind them.

Bryson glanced toward the manager's office. Inside, a man stood with his back to the window, probably paid to not look outside.

Once Bryson was on the driveway, he fought back, twisting his arm, loosening the grip only slightly. A fist punched into his kidney. His legs buckled. He fell, knees hitting the driveway, pulling his captor with him. They tumbled in a heap. Bryson clawed his way out from under the man.

A motorcycle whipped between the black car and the hotel.

LOS ANGELES, LEVEL 4—MONDAY, JUNE 12, 2141 6:29 P.M.

I rode past the Hotel Ruby, following an old man driving so slow I thought he was almost about to stop. It was perfect.

A black car was parked across the driveway leading to the hotel parking. A gate to the second-floor balcony stood open. As I passed the hood of the black car, three men stepped out of a room on the second floor. The two outside men were holding onto the middle one as if their lives depended on it. The one in the middle fit Bryson's description.

This had just gone from a simple pickup to a rescue.

My mouth went dry and suddenly every sound, every nuance of

the street came to the forefront. I wasn't ready for this. I didn't have any weapons. I hadn't finished my training. What the fuck was I supposed to do? I didn't have time to think either. Twisting the accelerator, I sped past the old man and whipped toward an alley, turning onto the sidewalk.

If there were more than two men, if there was one in the car, I was in big trouble.

I sped down the narrow strip between the buildings and the parked cars. My timing was as close to perfect as I could have hoped for. I locked the back brakes and shifted my weight, sliding the tail end of the bike out into a circle, hitting the first man as he was reaching to open the car door. He flopped over the carryall behind me like a sack of garbage. I knew without looking back that he wasn't going to be able to walk for a while.

The impact stopped my slide and I twisted the accelerator again, leaving a black half circle on the driveway. Bryson and the other man were down. I leaned over and grabbed the back of Bryson's collar, helping him to his feet.

"Get on."

It felt like he stood there for an eternity before swinging his leg over the bike and slipping between me and the carryall. I'd have to get rid of that damn thing. I zipped between the black car and hotel, speeding down the street.

Ian had rescued me last year on his bike, and here I was doing the same thing for someone else. Only this was different. Ian had a plan, he had experience. He had ACE.

Bryson and I had nothing.

I leaned the bike over, turning and racing between two oncoming cars. Bryson shifted his weight and the bike wobbled and veered closer to the moving vehicles. Shit. I had an inexperienced rider to boot.

I yelled over my shoulder. "Don't fucking move. Just sit still, no matter what the bike does." I had no clue if he heard me or not.

Bryson still had an active tracker. I'd have to find somewhere to stop and get the blocker on him. I slowed down to regular traffic speed, looking for a spot to pull over. Somewhere we wouldn't be boxed in.

A black car squealed its tires around a corner and pulled up beside us, driving head-on into traffic flowing in the other direction. He swerved toward us. I twitched the bike into the other track and kicked out at his door.

There was only one guy in the car. If this was the same one I'd seen at the hotel, then he'd left his buddy behind.

The driver swerved again, coming completely into my lane. We were riding the fine line between the parked cars and him. I grabbed my brakes and the black car raced ahead a full car length before slamming on his. It was all I needed. Pulling a U-turn, I flew along the yellow line separating the different directions of traffic and slid in between two cars, darting down a side street.

All of this was pointless if we couldn't turn off that damn tracker.

I kept going, aiming for the Level 5 up-ramp, not bothering to try to lose anyone following us. It didn't matter anyway.

I saw a chance up ahead; a delivery truck was parked by the curb. I jumped the small barrier up to the sidewalk and stopped as close to the middle of the truck as possible, hugging its side. I put out the kickstand and got off the bike.

"Why are we stopping?" There was a solid layer of panic in Bryson's voice, and he kept looking behind us.

"They can track you. We need to block the signal, or we'll never lose them."

"They . . . they put a tracker on me? Where?"

"Not on you, *in* you. It's been there since you were a baby. Now lean forward and lift up your shirt. All the way to your neck." I popped open the carryall and got out the blocker, peeling off the backing to expose the adhesive. Bryson did as he was told. This was a guy that was used to following orders.

His lower back was a massive bruise, as though someone had kicked him while he was down. I pressed the blocker in between his shoulder blades, exactly where mine had been, and pulled down his shirt. Now was the time to start doubling back to make sure we weren't followed.

The first thing I would do was head away from Level 5. They'd expect us to continue our route after they lost his signal. I hoped so anyway. Even if they didn't, they probably had eyes on the doc by now.

I slid back onto the bike, pushing Bryson as far back on the seat as he would go.

"Hang on. This might get a little rough," I said. "And for fuck's sake, don't shift around on the seat when we're in a corner. Or ever, for that matter."

I maneuvered the bike back on the road, cut across a side street, and started heading down to Level 2. Kai wouldn't be happy. Too bad. I wasn't about to head back to Doc Searls' office. Not right away.

I rode back down to Level 2. I had nowhere else to go.

CHAPTER 12

LOS ANGELES, LEVEL 2—MONDAY, JUNE 12, 2141 6:51 P.M.

BRYSON STRUGGLED TO GET OFF the motorcycle, his foot snagging on the seat, forcing him to hop as he tried to lift it high enough. He almost slipped and fell in the Level 2 filth. His body ached in places he didn't think *could* hurt.

How did Kadokawa find him? Could the tracker the girl and his dad told him about be real? At least he assumed it was Kadokawa. If he *was* being tracked, it could have been anybody. Knowing that didn't make him feel any better.

He watched the girl who had rescued him kick at the back door of a building and wait. When no one answered, she hoofed at it again.

Could he trust her? Sure, she had taken him away from the men at the hotel, but he didn't know her. He didn't even know her name.

That she was short and feisty were the only things he knew for sure. Maybe it would be best if he walked away.

Just as the thought entered his head, the back door opened. A taller woman launched from the doorway and grabbed the smaller one in a bear hug while an older Asian man stood in the background. Bryson's first instinct was to run. Asian meant Kadokawa. Before he could make up his mind, the short girl had grabbed his arm and dragged him inside. The door thudded closed behind him.

"Who is he?" asked the old man.

The short girl hesitated before answering. "Bryson Searls," she said. "Meet Kai and Pat. I'm Kris." She turned to face the other two. "I had some problems getting to my bike, and Doc Searls patched me up. Getting this guy was the return favor."

At the mention of Bryson's name, the Asian guy, Kai, looked at Bryson as if he recognized him.

"You went to an *ACE* doctor?" Pat cringed as she asked the question.

Bryson began to breathe a bit easier. Apparently his rescuer had been sent by his dad. Why hadn't she just said that earlier, like when she'd put the patch on his back?

Kai glanced at Bryson and slowly approached Kris, almost like he was scared of her. "Are you hurt? Let me see."

She backed away a step and Kai stopped. Bryson slumped against the wall. There was something going on between those two, but he really didn't care to know what it was. His life was already messed up.

"I'm fine. I don't know about him, though," Kris said.

"I was mugged yesterday, out by the hotel. One of the guys who grabbed me hit me where I'd been kicked."

Kai put his shoulder under Bryson's arm and started walking him to the office. "I can look at that."

"You a doctor?" Bryson asked.

"When I need to be. Mostly I am a cook."

Bryson missed a step and stumbled. Kai took more of his weight, leading him to a table by the side wall. The two women stayed out in the hallway by the door. He could hear them whispering to each other. Kai glanced at the hallway once or twice, but didn't join them.

"Where does it hurt?" Kai asked.

"The mugger kicked me in the ribs and back. Then one of the guys who tried to abduct me punched me in the kidneys."

"Okay. Take off your shirt and lie on your side, let me see your back first."

Bryson did as he was told and gasped when Kai's fingers started probing the bruises.

"Sorry. Let me see your front."

After a bit more poking and prodding Bryson had had enough. He sat up and hung his feet off the side of the table.

Kai took a step back. "You have got some pretty bad bruising, and you may be peeing blood for a couple of days, but other than that, you are fine. The cut on your face should heal by itself."

"So I can go?"

"I am not stopping you. But you may have a tough time getting past Kris." Kai moved to his desk and grabbed a bottle out of the drawer, removing its lid. He shook a couple of pills into Bryson's hand. "This is for the pain and to help relax your muscles. Do not drive any big machines after taking these." Kai grinned.

Bryson looked at the pills and threw them into his mouth, dry swallowing both of them at once.

"Wait here," Kai said. "I go get her."

The last thing Bryson remembered was Kai reaching for him.

LOS ANGELES, LEVEL 2—MONDAY, JUNE 12, 2141 7:05 P.M.

Pat and Kris sat on the cot in the storage room. As Kris leaned against the back wall, Pat saw her tense up for a split-second before she relaxed.

"Are you okay?" Pat asked.

"Yeah. The doctor said I wouldn't even be able to feel it tomorrow."

"Tell me what happened."

Kris told the story of getting to the greenhouses and into Doc Searls' offices. She had just finished giving Pat her comm unit back when Kai walked in the room.

"You left him alone?" Pat pushed herself to her feet.

"He is out cold. I gave him some pills, told him it was for pain. He will be out for hours." He looked at Kris. "You brought in some-one very important, all the corporations want him."

"Who is he?" Pat asked.

"Bryson Searls is the inventor of the quantum jump drive," Kai replied. "His invention is the reason the corporations are willing to go to war again."

"How do you know?" Kris asked.

"The insurgents. Although I usually only deal with a local group, they are scattered throughout San Angeles. They are not as large as ACE, or as organized, but they have sources."

"I'm bringing him back to his dad, not giving him to the insurgents."

Kai pulled his hand from his pocket, holding a memory chip between his finger and thumb. "This may be all we need. I put a special chip in its place, with a heavily encoded virus on it. If anyone breaks the code, their whole network will be infected."

"What's on it?" Pat asked.

Kai shrugged.

When Pat sat back down, silence filled the room. Kai stayed standing in the doorway, playing with the chip in his pocket. He looked at Kris without saying anything.

"Look," Kris said, finally breaking the silence. "Whatever happened in the past, it's something I can't think about right now. I have one goal, and that's to get Ian. No matter where he is, or who has him. I was hoping ACE could help me out, but I'm not sure anymore." She glanced quickly at Kai. "But I have to find out. If ACE is what you say they are, then William being there when Janice attacked us wasn't just a fluke. It could also mean that ACE has Ian. I have no idea why, and right now, I don't care."

"So, what do you want to do?" Pat asked.

"I want to talk to William and—"

"That is dangerous move," Kai interrupted. "He is a very difficult man to get alone."

"I don't care. I'll figure out something."

"We," Pat said. "We'll figure out something. That's the only way this is going to work." If Kris thought she was going to do this alone, she didn't know her friends.

Kris smiled and leaned her head against the wall.

"That is right," Kai said. "We. The insurgents can help us."

Without opening her eyes, Kris replied. "Like the two idiots in the car that picked us up? They couldn't pick theirs twins out of a lineup."

"That was an emergency. I did the best I could."

"You could have left us alone." Kris looked like she regretted raising her voice the moment she saw Kai's reaction. He was only trying to help. She pushed on anyway. "We could have made it out ourselves."

"I know you could have. I was . . . I was worried. I wanted to help." He sighed, looking at the floor instead of at Kris. "I am sorry."

"Instead of being sorry, help me get to William."

Kai exchanged a look with Pat. "That we can do."

Pat left the cot and moved to the middle of the floor, leaving Kris behind. As Kai moved to join her, she saw Kris slowly slide down the wall and lift her feet off the floor. Before Kai was even able to say anything, Kris's breathing deepened. Good, she needed it. Tomorrow would be another long day. She huddled with Kai on the floor, tossing ideas back and forth. Eventually he left and grabbed some paper from his office.

By morning, they knew what they were going to do.

LOS ANGELES, LEVEL 2—TUESDAY, JUNE 13, 2141 7:15 A.M.

I woke up with someone shaking my shoulder. I pulled away at first, dragging the blanket up to cover my face. Blanket? I didn't recall having one, or even falling asleep, really. The events from the day before crashed into me and I sat up, rubbing the sleep from my eyes.

Pat sat on the edge of the cot, a cup of hot coffee in her hands.

"Kai covered the windows with menus and tape," she said. "No one can see in now, so I made us some breakfast and coffee. It's the first time I've scrambled eggs in a wok." She tried to smile, as though to cover up her concern for me.

At the word coffee, the aroma filled my senses. It was all I could do not to grab the cup and slurp up the life-giving nectar. I burned my lips on the hot liquid.

"Easy there, slugger. I don't know how to cook cold," Pat laughed. "What is it with you and coffee? You were the same back at the compound."

I didn't answer her, slowly sipping the coffee instead. Pat eased the cup out of my hands and put it on the floor. "Maybe some food as well?" she asked.

Someone had brought in the plastic table and chairs from the front of the restaurant. A plate of food sat on the tabletop, still steaming in the cool room. I picked up my coffee cup and sat in one of the chairs, staring at the food. I didn't mind the smell of the eggs, but the texture in my mouth made me want to puke. I ate what I could before shoving the plate away.

Pat frowned. "Is everything okay?"

"I haven't been feeling well in the mornings. Nothing to worry about."

Pat raised her eyebrows at me.

"What?"

"Nothing," she said. "We'll talk about it later."

With a partial breakfast in my stomach and a third cup of coffee in my hand, I almost felt human, though I would have killed for a shower. The thought was barely formed in my head before I felt a wave of shame. Killing wasn't something to be done lightly, if at all. I knew that. Experience had taught me that.

"Where's Kai and Bryson?" I asked.

"Kai's trying to clean up after breakfast. They turned the water on for a while this morning, but it's off again. Bryson still hasn't woken up. I imagine he's going to be pretty pissed off when he does. Besides making breakfast, Kai and I came up with a plan for getting you in to see William. It's risky, and we need to bring in some outside help, but it could work."

I was about to ask her how when Kai walked in. He was smiling, carrying in a plate of food that he put on the table beside me before settling in the chair. It was almost as though everything was the same. Like this was just another evening I'd come into the restaurant, and we'd sit and chat about life. About everything. Not once had he mentioned how he knew my parents. That he had been there when they had died. It still didn't feel right that he had lied to me. I moved my chair farther away from him. His smile died.

If Pat noticed it, she didn't say anything. Instead, she started talking about the plan.

"Kai and I were up most of night, but we think we have it solved."

Kai laughed. "We? I listened to you and provided raw materials. You have got a great career ahead of you as a strategist."

I was pretty sure I saw Pat blush, something that I had never thought she was capable of. I almost teased her about it, but then I noticed something else. She was different this morning. Energized in a way I'd never seen before. As they started talking about the plan, I realized that she seemed more . . . complete. She'd enjoyed being a cook, but it was obvious she liked being in the action more. She couldn't be in the field anymore, she'd proven that when the transport crashed, and again at the greenhouses. But it was like she was whole again, planning, plotting, making things happen. It was good to see.

"Okay," Pat said. "ACE has a few locations on Level 4." She pulled a pad out of the pile and turned it on. "This is the building William is in, and this is another one of their closest assets. There's no way in hell you're getting in to see William if we don't create a distraction first. That's where some of Kai's people come in—"

"They are not *my* people. We sometimes work together."

Pat immediately looked contrite. "Right. Sorry. This is where the insurgents come in. Kai's worked with them in the past, and he figures they could help us out. A small group will plant explosives— nothing serious, just something to create a lot of smoke and make loud noises—around the second building. With the main building being the closest, ACE will have to send people out to check what is going on. At the very least, they'll be distracted, which will give us our opening. We can't just walk in the door and ask for William, so that's where the building across the street comes in. It's just an office building, nothing special about it as far as we can tell, except that it touches the ceiling, just like ACE's."

Kai pulled up building plans on his pad. "We get you to the top floor and go through a window to the ceiling. That will get you above the Ambients. You will climb along the girders until you get to ACE's building, lower yourself to a window, and break in from the top. We can get you right into William's office."

It almost sounded too easy.

"So, what's the catch?" I asked.

"Getting you out," Pat said. "They'll know the second you get inside. You won't have much time to question William. If he's in his office when you leave, once you're on the girders, you are pretty much trapped. Even just a lucky shot could drop you to ground level. There'd be no chance of surviving that."

"Then we'll have to move fast."

LOS ANGELES, LEVEL 2—TUESDAY, JUNE 13, 2141 8:17 A.M.

Bryson opened his eyes and stared at the ceiling. His fuzzy mind created images and patterns from the stains and shadows on it. A flowing river there, a quantum displacer in the corner, a bat flittering in the dark. He blinked and the images disappeared.

He was in a building on Level 2. Somewhere near or in China-town, he thought. The crazy ride yesterday, the failed abduction, the escape from his lab. It all came back at once, like a massive data dump. Bryson forced his legs over the edge of the bed and pushed himself off. He fell to the floor, holding in his gasp of surprise. The drop was farther than he had thought. As he stood, he knew why. He hadn't been on a bed; it was a table. He should have remembered that from earlier.

The old man had given him some pills for the pain. That was the last memory he could recall. They must have been more than that. He didn't even remember falling asleep or feeling drowsy, just waking up this morning. At least he assumed it was morning. For all he knew, he had been out for days. He jammed his hand into his pocket, feeling for the chip. His probing fingers felt it pressed into the fold at the bottom and he let out a sigh of relief. He still had all of his data.

Soft voices and the smell of cooking wafted through the curtained doorway, and he shuffled over. Once he was in the hallway, the voices became clear. He stopped and listened.

It was obvious they were planning something, and it sounded insane—climbing across the ceiling, lowering to windows with the help of ropes. His best guess was they were planning on breaking into a corporate tower of some sort. It didn't just sound insane, it *was* insane. A chair scraped across the floor, and Bryson slid along the wall until his back was against another door. This was the one he had come in through.

He was trying to get away from the corporations, not break into them. This wasn't someplace he wanted to be, or something he wanted to be part of. Kris, the small girl, was supposed to bring him to his dad. Instead he'd been brought here, drugged, and left feeling more like a prisoner than having been rescued. It was a feeling he knew all too well. He reached for the lock behind his back and slowly turned it. He was leaving this place, with the patch on his back, the one that supposedly stopped him from being tracked.

If he was untrackable, there was nothing stopping him from getting up to see his dad himself. The lock clicked open and Bryson stood still, his muscles vibrating. He was sure someone in the room had heard. The muted voices continued. He turned toward the door and opened it slowly, slipping out as soon as the gap was wide enough, and closed it softly behind him.

He was free, and he was going home. It had been a long time since he'd thought of seeing his dad as home.

Bryson didn't make it out of the alley to the street. Someone yanked his arm, pulling him farther into the shadows, and slammed him into the back wall of the building he had just left. Hands searched his pockets.

"I don't think he's one of them."

The pressure forcing him into the wall let up a bit, but they didn't let him go. A second person came up, dressed in black with a mask over her face and a nasty looking machine gun resting on her hip. She held a flashlight with a tight beam up to his face and scowled.

"He's not what we came for, but he is a bonus. We'll take him as well." She stepped closer. "Who else is in there?"

"I . . . I don't know."

The man holding him pulled him away from the wall and slammed him back into it.

"Who else is in there?" the woman asked again.

"Three people." The words tumbled out in a rush. "An old Asian guy, a young girl, and another woman. I don't know who they are."

The man pulled Bryson from the wall again.

"Wait! Wait, I know their first names. The old man is Kai, the girl is Kris . . . I think. I can't remember the woman's name."

The two people in black exchanged glances before the woman nodded. "Sounds right. Take Mr. Searls to the van and don't let him go. This one might end up being more important than the rest."

As soon as the woman said his name, all the fire and resistance bled from his body. If they knew who he was . . .

He didn't complete the thought before he was wrenched from

the wall and yanked down the alley to the street. A plain van was parked around the corner, farther from the building he had just left, its motor running and all the lights off. The back door was opened before he got there, and he was thrown in, landing in a heap near the front of the storage space. The door slammed shut behind him, leaving him in the dark.

<hr />

LOS ANGELES, LEVEL 2—TUESDAY, JUNE 13, 2141 8:20 A.M.

I watched quietly while Kai grabbed the plates from the table and left the room. We still hadn't said anything directly to each other.

"You've already lost your parents. Do you really want to lose a friend as well?" Pat asked.

Her abruptness took me by surprise. Pat was usually the kind of person to let people make their own decisions. She didn't like to interfere.

"We all have our demons, Kris. It's part of the job, part of our lives. I have to live with what I did in France, and what they did to me. You have to live with what happened to you last year. He has to live with his choices. Our actions, our choices, they all haunt us enough without other people judging us as well."

Pat's words cut into me, and Kai's suffering took on a whole new light. If he had stayed with my parents, would the outcome have been any different? Would there have been three bodies that night instead of two? They were questions I would never have answers to, and I wasn't sure I really needed them.

Kai came running into the room. "Bryson is gone and the back door was unlocked. I have no idea when he left. I peeked out the front windows, between the menus, to see if he was on the front street. I think we are in trouble." As he spoke, he moved to the shelving units and began to pull one away from the wall. Pat grabbed the pad off the table and ran to help him.

I stood like a fool. "What—"

"A sniper across the street, I think. I am not taking any chances." Kai looked at me. "Not with you here."

Behind the shelf, a section of wall came away, the cuts carefully hidden behind the struts of the shelf. The small opening revealed a dark hole just beyond it.

"Pat, you go first," Kai said. "Then Kris. I will be right behind you to close everything up."

An overwhelming feeling that I'd never see him again rushed through me. I knew then that I'd already forgiven him. That I couldn't lose him as well.

"Kai, I—"

"Later. Go! I will be right behind you."

He gave me a shove and I followed Pat down the hole. True to his word, Kai stepped onto the ladder and stopped to pull the shelf back into place. It closed with a quiet click, covering us in a blanket of darkness. From below, a faint light came on.

A loud bang from above made me freeze, until Kai's feet found my fingers. It sounded like they were tipping over the shelves in the room above us. I sped up and dropped the last little bit, landing beside Pat. She handed me another flashlight and we waited for Kai to join us. His breathing was hard and uneven, but he grabbed Pat's flashlight and waved for us to follow him, holding his finger up to his lips, cautioning us to silence. Voices echoed down from the restaurant as we raced down the tunnel.

This was different than the last time I'd been in the interlevel infrastructure, back when Ian had led me through the Level 4 floor to meet Nigel. Those weren't tunnels. Though some had been dark and unused, they had been built at the same time the levels were created. These were obviously hand carved out of the fibercrete that made up the floor. Stagnant, dusty air filled my lungs when I breathed, and I fought back a sneeze. The tunnel sloped downward, speeding us toward our destination. Kai ran, never stopping, never slowing, until we reached the end. The hole in this wall wasn't hidden or covered up. Chisels, hammers, and a wheelbarrow still sat in the dark where they had been left. Each item was covered in dust and settled dirt.

The hole opened into a room, most of its space taken by piles of rubble. Every step kicked up dust and dirt. I tried to keep my breathing shallow. Kai moved into a hallway and turned left. Pat and I followed. When I turned back to look at the floor, I could see our tracks. If they found the entrance to the ladder, it wouldn't take any effort to follow us.

As if on cue, a voice echoed from behind us. They had found the hole. Kai picked up his pace, practically running faster than his flashlight could illuminate.

"We're leaving a trail." I barely got the words out through my breathing. This had to be hell for Kai.

"Just a . . . bit . . . farther," Kai panted. His pace never slowed.

He finally stopped by a door, his head pressed against cold steel. He didn't rest for more than a second before he pulled the door open. We stepped into a maintenance hallway and turned right, no longer leaving tracks behind us. As I closed the door, the voices from the route we had just taken sounded louder.

When I had been led through the interlevel halls by Ian, the twists and turns, stairways and doors, had me more confused than anything else. Back then, I had no clue where I was, or how I would have gotten out if Ian had just left me. This time was better. Part of the ACE training had us being led through a maze blindfolded. At the end, the blindfold was removed and we had to find our way back to the start. We used sounds, we counted steps. The times we were taken in with a vehicle, we learned to feel the road under us and know when the vehicle turned.

I wasn't too good at it, but at least I wasn't lost. It didn't matter anyway. As soon as we started up the final set of stairs, my nose told me where we were.

The oily smell of fish permeated the air, sinking into every pore, coating my tongue and mouth with its familiarity. Kai pushed open a door to the alley beside the Lee Fish Market. The door slammed shut behind us, leaving a metal, handleless rectangle in the wall. Instead of moving toward the lights of Chinatown, he led us farther down the alley, eventually exiting onto a small street. A few vendors stood by carts, and as soon as they saw us, they started hawking their wares. I'd seen them before, in my previous life here, but I'd never stopped to see what they sold. Kai picked up three barbecue pork buns. They were still warm and soft, made fresh only an hour or so ago. As we ate them, he led us to a squat building. I devoured mine. It was the best thing I'd ever tasted. I asked for more, and Pat looked at me, concern on her face.

"My second home," he said. "We should be safe here. It is not under my name, and not related to the restaurant at all."

The furnishings were sparse, reminding me of what I'd had above the fish market. Not quite as bad, though. Against one wall Kai had a dark green sofa, old and worn, that must have doubled as a bed, and a small vid screen against the other. In the corner was a duplicate set of the white plastic table and chairs he had in the restaurant. By the blackened-out windows, I was surprised to see a small shrine where a skinny Buddha sat behind three small candles and a large plastic white flower. Kai motioned to the table, and we sat down.

"I spoke to my contact from the restaurant. They are getting what we need. We leave in an hour."

CHAPTER 13

LOS ANGELES, LEVEL 4—TUESDAY, JUNE 13, 2141 10:02 A.M.

I STARED OUT THE WINDOW, twelve stories off the ground. Above us, the Ambients shone with their midday brightness, and above that lay the stippled ceiling, crisscrossed with girders and air vents and now-empty water pipes. Like everything else on the lower levels, the ceiling was a dirty gray, made more so by the years of accumulated grime.

Looking down, my stomach clenched. I quickly reminded myself that I was scared of small spaces, not heights. But the instant exposure created by the sheer wall of the building still did its work. Six other people stood in the room with me. Five were joining me in the traverse to the ACE tower, and one was staying behind to keep an eye on the previous occupants of the office we had commandeered. They lay on the floor, trussed with zip ties and tape over their mouths. Missing was Pat. She had wanted to come with us, but I somehow managed to convince her she would be more helpful where she could look at building plans, in case anything went wrong. The real reason was that I couldn't trust her to not have another episode if we got into trouble.

No one spoke. They all pulled their climbing harnesses over the gray jumpsuits supplied by the insurgents and double-checked each other and the gear in silence. Three people had comm units: Phillip—as official leader—had one and the other two were handed to a couple of Phillip's team.

Once we got past the Ambients and up into the actual girders, the going would be relatively smooth. The jumpsuits were mottled and colored to match the ceiling, in case anyone took a quick glance outside and saw something through the Ambients. I looked out the window to the ground again and felt a sweat break out down my back.

The buildings were designed to prevent what we were about to do. The outside walls, as filthy as the ceiling, were as smooth as glass. There was no place to put a hand or a foot. No place to insert protection against a fall. The windows were sealed as well, and alarmed against any breakage. This particular building used air pressure to detect if there was a breach instead of sensors embedded into the glass. That's what the plans said, anyway. If that wasn't the case, this was going to be a short day.

Phillip beckoned us closer to the window. We had all been introduced, but their names stuck to me like oil to water. The six of us huddled in closely to the structure the insurgents had just built. It looked flimsy, barely strong enough to resist a slight breeze, in my opinion. They said they'd tested it, though.

"Okay, preparing to seal us in. Stay away from the walls and stand still," Phillip said.

Even though the plastic was clear, as soon as we were enclosed and pressed against each other in the small space, I began to hyper-ventilate. Someone shifted in front of me, and I shuffled backward into the temporary wall.

"I said stand still," Phillip said.

One of the others pulled a pressure sensor from their pocket and nodded. Phillip started cutting the glass with a miniature spinning blade.

If the barrier didn't hold, if the building sensors detected the pressure change, we had maybe five minutes to get out. Five minutes to get out of our climbing gear and exit the building with the regular workers. It would be tight.

I shuddered when I thought the word tight, feeling the people around me, the enclosed space suffocating me. I shifted my head, looking between two people at the window Phillip was cutting open. Put the smallest person that hates being confined in the back. Fucking great.

With a small pop, the glass fell inward out of its frame. Phillip held it and stared at the woman with the pressure sensor. We all held our breath. Finally the woman nodded and gave a thumbs-up; time to go. The glass was pulled completely inside and placed against the wall. Phillip leaned out the window and swung a grappling hook up to the girders while two others grabbed onto the back of his harness. The hook wrapped around a girder twice. Phillip pulled it tight.

The rope was anchored to the floor with a bright silver bolt and tied off, giving us a single line from the room to the ceiling. Phillip unclipped two mechanical ascenders from his belt and attached them to the rope. He clipped two slings into them, one attached to his harness and the other hanging at knee height. Moving to the window's ledge, he weighted the first sling before stepping into the second one. He stood, sliding the ascender attached to his harness up the rope before hanging off it again. Once his weight was off the foot sling, he slid up its ascender and stood in it. The process repeated until he reached the girder almost two meters above. When he was off the rope, the next person started.

It was my turn. The woman who verified the pressure checked my ascenders. I'd used prusiks before to climb, but the mechanical ascender was new to me. As I put my weight on the rope, I desperately wanted my prusiks back. I knew how they worked. I trusted them. After the first few moves the trepidation fell away. The ascenders did their job, grabbing onto the rope and letting me climb without any hand or foot holds. The last person started climbing before I had fully unclipped my gear, as eager as the rest of us to get moving.

It took us over half an hour before we were all on the girders. Leaving the rope in place behind us, we began the slow process of moving around the building toward the ACE tower. Once we got into William's twelfth-floor office, we could use a similar system to climb back out.

That was where the plan got complicated. We didn't know whether the ACE tower used a pressure monitoring system or a glass sensor to know if the building's seal had been broken. Pat and Kai had argued about it for a while before I told them it didn't matter. Once the seal was broken, without us being able to build a custom seal ourselves, the entire building would know the window was breached.

They'd changed the plan then, giving us an alternate way to evacuate the building. Under our climbing gear and jumpsuits we wore regular business clothes. Business casual is what Pat had called it. I called it uncomfortable.

If everything went to hell, we were supposed to separate and mingle, finding our own way out. It was a long shot, but one I was willing to risk. Phillip and his crew came along in case we met with resistance. I thought it would be better with a smaller group, but in the end I didn't care. As long as I had a chance to talk to William.

The Level 4 floor spread out underneath us, a miniature of the places I'd couriered through. From here, I could watch the ebb and flow of traffic, a small piece of humanity trying to get through another day. My stomach lurched.

Phillip began to move off, walking along the girders with no rope to stop him if he slipped and fell. Sudden vertigo gripped me, and I couldn't move. The image of the road rushing up to meet me imprinted on my brain. This was way different than rock climbing, where we had protection in case of a fall. This felt more like tightrope walking. The woman behind me gave me a gentle nudge, and I slid a foot forward, followed by another one. My grip on the supports turned my fingers white. When I couldn't hold on to the support anymore, I let go and leaned to reach the next one. My feet dislodged years of accumulated grime, knocking chunks off the girder. I made the mistake of watching one fall as it hit the top of an Ambient and disintegrated into dust before it reached the Level 4 floor. I teetered on the edge, the urge to follow it burning through me.

Apparently, I was scared of heights, too.

By the time we reached the ACE tower, I was still struggling with the heights and the lack of rope to save us if we fell. If my foot slipped, or my hand slid down a grime-coated support, I had to fight back the surge of fear. I knew roping up would have slowed us down and added extra weight, but I wasn't comfortable without it. This mission was supposed to be light and fast.

We crossed the girders until we came to one above William's office. Kai knew it quite well. He'd had meetings with Nigel here at least once a week when he was in charge of my parents. As soon as he'd said that, he had stopped talking and looked at me. I had tried to smile. It must have worked, since he had continued with telling us the plan. Inside, I'd felt empty.

A series of explosions filled the air with smoke a few blocks away. The diversion had kicked in. Phillip lowered a rope with a knot in the end and rappelled down the short distance to the window. He glanced inside, signaling back to us that the room was empty. I could feel the wave of relief coming off the others. I didn't feel the same way. We'd have to hunt down William now. Phillip got out his glass cutter and sliced a groove around the frame. Once it was done, he gave the glass a sharp kick, and it exploded inward. The rest of us lowered down the rope when he was inside.

The office wasn't just empty, it was unused. Dust covered almost every surface.

William hadn't been here in a long time.

LOS ANGELES, LEVEL 5—TUESDAY, JUNE 13, 2141 8:31 A.M.

Bryson bounced in the back of the van. Before they'd left China-town, a man had climbed into the back with him and turned on an overhead light, a dull red glow that didn't seem to do anything except create darker shadows. When the man had gotten in, Bryson had tried for the open door only to be kicked back. His head impacted the side of the van and stars danced in front of his eyes. By the time they disappeared, the van was in motion. His old habits kicked in, and he resigned himself to his fate.

That didn't mean he couldn't find out what was going on. These people didn't look or act like Kadokawa. Almost every Kadokawa employee he'd seen, those who weren't kept from Meridian anyway, had a certain way of moving, a certain way of talking to each other. When a person of lesser rank talked to someone higher up, there was a palpable deference in their posture and the tone of voice they used. He hadn't seen that when these people grabbed him from behind the building.

If it wasn't Kadokawa, he figured it had to be one of the other two major corporations, SoCal or IBC. He didn't think any of the smaller ones had what it took to do a daytime grab off the street. Not in San Angeles anyway.

"Who are you?" Bryson asked. When there was no answer, he rephrased the question. "Who do you work for?"

The man casually placed his hand on the butt of his gun. He didn't look at Bryson, didn't acknowledge the questions or that Bryson was even there, but the message was clear. Bryson took the hint and kept quiet. He alternated between feeling miserable and being angry at himself, then ended up sitting sullenly and staring at the floor for the rest of the trip.

He'd lost track of how many turns they had taken before they'd even left Chinatown. Though he had felt a couple of up-ramps, he hadn't counted them. What did it matter anyway? He was a scientist, not a soldier. If they were bothering to bring him somewhere, at least that meant they weren't planning on killing him. Maybe.

There were always rumors of people disappearing. Vanishing off the face of the planet as though they'd never existed. He was too valuable to have that happen to him . . . he hoped. With his history at Meridian, even without the breakthrough he'd accomplished just before leaving, almost every corporation would want to keep him alive.

All motion stopped, and he heard voices through the thin skin of the van. Feet pounded on fibercrete and ran off into the distance. When his door opened, he realized he was in interlevel parking. It made sense, he thought. They wouldn't want to show the world they'd caught the inventor of the quantum jump drive. He was pulled out of the van and his hands were shackled in front of him before he was led to an elevator. The door was already open when they reached it. The man shoved Bryson inside, pressed a button on the panel, and got out before the doors closed.

Bryson was left alone.

He pushed every button he could find. The alarm, the open and close door, all of the floors. Nothing happened. The lights didn't even turn on. The elevator was moving up and not making any stops in between. He gave up for the second time that day and waited for it to stop.

The doors opened on a waiting room as empty as the elevator. An ornate French writing desk stood in front of a door at the far end, with no chair behind it. Its surface was as barren as the rest of the room. He walked over and tried the knob on the door. Locked. The elevator doors stayed open. He took one more try at the buttons with the same results. Eventually he moved to the wall dead center between the elevator and the locked door and slid down it to sit on the floor. Occasionally he would get up and walk to the open elevator, trying again to press the unresponsive buttons. Then he would move across the room and try the door behind the desk before returning to his sitting spot.

By his best guess, he had waited over an hour before he heard the loud click of the door unlocking. He was about to find out who his new owners were. Bryson sighed and pushed himself to his feet, muscles aching in protest, and waited for the door to open, but it never did. Even though he hurt from head to toe, he forced himself to walk to the door and twisted the knob as if it was something he did every day. It opened, swinging inward.

The room beyond was windowless and plain. A single, closed door sat in the far wall, with a simple desk and a folding chair behind it. Another folding chair leaned against the bare white wall. The door opened and he got a brief view of a smaller room on the other side. A woman walked through and the door closed behind her. Bryson thought he heard a lock click shut. The woman ignored him until she was behind the desk. She pulled a pad of paper and a pen from the drawer and finally looked up. The extravagance of real paper shocked him.

"I am Ms. Peters. My job is to bring your jump drive into SoCal. Please, sit."

Bryson shrugged and stayed standing. Maybe it wasn't time to give up just yet.

"I'd ask you to suit yourself, but that would begin our relationship on the wrong foot. Get that chair, put it here," she said, pointing to the front of the desk. "And sit."

Bryson's heart beat faster, and a trickle of sweat rolled down his back. His first instinct was to do as he was told, to not make waves. He fought the urge and stayed on his feet.

"Just to be clear, Mr. Searls, you do have the ability to make your own choices. However, they are not whether you should sit or stand, but whether you will obey or be punished. You have a chance to make a friend today, or an enemy." She stared into his eyes. "Which do you want it to be?"

He took a step toward the chair and stopped. He wasn't going to do what she asked. The thought came as surprise. This wasn't what he did. It wasn't who he was. Why was he doing this now, when there was nowhere to run? Maybe he'd just had enough. Bryson held his ground.

"Since you have made your choice, I will follow through." Peters leaned back in her chair and knocked twice on the door. The guard that came through was massive, bringing a wooden stick with him. Bryson recognized it. He had played cricket at Harvard. As the guard rounded the desk, Bryson backed away, moving toward the still-open door to the room with the elevator.

"Please reconsider, Mr. Bryson."

He stopped. Ms. Peters raised her hand, halting the guard's progress. Bryson raised his shackled hands to wipe at the sweat that poured into his eyes. When the guard took another step, Bryson dashed for the chair, grabbing it and opening it up. He sat. He didn't have time to move it in front of the desk. His hands shook and his whole body vibrated. He looked at his knees, not daring to raise his eyes.

"Ah, Mr. Searls. Fear is a wonderful incentive, isn't it? But not the only one I have. If you're good, and do what I ask, you'll find that I can be a wonderful ally." She waved the guard away. "Now please, if you will, in front of the desk?"

He stood, using the chair to help support himself, and moved it to where she had pointed before lowering himself into it once again.

She smiled and lifted the pen, hovering it just above the paper. "Excellent, shall we begin?"

<hr>

LOS ANGELES, LEVEL 4—TUESDAY, JUNE 13, 2141 10:36 A.M.

Something was wrong. We'd been in the building for at least five minutes, and nothing had happened. Some alarm should have been set off by the broken window. In those few minutes, we'd left the unused office and checked every door we saw. It was as though the top floor of the building had been abandoned. There were no traces that anyone had been here in a long time.

Phillip pressed his hand to his ear and stood still for a second, getting intel from the insurgents. "We go down," he said. "There's a chance William's office is on the fifth floor."

"We find that out now?" I asked. "We have to go down seven stories in a building that is full of people that know we're here? It would have been easier to walk through the fucking front door. What if we make it to the fifth floor? It's a big building. His office could be anywhere."

By the time I was done, all five of the insurgents stood in a group looking at me.

"We go down," Phillip repeated. Two of his team, the ones that were handed comm units earlier, left the group and entered the hallway, taking point. The rest followed. My only way out was back the way we'd come in. But I knew I wouldn't take it. I had to find out if ACE had Ian. I double-checked my gun and followed them, catching up at the stairs.

The stairwell was as empty as the twelfth floor.

The point team stopped at the fifth-floor door and waited for us before throwing it open and disappearing inside. Moments later, I heard Phillip's earbud crackle with sound. He opened the door and stood in the hallway. Following him, I saw most of the office doors had been opened.

"Empty. As empty as the twelfth floor," he said.

I stepped around him and walked into the first office. Though there was some dust, I could easily see where stacks of information pads had sat. Unlike the twelfth floor, this place had been recently emptied.

"They didn't do this today, but it wasn't that long ago," I said. "Maybe that's why no one came to check out the broken window."

Phillip's earbud crackled again. "Bring her here," he said before turning to the rest of us. "We found someone carrying boxes."

The point team dragged an older lady down the hall. Her feet could barely keep up, and she kept tripping. The look on her face was one of pure terror. By my guess, she was well into her sixties, and the men were treating her like a sack of garbage. They threw her against the wall so hard, I was sure something had broken. As she slid down, one guy was already swinging his fist. I stepped in between them. The half-pulled punch hit my back and I flew into the wall. Before I realized what I was doing, I spun and heel kicked him in the gut. The guy ended up on the floor, his face white and his mouth open, gasping for breath. The others stood in what I thought was shock. They hadn't expected that response from a girl like me.

I ignored them and crouched down to speak to the old lady. "What's your name?"

She cowered on the floor, whimpering and clutching her sweater in tight fists. Her eyes flicked between the guy on the floor and me. I reached for her hand and she jerked away from my touch as though it burned.

"I'm not going to hurt you. I'm not going to let them hurt you either. Please, I only have a couple of questions."

The whimpering slowed and the old lady looked into my eyes. I'm not sure what she saw, but she nodded her head.

"Is William Clark still in the building?" I asked.

Another quick nod. Her eyes flicked to Phillip's team standing around us. I reached out and placed my hand on her shoulder.

"Ignore them. It's just you and me here. Where is he? Where is William?"

Her mouth moved as though she was about to answer. Before she did, a shadow fell across the wall. Phillip leaned in.

"Answer the question," he demanded.

When she didn't respond, he pulled back his leg as though to kick her. I jumped to my feet, twisting to face him, and pushed him against the far wall. Four guns swiveled to point at me.

"I have this. You fucking touch her, and I'll kill you myself."

Phillip grinned and raised his hands. "Whatever you say. This is your show."

I gave him one more shove against the wall and turned to crouch in front of the old lady again. My hands shook. I knew I couldn't let her see how rattled I was. If she did, I'd never get her to trust me enough to answer the questions. I took a deep breath, calming myself.

"Where is he?"

It took her a minute to answer. "His office, I think. Third floor, in the far corner." She pointed down the hall. Her hands shook more than mine did. I smiled.

"Where is everyone?"

Her look changed to one of confusion. "We've been emptying the building for months. All our offices are moving to Level 6."

Level 6 didn't sound right for ACE. One of the main tenets of ACE was to stay under the radar. If they became too obvious, too forward in their actions, it would be easier for the corporations to ferret them out and get rid of them. Doc Searls was right. There was something rotten in ACE.

"Okay," I said. "I can't just leave you here alone. I'm going to have to tie you up before we go. Do you understand?"

For the third time, she nodded. I reached to untie my shoes, planning on using the laces to tie her up.

A gunshot sounded behind me, close enough to deafen my ear, and the back of her head exploded into the wall. Blood splattered over me, red hot drops that seared through my skin. I blinked, and a red haze filled my vision. I fell back onto my butt and scrambled away from the already cooling body. My ear rang, blocking all sound from that side.

The fury started slowly. Creeping from my gut, pushing at the shock and revulsion that held me in its grip. My temper rose to the surface and my face felt flushed. I leaped to my feet. Phillip lowered his gun, shock on his face—as if he hadn't expected the carnage—changing to one that looked too much like pleasure. I took a half step toward him and froze. This time, all five weapons were pointed at me.

"You didn't have to do that," I growled. "She was under control."

Phillip smiled. It didn't touch his eyes. "My job is to get you to William any way I can. You remember when I said this was your show? I lied. This is our show. I'll do whatever I think is necessary to get you to William and get you out safe. Whatever *I* think is necessary."

"You didn't have to kill her. I promised—"

"You promised something you couldn't follow through on. I let you both believe it so we could get our answers. What if we restrained her and she escaped? The whole building would know we were in here. My responsibility is the safety of every member of this team, including you. I do what I have to."

Phillip glanced down at my hand. I hadn't even realized I'd moved it to my own gun.

"If that weapon moves even a millimeter, you'll never get to see William," Phillip said.

The man I'd kicked in the gut took a step closer and placed the muzzle of his gun against my temple, pressing it hard into my skin. I refused to let him scare me. The anger I'd felt settled into a dull roar, and I slowly moved my hand away. The man reached for my gun.

"Leave it," Phillip said. "She knows I'm right. You can see it in her eyes. Let's get down to the third floor. You two, back on point."

Phillip was wrong. Not only did I know he was wrong, if I had my chance, I was pretty sure I was going to show him how I felt. For now, we both had the same goal. For now.

We moved across the floor to a set of stairs closer to William's office. As we descended, the anger stayed in me, but it was wrapped in a blanket of doubt. Was this what I had signed up for? Was this what Ian did? I didn't—I couldn't—believe it. Phillip wasn't Ian. They weren't alike at all.

CHAPTER 14

UNKNOWN

MILLER WOKE TO THE soft familiar hum his brain associated only with pain. He jerked away from it, only to be pulled gently back.

"Hold still, this won't take much longer," Jeremy said from beside him. "Good, all done."

Squinting in the bright light, Miller looked toward the sound of the voice before realizing he no longer felt the pain of the burns. Instead, his arms and legs itched. He lifted his head and looked toward his feet. The skin on his thighs was a bright pink.

"You should feel better now," Jeremy said, giggling. "I can't do anything about your shoulder, unfortunately. But then, you won't even feel it in a while. Today will be our last time together."

Miller watched Jeremy push himself to his feet and stretch before walking to the stainless steel table. When Jeremy turned around, he held his briefcase in his hands, opened and angled so Miller could see what was inside.

He didn't need reminding.

Inside the case were the tools of a madman: sharp metal instruments, each one polished to a fine sheen. Jeremy held an ordinary scalpel in his hands, and reached for the fresh skin on Miller's thighs.

Someone knocked on the door.

Miller didn't take his eyes off the blade, but he heard the aggravation in Jeremy's voice.

"What?"

The door opened a crack. "We have intruders in the building. We're looking for them now."

"Wait outside until I call you. Bring this man's clothes when you come in." Jeremy slipped the scalpel back into the case.

"Yes, sir." The door closed again.

"Saved again. Do you think she's here? Do you think she'd try to save you in this place?"

Miller stared at Jeremy's face, watching the excitement build in his eyes.

"It has to be her. It *has* to be." He raised his voice. "Get in here."

Miller could barely raise his head to watch two blurry figures walk in. They untied him from the mesh frame and got him dressed before one chained his feet together and the other twisted his arms behind his back and tied his wrists. Miller bit down, refusing to show them how much it hurt. When they grabbed under his arms and hauled him to his feet, he couldn't stop the gasp that escaped his lips.

Jeremy stood in front of him. "Shall we go see if it is her? I'm sure she would do almost anything to get you free, perhaps even at the cost of her own freedom." Jeremy smiled before pivoting and walking to the door. Miller's captors dragged him behind. Every step sent needles of pain through his shoulder.

The hallway outside the door was barren. Miller closed his eyes in the sudden brightness and missed Jeremy turning. The guards threw him around the corner and a fresh wave of pain crashed through him, almost bringing him to his knees. He forced his eyes open. If he knew the way out—if they brought him back—he would need to know which way to go. This time he would find a way out of the torture chamber.

The stairs were the hardest. They had shackled his feet so close together he could barely lift his foot onto the next step. The guards ended up carrying him through each step, grunting as though the effort was too much for them. Miller's shoulder flared red hot. By the time they had reached the top, his hold on reality had dwindled to a fine thread. At the next set of stairs, Miller let go, letting the shadows pull him into their depths.

<hr/>

LOS ANGELES, LEVEL 4—TUESDAY, JUNE 13, 2141 10:40 A.M.

The third floor was as deserted as the rest we'd seen. I tried to slow down, to lag behind the team of insurgents, but they wouldn't let me. At least two always stayed behind, sometimes pressing on my back to make me keep up with the rest. They weren't pointing their guns at me anymore, but it still felt like the five barrels pressed into me. These guys were thugs and murderers. If this was the way the insurgents worked, I knew I didn't want to be a part of them.

Voices echoed down the deserted hallway. People were still here. We got to William's door and slipped in without being seen. The front area was a waiting room. Boxes lined the walls, some of them sealed while others still sat open, waiting to be filled. The receptionist, if there was one, wasn't in the room. Maybe it was her Phillip had killed upstairs. I felt some of the blame shift over to me. It was my idea to come here, to talk to William. In the end, whatever happened here was my fault.

Another door separated the reception area from the back office. The door was open a few centimeters, and a loud thud came from the other side. A rush of adrenaline flooded through me, and my heart beat faster and louder. I was sure everyone in the room could hear it.

I was going to get my answers.

The point team pushed open the door and entered the room, followed by the rest of us. The two who insisted on staying behind me closed the door after them. William stood by a deep red credenza, a look of confusion on his face.

Until he saw me.

This room was the opposite of Nigel's old office—the one we had seen on the twelfth floor. This one's corner windows showed a wide swath of Level 4. The furniture looked heavy and ornate. There was no work table where a small group could collaborate. Even though the room was larger, there were only two chairs at the front of the desk and a couch by the credenza. The rest was open space.

Phillip pulled William away from the window and made him kneel in the middle of the room with his hands on his head. William never stopped looking at me.

"Kris," William said. "I think the last time we met, I said you had done some very unexpected things. It seems you continue to do so."

I glared at him. Did he think I was stupid? "Wrong. Last time we *met*, you never spoke. Janice was waiting to kill us. You just stood by and let it happen. Were you there to make sure the job was done?"

"I was there to bring the three of you in. When Janice opened fire, I was as shocked as you were."

Anger crossed his face before being replaced by a look of concern. I would have missed it if I had blinked. He was lying. It must have looked that way to Phillip as well. Phillip pistol-whipped William, slicing open his cheek. I almost wished I'd done it myself before jumping to get in between them.

Is this how it started? First the physical violence because they deserved it, then killing unarmed people in hallways. Is this how I would change into a person like Phillip?

William got back to his knees but didn't raise his hands to his head. He ignored Phillip. "You need to control your dogs better."

"Desperate times," I said. "I had to get in here. I had to talk to you."

"You're part of ACE, Kris. You're welcome here anytime."

Part of me wanted to believe him, but I couldn't wipe the image of him standing by the greenhouse out of my mind. He hadn't seemed shocked by the gunfire, there hadn't been any concern for his own safety.

"Bring his chair," I said.

Phillip nodded at one of his team and they wheeled the chair from behind the desk. William lowered himself into it slowly. Zip ties appeared from one of the insurgent's backpacks, and William's arms and legs were roughly strapped down. The thought that they could have restrained the woman on the fifth floor flashed through my mind. I buried it. Now was not the time.

"No," I said. "You were there to make sure Janice got the job done."

William stared at me. I'd seen the look before, back in the safe house when he had tried to recruit me, and again in the shuttle port parking garage when he had decided I could help find Ian.

He nodded his head and sighed. "I've never lied to you Kris, and I won't start now. Miller is here, but he's not under ACE control. I can't explain it, but that's how it is. I know what's being done to him, and I didn't want to see the same thing happen to you."

Ian was here! I almost didn't hear the rest of what he had said. Blood thrilled through my veins. He was here, and we were going to get him. I didn't dwell on the fact that William's way to save me from whatever was happening to Ian was to kill me.

Phillip interfered. "What do you mean he's here but not under your control. ACE runs this building. There is no one else."

William didn't reply.

This was my interrogation, but Phillip's question was a good one. "Answer his question," I said.

A voice called from the front office, female, young by the sounds of it. My first thought was that we'd been discovered, but I couldn't see how. The building was damn near deserted.

"Mr. Clark. The men haven't arrived to take the boxes yet." There was a knock at the door and the knob started turning. "Mr. Clark?"

Phillip's gun pointed at William's head. William tensed up.

"Sorry, Tanna. I'm in a meeting. I should have locked the door."

The door, open only a few millimeters, pulled shut again with a click. William's body relaxed, even though the gun was still aimed at him. Everything told me he cared more about Tanna's well-being than his own. Why couldn't people be simple? Why couldn't they just be good or evil, black or white? It would make the world a simpler place.

Tanna's voice came muffled through the door. "Sorry, Mr. Clark. I'll go see if I can find them. Is there anything I can bring you before I go?"

"No, thank you, Tanna."

After a few silent moments, Phillip spoke again. "Answer the question."

"I can't."

Before I could intervene, Phillip's gun slashed across William's face again. The chair teetered but didn't tip over. For the first time, William looked at Phillip. Anger burned deep in his eyes.

"Where is he?" I asked.

William tore his gaze from Phillip, the anger gone before he looked at me.

"In the basement," William whispered. "You don't want to go there." An almost pleading tone entered his voice. "I don't want to see what he does to you. There's . . . there's parts of him I don't think I even know anymore."

"Who?"

"I . . . I can't. I still love him." The last words came out with a sense of wonder behind them.

I kicked William's chair, propelling it into the wall with a soft thud. Before anyone could move, I blocked him from Phillip's team, pulled my gun, and turned to face them. "We go down to the basement." If they noticed the gun shaking in my hands, they didn't say anything.

All five guns pointed at me again. I maneuvered the chair into a corner and stood staring at them.

"We can't leave him," Phillip said.

"We can, and we will. Give me something to cover his mouth and we leave." I could still feel the old lady's blood on my face. I was surprised William was able to look at me and not hate what he saw. "I won't let you kill another one." Even if he was planning on killing me.

Phillip put his gun away, disgust on his face. "Give her the tape and let's get out of here."

A roll of tape landed on the desk, and the four followed Phillip out the door. For a second, fear flitted through me like a cold wind. They had left me here. I was going to have to find my own way out.

I pushed the feeling aside. I didn't care. I refused to let this job turn me into an animal, into something I wasn't. My second thought was for Tanna. Was she still out there? If she was, I didn't think Phillip would hesitate to kill her.

Before I taped his mouth, William tried one more time. "Don't go down there. If he gets you—"

"Who? If who gets me?"

William stared at the floor. I covered his mouth with tape and turned to go.

When I got to the door I stopped, one hand on the doorknob. "I have to," I said, turning to meet William's eyes. He closed his eyes and nodded, understanding. I closed the door behind me, making sure it was locked. Phillip's team had gathered by the door to the hallway.

"We did what we came here to do," Phillip said. "Now we go back up and get out of here."

"No. We go down. He's here. Ian is here, and I'm not leaving without him."

"We don't have the manpower to do that. You have the information you wanted; you know that ACE is corrupt. Now let's get the info back to people who can help us plan the next step."

I pushed past them and ran to the stairs. The next step was to get Ian. I wasn't sure I'd get another opportunity like this one. Thankfully, the hallway was still empty. I was halfway down the first flight before I heard them following. I kept going.

The stairs ended at the first floor, without access to the basement. Phillip and his team caught up with me.

"We can't go out there," he said. "It's too dangerous."

I was blind to everything he said. All I knew was that we had to get to Ian. I eased the door open and peered through the tiny crack. The stairs opened into a foyer. From the slim sliver I could see, two security guards stood near the front entrance. I couldn't see any way down to the basement. I tucked my gun into my jumpsuit and pulled the door wider. It opened a couple of centimeters more before coming to a stop against Phillip's foot. His arm reached over my head and shoved the door closed. For a second, he was my uncle, wearing a dirty white undershirt and smelling of alcohol and pizza. My hatred for Phillip surged.

"We go back up," he said.

At his words, a door slammed shut above us and voices echoed down. Everyone fell silent.

"Shit. You two go look," he whispered.

The point team disappeared up the stairs, coming back only moments later. They leaned into Phillip and whispered. I picked up the words security and armed.

"Shit," Phillip said again. He began to strip off his jumpsuit and the others followed. It didn't take me long to do the same. We jammed the clothing under the stairs, tucked our guns under our shirts, and entered the foyer as a group. I kept looking for a way down.

The security guards exited the stairs seconds behind us. Phillip kept walking. We stayed in a loose group, just a bunch of coworkers heading out for an early lunch. One of his team, a young woman barely older than me, started to panic. I could hear her breathing ramp up, saw her hands shaking at her sides. I reached out to calm her. She jerked away from my touch and stopped, pulling her gun out. It spat fire with a loud bang, and one of the security guards fell. All hell broke loose.

More security emerged from a corner office. In no time, we were outnumbered and outgunned. Phillip grabbed my collar and jerked me into the middle of the circle created by his team. They opened fire and people started falling.

The woman who had fired the first shot crumpled, the front of her shirt blossoming red. I finally recognized her as the one that followed me across the girders. The rest of the team tightened the circle, firing their guns at anything that moved. I tried to push past the circle, tried to find a way to the basement.

This was different than training. It was real, and I was scared. We were two meters from the main entrance and moving fast. Then one. Phillip kept his hand wrapped in my collar, pulling me with the group. Two more of our group had fallen and someone was partly dragging, partly carrying another.

"Kris Merrill."

The voice reverberated through the foyer. I stopped moving and felt my shirt tighten around my neck as Phillip continued to pull. I searched for the source of the voice.

Ian stepped around a corner. One of the insurgent's guns pivoted toward the movement and I struck out. The bullet dug into the floor, throwing chunks of tiling on Ian's feet.

A familiar face peered over Ian's shoulder. The hand continued to pull at the back of my collar, dragging me farther away.

"Ian!" I screamed. His eyes flickered to me and back down to the floor. Behind him, Jeremy Adams laughed, a crazed look on his face.

The doors shut in front of me. Jeremy yelled something, pointing at me, his cheeks flushed. The only words that made it into my brain were *Level 6*. Through the glass, I could see Ian. He looked broken. I twisted, breaking free of Phillip's grip. I had to get Ian. Before I could take a step, an arm looped around my neck and jerked me off my feet. My gun slipped from my fingers.

Guards rushed for the door, no longer firing their guns.

Some sort of vehicle squealed behind us. I was thrown in, rolling across its floor. I struggled to my knees, trying to get away, trying to crawl back to Ian. The doors slammed shut and the acceleration threw me sideways. Hands grabbed me, holding me down.

―――――

LOS ANGELES, LEVEL 2—TUESDAY, JUNE 13, 2141 10:37 A.M.

Pat's whole body jerked at the sound of the single gunshot coming from the comm unit on the table, followed by Kris's voice. Pat didn't hear what she said.

Standing in the corner of the room by Kai's sofa was a little girl holding a broken doll. *Pourquoi?*

A warm hand touched hers and she yanked it back. The hand refused to let go, squeezing tighter. Eventually, Kai's voice broke through.

"Pat. Come on Pat, we need you here. That is it. Focus."

She drew a shuddering breath and closed her eyes, willing the memories to go away. When she opened them again, the girl was gone and Kai sat beside her, a wrinkled smile on his face.

"Good," he said. "Good! Now concentrate. Things are changing, and we need to help Kris. We cannot do that if you let go."

Pat nodded, pulling the pad with the building's floor plan closer to her. "Right. I'm good." Her voice sounded shaky. She could still feel the pain and the fear and the memories threatening to pull her in, but this time they stayed in the periphery.

Kai let go of Pat's hand and pointed at the pad, to a set of stairs in the corner opposite where the infiltration team stood. "If they use these stairs, it should let them out closer to William's office. It will be easier to get there now, rather than lower down where there might be more people."

Pat nodded again and reached for the comm unit. Before she touched it, the voice came on again, letting Phillip know of the stairs. They heard the double-click acknowledgment from Phillip. They both listened quietly as the team moved across the building.

"Can we really trust these guys?" asked Pat.

Kai didn't respond.

"Kai, can we trust these guys? They just killed someone in cold blood. They're acting more like hit men than an infiltration team."

"We have all had to do it when we were in the field."

"Not on purpose, not like that."

Kai closed his eyes. "No, not like that."

"So, can we? Trust them?"

"I do not know. I used to think we could, but now. It is almost as if life means nothing to them." Kai told her about the team that had gained access to Level 6 via the broken water pipes. "They sent in kids. How could they do that?"

He didn't look like he expected an answer.

"We need to make plans in case this thing falls apart," Pat said.

"And tell who? Phillip? We should have equipped Kris with our own comm unit."

"That's a mistake we won't make again." I should never have taken mine back, she thought.

They both went quiet as voices came from the comm unit. Both Kai and Pat leaned forward when they heard Miller's name.

"Where is the layout for the basement?" Kai's voice was excited and concerned at the same time.

Pat flipped through the pad. "We don't have one." She paused, a look of shock on her face. "Kris wouldn't go in, would she? Phillip will stop her."

Kai just looked at Pat. "That is what I am afraid of."

LOS ANGELES, LEVEL 2—TUESDAY, JUNE 13, 2141 10:49 A.M.

I fought.

I used everything I had—biting, punching, kicking. I used all the training I'd received at boot camp. None of it helped. Images flashed through my mind. Ian. His shoulders stooped, his hands and feet in chains. The way he seemed beaten, lost.

The look on his face.

When the van stopped I lunged for the door, getting it open a crack before four bodies pounced on me, pinning me down. I twisted, trying to get free, and a knee hit my forehead. I didn't care. I had to get back to Ian. A hand clamped over my mouth and nose. I couldn't breathe. My vision dimmed, and I stopped fighting back.

When I came to, my hands and feet were taped together. I started screaming and they taped my mouth. I had found Ian, and they had stopped me from getting to him.

A voice talked quietly in the front seat. "She'll be outside the side door of the fish market" was all I heard. The van stopped again. This time, someone else opened the sliding door, and I was carried out and placed on the ground by the two dumpsters. The van was gone before its door closed, tires slipping in the fish-encrusted slime. Tears streamed down my face. I gasped for breath, only to taste the tape. I couldn't breathe. I choked and coughed, filling my mouth with phlegm. My body jerked, my lungs expanding to get air. I gagged on my own mucus and tried to suck in more air, making it worse.

A hand grabbed my shoulder and the tape was ripped off my mouth. I hacked out what felt like a lung, desperately sucking in the putrid air between coughs. Someone alternated between pounding and rubbing my back. By the time I was almost under control, my hands and feet were cut clear of the tape that bound them. I struggled to stand, staggering against the building as another coughing fit took control.

Ian!

I flung myself from the wall and almost fell. I put one foot in front of the other and repeated, staggering away from the building toward the bright neon of Chinatown. Hands reached for me. Someone blocked my way. I swerved and they moved to stay in front of me.

"There's nothing we can do."

The voice came through blurry. *I have to get Ian.* I didn't know if I had said it out loud or screamed it in my head.

"There's nothing we can do."

The voice belonged to Pat. I stopped trying to get past her and fell into her arms. She caught me, held me close. Half carried me to Kai's apartment.

"We know he's alive. We'll get him." Behind the promise I thought I heard doubt.

Kai's apartment was dim and the air was thick. A small fan pushed a breeze around the room in a losing battle. I sat on the couch and stared at the far wall. The vid screen was on, talking heads with background images of riots.

Kai emerged from the kitchen, carrying a mug. "Drink this."

I pushed his hands away.

"Drink. You will feel better, I promise."

I didn't want to feel better. Kai held the mug to my lips and tilted it. Lukewarm green tea flooded my mouth. I swallowed and took the mug from him.

"I saw Ian," I said. With the words came tears.

"We know," Pat said.

"I couldn't get to him." I let my tears fall. I felt hollow, as though someone had ripped out my insides and left only a shell.

"We know who has him now, and we know where they're going. When we get all the details, we'll figure out a plan."

A plan. We'd had a plan when we went in to talk to William. The insurgents had a different plan. "When?" I asked, my voice weak.

"We're working on it."

I just nodded and drank some more tea. When the mug was empty I got up to put it away. The world spun, and I balanced on Pat's shoulder for a second before trying to walk. Everything hurt. It felt like my hollow body had been thrown into a commercial dryer and was spinning around in the drum. I made it to the kitchen and leaned against the small counter. Pots filled with water lined every possible surface. Some of them were already empty. Kai must have seen me looking.

"They still do not have the water on all the time."

I didn't answer. I didn't care. After watching me for a while, Pat and Kai went back to the plastic table in the corner. I didn't pay any attention to them until I heard Ian's name.

"When do we go back to get him?" I asked.

The conversation stopped, and Kai turned in his chair to look at me. "He will not be there. We know ACE is moving to Level 6, and we think they will take Miller with them. We do not know where on Level 6. That is what we are working on."

"Why Level 6?"

"It is what the woman on the fifth floor said, and what the man that had Miller said when he was taunting you."

"Jeremy." The hollow feeling in me grew. I had seen him shot by a team from ACE. The reality finally sunk in. Jeremy and ACE were working together. I fell back on the couch.

"Sorry?"

"Jeremy," I said. "Jeremy Adams from Meridian."

"I thought he was—are you sure?" Kai asked.

"It's a face I won't ever forget."

"Jeremy Adams and ACE. That I would never have thought of. I knew Meridian was linked, but Jeremy still alive?"

An uncomfortable silence enveloped the room. Kai turned back to the table, facing Pat. They both sat there, as though they were afraid to say the wrong thing. I walked over to them and sat down in the only empty chair, pulling it closer to the table. Its feet scraped along the floor.

"How do we find him?" I asked.

"The insurgents—"

"Fuck the insurgents." My voice had gotten louder, sounding out of place in the small room. "I don't trust them."

"They saved your life," Pat said. "You don't have to trust them to use them."

I opened my mouth to interrupt her. Pat rushed on.

"They have resources we don't. If they can find out where he is, Kai and I can figure out how to get to him."

I knew she was right. I slumped in my chair. "Information only, nothing more," I said, sounding like a small child.

"That's it. We do this one alone."

I bowed my head. "Okay."

CHAPTER 15

LOS ANGELES, LEVEL 2—TUESDAY, JUNE 13, 2141 11:34 A.M.

KAI GENTLY PLACED his comm unit on the plastic table, but his hands were shaking. The frustration he felt inside echoed in his voice. "They keep telling me how pissed off they are instead of giving me what I want."

"Is there any other way?" Pat asked.

"I do not know, maybe. I still have some contacts in ACE, but after this, I am afraid to use them."

Pat shook her head. "We can't go to ACE. With Jeremy there, who knows how corrupt the whole thing has become."

Kai knew she was right, but the roadblocks he was getting from the insurgents were starting to pile up. That, and the fact that Jack was trying to run what amounted to a civil war, made everything more difficult. It seemed like once he had lost his usefulness as a doctor of sorts, the insurgents didn't want to talk to him anymore.

He got to his feet. It was time to meet face-to-face and call in the favors they owed him.

"Where are you going?" Pat asked.

"To get what we need." When he saw Pat start to stand, he stopped her. "Stay with Kris. I do not want her to be alone when she wakes up. Who knows what she will do?"

Kai left the apartment, locking the door behind him. When he exited the building, he stopped short. He had expected the street to be full of vendors and their carts, the same as every day. Instead most of them were gone. The few who had stuck around were the poorest of them. The ones who couldn't afford to go into hiding when things went bad. He had to admit, at least to himself, that the empty street unsettled him. Without the general noise the city normally made, he became aware of the background, the slight buzz of the Ambients and the hum of the ventilation fans.

When he walked the block to the front of the fish market, the emptiness sunk into his bones. Most of the stores and restaurants looked open, but only the homeless were on the streets. No one would be doing any business today. Kai's steps turned tentative, and he almost changed his mind.

No.

He'd run away from helping people he had cared for in the past. He wasn't about to do the same with their daughter.

The sound of vehicles rattled from down the empty street. Panic gripped Kai. He rushed to the entryway of an acupuncturist and twisted the knob. The door was locked. He could see trucks turning onto the street only a few blocks away. He had nowhere to hide. Glancing in the opposite direction, even the bums had all but disappeared, hiding under garbage or pulling themselves deeper into shadowed doorways. Kai dropped to the ground, his old bones complaining, and curled into a ball against the locked door. He wasn't sure if the pounding he felt was from the trucks as they drove past or his heart threatening to beat itself out of his chest.

Kai lifted his eyes, hiding his face behind his gnarled hands. The trucks were military. SoCal's logo, a representation of the entire west coast in matte black, lay against the speckled gray of the trucks. They were camouflaged for use in the city. Gray on gray on top of gray. There was something wrong with needing special equipment to control the population.

He waited for a few minutes after they passed before he got back up and started walking. The dirt from the sidewalk clung to his clothes. He left it there, knowing it would help him if he needed to hide again.

The walk was only twenty-five minutes due south, even with his muscles stiff and sore from the morning's run from the restaurant. He was getting too old for this.

The closer he got, the more people he noticed. Some peered from behind curtains, others sat with what appeared to be their worldly possessions clutched beside them. Yet it wasn't quite right. There were too many of them for a residential neighborhood. Homeless people tended to migrate from one commercial area to another. Very few picked one area as their home and never left. That they were lookouts was too obvious. He would have to say something to Jack.

Kai entered an apartment block. It looked like every other one on both sides of the street. Gray fibercrete blocks stacked on top of one another. Small slits for windows that barely let the Ambients shine in. It always reminded him of a prison complex rather than a place to live.

He didn't make it to the stairs before a man emerged from the shadows and blocked his way.

"There's nothing here you want."

"I would like to see Jack."

"I don't know what you're talking about, old man. There's no Jack here. We just don't want bums in our building."

Kai pulled himself to his full height and still had to look up at the man who blocked him. "You did not say that when I pulled three bullets out of your backside last year."

The man moved his hand to his butt and took a step back. He squinted at the dirty clothes. "Kai?"

"Who else? I need to see Jack."

"He's pretty busy."

"I can see that," Kai said. "Busy starting a war he can't possibly finish. But that's not why I am here." Kai moved to walk around the man.

"I can't—"

"Then I cannot help you next time you show up on my table." There were others who could do Kai's work, but he hoped the man didn't think it through.

"Wait . . . wait here. I'll see what I can do." The man beckoned another guard dressed in black and asked him to keep an eye on Kai.

Kai leaned against the doorframe, suddenly more tired than he'd ever felt before. Years of conspiracy and hiding, bloodshed and death. With a sudden realization, like a Zen epiphany sparking through him, Kai knew he'd had enough. He would help Kris get Miller, and that would be it. He had given enough of his life to causes he had never really fully been behind. It was past time to get out. Except for Kris.

The man returned, and Kai followed him wearily back up the stairs.

LOS ANGELES, LEVEL 2—TUESDAY, JUNE 13, 2141 12:40 P.M.

When Kai came back he didn't look happy. I started questioning him, but he held up his hand, asking me to wait. I bit my tongue, anxious to hear what had happened.

The water had come back on while he was gone, so Pat and I had filled the pots and managed to get cleaned up a bit. Kai needed to wash as well, but by the time he'd made it back, the water was off again.

According to the news, the riots were spreading, and the violence with them. The rioters equipped themselves with anything they could find, from sticks and rocks to fully automatic weapons. The broadcasters had no idea where the guns were coming from. From the sounds of it, neither did the people using them. Most of the time, they ended up shooting their own people, sometimes friends and family, instead of the SoCal soldiers. It didn't take a ton of training to fire a weapon, but when you had never used one— heck, never even *seen* one before—it didn't take long for mistakes to happen.

The water trucks had stopped coming, though soldiers still guarded the transfer stations. Water rationing on the lower levels was still in effect. The rioters didn't know what to do now that they didn't have a target. Eventually they figured out the water valves feeding the city were located in the stations. That meant when the water was turned off, the only way to turn them on again was to get inside.

They actually did it once. The protesters outnumbered the soldiers by at least five to one. The people in the back kept pushing forward, and they didn't stop when the gunfire started. They didn't stop when they walked over the bodies of the people in front.

Eventually they got inside and turned the water back on. Seconds later, the whole place blew up. Hundreds died, and the water situation got worse. The soldiers had booby-trapped the station.

SoCal made an announcement then, saying they had been ready to turn the water back on full-time. They blamed the new shortages on the rioters and clamped down even harder. Rumor had it that parts of Level 1 hadn't had water since the transport crash.

Kai grabbed a glass and dipped it in a pot. He used some of it to wet a cloth and drank the rest, using the damp cloth to wipe his hands and face. He went back for more and hesitated before putting the glass firmly back on the counter and moving to the sofa. He sat with a soft sigh and rubbed his eyes.

"They have put barriers across the Level 6 up- and down-ramps. In some places, they even raised walls."

"So how do we get up there?" I asked.

He looked at me for the first time since he'd walked in. I could see defeat in every part of his face. "We do not."

Silence filled the room. I shook my head. I wasn't going to accept that.

"There's got to be some way. I can control my ID tag. I can sneak past whatever security they have in place. I've done it before."

Kai just looked at me.

"If we—"

"No, Kris. There are no ifs, no secrets. There are maybe two locations where they are letting people up to Level 6 in Los Angeles. From what I heard, the lineups are hours long. They are checking ID tags, fingerprints, retinal scans. Everything."

With every word I felt emptier, and my anger at him grew.

"You're just running away again," I said quietly. I thought I should yell and scream, but instead I just said it. My lack of emotion looked like it hit him harder than if I had raised my voice.

"Kris, I—"

It was my turn to interrupt him. "I don't care." I turned my back and started looking for my jacket.

"There might be a way," Pat said. She touched my arm. "Don't go yet."

I stopped. "How?"

"Let me talk to Kai about it first. If we can work out some details—"

"No. Tell me."

Pat sighed and dropped her arm. For a minute, I didn't think she was going to say anything, and I could feel my anger starting to build.

"We can climb up the outside," she said.

"The water pipe has been repaired, and soldiers are guarding the hole in the wall." Kai's voice came from so close, I almost jumped.

"Not the pipe," Pat said. "The wall."

I moved out from between them and waited.

"I do not understand," Kai said.

Pat turned to him. "Kris knows how to climb. She's spent most of her mornings and free time out at the cliffs by the compound. We've climbed together there. We know how to work together."

"The wall is almost two hundred meters tall."

"I know. We can do it. We all know the wall is weathered and cracked from exposure and earthquakes. They try to fix it, but it's too much for them to keep up." Pat looked at me. "We can do this."

I felt hope start to fill my chest. It bubbled out and I tried to control it as I spoke up. "I saw the wall when we were flying by. It looked doable."

Kai shook his head. "It is a suicide mission. You would be exposed the whole way up."

"Not if they're not looking for us," Pat said. "If we wear gray clothes, use a gray rope. Maybe get headsets to communicate, so we don't have to yell at each other. Depending on how the climb goes, it would only be maybe five or six pitches. Not that much, really."

Kai held up his hand. "What is a pitch?"

"A single section of a climb, where the lead climber stops to bring up the second. You can't do the whole thing in one go, they don't make ropes long or light enough. A rope is usually fifty or sixty meters long, so we're looking at a minimum of four pitches."

"I've never climbed multi-pitch," I said.

"See, you are putting your lives in danger for nothing," Kai said.

I exploded at the word *nothing*. How dare he? "Nothing? Fuck you, Kai. Ian isn't *nothing* to me. I would—"

"No! No, I did not mean it that way."

I didn't care. I turned to Pat. "Let's do it."

Pat grabbed a chair at the table and an information pad. I sat beside her, and after a while, Kai joined us. As he sat, Pat passed a list to him.

"This is what we'll need."

Kai grabbed the list and read it. His lips tightened at a few of the items, but he nodded anyway. After a glance at me, he stood and walked out of the apartment to see the insurgents again.

"He didn't mean it that way, you know," Pat said.

"Do I?"

Pat smiled and pulled another pad closer. "You do. Just give it time."

Time was something we didn't have. I knew Jeremy. If he didn't think Ian was of any use to him . . . I tried to throw the idea out of my head. It didn't work. All we had to do was hurry.

When Kai came back for the second time, we'd figured out almost everything. Except how to get through the damn hole.

CHAPTER 16

SANTA BARBARA, LEVEL 1—TUESDAY, JUNE 13, 2141 2:36 P.M.

WE GOT OUT OF THE CAR about a kilometer from the crash site and started unloading the trunk right away. I could already smell the chemicals Kai had said were dumped here years ago. We were in the no-man's zone, and weren't too worried about the authorities, not until we were closer to the hole in the wall. Gangs were another issue, if they were stupid or desperate enough to live in the contaminated area. There was always someone desperate enough.

Kai stood and watched while Pat and I got into our gear. The wall behind us was dirty gray fibercrete covered in graffiti. Some of it I recognized from what I had seen in downtown Los Angeles when I was a courier, but it all looked old. The new stuff—the stuff not layered in grime—looked like simple signatures or gang markings.

I got into my coveralls. They were too big for me, flowing past my hands and feet by over ten centimeters. Kai gave me shoelaces to tie them up, and the extra material billowed around me. I'd wanted to just fold up cuffs, but that would have stopped the coveralls from doing their job. The material helped disperse any thermal imaging readings. The side effect of that was I got warm fast. I pulled the hood up anyway. The insurgents had been stockpiling equipment for years, preparing for a civil war. None of it seemed to be in my size.

Pat crouched at the base of the wall, filling a small backpack with our street clothes and a little bit of food and water. She had refused a gun. When one of the insurgents tried to give her one, Pat had almost reacted violently. She wasn't offered another one. Her reaction made me think twice about teaming up with her, but I trusted her during the climb, at least.

If everything went well, we'd only be climbing the wall for about three and a half hours. Add the time it would take to get past the military, out the hole, and far enough away to not be seen, and we were closer to five hours. Kai was surprised at how long it would take, until I asked him to climb the outside of his apartment. He looked at it, and accepted our estimate.

The timing would put us at the top of the wall shortly before sunset. We were cutting it close—any serious mistakes would have us on the wall at night. At that point, we'd be stuck. There was no way we wanted to use lights, not where they could be seen so easily by anything outside the wall.

No one seemed to know if the exterior was patrolled or monitored in any way, except for the cameras at the top. That's where the thermal coveralls would come into effect, making us almost invisible. We hoped.

The color of Pat's coveralls almost matched the color of the fibercrete. That was the second part of not being discovered. The plan was to blend in with the outside wall. If we could have waited another couple of days, there was a chance we could have gotten some military-grade camouflage. That stuff had the ability to match almost every background, as long as you had something close to the right color to start with. In the end it didn't matter; what we wore *had* to be good enough. We'd turned off our trackers as well, in case SoCal or their army had set up sensors along the way in. We were essentially invisible.

Kai had contacted the insurgents to get most of this stuff. The part I was uncomfortable with was the rest of the deal. The plan was that they would divert the attention of the soldiers around the hole, and in return, we would join the group that had blown up the water stations on Level 6, helping them get out. SoCal had figured out the team was a man with two kids. Pat and I were supposed to break that up, posing as a family as we went back down. I was fully prepared to back out on that deal if things got bad. My plan was to get Ian, Pat, and myself somewhere safe. The only problem was that two of the Level 6 insurgents were just kids, and I knew I couldn't leave them there.

My backpack contained most of the climbing gear: our shoes, slings, and harnesses, our best guess at the climbing protection we'd need once we were on the wall, and my gun. Pat threw the sixty-meter rope over her shoulders and tied the loose ends around her waist. Finding a gray rope was one of the tougher things to do. Climbing ropes were usually ultracolorful, verging on the neon.

When we were ready to go, I gave Kai a quick hug. The old man was crying again as we started walking along the base of the wall, testing our comm equipment. He got back in the car. The comm link between Pat and I had a short-range setting so no one could overhear us, as well as a standard comm unit. We weren't sure if the standard comm unit would work outside the walls, or even if there were comm towers we could have used.

Pat and I crept along the base of the wall toward the hole.

Intel told us that the soldiers were set up in a ring about a hundred and fifty meters from the hole, just outside the wreckage perimeter. They had built a temporary fence around themselves with only one way in or out for the repair crew. As we got closer, I noticed something the insurgents had forgot to mention. Watchtowers. And the wall wasn't all that temporary. At least it didn't look that way to me. It looked like solid fibercrete.

I tapped Pat's back and she stopped.

"What's with the wall?" I asked.

Pat frowned, obviously concerned. "That's standard military-issue fortifications. Ten meters tall and about a meter thick. The towers will have at least two people in them. They supplement the drones."

"How the hell—"

"There'll be a seam in the corner where the temporary wall meets the outside one. We'll climb up there and down the other side."

I looked at her like she was crazy. They had to know the corner was a weakness. Wouldn't they have extra guards and drones watching it?

It was like Pat read my mind. "It's usually pretty well protected, but we're hoping the diversions pull some of the attention away, at least long enough for us to get over."

I grimaced and nudged her forward again. It felt like we were placing too much trust in people we didn't know.

The perimeter of the wall had been cleared of anything that could hide us. We hunkered down just outside the clearing and waited. Drones flew overhead occasionally. I tried to find a pattern, but couldn't. The longest stretch between flights was about five minutes, the shortest less than one. Not nearly enough time for us to scale the wall.

Pat wasn't happy. "I think they're on high alert," she whispered over the comm unit. "It might be the fighting at the water stations."

Another drone flew overhead, followed quickly by two more. Farther down, I could see even more flying toward the wall. A spate of gunfire sounded from the tower, and a drone fell out of the air, crashing into the temporary wall and sliding down to the base in a pile of wreckage. Five more drones flashed by with the same results. If this was the best the insurgents could do, we were fucked.

The battle, if you could call it that, went on for a few more minutes. Over fifty drones lay around the perimeter barrier when it was all done, and those were the ones we could see. Even more had flown in around the wall out of sight. None of them made it over the wall. Some didn't even make it to the cleared area.

The next thing I knew, I was flat on my back. The sound of multiple small explosions echoed between the wall and the ceiling. Pat lay beside me, a stunned look on her face. For just a moment, I thought I saw fear and the wash of memories. It was gone so fast, I wasn't sure it had even happened. Pat jumped to her feet and pulled me up. The air was filled with a thick, billowy smoke. Every crashed drone had flared and exploded at the same time. I could already hear the constant thrum of the exhaust fans speed up. We didn't have much time.

Pat and I bolted across the clearing together, sliding into the corner. Gunfire sounded from around the wall, some of it much too close. The seam between the barrier and the wall looked to be about two centimeters wide, maybe a bit more. Too small to get our toes into, even with the climbing shoes. We had good friction in the corner, but I really didn't want to do finger jams or a layback for ten meters.

I pulled open my pack and yanked out some of the gear. Finding the right equipment didn't take long. I picked six small camming units. When you pulled on the axle, the cams squeezed in, making them smaller. When you let go, the cams expanded again, putting outward pressure on the crack they'd been placed in. Falling or putting weight on them increased the outward pressure, making them even more secure. We moved fast, climbing simultaneously to make better time, trying to beat the quickly dissipating smoke screen,.

I peeked over the top of the temporary wall. The other side of the barrier hadn't been touched. Pieces of transport lay scattered between chunks of fibercrete. Seats lay sprinkled among the debris. From here, I thought I could see where I had left Ian trapped under a pillar. I looked away, my throat feeling thick. I was ashamed of what I had done. I didn't want to be reminded of that day. It was a mistake. One of the worst I'd ever made.

A drone flew overhead, only a few meters above the barrier. The smoke cleared, pushed away by the drone's downdraft. I pressed my face into the corner, praying the coveralls worked. The drone hovered for a while, before it changed direction and followed the top of the wall away from us. The smoke thickened again as it left.

I quickly slid over the top on my stomach, reversing the procedure I had used to climb up to get down the other side. Dropping to the ground, I cleaned out my gear and sprinted a few meters away to wait for Pat. She wasn't far behind. We hugged the city wall as we crawled to the opening created by the crash, stopping behind anything that would give us cover. From here, we could hear drones swarming on the other side of the barrier. The smoke had almost cleared, but gunfire still echoed from the ceiling, and I could see bright flashes from the towers.

Two drones positioned themselves above the corner we had just climbed. They were joined by a pair of soldiers. If we had still been climbing the corner, we wouldn't have seen them. We would have been dead. Now that we were past, the soldiers stood out, hiding behind a toppled support pillar.

We reached the hole and crawled out onto the top of the cliff without being seen.

Once we were outside, our cover disappeared, but so did the security. We crept along the base of the wall between tufts of grass and open air, letting the coveralls camouflage us as best they could.

——————

LOS ANGELES, LEVEL 6—TUESDAY, JUNE 13, 2141 11:20 A.M.

Miller lay in the back seat of a large sedan. The windows were tinted almost black, and a set of bars lay across the glass. More bars and thick glass separated the driver's seat from where he was. It was almost like a prisoner transport vehicle, with his hands zip-tied behind his back and his feet anchored to a bolt in the floor. He tried to open the car door, even if it was just to be seen by someone. No one would help him, *that* he knew, but they would remember, and some would talk if asked the right questions. The door was locked. He hadn't expected much more. He leaned back in his seat, suddenly more exhausted than he had ever felt in his life.

He had seen Kris at the ACE building, being dragged out by people he didn't recognize. He hoped they were good people, that she had found someone to help her get someplace safe. He held no hope of ACE ever being a safe place for her. Not after he'd seen William.

The car stopped and Miller heard muffled voices through the windows. The back window opened, and he felt a rush of fresh air enter the car. Miller raised his head and looked out. A man dressed in a SoCal uniform, standard-issue for anyone on security duty for entrance to Level 6, stared back at him. Before Miller could say anything, the window closed again and the car started to move up the ramp. Apparently, SoCal didn't care about him either. Maybe if they knew who he was, they would have grabbed him. It wouldn't have meant freedom.

The car drove for another forty minutes before Miller felt the nose of the vehicle dip down again. Interlevel parking. From the twists and turns the car had made, he figured he was somewhere in downtown Los Angeles. It still had to be Level 6, since he hadn't felt another up-ramp. When the car stopped, his door was opened and someone reached in to unlock him from the bolt in the car floor. Miller feebly tried to kick out, a last weak attempt for freedom, and the woman just laughed. She hauled him out and stood him up in front of Jeremy.

"Welcome to your new home," Jeremy said. "SoCal is closing off Level 6 and up, so I doubt your girlfriend will make another attempt to get you. Still, she has proven to be most resourceful in the past. She may even make it here. I think I'll keep you around for a few days, just in case. Besides, I'm having far too much fun with you." He turned and walked away, laughing.

The woman and another guard grabbed Miller by his arms and jerked him forward. They didn't follow Jeremy to the elevator, but instead went to a door in the parking garage. Lights flickered to life when the door was opened, revealing a long hallway with rooms off to the side. Miller recognized it for what it was. A prison. The guards threw him into a room at the end of the hall and locked the door behind him. Miller sprawled on his face on the rough floor.

Before the lights were turned off, he saw a parrilla in the corner.

LOS ANGELES, LEVEL 7—TUESDAY, JUNE 13, 2141 12:26 P.M.

Bryson limped across the white and gray tiles of the Los Angeles shuttle port, two large men on either side of him and Ms. Peters walking a few paces ahead. His knees still ached when he walked, but the pain was manageable. Ms. Peters had called in a doctor to take care of him when she found out he'd been mugged. The doctor had suggested he stay off his feet for most of the day, but that wasn't part of SoCal's schedule.

He didn't remember most of their meeting. It had turned into an endless barrage of questions, sometimes the same one rephrased to make sure his response stayed the same. By the end of the meeting Ms. Peters had the memory chip and the decryption key with the complete plans to the jump drive and new shielding.

After she had finished with him, he waited back in the room just off the elevator for another hour until someone came to get him. He'd spent the time lying on his back, staring at the ceiling, trying to figure out how a physicist went from writing a thesis to being interrogated like a criminal by one of the big three corporations in ten short years. He wished he could call his dad to tell him he was right. The corporations were evil.

The two men at his side had escorted him down to the parking garage and into a limousine where Ms. Peters waited. They didn't talk during the drive.

At the shuttle port, instead of going through standard security, Ms. Peters led them down a hallway to the far end of the concourse. She walked through a security checkpoint without showing any identification. Once through the doors, the general background noise of the shuttle port disappeared and the floor changed from tiles to thick gray carpet. A waiter carrying a tray of drinks appeared almost instantly. She waved him away.

Without stopping, Ms. Peters walked to a gangway and boarded a small shuttle. The four of them were the only passengers. Within minutes, they were in the air.

"Where are we going?" Bryson asked.

"Home." She paused and turned to face him. "SoCal Sat City 2. We have your lab configured and your staff ready. You'll begin work tomorrow."

"My staff? You got my staff from Kadokawa?" He could barely keep the elation out of his voice. His leaving didn't cause any hardship on his staff.

Ms. Peters laughed. "No. These people are some of the greatest minds in quantum theory. They've been studying your designs since we got hold of them last year. Sadly, they haven't gotten very far. They are very much looking forward to working with you."

Bryson couldn't help but wonder how many of them worked for SoCal, and how many of them were, like him, prisoners.

An hour later, the massive satellite came into view. The shuttle docked with no delay, even though he saw other transports waiting. Bryson realized that when you had the power of SoCal behind you, anything was possible. The power of corruption.

They were picked up almost immediately by a small open-air car. Ms. Peters sat in the front while Bryson and his two guards crammed themselves into the back seat. The guards had visibly relaxed once they'd docked.

Bryson stared. He had lived for so long in Meridian Sat City, he'd forgotten how big these things could get. The promenade they drove through was three stories tall, with walkways and roads along each edge and open air in the middle. In the open space grew trees that almost touched the ceiling. Drones flitted everywhere, delivering items or monitoring the populace.

The car turned off the promenade, driving for a few more

minutes before entering an elevator. The doors closed, and he felt the familiar sensation in his stomach as the elevator sped down. When the doors opened, the atmosphere had changed. Gone were the soaring open spaces and trees, replaced by plain composite and exposed conduits. Ms. Peters got out of the car and led Bryson down the hall.

They stopped in front of a simple door marked C3-LAB 42. She held her hand up to a sensor, and the door opened to an airlock. Behind it lay something Bryson recognized almost right away.

It was a duplicate of his lab at Meridian. As he stepped through the door, the background vibration of the city disappeared, yet he hadn't seen the eight centimeter gap between the lab and the Sat City that Meridian had used to accomplish the same thing. Ms. Peters stepped in with him, leaving the guards outside. They both slipped on the clean room suits and waited for the airlock to cycle. When the inner door opened, Bryson led the way in.

"Welcome home, Mr. Searls," Ms. Peters said.

SANTA BARBARA, OUTSIDE—TUESDAY, JUNE 13, 2141 3:40 P.M.

Pat and I had walked a good kilometer before we started looking for a place to climb, which put us almost opposite where we'd been dropped off. Kai would be long gone by now, though. As we walked, Pat pulled out a roll of fabric tape and we covered our hands with it, doubling up over the back.

We tried to be as careful as we could, staying close to the wall so our coveralls helped us blend in. We thought we saw a drone once, off in the distance. Just a speck that followed the wall. Other than that, we were alone.

Scouting a route was difficult. We couldn't get more than three meters away from the wall before we hit the edge of the cliff, which stopped us from being able to see up too high. In the end, we chose to climb in a rounded inside corner that tightened up as it went higher. Pat had taken the first lead, using the cracks and missing pieces of wall to climb. It took her over twenty minutes to get fifty meters high, and this was the easy part of the climb. She threw in some extra anchors and prepared to belay me up. We had been silent until that point.

"Off belay," Pat said into her short-range comm unit.

"Belay off." I unclipped the rope from my belay device. As soon as I did, I reached for the end of the rope and started to tie myself in. My stomach knotted, and fear pulled at the corners of my mind. I pushed the memories of the girders on Level 4 away. I had a rope, was tied in, I'd done this a million times. Never so high, but—I couldn't think about it. My hands shook as I completed the knot.

It seemed to take forever before Pat's voice crackled through the comm unit again, surprising me. "Taking up." The small coil of rope on the ground started unwinding as Pat pulled the slack out of the line. When the rope was tight she called out again. "On belay."

After a quick "climbing" reply, I started up the wall. Fibercrete felt different than the limestone near the compound. The fibercrete was rougher, and where pieces had broken off and on the insides of the cracks, it was like grabbing onto sharp crystals. Even with the tape on my hands, it felt like my skin was being shredded. I came up to the first piece of protection Pat had placed in the wall and pulled the trigger on the cam. The piece came out easily and I clipped it to my harness. The regular pattern of climbing calmed me, and I got into the rhythm.

Fifteen minutes later, I pulled myself up beside Pat and she told me which anchors to clip into. I equalized my sling, distributing my weight evenly between the anchors, and hung off the protection, my feet pressed against the wall. The shoes the insurgents had given me were too small, even for climbing, and my toes throbbed in the tight confines. It was still better than going too big. We'd made good time on the first part of the climb at under an hour. If we could keep it up, we'd be ahead of schedule.

I'd only ever seen the ocean through the windows of a transport, and once from the parking garage of the shuttle port. Out here, out in the open, I could really smell the water. I could feel the wind blow up the wall from the base. For the first time since we left the compound, I felt myself relax.

Pat smiled at me. She felt calmer as well.

The zigzag crack we were following continued up as far as we could see. I gave Pat back the pieces of protection I had removed, along with their slings, and she flipped the rope over my equalized anchors. With the standard routine of "On belay," she took off up-ward. I fed the rope out as she needed it, feeling the tension and the slack in the line rather that straining my neck to follow her every move. Instead, I looked over the water below us. When this was over, I would find a way to bring Ian to the ocean.

The rope slackened and Pat's voice echoed in my ear again. "Off belay."

The second pitch was harder than the first, though shorter and slower. The wall became more vertical, and the crack narrowed in places down to barely a fingertip wide. I placed the balls of my feet into the edge of the cracks, pressing the shoe's soft sole against the hard corner, and pushed myself up, only to jam my fingers in a new spot, weight them, and walk my feet up again. My muscles burned under the repetition. It felt good.

At the belay station, Pat handed the equipment rack to me. I slung it over my head and under my arm and began replacing the gear I'd pulled. I stared at the wall above me. The crack widened again into a fist-sized fissure. I started up, pressing my feet into the small cracks again until I got to the big stuff. I jammed my hand into the crack and made a fist, feeling the crystals bite through the tape before I moved a foot, twisting it in the crack to get more friction. I stepped up, moved my hand, jammed in the next foot, placing protection every three meters or so. My breathing deepened and joined the rhythm of my hands and feet. I only stopped when the crack narrowed again. I threw in four of the large cams and equalized an anchor before clipping myself in to them.

The sun had settled lower in the sky. It beat on our backs as we climbed, removing the chill of living in the lower levels. It would have been nice to take off the coveralls, but we still needed them to help us blend into the wall.

By the look of it, we had maybe three hours of daylight left. Things had been easy going so far, but that still didn't give us much time. Pat and I passed off the gear at the belay, and she took off again. My rope handling wasn't as good as hers, and when the rope got taut from coiling around itself, I heard her swearing under her breath.

I started climbing again when it was my turn. I hadn't made more than three moves before I heard the familiar sound of a drone.

The whine of its electric motor echoed off the corner we were climbing and bounced up the wall. I froze, both fists jammed deep into the crack and my feet pressed against the outer walls of the corner. I glanced up at Pat. I couldn't see her. The gray rope disappeared in the distance, dwindling to almost nothing. The wall itself was perfectly straight, so there was no reason I shouldn't have seen her, except for the gray coveralls we were wearing.

A flash of motion caught my eye. The drone was maybe twelve meters away, flying horizontally almost a meter below me. If I was still anchored in at the belay, I would have been below it. I had no idea if it was examining the wall or the ground. If SoCal had found some indicator we were out here, it could be looking for us. Would the camouflage of the coveralls help?

"Why did you stop," Pat asked.

"A drone. Ten meters to my left, about a meter below me," I whispered back.

"Shit. Don't move."

"Yeah, good plan." I couldn't keep the sarcasm out of my voice. It helped hide the terror I felt.

My shoulders began to throb, the right one feeling like it was going to burst into flames. It had never been right since I popped it trying to open a locked door last year. I wanted to move my feet into the corner, jam them into the crack, and get the weight off my hands. But I didn't dare move. I stopped breathing.

CHAPTER 17

SANTA BARBARA, OUTSIDE—TUESDAY, JUNE 13, 2141 6:27 P.M.

THE DRONE SLOWED DOWN and gently lowered itself almost to the ground. It backed up and followed the wall along where Pat and I had walked.

Had we left footprints behind? Had Pat dropped a piece of protection? No, she would have called out if something was coming my way. What could the drone have seen that interested it? Panic made my hands sweat, and I felt my grip in the crack loosen as the protective tape slipped. I gently slid one hand out, wiped it on my coveralls, and reinserted it into the crack before doing the same with my other hand. It didn't help.

In the time it took me to do that, the drone reached the corner we were climbing and slowly rose again. The closer it got to me, the more panic started consuming me, until my entire body was numb with it. The drone settled just below my feet and moved off, eventually rounding the outside corner and disappearing from view. I breathed a sigh of relief and moved my right foot into the crack, standing on it and relieving the burn in my shoulders.

Pat must have felt a change of tension in the rope. "Is it gone?" she asked.

"Yeah," I whispered back. "That was too fucking close. I thought I was going to have to smash it with my feet."

"That close?" I could hear the stress in her voice.

"Yeah."

I shook out my shoulders one at a time and started the repetitious climbing again.

Once I reached the belay station, Pat made us eat and drink. The sandwiches Kai had made for us had squished in the pack, but they were still some of the best I'd ever tasted. Working in the sun, feeling the fresh air, breathing it in, always changed my perspective. The world became a better place. At least for a while. When we were done, Pat put everything back in her pack and passed me the rack. It was my turn to lead again.

The crack ran out fifteen meters up.

I braced my feet wide in the corner, pushing them into the wall, and twisted two fingers into the final part of the crack. I leaned back as far as I could, feeling my grip slip, and twisted my fingers tighter. Just over a meter above, a horizontal crack started. It wasn't much, but with the friction of the fibercrete, I figured I would be able to traverse across until I found another way up. Leaving the corner didn't make me happy, but the only other way was down.

I called down to Pat. "Watch me."

"I am, girl, I am."

The only way to place more protection was to move my fingers. I leaned in close to the wall and untwisted them. My left foot slipped and then popped. I launched away from the wall. For a split second,

I felt like I was floating. My world slowed to a crawl, every detail of the wall jumping into sharp focus, and then sped up beyond belief. I plummeted.

I felt a tug on the rope and continued my descent. Another one. I held a scream in my throat, not daring to let it out. The rope tightened a third time and I bounced upward before settling back down.

I opened my eyes. Pat stared back at me, her eyes so big I felt like I could climb in and rest for a while. She came out of it before I did, reaching out and pulling me into the belay station. She clipped me into the anchor and let some slack in the rope. I almost screamed before the anchors took my weight.

"You okay?"

It took me a bit to answer. My stomach still felt as though it nestled against my larynx. "Yeah," I said. "Yeah." I looked at the wall stretching above me. "My first real lead fall."

Pat grinned. I couldn't help but laugh and smile back as the tension tumbled from me. Hanging on the rope were two pieces of protection. They must have popped as I fell. The last one had stayed in place. If that one had popped, I would have ended up below Pat and been forced to climb up to the belay station. My stomach roiled, and my hastily eaten lunch splattered against the wall below us. I grabbed some water and rinsed out my mouth.

"Christ," I said.

Pat was still grinning. "Time to get back on the horse, as the old saying goes."

I stared at her.

"You're already tied in," she said. "The first part is a bit of top-roping, then the stuff you already climbed. No point in switching leads. We'd have to untie from the rope."

Going back into a lead situation was the last thing I wanted to do. My hands still tingled from the sudden drop. I pulled myself toward the wall, and Pat instinctively tightened the rope.

"Give me a minute," I said.

Pat stayed quiet. Five minutes later, she finally spoke.

"You have to go. We can't hang around here all day. The sun will be down before you know it, and we can't climb in the dark."

I nodded and took a deep breath, trying to steady my frayed nerves. "Climbing."

"Climb on."

I made it three moves before my leg started twitching so much it popped from the crack and I fell again. They called it Elvis leg. I wasn't quite sure why, but this time at least I knew who Elvis was. I rested my forehead against the warm wall and counted to ten before I started up again. Elvis came for another visit and I stopped.

This was stupid. I was top-roping. I'd done this a million times. Granted, not a hundred and thirty meters above the ground, but the logistics were the same. With the rope anchored above me, the most I could fall would be the rope stretch plus whatever slack Pat kept in the line. I rubbed my hands against the coveralls, wishing we'd brought some chalk powder to keep them dry, and prepared to start up again.

"Keep me tight," I said into the comm unit.

The top piece of protection had held a huge fall, and another small one after that. I told myself it wasn't about to come out now. I jammed my left foot and right hand into the crack and stood, then my left hand higher up, followed by my right foot. I started the pattern again.

Before I knew it, I had passed the piece that had held my fall. The fibercrete around it had crumbled a bit, but the cams had expanded under weight and held. Once my weight was off the piece, I reseated it, pushing it deeper into the flaring crack. Pat would have a hell of a time getting it out. I didn't much care.

It took twice as long for me to place the next pieces as I continued upward. I saw where the old ones had been, where the fibercrete had crumbled, softened by the weather. I placed the next protection in a different spot, as deep as I could.

Not giving myself the chance to think, I moved above the last piece, pressing my feet into the corner walls. I moved my hands up, pushing against the walls as hard as I could, holding them there as I walked my feet up. I reached the horizontal crack before I knew it, sinking my left fingers into it and transferring my weight onto them. My foot stood on the last piece of protection I'd placed. I wedged a cam into the crack without caring about the placement, desperate for even the semblance of safety. My heart thudded in my chest as I reached for the rope and clipped it into the protection before grabbing the piece with my right hand and hanging on it. Everything about what I had just done reeked of bad climbing etiquette, but I didn't care.

Once I'd gotten myself under control, I moved along the horizontal crack until I reached a vertical seam in the fibercrete. I stopped and placed anchors. Just above, the seam widened into another crack.

"Off belay."

SANTA BARBARA, OUTSIDE—TUESDAY, JUNE 13, 2141 8:06 P.M.

Pat and I hung below the top of the wall. Above us sat a high-end residential sector with massive yards and pools and security systems. The sun was a bright red ball sizzling as it touched the ocean below us. We were waiting for dark.

Where the fibercrete ended, a strong ornate metal fence started. The wall rose a meter higher than the ground all the way around Level 7, so it was about a three meter drop on the other side.

Pat waited as the sun dipped under the water and the clouds churned into a deep coral. It would be a while before it was dark enough for us to move. The cameras placed along the top of the wall used infrared at night. They were the main reason we had the coveralls. With the hoods up, the only thing the cameras would be able to pick up were our hands and feet. And then only if they got lucky. That's what we hoped, anyway.

The sunset brought me back to my first trip to Level 7. I had left Ian in the hospital, surrounded by police. He had just killed Abby. I was as taken by the beautiful red-orange shimmering on the ocean waves today as I had been a year ago. Over the last year, I had grown to love the mountains, but sunsets like this just didn't happen there.

Pat hissed at me from above. She had already climbed over the fence and was waiting for me. I pulled on the anchor, walking my feet up the wall until I could grab the fence with one hand before unclipping myself. I wasn't comfortable until I had both my hands and feet firmly planted on the metal.

As planned, we had landed in a backyard. A deep blue pool shone near the house, a good sprint away from us. I could smell the chemicals used to keep it clean. To the left, a row of tall trees indicated the edge of the property. We ran, crouching along the wall until we reached them. Behind us, sprinklers turned on, washing the lush green grass. Everyone below Level 6 was on water rationing, and here they were still concerned about keeping their grass looking green. There was a reason SoCal was blocking access, and it wasn't just the unrest. If everyone knew what was really happening, the riots would turn into an all-out war.

Once we were in the trees, Pat stripped off her coveralls and pulled on the clothes from her backpack. Even in the dim light coming from the distant houses, I could see scars down her back, wrapping around her torso. They were so deep, even tissue regeneration wouldn't have gotten rid of them. I quickly changed before she caught me staring, before she saw the pity that I was sure was written across my face. It was no wonder she was constantly haunted by memories of what had happened to her.

The last item out of my backpack was my gun. I slipped it into a holster under my jacket.

We'd both chosen darker clothes. We needed to blend in with the general populace, but still wanted to be able to hide in the shadows. First we needed to contact the insurgents who were blowing up the water stations. We knew they were in Santa Barbara, but we didn't know where.

Needing them still churned up my insides. Even though they had meant well when I saw Ian in ACE's building, I couldn't help but distrust them. But Pat and I had no other contacts up here. If we . . . No! *Once* I got Ian out of the building, we were going to need a quick getaway, and they could provide it.

Pat and I crept through the trees to the street in front of the house, and from there to, according to the sign, New Cliff Drive. Once free of the houses, Pat pulled out her comm unit and called Kai.

"We're here." She listened for a while and closed the connection. "They're waiting for us with a car at the charging station about two kilometers south of here by Highway 7-97. Keep your comm unit active."

As we were walking, I started thinking about what I would do. First, I had to get rid of Pat. I tried to convince myself that it wasn't because I didn't trust her, but I knew that wasn't a hundred percent true. I had no idea when she would lose it again, when her memories would rip her from the present into the past. She had been much better lately, but that didn't change how I felt. I knew that if we went in together and found Ian and she had another episode, I wouldn't even stop to think about it. I would get Ian out and leave her behind. I didn't want that on my hands. Once I found out from the insurgents where Ian was, I would dump them all and go in alone.

LOS ANGELES, LEVELS 6 & 7—TUESDAY, JUNE 13, 2141 9:52 P.M.

Only one of the insurgents picked us up. Albert drove us past the Griffith Observatory Museum on the way to downtown Los Angeles. The observatory sat on a small hill above Level 7, bathed in lights so bright there was no chance it was being used for its original purpose. Residential areas sat carved into the hills surrounding it. The homes were spread far apart, some of them dwarfing the size of the observatory. The obvious cost of what I saw sickened me.

Ahead lay downtown itself. The three tallest buildings belonged to SoCal, IBC, and Kadokawa. From what I understood, each building was sovereign land of the corporation that owned it, just like an embassy. The rest, theoretically, belonged to the United States, but in reality were controlled by SoCal. The plazas around the towers would be barricaded now, patrolled by militia, and would stay that way until the hostilities between the corporations ended.

We skipped downtown, moving closer to New Pasadena, and took a down-ramp to Level 6, pulling into an industrial complex. At this time of night, the parking lots were quiet. I caught a faint glimpse of movement just outside the lights before someone walked toward the car. She was only a child, cradling a rifle in her arms as if was too heavy for her. One of the insurgents. The look on her face reminded me of my time on Level 1, when I had been only a little older than she appeared to be. I saw the same mixture of haunted and scared, the same refusal to let anyone know.

She spoke quietly to Albert before returning to her post in the shadows.

After we parked, the driver walked to the door of the closest building and typed in a code, blocking our view with his body.

Pat stepped closer. "What's the code?"

"Oh, sorry." He punched it in again as she watched.

"If we get separated, is this a safe place to come back to?"

"Yeah," he said. "No one knows we're here, and since we back-tracked from the last station we hit, I don't think anyone will be looking for us. Not here." He pulled open the door and entered. Pat and I followed.

He unlocked another door at the end of the hall on the second floor and let us in. The room was barren, except for some rickety looking chairs and a folding table covered in stained green vinyl. A young boy sitting at the table stood when we walked in and moved to the back corner. He had the same look in his eyes as the girl outside.

Stacks of information pads lay scattered on the surface of the table. Albert put his car keys beside a pile and fished through them, pulling a pad out. He tossed it to Pat.

"This is the plan of the building ACE moved into. It took a lot to get that. I hope this guy is worth it."

Pat turned her back on him and powered up the unit. I stood beside her, watching as she flicked through the screens.

"When do we go in?" I asked. I wanted to leave now.

Pat flipped through more displays before answering. "It'll take me a while to figure this out." She looked up at our guide. "Do you know where the guards are?"

"Keep looking."

Pat went through the screens faster until she found what she wanted. She sat down, tuning the world out, and stared at the glowing screen.

"We already have a plan for you to get in," Albert said.

Pat kept staring at the display, already engrossed in what she was seeing. "Give the information to Kris. We'll compare notes in an hour."

At the table, Albert pulled out another pad and I took it from his hand. It showed the weaknesses in ACE's defenses.

"According to our sources, ACE built holding cells in the sub-basement. One of them was specially outfitted with stainless steel tables, metal mesh frames, and other unmentionables. We figure that's where they're keeping your guy."

"And how do we get in?" Outwardly, I ignored the description of the torture chamber equipment, but inside it felt like I was being ripped apart.

"*You* two get in through here." He zoomed in on a detailed map. "This is the building right beside ACE. It used to be a single structure, but they built a solid fibercrete wall between the two sections. There's a wet wall right here in the corner. It's where the main plumbing and electrical is run for both buildings. You have to go through half a meter of fibercrete reinforced with silica nanorods to get to it. Once inside, you have the freedom to move to any floor. The only problem is, there's another half a meter of fibercrete and silica nanorods to get through on the other side. It took us most of today to crack through into the wet wall, which means it'll take you most of the night to get inside ACE."

"If the wet wall is used for plumbing, there should be access for repairs, shouldn't there?" I asked.

"Yeah. If you were ACE, would you leave those unprotected?"

"Maybe."

"Nah. That ain't happening. They'll be wired or something."

"Where are the access points?"

He looked at me like I was stupid and shrugged. "There's one every third floor, so four in total. One in the basement, third floor, sixth floor, and ninth floor. In both buildings."

"How tall is the building?"

"Ten floors."

"Nothing on the roof for access?"

"Not that we know of."

I nodded. Taking the whole night to go through the wall was out of the question. I didn't want to be in the ACE building during the day when everyone was there, so I would have to wait the entire day before I broke through the last bit. That was way too long to leave Ian alone with Jeremy.

"Where's your entry to the wet wall?" I asked.

"From a bathroom under construction on the second floor."

My plan was starting to form. If I used the second-floor hole and climbed down to the basement, I could get into ACE through the access panel. Then I would only have to go down one more level before reaching the holding cells in the subbasement. It was only a guess that Ian was being kept there . . . a pretty good one though. Then I would have to get back into the wet wall and help Ian to climb up two floors, back to the hole. I'd seen the condition he was in.

I wasn't sure he could make it.

A sudden feeling of despair came over me—this was turning into an impossible job. But I knew I had to try. I put the pad back on the table and walked to the office door.

"Where are you going?" Albert asked.

"I just need some fresh air. Your girl can keep an eye on me."

Closing the door softly behind me, I resisted the urge to sprint down the hallway. I pretended to be deep in thought, but I'd already made up my mind to go in alone.

I put my hand in my pockets and closed my fingers around the keys I'd stolen from the table.

CHAPTER 18

LOS ANGELES, LEVEL 6—TUESDAY, JUNE 13, 2141 10:16 P.M.

THE ACE BUILDING was on the outskirts of downtown. On Level 1, I would have seen buildings truncated at the fifth floor, cut off when the levels were first built. Here, the towers soared into air, though none of them touch the ceiling over sixty meters above me.

My slow drive past the building had shown me nothing. Unlike the corporate towers, there was no outward sign that anything important went on inside. At first I thought the insurgents had gotten their information wrong, but as I drove past, I realized that this is exactly the way ACE, the old ACE I knew, would have it. There would be eyes on the outside, hidden cameras and people during the day, but everything else would be behind the building's facade. Jeremy might have somehow gotten control of ACE, but some things would never change.

I only saw one person. He was sitting near the delivery entrance of the adjacent building, a sandwich in one hand and a pad in the other.

I could almost feel Ian pulling at me from inside, calling me to help him. I couldn't—didn't want to—resist.

The lot I pulled into was a couple of blocks from ACE, and empty. I parked the car and threw the keys under the seat. If I didn't make it out, the insurgents would still be able to find the car and drive it away.

The walk to the building beside ACE took only a few minutes. By now, Pat probably knew that I was gone, but without the car it would take her longer to get here. I planned to have Ian out in the next twenty minutes. If it took longer than that, we probably wouldn't make it.

My timing was already starting out bad. The building that shared the wet wall with ACE was locked. I walked toward the delivery doors, hoping the man I'd seen earlier was still there, and that he wasn't an ACE lookout. When I got to the short driveway, even the box he had been sitting on was gone, but the door still stood open. I crept down the drive toward the loading dock at the end.

The sandwich eater stood in the corner created by the open door, holding it open so you couldn't see him from the street. A stream of urine ran between his feet. And they said people who lived on Level 2 were disgusting.

Before he could turn around, I dashed through the open door. The hallway I found myself in was short, ending in double doors on the left. On the right was an open entry leading to a janitor's closet. I heard voices behind the double doors, getting louder as they came closer. The man outside must have heard them as well. The outside door slipped from his grip and almost shut, blocking out the background noise of the city.

I jumped into the closet.

The closet was bigger than I had thought, and a complete mess. Bottles of cleaning chemicals lined the shelves set against one wall. A dried-up stain showed where one of the bottles had fallen some time ago, leaving a track to the drain in the floor. A mass of used mops with broken handles and missing heads had been thrown into a corner. It was the only spot I could find to hide. The mops shifted as I crawled behind them. One crashed to the floor. I crouched, one hand on my gun, sure they would find me.

The man that had been outside walked in, kicking the fallen mop out of his way. It clattered against the pile I hid behind. I tried to push myself deeper into the corner.

"What are you doing?" a voice asked from the hallway.

The man jumped as though startled. "I'm just getting some garbage bags."

"Well, hurry it up. I'm tired of doing half your work for you."

"You do no such thing," the man said as he grabbed a box off the shelf beside me and left the closet. "I do more than my share."

"Ha. If you did your share, we would be home already . . ."

The voices got quieter as the cleaning staff walked away, fading to nothing as they went through the double doors. I breathed a sigh of relief and crawled out from the behind the mops.

A silhouette blocked the light from the hallway as I stood up. I raised my gun, pointing it toward them. Where the hell had the person come from? They took a step backward.

"Don't move," I said.

The silhouette changed into an old woman as I stepped from the closet. Her hands were raised in the air, shaking like leaves on a tree.

"Please, no . . ."

"Be quiet." I searched her with one hand, finding nothing but a bunch of keys. "What are these keys for?"

"Please, I just the cleaning lady. I don't know anything."

"What are the keys for?"

"They open offices, so we can clean."

I'd already figured out that much. What I really wanted to know was if the keys opened the access to the wet walls.

"What else?" I asked.

"I don't know. Please?"

Her body radiated fear so intense, I could almost taste it. But I knew it wasn't over yet. Not for her. It made me feel like scum, but I had to keep the end goal in mind: get to Ian. I pushed her into the closet and forced her to lie on her side, tying her hands and feet with the electrical cord from an old vacuum. I wanted to cover her mouth, but I remembered how it had felt when the insurgents had taped over mine. I didn't want her death on my hands.

Before I closed the closet door, I leaned in close. "No sounds, no noise. If I hear you, I'll be back."

I must have sounded more convincing than I felt, because even her quiet whimpering stopped.

I leaned my forehead against the closed door. ACE had trained me for this, but I had never felt this way. Never felt like I was villain. It had never felt *real*.

I moved to the double doors and listened before pushing through. One of these keys *had* to fit the wet wall access hatch. It would save me from having to haul Ian up three floors to the hole the insurgents made. I didn't even know if there would be a ladder to help.

From the floor plan on the pad, I knew where the stairs were. I ran to them and into the basement. The wet wall was easy enough to find.

None of the keys fit.

LOS ANGELES, LEVEL 6—TUESDAY, JUNE 13, 2141 10:33 P.M.

I was out of breath from running up two flights of stairs. With my ear against the second-floor door, I slowed my breathing as best I could and listened. I didn't hear anything. I wasn't sure how long I had before the other two cleaners would get worried and start looking for the old lady. I opened the door and ran down the hall to the bathrooms.

The washroom was under renovation. Cans of paint sat on a plastic sheet in the corner, and beams lay stacked in the middle of the room. The place looked like it had been separated into smaller sections at one time, but now it was gutted with piles of busted building materials everywhere. One of the piles hid the hole to the wet wall.

The insurgents couldn't have been working on it for long. The hole was barely big enough for a grown man to fit through. It was more than big enough for me. No matter what size it was, it would have to do.

Pipes, ventilation, and wiring ran up and down the wet wall, but nothing else. There were no ladders, no platforms for workers to use. Nothing to grab on to. The size of the hole didn't matter anymore.

Getting Ian out this way would be impossible.

I stuck my gun back into its holster under my jacket, gave Oscar a quick good luck rub, and stretched out to reach a pipe on the opposite wall. I jerked my hand back, seared from the hot water running through it. Shifting my position, I reached for a different pipe and slowly transferred my weight to it, ignoring the pain in my hand. The pipe shook, but held. I slid down, the light from the hole above me getting dimmer and dimmer. I hadn't even thought of bringing a flashlight.

The comm unit in my ear crackled, and I almost let go, scared by the sudden noise.

"Where are you?" Pat asked.

"I went for a walk," I grunted, trying to keep my grip on the slippery pipe as I moved down to the basement.

"Bullshit. You stole their car. This guy is pissed off enough to shoot you if he sees you."

"The keys are in it."

"Where . . ." I could almost hear the realization dawning on her. "Where are you?"

My toes caught the edge of the basement access door, a small lip on the sill. It wasn't big enough for me to stay long, but it gave me a bit of a rest. I crouched down, holding onto a pipe with one hand and feeling in the dark for something to open the door with the other. "I'm not going to get anyone else I know hurt." That was only part of the truth. I wasn't about to tell her I didn't trust her.

"Don't do it, Kris. Don't go in. Alone isn't going to work."

My fingers found what I hoped was a safety release for the access door. I pried it away from the door with my fingernail, scraping through years of rust to get a better grip on it, and pulled. The access door popped open a centimeter. I pushed it the rest of the way with my feet and slid into darkness.

"Too late, I'm in." I closed the connection.

Pat wouldn't be the only one who knew I was in. ACE would have had the access door monitored. I hadn't felt any resistance as it opened, but Albert was right, they weren't dumb enough to leave a back door into their building wide open.

I assumed I'd entered another bathroom, it would only make sense. I felt my way to the door and opened it. Light flooded in from the hallway, illuminating urinals lining the wall.

I pulled out my gun and dashed to the stairwell, forcing myself to slow down on the stairs to the subbasement, keeping as quiet as I could. I heard feet pounding on the steps above me. People coming to check on the alarm I triggered when I open the access door.

Getting out wasn't going to be easy.

I didn't have time to think about that now. I needed to find Ian. I buried the fear growing inside me as deep as I could and ran down the hall.

Doorways lined the corridor, all of them open. Each room was the same, tiny with nothing but a frame anchored to the wall for a bed and a metal toilet. The rooms were empty. Ian wasn't in one of the cells. My step faltered.

There was only one more door, and it was closed. I knew what was behind that particular door. I'd gotten the inventory list from Albert. I pulled it open and looked inside.

Ian was strapped to a metal frame. His bare feet were off the ground; metal strips held them snugly. His arms were tied together above him and he hung from them, his head rolled onto his chest. Small incisions covered his chest where his shirt had been ripped open.

Voices echoed down the hallway. I closed the door as quietly as I could, desperate for a place to hide. Just before it latched shut, I realized there was no handle on the inside of the door, just a slot for a key. I pulled Oscar out of my pocket and slipped the keychain in between the door and the frame, just below the hinge. If they saw it, we'd never get out of this room.

Ian lifted his head, his eyes opening a crack. He looked straight at me, but I didn't see any recognition in them.

Bare white walls made the room appear large. Two stainless steel tables sat on spindly legs by the far wall. I could see only one place to hide, and I really didn't want to use it. Voices penetrated the partially closed door, and I had no choice, sprinting toward Ian and slipping behind the mesh frame just as the door to the torture chamber opened. I climbed up the mesh, hiding myself behind Ian's torso.

I froze where I was. My gun, still in its holster, jammed into my ribs, but I didn't dare reach for it. Even if I could, the noise might draw in even more guards. Footsteps entered the room, sounding like they stopped just inside the door. I was sure the person could hear my breathing or smell my sweat from across the room.

"Anyone in there?" A second voice from the door.

"Just this poor bastard."

"Yeah. Hey, I know him! That's Miller. He was with us when Nigel was shot last year."

The footsteps got closer. I held my breath. So much needed to go right for us to get out. I wanted to take a look at Oscar, make sure he was still in the door. I knew I couldn't.

"You sure?"

"Yeah. I never forget the face of a pretentious ass."

There was no response.

"Come on, we've got a call of another access panel open on the sixth floor. There's no one here. If someone came in, they didn't head in this direction. It's probably the new system working out its bugs."

The footsteps got farther away and I heard the door close. I hung where I was for a few seconds before I dared to move. Lowering my feet to the floor, I unhooked my cramped fingers from the mesh. Moving to the front of the frame, I unclipped Ian's feet. I had to climb the mesh again to do the same to his arms. He collapsed to the ground, landing in a heap like a rag doll.

I jumped down and rolled him over. He groaned, opening his eyes again.

"Ian. Ian, you have to be here, with me. We need to get out."

His eyes focused on my face and he lifted his fingers to my cheek. "Kris?" His voice sounded weak and raspy.

Tears flowed down my face. "We need to go."

"You shouldn't have come."

"I didn't have a choice." I wiped my eyes, angry at myself. Now was not the time for crying. It never was. "Come on, you need to get up." I stood and grabbed him under the arm. Ian grunted in pain and I let go. "Are you okay?"

It was a stupid question. I knew that before I'd finished saying it.

Ian pulled himself up using the mesh frame and his other arm. He stumbled and fell, leaning against the mesh until he could almost stand on his own. I moved in and slung his good arm over my shoulder. He leaned into me, the sudden weight almost bowling me over. We walked slowly to the door, and with each step he seemed to get stronger, though he still rested against me.

Oscar had moved, the keychain barely stuck in the doorframe. It had to be enough. The door resisted the first push, but the second budged it open slightly. I leaned Ian against the wall and reached down to retrieve Oscar.

I pushed the door open the rest of the way and looked down the hall. It was empty. Ian and I stepped out and trudged down toward the stairs.

"Where are we going?" he asked. "Who else is with you?"

I didn't answer for a minute. I knew he was too weak to climb back up the pipes to the second floor. Even I would have a tough time, and I hadn't been in Jeremy's company for days. "I don't know."

Ian stopped. "How did you get in?"

He listened quietly as I told him.

"You could make it out of here. Leave me your gun, I'll get out on my own. We both know I'm in no condition to climb."

The idea was so far from where I was, I almost laughed out loud. I opened the door and we moved into the stairwell.

William was waiting for us, a gun in his hand and a look of exasperation on his face.

LOS ANGELES, LEVEL 6—TUESDAY, JUNE 13, 2141 10:35 P.M.

Pat heard the comm link close and fell back into her chair. What the fuck was Kris thinking? She was going to get herself and Miller killed. Maybe that was her plan. Maybe she'd had enough and wanted to end it all. Pat almost believed it, except Kris would never do anything to harm Ian. She loved him too much.

Now she was in the lion's den.

"I need to get to the ACE building," Pat said.

"And how the fuck do you plan on doing that? Your friend stole our car. As far as I'm concerned you can . . ." Albert paused, his eyes widened. "She went in alone?"

"Yes, she went in alone. How do we get there?"

"We don't. She'll be dead before we do."

"Would you give up that easily if it was one of your team out there?"

"If they just left without saying anything, if they broke up the team like that? Yeah, I think I would."

Pat knew he was right, partners never abandoned one another. She wasn't about to give him the pleasure of knowing it, though. "Well, I can't. Will you help me?"

"There's nothing we can do."

Pat turned her back on Albert and walked to the door.

She shivered in the cool night air. The ACE building was about a kilometer and a half away, just over twenty minutes walking. She started running. Her best time for a five-kilometer run was under twenty-five minutes. That made for about a seven minute run to ACE. Too late to be of any help.

Pat sped up.

The downtown streets were empty, which was a good thing. Pat didn't stop or slow down at the intersections. She passed the car sitting in a dark lot before her brain caught up to what she had seen. She skidded to a stop. Her lungs felt like they were going to burst. She almost doubled over, but forced herself back to the parking lot. Kris said she'd left the keys under the seat. Pat tried to run again and ended up only stumbling to the parked vehicle.

The door was unlocked. She pulled it open and slid behind the wheel. Her hands were shaking and her sight got blurry. She wasn't getting enough air. She didn't care, she didn't have time to rest. Pat found the keys and unlocked the motor, throwing the car into reverse. She almost slammed into the charging units behind her. The front tires squealed as the car left the lot, heading the wrong way down a one-way street.

$$\Longrightarrow$$

LOS ANGELES, LEVEL 6—TUESDAY, JUNE 13, 2141 10:41 P.M.

"I knew it was you as soon as the alarm went off," William said, shaking his head slowly. "What a waste, both of you."

Ian slumped against me, pushing me into the open door. I stared at William as he lowered his gun. He was standing way too close, in the confines of the stairwell. I knew I'd be able to take him out at this range, but I wouldn't be able to do it without dropping Ian.

"This isn't what I wanted, you know. ACE was doing good. We were making headway." William's voice got softer. "There's really nothing left anymore."

"What do you want?" I couldn't keep the venom out of my voice.

William sighed. "I set off an alarm on the sixth floor. I opened another access point to the wet wall. I didn't even want this building, you know. Didn't want Level 6. It's too open to scrutiny. He didn't care."

I asked the question again. "What do you want? What about us?"

William stepped away from the stairs, moving even closer to me. "Get him out of here."

I didn't move.

"Go! You don't have much time. As soon as they realize no one is on the sixth floor, security will go back to their rounds."

"So you can be Jeremy's hero and shoot us in the back?"

William stared at us for a second. "No. So you have a chance to get away from here. Away from what ACE has become. Maybe get out of the city and have a life together."

I wasn't sure William was talking about Ian and me any more.

William put his gun on the floor and kicked it under the stairs. "Too much has gone wrong, changed. This isn't what ACE is. It's not what *I* am."

As soon as the gun was down, I lashed out with my foot. William crumpled to the ground at the same time Ian did, pulling me with him.

I struggled back to my feet, wedging my shoulder under Ian's. "Come on, we have to go."

"I won't make it up the pipes," Ian said.

"No. With the fake alarm on the sixth floor, we have a chance to make it through the front door. Now come on."

Ian made it to the bottom of the stairs and stopped. I took the first step up and lifted him with my shoulder. He followed slowly. With each step, Ian got slower and slower. He had taken more of a beating than I'd thought. William watched from the bottom, still laying on the cold fibercrete.

By the time we reached the first-floor door, Ian was panting with the strain of keeping up with me, barely containing the pain that must have been consuming his body. How I wished I could take some of his pain as my own.

I could already hear people on the stairs above. We stepped

through the door without looking, into a carpeted lobby. Ian tripped again, almost taking me down.

A security guard came around the corner from the front desk. When he saw us, he reached for his gun. Without thinking, I lifted mine and pulled the trigger. The guard crumpled to the ground, blood pooling underneath him. The overhead lights reflected off the thin gold ring on his left hand. I tried not to think about it. Ian and I lurched past the body. The door was only a couple of meters away.

"Kris Merrill."

The voice was calm, authoritative, and in control. I recognized it right away. Ian and I stopped and turned around. Ian forced himself to stand on his own, and a wave of pride flushed through me.

Jeremy stood by the security desk, just in front of the dead guard. The gun nestled in the palm of his hand, looking like a toy: small and pure black. I recognized it from training. It looked like a Ruger CRH, a close range, low-powered weapon. Jeremy was too far away to kill us with it, but it would still be able to stop us from leaving. He pointed it straight at me.

"You almost made it," he said, taking a couple of steps closer, getting in range.

We stood there, not saying anything.

"Be a dear and drop the gun. You won't be needing it anymore."

Instead of dropping it, I raised it and aimed at him.

"I thought you were smarter than that." The gun in his hand moved to point at Ian. "Perhaps if I shot him you would cooperate better."

The stairway door burst open and Jeremy twitched. William jumped out behind him, his gun pointing at Jeremy's back.

I pulled the trigger at the same time Jeremy did. Three gunshots echoed in the space.

Ian and Jeremy both crumpled to the floor, and my world collapsed. I stood in shock as William sprinted to Jeremy and dove to his knees, sliding on the carpet beside him. The gunshots still rang in my ears. William dropped his gun and lifted Jeremy's head into his lap as I grabbed Ian under the arms and dragged him to the doors, my own gun forgotten on the floor. I watched William as I pulled. Jeremy tilted his head, his lips moving, before slumping back to the floor. William wilted.

The doors pushed open when my back pressed against them, slamming against Ian's legs as I pulled him through. Security piled out of the elevator and stairwell. They took one look at the three men on the floor before seeing me. One took aim and fired at me through the glass doors, and the rest of the guards followed suit. I yanked Ian behind a pillar. More bullets shot through the window beside me. Glass blew over the sidewalk and into a planter filled with delicate white flowers. Suddenly it all stopped.

Headlights flashed down the street, cutting through the dimmed Ambients. The first thought that entered my head was more security. The car skidded to a stop in front of me. The rear door flew open.

I recognized Pat behind the wheel and lunged for the back door, crawling in and pulling Ian behind me. The car accelerated, slamming the rear door shut with a loud bang. Glass shattered, spraying Ian's legs with tiny blue crystals.

I looked out the broken window before we raced away. The guards milled around William. A few watched us leave. Pat whipped around a corner and left downtown, heading east.

My legs felt wet from the blood that soaked through my pants. I crawled out from under Ian and lay him on the seat. He was too tall to fit, making it harder to roll him over without both of us ending up on the floor.

I found the wound right away. The bullet had entered his chest, a few centimeters left of dead center. A bit more to the right, and the bullet would have hit his heart. Blood pumped from the hole, and with each breath, bubbles formed. I pulled off my jacket and pressed it against the wound. I felt myself going numb and fought against it.

"How bad is it?" Pat asked.

"We need to get to a hospital." I felt the car slow down as it entered a sweeping turn.

"You know we can't do that. As soon as we do, Jeremy will have him again."

"Jeremy's dead. I killed him." Saying the words out loud sent a shiver of released tension through me. Jeremy was gone, this time for good. Only, I wasn't sure it was me who had killed him. There had been three shots.

Pat pulled over to the side of the road. Outside the window, I could see we were sitting on an interchange just off a major freeway. She leaned over the seat and looked at Ian. I pulled the jacket away from the wound and heard her suck in a breath. She turned around again and accelerated down the highway, pulling up directions on the car's comm unit.

I slumped against the back of the seat, still trying to stop the flow of blood. Everything crashed down on me and tears pooled in my eyes, rolling down my cheeks. I wished it was me on the backseat instead of him. Ian lay motionless on the seat as the car raced down the road.

According to the comm unit, we were forty-five minutes from the nearest hospital.

LOS ANGELES, LEVEL 6—TUESDAY, JUNE 13, 2141 11:02 P.M.

Ian reached out to me, his hand moving slowly, shaking as though it was barely under control. He pulled my hand away from my face, wiping at my tears with an unsteady thumb. He was smiling, the same smile he gave me on the transport before it crashed. Behind his eyes I saw pain. His hand slipped, and I shifted onto my knees to be closer to him. I rubbed at my eyes with the back of my hand.

His smile turned into a grimace as the car went over a bump.

In the back of my mind, the scenario played through over and over. I timed it in my head so that I jumped in front of the bullet. I timed it so we got upstairs sooner, before Jeremy was there. None of it mattered.

I wished there was more I could do, I *needed* to do something, but there was nothing I could do. My jacket wasn't holding back the blood at all anymore, wasn't even soaking it up. Ian's face was a pale blue, noticeable even in the dim lights of the Ambients that pulsed through the car windows as we raced down nearly deserted streets. His breathing was shallow and quick, short sharp inhales followed by a rattling exhale.

He tried to smile again, his face changing in that split instant to one full of lies, full of love. Protection. I tried to smile back, to be brave. My hands were covered in his blood. Less seemed to be seeping out from under the jacket. I didn't dare lift it to see what was happening.

With one hand pressing down on the bullet wound, I searched the back seat of the car. There had to be something else I could use other than my fucking jacket. I groped under seats, finding nothing but a useless wadded-up tissue.

Ian reached out to me again, touching my cheek in a gentle caress before pulling me in closer. I leaned in as he whispered something I couldn't hear. Tilting my head, I felt his lips on my cheek, cold and hard instead of the beautiful warmth he always kissed me with. His arm fell limply back to the seat, sliding off, his fingers hitting the floor. His eyes closed.

I screamed his name.

"You can't die on me. Not now. Not after everything you've been through." I slapped his face until his eyes opened, out of focus, staring at nothing. The blue tinge to his skin had deepened. "Breathe. Stay with me. We're almost there. Stay awake. Please stay awake." I slapped his face again.

Ian blinked, his eyes shifting back into focus, looking at me.

I knew he was dying, and there wasn't anything I could do. I screamed over my shoulder. "Drive faster." I didn't get a response.

His lips moved, another soft whisper. I leaned in close again, desperate to hear his voice. Ian whispered in my ear, warm breath blowing gently on my face.

"Not your fault."

Part of me wanted to believe him, part of me just wanted to curl up and die with him, to trade places with him. Ian was my life, was the reason I was still here in this fucking city. He was the only man I'd ever loved. But I knew it was my fault.

His words were like acid, burning a hole deep in my soul.

The quiet sounds of his breathing slowed and stopped. I lifted the jacket. No bubbles formed around the bullet hole, and the blood had stopped seeping from the wound. My world meant nothing.

The car braked hard and swerved, almost throwing Ian's body from the seat onto the floor before accelerating again. I crawled on top of him, placing my hands on his sternum, and started pumping. Fresh blood leaked out of the hole. I counted out thirty and stopped, tilting his head back and forcing air into his lungs. His chest barely rose. I repositioned his head and tried again, with the same results.

I went back to his chest, trying to force his heart to pump blood through his body. Breathing, compressions, breathing, compressions, breathing . . .

I could barely see what I was doing anymore. Blood had soaked through my pants where it had pooled under Ian. I could barely get enough control of myself to start the next cycle. Compressions, breathing, compressions . . .

The car slowed down. We were here. The doctors could bring my Ian back to me. The back door opened and I felt hands pull me off of him.

"Come on, Kris. You're not helping anymore. It's been too long, he's lost too much blood."

I struggled and kicked throwing myself back into the car. Compres—

Pat pulled at me again, harder this time, yanking me out of the car before she slammed the door shut. I lunged for the door and she grabbed me, holding me in her arms like a wild beast. I fought back, screaming, punching, scratching. Anything to make her let go. She only held me tighter.

"He's gone, Kris. He's not coming back."

"NO!"

"There's nothing more we can do."

"No! Take us to the hospital, the doctors—"

"We're still thirty minutes away. There's nothing they can do. All they'll want is answers that we can't give, and then they'll hold on to him because there's no family to pick up the body."

It was like she had flicked a switch in my head. I couldn't talk any more, couldn't fight. I slumped in her arms and cried until I couldn't even do that anymore.

She put me in the front seat of the car and drove back to the insurgents.

LOS ANGELES, LEVEL 5—THURSDAY, JUNE 15, 2141 9:45 A.M.

Pat, Kai and I sat at a café table, the hard chairs prompting us to move on, to not stay so long. Across from us, the public greenhouses were almost empty this early on a Thursday morning.

I had one bite from the muffin sitting in front of me, and my coffee cup was still full and cold. I hadn't woken up feeling sick this morning, but I wasn't hungry. Not now. I'd eat later in the day. I had more than just me to take care of. I'd called Doc Searls. I was more than six weeks pregnant. A boy. My hand moved to my belly. My little Ian. I didn't tell anyone.

We'd waited for the greenhouses to open at seven o'clock, me, Pat, Kai, and Ian; waited for the gardeners to disperse before we walked into the one filled with tall, slender birch trees. I'd looked up what *shinrin-yoku* meant. Forest bathing. A beautiful phrase for how being in the wilderness made me, made *us*, feel. Clean, peaceful.

It was the closest the city could get to my memories of the Canadian mountains. The only place Ian and I had ever felt free. Free from the corporations. Free from our jobs. Free to love each other.

We had left the path, walking further into the depths of the manicured forest. When we thought no one would see us, we'd dug as deep as we could, leaving Ian's ashes at the bottom. Before we covered him, I placed Oscar on top of the box. Everyone needs company. We left him there, barely a bump in the grass to remind us where he was. I carved a tiny heart in the closest tree, right at ground level.

Kai reached into his pocket and pulled out three slightly crinkled red envelopes. He grimaced slightly as he tried to flatten them out again. Before we left, he handed one to each of us, keeping one for himself. Inside was a single circular coin with a square hole in the center.

"Be sure use it before you get home," he said. "For luck. All the stores in Chinatown will accept it."

I barely heard him.

We'd walked out again, and sat at the café until the waiter asked us to leave.

Pat paid with her throwaway comm unit and stood, placing her hand on my shoulder before going back to the car with Kai following her. I sat for a bit longer.

The insurgents had started a revolution, and I was a part of it. I had to create a better world for our child. I stood and walked to the waiting car.

On the drive back to Level 2, I started planning. I couldn't win against the corporations, not alone. ACE was falling apart with all that had happened, and William had been seen boarding a shuttle to St. Thomas. No one was helping the people below Level 6 anymore. But I could. Whether they knew it or not, we were all corporate slaves. We weren't free to leave the city, we weren't free to move above Level 5.

We had work to do.